STAR LAKE BOXED SET

THREE STAR LAKE SMALL TOWN ROMANCES

LORANA HOOPES

DEDICATION

Dedication Page:

To my family who lets me write. To my friends to who inspire me. To Brandon M. Thanks for being my muse for this book.

NOTE FROM THE AUTHOR

This book is dear to my heart. I've always loved the small town feel and the crazy characters that generally live there. I hope you enjoy the story and the characters as they are dear to my heart. If you do, please leave a review at your retailer. It really does make a difference because it lets people make an informed decision about books.

Below are all the books in the small town series. I would love for you to check them out. I'd also like to offer you a sample of my newest book. Free Sample!

WHEN LOVE RETURNS

CHAPTER 1

There it was. The one stoplight Brandon thought he'd never see again, still blinking its irregular red pattern that no one ever paid attention to. As most of the shops were centrally located, few people drove in town. Their cars were used for driving to neighboring cities when what they wanted wasn't available in town. There was no real need for the stop light, but the people had decided the town needed at least one stoplight to be called a proper town, and so it had been erected.

There had been a huge ceremony the day it was christened; the whole town had shown up. The mayor had been forced to stand on a ladder to cut the red ribbon as someone had placed it too high. Once he was up the ladder, another member of the city board handed him a giant pair of silver scissors. Then it became a balancing act as the mayor tried to open the giant scissors without losing his balance – that had been comical – and the town had watched in awe as the stoplight blinked, blinked, long pause, blinked, blinked.

The awe had faded quickly, and a squabble had broken out

among the adults about the brand new broken light. The whole affair had been rather disappointing to a sixteen-year-old, who had been looking forward to getting his driver's license. That day was the nail in the coffin that solidified Brandon's idea of leaving the tiny backwards town and returning to normalcy.

Then he had met Presley, and his life changed.

"Are we there yet, Daddy?"

Brandon glanced in the rearview mirror at his daughter, Joy, strapped in her car seat. Her dark curls came from him, but her blue-grey eyes were her mother's. Joy was the one good thing that came out of this town.

"Almost, Bug."

She resumed her stare out the window as they continued down Main Street. The Diner still sat on the corner, probably still run by Max, the same uninspired owner who wore a ball cap and plaid flannel shirt to work every day. His choice of attire left a lot to be desired, but he was a good cook. To this day, Brandon was not sure he'd had a better burger.

Next to the diner was the small Post Office. Brandon had never spent much time there growing up, but he knew the man who worked there, Bert. An odd man to say the least – always trying out new ideas that never seemed to work. One year, he had tried raising chickens to supply eggs for the general store, but he had become attached to one of the chickens, naming her Stella and carrying her from place to place in a little bag like wealthy old women do with tiny dogs. The chicken had escaped the bag one day in the middle of The Diner and wreaked havoc, incensing Max. Stella disappeared after that, and Brandon was fairly certain she ended up on Max's menu, but he could never prove it.

The general store appeared next. It carried groceries and a small selection of clothing and household goods. Brandon had been shocked by the meager selection when he first arrived, but the town wore on him and had a way of making him forget the outside world moving on around it. By the time he graduated high school, Brandon had been accustomed to the small offerings until he arrived in Dallas and felt like a total hick, at least three years behind the times.

"Daddy, look, cupcakes. Can we get one?"

Twisting in the black leather seat, Brandon followed her finger pointing out the opposite window. There had been no cupcake shop four years ago, but there was indeed a shop there now, where the laundromat had been, sporting a colorful cupcake sign and logo on the window. Sweet Treats. Not a highly original name, but neither were most of the stores in town.

"We'll come back by later." Brandon was curious about the owner. Who would choose to put up a new shop in this sleepy little town?

Her bottom lip turned out in an adorable pout, but she didn't continue to fight him. For her, this trip was like a vacation to a new and unusual place. The two rarely ventured from Dallas, mainly because Brandon's work kept him too busy for vacations. For him, it was a return to a past he had hoped to forget. Too much pain and too much sadness resided in this little town.

Brandon made a right down Cooper Street, the road that led to his parent's house. Though it had been years since he had been back, he could drive the route blindfolded, partly because it was a simple route, and partly because he walked it so many times as a teenager.

The two-story yellow house looked exactly as he remembered it, though the paint was chipping in a few more places and faded in others. The gravel of the driveway crunched under the tires as he pulled in. Brandon parked the car and took a deep breath.

"Let me out Daddy," Joy called from the back seat.

Sighing, he opened his door and then reached in to unbuckle her. Though five, she was still too small to qualify for a booster seat, and Brandon felt safer having her in the bigger car seat anyway. No one ever told him that when he became a parent, he would have crazy nightmares about all the ways he could lose his daughter. The car accident was always the worst.

Joy scurried out of the car, her faded pink bunny clutched in one petite hand. On the day she was born, Brandon's mother had given her a soft pink cuddle bunny. Joy latched onto it, sleeping with it every night. When she began crawling, she would often pick up the bunny in her mouth, dragging it across the floors. Even after she began walking, the bunny would go outside with her to play in the dirt or be flung around the room. The bunny had seen better days, but she refused to part with it for any longer than an occasional trip in the washing machine, and of course, no one sold this bunny any longer. Brandon had scoured the internet one day looking for a replacement, but come up empty. He dreaded the day it fell apart, and he couldn't replace it.

As Joy scrambled up the wooden porch, Brandon popped the trunk and grabbed the two suitcases he packed the night before. His hope was that they'd only be here a week, but he had no guarantee and therefore packed for at least two.

Joy was banging on the door when Brandon reached her side. She hadn't been around his parents much, as Brandon had moved to Dallas shortly after Joy's first birthday, but they had visited a few times. Joy always clung to them when they did as if she knew the time wouldn't be for very long. Now, she had created this idea in her head of what they would be like while she was here and regaled Brandon with it the last few days. He hoped she wouldn't be disappointed, but was afraid she might. His mother probably wouldn't be able to spend much time with her as she would be taking care of his father, at least when he got released from the hospital.

Brandon's mother opened the door and broke into a smile. She looked older than he remembered. More lines crossed her face and more grey streaks colored her hair, but her eyes still twinkled the way they always had.

"Joy." She bent down with her arms out.

"Nana." Joy ran into her arms, squeezing the woman tightly about the neck. "You smell like cookies."

A smile played across Brandon's lips. His mother always smelled of vanilla and sugar, and while she had often had a plate of cookies waiting for him when he arrived home from school, she hadn't every day, and he wondered how she still smelled of cookies on those days.

"That's because I have some in the kitchen." She tapped the end of Joy's nose, earning a giggle. "Now, come in, and let's get you settled."

"Then can we have cookies?" Joy bounced up and down, sending the lights in her pink sneakers into overdrive. His mother nodded, smiling at her enthusiasm.

Brandon pulled the two suitcases into the homey entrance and shut the door behind him.

The house hadn't changed a bit. A wooden coatrack still sat just to the right of the front door, holding his father's derby cap and a few coats, and the sign, announcing "As for me and my house, we will serve the Lord," still hung prominently on the wall. Brandon shed his coat, adding it to the rack and then removed Joy's as well.

"Let me show you to your room." His mother grabbed Joy's free hand and led her down the beige carpeted hallway. Pictures of Brandon and his sister, Anna, lined the walls. His mother never let an opportunity to take a picture go by, and Brandon was almost certain she bought every school picture they ever had so she could display them all on the walls. He had tried to remove one once and replace it with something else, but she noticed right away and forced him to rehang the picture.

His mother opened the door to the guest room. She had obviously added some decorations for a younger child to enjoy. The daybed had been covered with a flowery pink and purple bedspread, and a blond doll sat propped on top. An old dollhouse was near the dresser along with a faded toy box filled with toys.

"This is all for me?" Joy's eyes were wide as she looked up at Brandon's mother.

The lines around his mother's eyes grew more visible as she smiled. "Yep, all for you. A girl needs proper toys."

"Especially in this town," he said under his breath. Not quietly enough though as his mother shot a look full of daggers his direction. How quickly she could change from sugar to fire. Brandon held his hand up in silent apology.

"Where is Daddy staying?"

"Right across the hall." His mother opened the door to Brandon's old room which looked very much like it had in high school. His football awards still lined the shelf, though a fine layer of dust coated them now, and the tattered posters of his favorite bands covered the walls.

"Didn't feel like updating this one?" he asked.

His mother shrugged. "Maybe I would have if you came around more often."

Brandon wanted to reply, but he didn't want to start a fight, so he bit his tongue and carried the suitcase inside. After dropping off Joy's suitcase as well, they followed his mother back towards the open living room and into the country-themed kitchen. Brandon hated the flowered wallpaper trim that circled the kitchen, but his mother hung it herself and had always loved it.

A plate of chocolate chip cookies sat in the middle of the scratched kitchen table. The usual wild flower display had been pushed to the side. Joy turned eager eyes on Brandon, the unasked question evident.

"You may have one." He held up a finger. "I don't want you to spoil your dinner."

She climbed up in a chair and snatched a cookie off the top of the pile, shoving most of it in her mouth.

Brandon shook his head. "You could chew more slowly."

Her ravenous munching changed to a thoughtful chewing, and he joined her at the table, plucking a cookie for himself off the pile.

"How is Dad?" Brandon asked before taking a bite. His father was the whole reason he was here. He was in the hospital after falling off a ladder and fracturing his skull. Though Brandon's mother claimed he hadn't needed to come, he couldn't very well stay in Dallas if there was a chance this was life threatening, and brain bleeds often were.

Plus, he figured his mother might need some help with his father when he got released. He would probably not be as active as he was before the accident. However, Brandon was in the middle of a big presentation, one that could set him up for life with an even bigger company, so he had left strict instructions with his assistant to keep him in the loop.

A flicker of doubt erased his mother's twinkling eyes for a moment before she recovered. "He is doing better today. The nurses say he only had a few instances of confusion yesterday, but they want to run another CT tomorrow."

"Any idea on when he'll be released?" Brandon took a bite of the cookie, enjoying the warm chocolate goodness. He had missed his mom's cooking.

"Probably another few days, but it depends on what the scan shows. He has a pretty big brain bleed."

"Your brain can bleed?" Joy's head popped up, her eyes as wide as saucers.

His mother shot an apologetic look and without saying it, the two agreed to finish the discussion later when little ears were not present.

"Don't worry." Brandon patted her arm. "The brain is amazing and can heal itself. When does Anna get in?" Anna, his younger sister, was away at college studying to become a nurse.

"She has finals this week, so she's coming as soon as she finishes the last one. Oh, and guess who else is back in town?"

Brandon raised an eyebrow at her; he had never been a fan of the guessing game.

"Presley Hays."

Presley Hays. The name knocked the wind out of him like a sucker punch. He hadn't thought of her in years. In high school, Presley had been his best friend – the one person who had made this town bearable – but for some reason they had grown apart when Morgan entered the picture, and then one day Presley had come over to tell him she was going to France to attend Le Cordon Bleu.

"The cupcake shop?" Brandon said the words for himself, but his mother smiled and nodded.

"Who's Presley?" Joy looked from Brandon to his mother.

"Just an old friend," Brandon said. *Just an old friend.*

CHAPTER 2

*A*s the last customer finished their treat and waved goodbye, Presley locked the door and smiled to herself. This might not have been her original dream, but she was starting to really like it here. There was something about the small town feel that she had missed.

She grabbed the cleaning rag that hung over the silver faucet of the big basin sink and began wiping down the glass table tops. There were only five tables; the room was rather small but big enough for her needs. Each table boasted two white wrought iron chairs — the fancy ones with the decorative backs and padded seats. They had cost her a fortune, but they reminded her of Paris, so she couldn't pass them up.

She glanced up at the Eiffel Tower. Trudy, the local artist, had painted it on one wall for her. It wasn't quite the same as when she could see it out her apartment window, but it was a close second, and Trudy had done it for a month's worth of treats. Presley was certain she came out on top of that deal, and at least this view didn't come with a cheating boyfriend.

Her eyes narrowed as she pictured Pierre, the handsome Parisian she had been dating in Paris. He had seemed too good to be true and now she knew why. For all his good qualities, Pierre had the nasty habit of being unable to be faithful to one woman. When Presley had hinted she knew he was cheating, he hadn't even denied it. Instead, he had played it off like philandering was acceptable in France, and maybe it was, but it was unacceptable to her, so she had packed up her things and come home.

Star Lake, Texas was never her dream, but she was no longer sure what her dream had been before Brandon Scott walked into her life. The day she met him, her dream began to include Brandon and a five-star dessert shop in some upscale city, maybe even Paris. They used to talk for hours about how they would get away from the small town and live life in a big city, but part of that dream had ended the day he told her Morgan was pregnant.

Presley had hoped Morgan would be a leaf in the wind like all the rest of the women had been. Brandon never stayed with one woman for long, and he couldn't stay single between them for long either. It was obvious he was looking for something and not finding it. Presley had always hoped it was because he was looking for her, but Morgan had been different.

She had been exotic and wealthy, vacationing for the summer to get away from her busy city life. With her beautiful dark hair and stunning blue eyes, she had hooked him from the beginning, and they had been inseparable. Presley had lost her best friend that summer long before she left town.

She should have told him how she felt before Morgan came along, but she had been too afraid, and she'd always thought she would have a little more time.

An incessant rapping at the front door broke her reminiscing, and she looked up to see Trudy frantically waving from the other side.

This had better be good. She knows I close at six.

"You'll never guess what I just heard." Trudy's excitement was punctuated by the squealing of her voice. Her trademark overalls were covered in paint splotches and a few random splatters dotted her face and outer coat as well. A red bandanna covered her dark hair. She must have been painting recently, though it was too dark for her to have been painting outside.

"What?" Presley asked, though she was not very curious. In Star Lake, people got excited if Max put a new dish on the menu. Well, some got excited. The old, crotchety people complained that the menu wasn't the same, and they couldn't find their favorites.

"Paula said she saw new blood come into town today. A hottie."

Presley took this with a grain of salt. For one thing, Paula was the town's gossip, and if she didn't have truthful tidbits, she tended to make them up just to have something to share. For another, Paula was in her forties, but still dressed like she was twenty in tight skirts and cleavage baring tops. She was so man hungry that she thought anything male on two legs was a hottie. She once tried to date the preacher who had to be close to seventy.

"Well, then good for Paula."

Trudy shook her head and rolled her eyes. "No, Paula said he was young. Like your age."

Trudy wasn't much older than Presley, but she had decided she was too artistic for men. She didn't want to be tied down with a relationship or a man wanting her attention when she wanted to be painting.

"Then I'm sure I will meet him eventually." Presley was not taking the bait. Ever since she returned a few months ago, the town had been trying to set her up with the few remaining single men she wasn't related to. And seeing how the town wasn't very big, that consisted of about three men.

Justin, the recent high school graduate who bagged groceries at the general store and hadn't decided what he wanted to do with his life yet; Bert, the odd mail carrier who was single for very good reason – the man once tried to establish a chicken petting farm for the elderly; and of course, the seventy-year-old preacher. Most of the other people Brandon and Presley had gone to school with either moved away like they had or stayed but got married. Star Lake was a great town for families, but it was not a hopping singles spot.

"You're hopeless," Trudy said, but she helped Presley turn the chairs over on the tabletops, so she could sweep the floor. "You need to get back out there."

"What do you want me to do?" Presley grabbed the broom from behind the counter. "Camp on a rooftop with a pair of binoculars scanning for this hottie? It's a small town. If he *does* exist" – she emphasized the word does, drawing it out to two syllables to make her skepticism unmistakable – "then he'll come in here sooner or later."

Trudy stuck her tongue out, but dropped the subject and continued turning over chairs.

Though Presley was not looking for a relationship after the disaster with Pierre, she couldn't help thinking that a man wouldn't be a terrible thing to have around. The limited dating pool was the one thing she didn't like about this small town.

After the floor was swept, Trudy ducked out – citing the need to finish her masterpiece, but really it was because she didn't like menial work. Presley didn't mind though. She took the remaining pastries out of the display case and wrapped them up. They would only keep for another day, but she was hopeful they would sell tomorrow. Business hadn't been booming since she started, more like a steady trickle, but it had been good enough to keep the lights on so far. However, if something didn't change soon, she might have to close the doors, and she had no idea what she would do then.

Sparing one final glance to make sure the place was tidy, she donned her coat and hat. The December air had chilled considerably the last few days, and by the time she left at night, it was almost always near freezing. The first snow ought to be right around the corner. Shoving her hands in her pocket, she began the walk home.

Her breath created tiny wisps of smoke as she exhaled, and the tip of her nose grew cold. Presley was glad she didn't live far from the shop. She glanced down Cooper street as she passed and could just make out Brandon's parent's house.

She didn't know why she bothered to look when she knew he wasn't there, but it was a gesture she couldn't seem to stop. Maybe it was from so many times of looking down the street when they were younger. The few times the two had snuck out, they would meet on the street corner before driving to nearby Mesa for a party. And every time after leaving his house, Presley would stop and turn back, hoping to find him running after her to sweep her up in a kiss.

She'd heard his father was still in the hospital after his fall, and she wondered if Anna would come back to see him. She knew Brandon wouldn't, as the last she'd heard, he hadn't been home since moving away. Probably too busy with his business and his family.

Unbidden, thoughts of Brandon filled her head, and Presley wondered about his child. Was it a boy who looked like him or a girl with the beauty of Morgan? The child would be about five now, possibly even in Kindergarten. Presley pictured Brandon sitting with the child at a table and doing homework. In her mind, it was always a girl with Morgan's eyes who would hold a piece of Brandon's heart that no other woman would ever touch.

Shaking her head to clear the traitorous thoughts, she continued walking. Though she hadn't spoken with his mother recently, Presley decided to bake the family something special to let them know she was thinking about them. After all, for years they had been a second family to her.

Half a block later, she reached her apartment. It was a mother-in-law suite attached to her mother's house but with its own entrance. Presley liked to call it her own apartment, and her mother worked so much that she rarely saw her anyway. Entering, she tossed her coat on the rack before calling for her cat, Niko.

Niko was the perfect man – considerate, always happy to see her, and shared her bed without taking it over. If only he were a man and not a cat. He climbed up on her lap as she sat on the couch and flicked on the TV. The images flashed in front of her eyes, but Presley's mind was on the hottie. Whether he lived up to his title or not, she curious as to who he was and why he was here.

The big tourist season was usually in the summer, when rich families from the city decided to test out rustic life for a few weeks. A small handful came in the winter though because the town typically got at least one good snowfall. Maybe the hottie was a food critic who'd heard about her shop and come to taste the wares. Smiling at the thought, she allowed herself to be sucked into the dream.

CHAPTER 3

"So, it's true. The prodigal son has returned."

Dropping his fork, Brandon turned to his sister, who was staring at him, a bag still slung over her shoulder. She must have just gotten in. Her blond hair, so unlike his darker shade, skimmed her thin shoulders. All their lives people wondered how they were related as she had inherited their mother's pale skin and blond hair while Brandon got their father's darker Italian skin and hair.

"Hey Anna." He crossed to her and enveloped her in a hug. She was taller and thinner than he remembered, and a flicker of regret at the years he has been away rose inside him. When the family first moved to Star Lake, the two of them had joined forces in trying to convince their parents to move back. It was only after meeting Presley that he and Anna started to grow apart.

"How long are you staying?" She dropped her bag and grabbed a plate from the cupboard, joining him at the table. Her fork stabbed three pancakes, and she doused them in Maple syrup before taking a giant bite. She was either not eating at college or had taken up a grueling exercise regimen to be able to eat like that and stay thin.

"Until Dad is better, but I'm in the middle of a huge presentation deal right now, so I'll have to get back soon."

"Look who I found." His mother entered the kitchen with Joy attached to her hand.

"Morning, Bug." He opened his arms, and Joy ran into them.

"Who are you?" Joy asked when she noticed Anna.

"This is my sister Anna. She's your aunt." Due to school, Anna had only come with their parent's once, so Joy hadn't seen her as often.

"Aunt Anna?" Her nose wrinkled, and she shook her head. "That doesn't sound right. I'll just call you Auntie Anne, like the pretzels. Can we have a pretzel Daddy?"

"Not right now." He deposited her into her own chair. "Right now, it's breakfast time, and your grandmother made pancakes, but maybe we can go into town later and check out the new bakery."

"The bakery or the baker?" Anna asked between bites of pancake, a teasing glint in her eye.

Brandon shot her a warning glare while placing a few pancakes on Joy's plate, but he wondered at the question himself. He hadn't seen or spoken with Presley in over five years, so why was he so curious about her now?

After breakfast, the four loaded into the car and drove the few miles to the hospital. It sat just outside of town, and unlike Star Lake itself, the hospital was state of the art. Most of the surrounding towns were more up to date, but it was like Star Lake had gotten stuck in a time warp or something.

Brandon's mother always said it was because the leaders of Star Lake enjoyed the slower pace of life in a small town, but it baffled him how anyone could enjoy the town. Maybe he was disillusioned because he had once thought of settling down in this town. Until Morgan left.

His throat began to close as they pulled into the parking lot. He hadn't been in this hospital since Joy was born, and while that was a happy event, it related to Morgan leaving, which was not. Brandon was thankful Anna and his mother were along as well.

"How about I show Joy the toys?" The look on his mother's face told him his father was evidently still bruised up. He mentally prepared himself for what he would see, but was still shocked when they entered the room. His father's left eye was swollen shut and colored a bright purple. A monitor was hooked to his finger, and an IV pumped fluid in his arm. He heard them enter nonetheless and opened his good eye.

"Brandon? Is that you?" His voice was clear, which gave Brandon hope that he was better than he looked. He appeared old and frail beneath the white sheet. Brandon wasn't sure if it was from his injuries or the hospital bed itself. Either way, another pang of regret surfaced, but he pushed it aside. Even if he lived closer, he couldn't keep his parents from aging or falling off ladders.

"Hi Dad. Anna's here too."

She stepped around Brandon and crossed to the other side of the bed. "Hi Daddy. You look awful." The words were her defense mechanism. Fear was evident in her eyes as she grabbed his hand and held it tight.

A labored laugh escaped his mouth before he grimaced in pain and grabbed his stomach. "Sorry, broken ribs."

"What were you thinking Dad?"

His one good eye focused on Brandon. "I guess I wasn't. I thought I was standing on something sturdy until I tumbled off it."

Anna's sniffle caught both of their attention.

"Don't worry, honey, I'm going to be fine."

She nodded, but a few more silent tears snaked their way down her cheek.

"Joy is here too, and I'll bring her to see you, but I'll need to explain your face first."

"And Morgan?"

His father had never given up hope that he and Morgan would get back together. Though he wasn't a fan of hers in the beginning, he was a strong believer that a home consisted of two parents.

"Morgan's not coming back, Dad. She's moved on to bigger things."

In truth, Brandon had no idea what Morgan was doing. He hadn't heard from her since the day she walked out. She sent no cards, no gifts, nothing. It was like she'd erased them from her memory completely.

"I'll keep praying," he said.

Brandon was about to tell him he could keep his prayers for himself when a nurse entered and stated she needed their father for more tests. Brandon and Anna leaned down to give him a hug and then watched as he was wheeled out of the room.

"Do you think he's okay?" Anna wiped the last tear from her cheek. She had always been the more emotional of the two of them.

Brandon wrapped an arm around her shoulders. "Yeah, he looked strong though bruised, and his speech sounded okay to me." His mother had told him the night before they were keeping his father for observation because his brain bleed wouldn't stop. They were hopeful it would clear up on its own after a few days because the other option involved drilling a hole in his skull.

After stopping at the nurse's station for directions, they continued down the hall to find their mother and Joy. Neither spoke, and Brandon was certain they were both entertaining the thought of what they would do if their father didn't come home. It was a sobering thought, and not one he wanted to dwell on very long.

The playroom wasn't very big, but it had a small play structure, a few old computers, and a table with puzzles, which was where Joy was parked. Brandon smiled, watching her. The girl had loved puzzles since she was three. Often, he would realize how silent the house was and go searching for her only to find her at a table in her room turning pieces and sticking them in formation. At almost six, she was now working five hundred-piece puzzles.

"That was short," his mother said when she saw them.

"They took him for more tests. How was Joy?"

She smiled and pointed. "She's been there since we got here."

"Hey, Bug, you want to go get that pretzel now?"

Her head popped up, but there was indecision in her eyes. She bit her bottom lip, her telltale sign of concentration as she tried to decide between the puzzle and a pretzel. Food won in the end, and she placed the piece in her hand back on the table. That was a trait she got from Brandon. Morgan hardly ever touched food, but that was probably how she stayed so thin.

He made a mental note to check the general store for a puzzle for her. There wasn't much to do in this town, and at least that would keep her busy when he needed to work.

They piled back in the car and drove back to Star Lake. Brandon parked in front of Max's, and they filed out. "It is still okay to park here, right?" Max had always lived above his diner, and though he owned an old beat up truck, he had always parked it in the alley.

His mother nodded. "Yes, Max hasn't changed much, though I hear he's seeing someone now."

"Who?" Anna asked. Brandon could have cared less about any town gossip, but Anna ate it up. She had always liked to be in the know. "Oh, please tell me it's Layla. I'll just die if it's anyone else."

"It is indeed Layla. They finally got together after she almost married Mr. Jones, remember him?"

"Daddy, can we go see if they have pretzels now?" Joy tugged on his pant leg and eagerly pointed to the shop across the street. Brandon was glad for the distraction and the ability to focus on something other than Max's love life.

After checking both directions for traffic, though there almost never was any, he let her scurry across the street. "I'll be right behind you. As soon as these two yentas stop yakking."

Anna punched his arm, but they followed Joy across the street.

"I'll be right there. I'm just going to check the store for something."

As Brandon hurried to the general store, he hoped he wouldn't run into anyone. It wasn't that he didn't like the people of this town, but he knew that after being gone for a while, everyone would want to hear his life story, and he just didn't feel like sharing right now.

CHAPTER 4

The silver bell above the door announced visitors, and
Presley looked up to see a small girl with dark curls
enter. Her coat and shoes were the same color of pink, and her
shoes lit up as she crossed the floor. Presley was terrible at judging
ages, but she guessed the girl to be five or six. She carried an air of
confidence for her young age as she sidled up to the dessert case.

"Well, hello there. What can I get for you?" Placing her arms on
the top of the counter, Presley smiled down at her.

She scanned the offerings, her index finger tapping against her
pink lips, before glancing up at Presley. "Do you have pretzels?"

Presley saw the girl's mouth move, but the words barely
registered as her focus was on the girl's eyes. Those eyes were
blazoned in her memory, the eyes of the woman who stole her love
– although she hadn't known he was her love. Could she be looking
into the eyes of his child?

Her questions were confirmed a moment later when his mother,
Beverly, and his sister entered her shop. Though Presley had seen
Beverly a time or two around town since returning, this was the

first time she would have spoken with her or with Anna since she left.

"Hello, Presley." Beverly's voice was nice and calm. She hadn't always been that way, but once she had mellowed out, her calm demeanor had been one of Presley's favorite things about Brandon's family. Her own mother was always rushed and hectic, but it was because she had to be, working two jobs to support Presley and her brother, Ryan, after their father left.

Beverly, on the other hand, had never had to work. Her husband, Bruce, had owned a software company, and when he retired, they had moved to Star Lake. When Presley first met Beverly, she had still been uptight and obsessed with money, but a few months in this town wore anyone down, and by her first Christmas, she was wearing jeans and sweaters instead of business suits and pearls.

"Hello Beverly, Anna." Presley nodded at each of them. Anna looked grown up, with her hair down around her shoulders instead of always in a ponytail the way she had worn it in High School. She was also thinner, and her face had taken on a more womanly, angular shape. Anna was only a few years younger than Brandon and Presley, but at sixteen and seventeen, those few years of maturity mattered. Now, Presley imagined they would be close friends, if they didn't have the giant elephant of Brandon between them.

The little girl, young as she was, was smart. Her eyes traveled from her family to Presley and back again. Though she might not have understood everything, she caught on that something was amiss.

"What did you want again, honey?" Presley hoped it was something in the back she would have to go look for. Her guess was that if his daughter was here, then Brandon was too, unless he and Morgan shipped her off to have some time alone. Regardless, she wanted to check her appearance in case either Brandon or Morgan entered her store.

Her words, "a pretzel," filled Presley with relief. She didn't have any of those in the front counter, but there were a few frozen in the freezer.

"I have some in the back. Would you like one as well?" Presley glanced up at Beverly and Anna.

Anna shook her head. "Not for me. I'll have one of those." She pointed to a chocolate éclair on the bottom shelf.

"That looks delicious. I'll have one too," Beverly agreed.

"Wonderful, I'll be right back."

The freezer was at the back of the shop, but just across from it was the bathroom. Presley ducked into the tiny room first and cringed at the face in the mirror. Her hair was piled in a messy pony; the purple streak hanging loose near her face, and a smudge of white flour resided on one cheek. Wiping at the smudge with one hand, she pushed the loose hair back behind her ear with the other. It was not a perfect look, but it was the best she could do for now.

Darting into the freezer and grabbing the pretzel, Presley unwrapped it as she headed to the toaster oven. In it went, and she set the timer for two minutes, just enough to warm it without making it hard and chewy. When the oven dinged, she wrapped the pretzel in some wax paper and took it back out to the girl.

A smile lit up her face as she reached her tiny hands out. As soon as the prize was in her grip, she chomped on the pastry. Suppressing her laughter, Presley extracted two chocolate eclairs and held them out to the women. Beverly handed her a twenty, and Presley dropped her head to make change. Then the bill jingled again.

A shudder ran down her spine, and she knew who it was before even looking up. She handed the change to Beverly, but her eyes were not on the woman. They were on the man with the chocolate brown eyes and the full beard. He looked older with the beard.

Masculinity rolled off him in invisible waves, but she was the only one affected.

His eyes caught hers, and just like that Presley fell again. There was something about those intoxicating brown eyes that had always sucked her in. The day they met flashed in her mind.

"What are you drawing?"

The voice over her shoulder startled her, and she slammed the sketchpad closed. Presley didn't share her drawings with anyone. They weren't very good, just one of her ways to escape reality. The other was baking, but that was harder to do at school. "Are you talking to me?"

He swung his lean frame onto the bench next to her, and the smell of him floated on the air. Soap and sandalwood. She lifted her eyes to his face. Liquid pools of chocolate gripped her gaze, and her heart stopped in her chest.

"I don't see anyone else drawing around here, do you?" His eyes twinkled as if he was teasing her, but why would he do that? He didn't even know her.

What was he doing talking to her? Didn't he know he should be hanging with the other rich kids, and not with her? "But why are you talking to me?" She tucked her purple streak behind her ear and tried not to turn the shade of red she felt inside, but the heat climbing her ears told her she was losing that battle.

"Well, I thought you seemed interesting, and you were sitting over here all by yourself. I'm Brandon by the way." He stuck out his hand, and she stared at it, afraid to shake it. What if her hand was sweaty? What if she had paint or charcoal on her fingers? She didn't usually care about those things, but this was Brandon Scott, hottie new arrival to town and every girl's dream.

"I know who you are." Her eyes dropped back down to the sketchpad in her lap. "Everyone knows who Brandon Scott is."

"Hey, Presley." He said the words as if it had only been days since they'd seen each other and not six years. "You look good." His voice was deep and rich, different than when they were in high school and yet still the same.

"Hi Brandon. It's been a while." She wanted to slap her forehead. Six years she had dreamed of this moment, and that was all she could say? Where were the flowery words she practiced over and over in her head for the time she saw him next?

A smile tugged on his lips, and she knew he could tell she was uncomfortable. He had always been able to read her like an open book, which she used to love, but now she wished he'd slam the cover closed and put the book back on the shelf. They didn't have that relationship anymore. He didn't deserve to be able to read her.

"I see you've met my daughter, Joy."

Presley's eyes fluttered to the girl, who was nearly finished with her pretzel. Joy was a pretty name, and it suited her. It was easy to imagine that she brought joy to those around her with her mesmerizing eyes and Brandon's contagious smile. As the women rose from their table, Presley realized that Beverly and Anna had moved away and seated themselves. She had no idea when.

"She seems lovely." Though she meant the words, they sounded forced and trite as they came out. "Would you like a pastry too?"

He smiled at her, and the world went silent. The surrounding noises and shapes faded away, and it was just her and him. "Of course." He pointed to one of the double chocolate espresso brownies, and on autopilot, she removed it from the case and handed it to him.

She didn't even remember to charge him, but he placed a five next to the register for her. "It was good to see you," he said, and then the four of them walked out of her shop. The little girl turned and waved, breaking the spell.

When they were out of sight, Presley sank to the floor. Her heart was racing as if she had just downed five cups of coffee. She placed a hand over it to slow the beating. She had thought she was over Brandon, but she was clearly just denying her feelings.

CHAPTER 5

*A*s the door closed behind them, Brandon couldn't help but sneak one final glance at Presley. She had always been beautiful, though she didn't know it, but age had defined her features even more. Her face had shed the extra roundness from childhood, accentuating her soft cheekbones and the slender curve of her neck. Her eyes were still the same arresting blue they had been back in high school, the kind that was hard to look away from. It had been her eyes that first drew Brandon to her.

When he had arrived in Star Lake as a Sophomore, he had known no one, and was angry at leaving his friends behind. His father's money had attracted people, but none he wanted to call friends. When he saw the quiet blond girl across the way in the lunchroom, he felt drawn to see what she was all about.

"What are you drawing?" Brandon leaned over her shoulder to try and get a glimpse of her sketch pad. She always had it with her, and he was curious what she drew in it. She rarely spoke though they had several classes together.

She tucked the purple strand of hair that always fell in her face behind her ear and looked up with piercing blue eyes that sent his heartbeat speeding up in his chest. They were beautiful and breathtaking. "Are you talking to me?"

He swung his lean frame onto the bench next to her and turned on his charm. "I don't see anyone else drawing around here, do you?"

She stared at him, unaffected. "But why are you talking to me?"

Brandon blinked; he was unaccustomed to his charm not working. "Well, I thought you seemed interesting, and you were sitting over here all by yourself. I'm Brandon by the way." He stuck out his hand, and she looked at it but didn't take the offer.

"I know who you are." She dropped her attention back down to her sketchpad. "Everyone knows who Brandon Scott is."

That had been the beginning of his interest in her. Brandon wasn't used to someone who didn't fall at his feet right away, and at first it had been about the challenge. He had wanted to get her to open up to him, but the more he'd gotten to know her, the more he realized she was an amazing person who completed him in a way he didn't understand.

Though quiet in large groups, she was fiercely opinionated in private, and she always called him out on his crap, which no one had ever done before. Her calm and quirky manner also soothed his irritation at being in this new town, and their friendship had grown.

At some point, he had fallen in love with her, but was too afraid to tell her. Too afraid to lose his best friend and his link to sanity in this tiny town. So, he had buried his feelings and sought comfort in the arms of other girls, but none of them made him feel the way he did when he was with Presley. At least not until Morgan came along.

"Daddy, let's go." Joy tugged on Brandon's hand, pulling his thoughts back into the present. "I want to see the ducks."

"Yeah, Romeo. Get your head out of the clouds and join us." Anna's eyes twinkled as she teased him.

Brandon flashed her another warning glare. There was no time for romance; he was only here until their father got a little better, and then he was going back to the city and his job. Still, it would be nice to see Presley again, just to catch up on old times.

He allowed himself to be drug down the sidewalk and tried to see the town from Joy's eyes.

"Look, an ice cream shop." Her little finger jabbed to the right. "Can we go sometime, Daddy?"

If it hadn't changed, Mr. Perkins ran the ice cream shop. It used to be one of his and Presley's favorite hangouts. They would often stop in after school and sit on the red padded barstools and order milkshakes, making faces at each other in the large mirror that hung on the wall behind the counter.

"Sure, we can." But she had already lost interest and was pointing at the old dollar cinema, which still appeared to be playing movies and then at Ms. Paula's dance studio. Relief flooded Brandon as the shops of downtown faded, and they reached the more residential part of town.

The trees had all lost their leaves for the winter, and the remnants of them crunched under their feet. A cool breeze blew a few tattered pieces across the sidewalk and lifted strands of Joy's hair.

"There it is." Her voice was shrill with excitement as she dropped his hand and ran to the lake. It hadn't iced over yet, but it would with the first big snow. Star Lake never had a long winter, but it generally had at least one or two good snows between December and February.

The few ducks on the lake scattered as Joy ran at them, sending her into gales of laughter. As they flew off, she ran after them. If nothing else, she would expend some energy here.

"She looks happy," his mother said placing a hand on his arm.

"She's happy in Dallas."

"Is she?"

His mother left it at that, but her damage was done. Watching Joy running after the ducks and tossing rocks into the lake,

Brandon wondered if she was happy in Dallas. Due to his work schedule, she was usually taken to school by his nanny, Amber, who dropped her off on the way to her own college classes. Then Amber picked her up from school and stayed with her until Brandon returned home around six or seven in the evening. He and Joy would then have dinner and play for an hour or two before time for bed.

The thought plagued him the remainder of the time they stayed at the park and during the walk back to the car. He decided to make the most of this trip. There might not be another chance like this to hang out with Joy if the proposal he was working on got accepted.

CHAPTER 6

"So, the hottie is Brandon Scott?" Trudy asked before shoving a fry in her mouth. The two were eating a late dinner at The Diner.

Presley dropped her head in her hands. "Yes, and I thought I was over him, but I am clearly not."

"Why don't you just tell him how you feel?" Max placed a hamburger and fries in front of Presley. His ballcap was turned around on his head in his signature style, and his plaid today was a blue and white. He and Presley were not close, but Max had a habit of listening to conversations and butting in with his advice whether it was asked for or not.

"Because I don't know if Morgan's still in the picture for one," Presley said rattling the reasons off on her sparkly painted fingers. She should give up glitter nail polish now that she was in her mid-twenties, but like her purple streak it had been a part of her for so long, she was not sure she could part with it. "He lives hours away from here for another, and I don't even know if he likes me. What if he's never thought of me as more than a friend?"

"Seems to me that since you aren't really friends anymore it wouldn't matter." Before Presley could respond, he whirled around and returned to the kitchen, but she heard him mutter "women" as the door closed behind him.

"You know, he might be right," Trudy said. "You haven't spoken to him in years, so it's not like you'd be losing anything."

Except my fantasies. Presley was ashamed to admit that part of her fear was hearing Brandon say he'd never thought of her as more than a friend and no longer having hope to cling to.

"Here's an idea. Why don't you take him and his daughter to the holiday fair this weekend? Layla is going to have a pie tasting competition and Bert is planning to make candles. If nothing else, it will be some cheap entertainment."

Presley rolled the thought over in her head as she took a bite of the burger. It would be fun to spend more time with him and at least catch up on old times, that was if Morgan wasn't in the picture.

~

The next day, gathering her courage, Presley packed a basket of pastries for the family. She'd been planning to bring them over anyway, but realized now they would make a great excuse if Morgan was around. After donning her coat and locking the shop, she forced her feet to follow the familiar path to Brandon's parents' house. The yellow house was just as she remembered it, if not a little more worn.

The porch step creaked under her footstep, and she cringed at the sound. She should have remembered that step. It was what got them caught one night when they arrived back after curfew. The image of his mother, irate and red, brought a smile to Presley's face. If only they had been doing something worth getting so worked up over instead of innocently studying for a test at her place and simply losing track of time. She almost lost her nerve and turned back, but her finger touched the doorbell before she could retreat.

Anna opened the door and smiled, knowingly. She was not fooled by Presley's ruse of freshly baked goods.

"Come in." Anna opened the door wider, and Presley shuffled inside, ducking her head to hide the pink flag across her cheeks. "Brandon and Mother are in the family room." She began to lead the way, but Presley's hand reached out to stay her arm. Curious, Anna turned back.

"Anna, is . . ." Presley didn't really know how to ask what was on her mind, but she couldn't go in there without knowing. "Is Morgan out of the picture?" She spat the words out before she could change her mind about asking them. Waiting to hear her fate, her hands gripped the basket tighter.

Anna's eyes twinkled, and she nodded. Relief flooded Presley's body so quickly that her knees buckled. Anna grabbed her elbow before she tumbled to the floor, and Presley mouthed a silent thank you. When her legs regained their strength, the two resumed the walk to the family room.

She felt him before she saw him. His presence was like a giant magnet, drawing her to him. He looked up from his phone as she entered.

"Presley? What are you doing here?"

Her ears flamed, and she was glad her hair was long enough to cover them. "I heard about your father, and I wanted to bring you some pastries. It isn't much, but . . ."

"It is wonderful, my dear. Thank you." Beverly stood and took the basket, exiting the room and pulling Anna behind her. Presley was left alone with Brandon, who looked as uncomfortable as she felt.

"Here, sit," he said finally, pointing to an empty space on the couch next to him.

Despite being afraid to sit next to him, afraid to be too close to his magnetic pull, her feet propelled her there anyway. "It was good to see you yesterday."

"Yes, you too."

An electricity ran between them. Presley could hear the soft buzz of it, and the hair on her arms stood up. She was drowning in those dark pools once again.

"How was Paris?"

The breathiness of his voice told her he was feeling something similar. Could it be that he had feelings for her as well?

Her tongue swiped her bottom lip, and his eyes followed the movement before returning to hers. "It was nice, until it wasn't. I met a guy there, but it . . . it didn't work out."

His free hand grabbed hers. "Presley, I'm sorry to hear that."

A fiery tingle ran up her arm at his touch, and her eyes dropped to their entwined fingers. Her throat had gone dry, and it was hard to form her next words. "I'm sorry about Morgan." She pulled her gaze up as she finished the words to judge his expression.

His posture stiffened, and his eyes hardened for just a second before returning to their normal soft gaze. "It was unfortunate, but I'd rather her be gone than stay and not be the mother Joy needs."

Though a beard coated most of his face, his lips were still visible, and her gaze couldn't help but fall to them. They were thin, pink, and perfect. "Um, so there's a festival tomorrow. I thought maybe you and Joy would like to go with me?" Her breath caught at the last word as she waited for his answer.

The twinkle that haunted her dreams lit his eyes, and he squeezed her hand. "I'd love that, as will Joy. What time is it?"

Relief washed over her, and the breath released. "It starts at noon and runs all afternoon, so I'll meet you here at 11:30 and we can walk in together."

"Great. I'm sure Joy will be excited." He tucked his phone in his jeans and stared back at her.

Another silence stretched out between them. Presley hated

that they were reduced to small talk. She missed the friend she could tell anything. "Okay, well, I should be going. It's getting late, and you probably want to get some sleep." Not wanting to, she rose from the couch, which separated their hands. They cried out at the missing warmth, but she refrained from reaching for him.

A look crossed his face through Presley was not sure if it was disappointment or if she just wanted it to be. "Let me walk you home then."

"Oh, you don't have to do that. It's not far."

A genuine smile lit his face. "I know it's not far. I used to walk there every day, remember?"

I remember. How could I forget? It was generally the highlight of my day. "If you want, but you don't have to."

"I want," he said, and for a moment she saw the old Brandon, the teasing twinkle in his eyes and his trademark lopsided smile. She followed him to the front door, where he grabbed his coat and scarf.

The winter air slapped their faces as they stepped out on the front porch. Pulling her coat tighter, Presley sank deeper in it to keep the heat locked inside.

"Are you cold?" He unwrapped his scarf and held it out to her. It wasn't quite the gesture she was hoping for, but she accepted and wrapped it around her neck, enjoying the little bit of warmth it added and the scent of Brandon that now filled her nose.

The stars were out, reminding her of the many times they laid in the back of his pickup bed and watched them. She had forgotten how bright they were here with few lights blocking their shine. "They're so beautiful."

"What?"

"The stars." She pointed to the sky. "I never saw them this bright in Paris. Too many lights."

His eyes followed her hands, and he paused. She stopped beside him. "Do you remember the time our Senior year we fell asleep in the truck after watching the stars?" he asked.

Her ears began their slow burn again. She had been replaying the exact memory in her head. He had fallen asleep before she did that night, and she could have woken him, but instead she curled against his chest, enjoying the beating of his heart in her ear and the steady rise and fall of his muscular chest under her hand. "Mother was so mad when I came in the next morning. She didn't believe me that we didn't do anything but sleep."

"Mine either." His laugh was as she remembered it, deep and melodious, and it elicited a laugh from her in return. "Maybe we should do it again."

"We would freeze," she said punching his arm. "We'll have to wait until summer when it warms up."

Immediately she regretted the words as his smile faded. "Right, summer. I'll be gone by then. Back to the city."

Presley cursed her bad timing. She had ruined the mood. They continued the walk, but a tension filled the air this time. "How long are you staying?" She didn't want to hear the answer, but her heart needed to. It needed to be reminded that whatever it was feeling now, it would not last. Brandon would go home in a few weeks, leaving her alone again.

He shrugged. "I'm not sure. A week, maybe two. Until my father is released and then probably a few more days to make sure Mother can take care of him."

It was as Presley expected, not near enough time or maybe too much, depending on how she looked at it. They finished the walk in silence. When they reached her door, she turned to him. "Thank you for the walk." There was so much more she wanted to say, but the words wouldn't form the way she wanted them to.

His eyes stared into hers, and she wondered if he was having the same problem. He took another step toward her, closing the distance, and his hands grabbed hers again. His fingers were cold, but she didn't care. There was a heat between the two of them when they touched.

"It really is good to see you, Presley. I didn't know it, but I've missed our friendship."

The word was like an icy dagger to her heart. Friends. She forced a tight smile. "Me too."

His eyes lingered a moment longer, and Presley thought maybe, just maybe, there was something more than friendship in them. Maybe he would lean across the few inches separating them and place his lips on hers. Her hand fought the urge to reach up and touch his beard. She wanted to feel it, to see if it was soft like his hair. She swallowed as she held his gaze, and then it was gone.

He cleared his throat and released her hands. "I'll see you tomorrow."

"Good night." Though the air was still cold, Presley stood and watched him as he walked away.

CHAPTER 7

*P*resley's eyes opened before the alarm went off. She was not much for sleeping in on the weekends anyway, but the thought of spending the day with Brandon kept her up half the night. She should be tired, but a stream of adrenaline coursed through her. Still, she knew this high wouldn't last, so after dressing, she started a pot of coffee.

Niko found her lap as she curled up with the steaming beverage. His back arched against her free hand, begging to be petted. As she stroked his black and white fur, his purr reverberated against her leg, and his paws kneaded her jeans. Thankfully whoever owned him before had him declawed.

A week after Presley moved back to town, Niko had shown up on her doorstep. It was like he knew she was lonely. She had asked around town as he looked well cared for, but no one could remember seeing him before. That had been her sign she was supposed to keep him.

"What am I doing, Niko? I shouldn't be falling for him again. His life isn't here. This is only going to end in heartbreak again."

Niko said nothing, which was another thing she loved about him. He was the only man who'd ever been in her life who just listened.

When the coffee was finished, she rinsed the cup in the sink, placed it on the small counter, and checked her appearance in the hall mirror one final time. She was no Morgan, but her hair had agreed to hold a curl today, and it fell gently on her shoulders. Her tiny bit of eye makeup accentuated the intensity of her blue eyes, and her lips even had a sparkly sheen. Not bad.

Though late morning, the air was still chilly, and she shivered inside her coat. By the time she reached Brandon's, her fingers were nearly numb. Hopefully most of the festival was going to be indoors, or they wouldn't be able to stay long.

She stepped over the creaky third step this time, placed her finger on the small ornate doorbell, and waited, her heart pumping loudly in her chest. Hopefully, Brandon wouldn't be able to hear the sound.

The melodic chime echoed through the door, and it swung open, revealing Brandon still in sweats. His disheveled hair gave the appearance of just crawling out of bed. Presley glanced at her watch. It was past eleven thirty am.

"Did you just wake up?" She didn't bother to hide the incredulity in her voice.

"Hello to you too." He ran his hand across his beard. "I slept in later than normal. It must be from traveling."

Presley's eyebrows raised. She had no idea where he was living now, but she had thought it was still in Texas. "Okay, well are you still up for the festival?"

He nodded and opened the door wider. "Joy has been talking about it non-stop, so even if I weren't, I have to be." His lopsided grin reflected how much love he had for his daughter. "Go on into the kitchen. I'll clean up and meet you there."

Her eyes lingered on his face a moment longer, but she looked away when the thought of him in the shower began to heat her cheeks.

Oblivious, he turned and walked down the hallway, and Presley continued into the kitchen. Beverly and Joy were at the table, coloring in old coloring books.

"Good morning, Presley," Beverly said looking up from the book. "Would you like to join us?"

Presley tried to conceal the smile tugging at her lips. Coloring had long been a favorite pastime of hers. She pulled out the chair next to Joy and picked up one of the other books on the table. It was an old one of princesses. Flipping through the pages to find a clean one, she glanced over at Joy. Her face was focused on her coloring, and she reminded Presley very much of Brandon whenever he was studying for a test. She had the same habit of scrunching her nose and occasionally sticking her tongue out of the corner of her mouth.

"So, Joy, are you excited about the festival today?" Presley asked as she reached for a light blue crayon.

Joy's crayon paused, and she looked up, eyes sparkling with delight. "I am so excited. I have been thinking about it all night. Nana says there's a pie tasting and hot chocolate and popcorn stringing. I've never strung popcorn." Her words tumbled out like a waterfall.

"There's that and a whole lot more. When I was young there were lots of ornament decorating tables. Those were always my favorite."

"That sounds fun." Then her face clouded over. "Course we don't usually put ornaments on the tree because Daddy is too busy."

Presley looked to Beverly who shrugged. Somehow, she couldn't imagine Brandon not celebrating Christmas. It was always their favorite holiday.

The first Christmas they spent together, he snuck her into the forest just outside of town and they wandered through the trees for hours until they found the perfect one. He whipped out a saw and cut down a Virginia pine. It wasn't quite the same as the pine trees he was used to in Washington, but it was a close second. They drug the tree back through the forest, losing a lot of the needles in the process, loaded it into his truck bed, and drove it to his house.

Once there, they turned on some Christmas music and unloaded the box of ornaments his family had brought with them. Hours later, they laid under the tree and stared up at the lights, exhausted and proud. Presley couldn't imagine the man who did all that with her no longer excited about Christmas.

"You mean he doesn't decorate a tree with you?"

"He doesn't usually even remember a tree until the last few days." Her voice took on a melancholic tone as she turned back to her coloring. "Then we go to whatever local store still has some and get whatever is still there. Sometimes Amber helps me decorate, but Daddy doesn't have much, so the tree still always looks sad."

"Like a Charlie Brown tree?"

"Who's Charlie Brown?"

"Never mind." Presley shook her head.

As she shrugged her tiny shoulders in defeat, Presley made a mental promise to remind Brandon of the fun they used to have here. Whatever Morgan and living in a big city had done to him, her hope was that it could be cured with a little small-town magic.

Her crayon moved across the picture adding shading and depth to the gown the long-haired girl was wearing, but her mind was a million miles away thinking about how best to reconnect Brandon with the roots he seemed to have forgotten.

"Are we going to sit around and color all day?"

His voice startled her, and the crayon jumped in her hand, sending a blue line outside of the dress and across the girl's arm. A small sigh of frustration escaped her lips. It was just a silly book, but as an artist, she took pride in her work, and now this piece was ruined.

Joy slammed her book closed with such force that the crayons bounced on the table. "Yes, let's go."

"You better dress warm. It was quite cold on the way here," Presley said, carefully closing her book and stacking it back in the middle. "Beverly, are you coming with us?"

"Of course, I wouldn't miss it for the world," his mother said closing her own book and putting the crayons away in the box.

"What about Anna?" Presley's preoccupation with Brandon had kept her from noticing Anna's absence until now.

"She's still sleeping," Beverly replied, "but I'll leave her a note to tell her where we've gone. I can't stay too long though. I need to get out to see Bruce today."

"How is he doing?" Presley asked as they moved to the living room to grab coats. Joy was already in hers and tugging on Brandon's sleeve in excitement.

"Better. They think he'll get to come home soon, but he won't be able to drive for at least a month."

"Good thing there's nowhere to drive around here." Brandon's words were followed by a snort, another new and unattractive habit he had picked up since the last time she saw him. He nodded an apology after Beverly shot him a dirty look and opened the door.

The winter wind rushed in the house, as cold as when Presley arrived. Brandon wrapped Joy's scarf tighter, and they ventured out into the frigid air. Grey clouds had moved in, creating a darker feel than almost noon.

"Looks like snow," Presley said as her nose began twitching. She had no idea why, but her nose could almost always tell when snow was coming. Her mother swore it was her artistic nature that had her in tune with the weather around her, but Presley always wished it would have picked a different way of alerting her. The twitchy nose always made her want to sneeze.

"Oh, I hope it snows. We never get snow in Dallas." Joy

spread her arms and turned in a circle as if the snow was already falling and she was spinning in it. "I can't wait to see how it feels."

Presley's head dropped forward in surprise. "You mean you've never seen snow?"

She shook her head, her eyes serious under her pink fuzzy hat. "Only on television, but I've always wanted to."

"Well, if it snows, I will come help you build the best snowman after church tomorrow."

"Yay!" She shouted the word and accompanied it with a skip around each of the adults. Her exuberance and joy was contagious. Even Brandon cracked a smile, but then again, he always seemed to have one for his daughter.

As they neared the diner, Max stepped out the door, grunting under his breath, and flipped his sign to closed. He had a heavier flannel shirt on today, but no coat and his faded ball cap was in its trademark place turned backward on his head.

"Are you going to the festival, Max?" Presley didn't mean to sound so surprised, but big crowds had never been Max's thing.

He rolled his eyes. "Layla roped me into judging this year, so I have to go. Not that I want to. Got better things to do here." He hooked a finger back toward his diner.

Presley stifled a laugh at his predicament. "But Max, everyone is going to be at the festival. No one would be coming in anyway."

He shrugged and harrumphed in his usual manner, but joined them in the short walk to the town barn. Joy stared at him with wide eyes as if unsure whether to be afraid of him or amused by him, which brought another smile to Presley's face.

Country music flowed from the barn before they hit the front door. An actual old barn, the building was now a faded red. The inside stalls were removed years ago to open the floor for larger events. Paula used the space for her dance recitals, but it also served as the meeting place for town halls and festivals like today.

"There better not be dancing," Max grumbled as he pulled open the door.

The bright lights inside illuminated the large structure and the booths set up inside. A heat wave rolled out to meet them, sending a shiver down Presley's spine as it collided with the cold outside.

"Wow!" For once Joy's energy was stilled. Her eyes darted back and forth but her feet seemed rooted to the spot.

To the left was the popcorn booth. Paula had squeezed her voluptuous frame into a tight red dress, and was eating about as much popcorn as she was popping with the air popper that was plugged into some unseen outlet with a long orange extension cord.

Trudy's table was next, a popup table sporting a myriad of different colored paints, aprons, and wood ornaments. Trudy herself was clad in her overalls – a stark contrast to Paula's formal dress.

A few feet from Trudy, Bert, in his button-down gingham-checked shirt and bow tie, stared down into a crock pot, which Presley assumed held wax. He dipped a string in the pot, squealed in pain, and plunged his finger into his mouth.

A chuckle escaped her lips as she continued scanning the room. There was a table across the back lined with pies and hot chocolate. To the right were tables to sit at, a wreath making table, and Justin, who was playing the music off his computer.

"Where do you want to go first?" Brandon asked Joy, masking his own annoyance though Presley could see it in his eyes.

Her eyes jumped from one place to the next. "There." She pointed to Trudy, which pleased Presley. Artistic outlets were right up her alley.

Trudy raised her eyebrows as they approached, and Presley shook her head a tiny bit in an effort to tell her she would spill all later.

"Well, who is this angel?" Trudy asked staring at Joy.

"I'm Joy. Who are you?"

Her lack of shyness was surprising.

Trudy smiled back. "I'm Trudy. What would you like to paint?"

Joy scanned the offerings. Trudy had carved out bells, trees, stars, and plump Santas. Joy's hand hovered over each as if she couldn't decide before she picked up the tree. Trudy handed her a brush and poured some green, yellow, and red paint in tiny tubs. Joy dipped the brush cautiously in the green and began to sweep it across her tree.

Unable to help herself, Presley picked up a Santa and a brush and began coloring her own. Brandon and Beverly watched in amusement. The flicker of annoyance left Brandon's eyes as he watched Joy finish the green and then dot the lights with meticulous strokes.

"She's a natural," Trudy said and Presley couldn't help but agree.

"Can we get a real tree this year, Daddy?" Joy's voice was hopeful as she turned her big eyes up at Brandon.

He laughed in response. "Yes, this year we can get a real tree."

"In fact," Presley said, "why don't we take her to the farm you took me my first year?"

He cocked his head as if trying to remember; then his eyes lit up. "Oh yeah. Okay, tomorrow evening?"

"I'd love to. The shop closes at six, so we can go any time after that."

Joy looked from Presley to her father and a tiny smile alit on her lips.

After ornaments, they strung some popcorn. Presley was thankful that Paula kept her leering eyes off Brandon. It probably helped that he was nearly half the woman's age.

They even stopped at Bert's candle making table, though he had forgotten some important element and they were unable to make a candle. The faux pas was typical Bert, but a part of Presley still felt a little sorry for him.

"Brandon Scott, is that you?" The shrill voice was unmistakable. It belonged to Krissy, the high school cheerleader who dated Brandon on and off throughout high school. Though not her lithe, slender self, the years had been good to her, and she was still as pretty as ever.

"Hi, Krissy, how are you?" Brandon's voice was stiff, almost hesitant as if he was afraid she would try to hit on him.

"I'm good. I married Tony. He worked on the school newspaper, remember? We have one child so far and another on the way." She patted her nearly flat stomach as she said this. It must have been very early or else she didn't show much until later.

"That's wonderful, Krissy," Presley said jumping in. "Congratulations."

"Daddy, is it pie time?" Joy asked tugging on Brandon's sleeve.

"Sorry, I guess we have to go, but it was good to see you Krissy."

"Yes, we'll have to get some of the old gang together sometime," she said.

Brandon nodded, but it was noncommittal, and Presley could tell he wouldn't be setting up a meeting anytime soon.

They continued toward the back, and Joy's eyes danced in excitement as she neared the pie table. There were a myriad of pies decorating the table – apple, cherry, chocolate, pecan, and pumpkin. She licked her lips as she surveyed the offerings. "Can we try them all?"

The laugh that burst from Brandon's lips reminded Presley of old times. Joyful and full. "No, that would ruin your dinner, but we can each pick a pie and share. How's that?"

She nodded enthusiastically as she reached for a large cherry slice.

"Did you enter a pie?" Brandon asked as he debated over which slice to pick.

Presley shook her head. "I forgot about the festival until Trudy reminded me, but I don't think it would be fair for me to enter anyway."

"Probably right." Brandon smiled and selected an apple slice. Beverly grabbed a pumpkin, leaving the chocolate for Presley. Then Brandon filled everyone a cup of steaming hot chocolate, and they took their goodies to an empty table.

The Porter family, who owned the General Store, was sitting at a table nearby. They had a large brood with five children, the youngest in diapers. Sid Porter was a few years older than Brandon and Presley and took over the store after his father retired. His sister, Misty, was a grade younger, and she married out of college and only returned for holidays.

Max was at another table along with Barnard, the mayor, and Layla. Max had his usual grumpy stare on as he tasted the pies. Barnard was treating each one like a wine tasting, delicately chewing each bite and tilting his head back and forth before marking on his pad. Layla was simply cleaning up each dessert. Presley had never seen a woman eat so much and stay as thin as she did, but it might be from the fact that Layla never seemed to slow down.

Presley took a few bites of the chocolate pie and then passed it to the right as Joy's pie came to her. In this manner, they sampled a little of each pie without feeling too gluttonous, though Presley's stomach still bulged against her jeans as they finished.

"Let's dance, Daddy." Joy grabbed his hand and pulled him over to the makeshift dance floor. As it was really the part Paula used for her dance recitals, there was a mirror behind them that allowed Presley to see Brandon's face as he twirled around with his daughter.

"You still care for him, don't you?" Beverly's voice broke Presley's daydream of dancing in Brandon's arms, and a blush crawled across her face.

She opened her mouth to answer, but Joy and Brandon

returned at that moment. "Presley, may I have this dance?" Brandon held out his hand and finished the gesture with a bowing flourish.

How different he seemed from the man who walked in an hour ago. Small town magic. She placed her hand in his and happened to catch the wink Beverly threw her direction.

The music changed to a slow song as they hit the floor, but Brandon didn't skip a beat. His left hand closed over her right as his arm circled her waist. When he pulled her closer, her body aligned with his, and she could feel every curve of him. His scent – dark and woodsy filled her nose. She wanted to lean her head on his shoulder, but she didn't know if it would be appropriate. So, she closed her eyes and focused on the feel of his hand on hers and the heat radiating between their bodies.

Though they had danced in high school, this time felt different. Was it the difference in their age? Was it the unspoken of past between them?

When her eyes opened, Brandon's deep brown eyes were there, staring down at her. An intensity shone in them she had never seen before. Her breath caught, and her lips parted, following a will of their own. Brandon's grip tightened on her back, and his head lowered down.

"Daddy." The spell was broken as Joy hurried up to them. Brandon pulled back, dropping Presley's hand and running his hand over his bearded chin.

"They're about to award a winner." Joy grabbed his hand and pulled him back to the table where Beverly sat. Presley followed, trying to erase the almost kiss from her mind.

Barnard stood on the makeshift stage that had been brought in and tapped the microphone. "Can you hear me?" His voice echoed around the room, and he took a step back to lessen the volume. Dressed in slacks and a button-down shirt that barely covered his rotund belly, Barnard was that man who saw one thing in the mirror while the rest of humanity saw something different. Presley had always admired his confidence even if she hadn't admired his wardrobe choice.

"Thank you all for coming out today. I hope you enjoyed the festival so far. Everything seems to have been a hit except for Bert's candles."

"I did my best," Bert shouted from the crowd. "I was working with my dead Aunt Frannie's recipe, and I think she forgot to write something down."

A titter of laughter scattered through the room.

"Anyway," Barnard drew the words out to grab the room's attention again. "Feel free to go back and do more crafts. I think we'll have to get more popcorn, but the booths will be open another few hours. Then tonight, you can come back for the Star Lake dance. We're going to clear this floor and kick up our heels." A cheer erupted from the small crowd, and Barnard raised his hands to quiet them.

"Now, the moment you've all been waiting for. I, and my humble associates, have finished tasting all the pies, and we have decided on the winner." He pulled three index cards out of the pocket of his shirt. "In third place, we have Paula's pumpkin pie."

"Ooh, thank you," Paula said as she pushed her way to the front. Even as she accepted the ribbon, her eyes scanned the crowd, probably looking for her next victim.

"In second place, we have Bert's cherry pie."

"Aha, at least Aunt Frannie got that recipe right." Bert stood and pointed his finger at the ceiling.

Barnard rolled his eyes and shook his head. Presley sneaked a glance at Brandon, who smiled back. Some things never changed. Their glance held a moment longer, and she wondered if he was thinking about that almost kiss as much as she was.

"And first place goes to … Oh my, it goes to my apple pie. I'm honored."

"You can't award your own pie, Barnard," Trudy called from the crowd.

"Well Max and Layla voted as well," he said, puffing up like a turkey. "It's not like I was the sole judge." This was another common occurrence. Barnard had a habit of always entering contests and making sure he won.

"It's not right," Trudy said, but most of the crowd had already lost interest.

"What did I miss?" Anna asked, popping in between Presley and Brandon.

"Everything," Brandon said. "The festival is basically over."

Beverly glanced down at her watch. "Well, I have to go check on your father." After hugging Joy, she waved goodbye to the rest of the group and hurried out of the door.

"Can we go to Star Lake?" Joy asked once again bouncing on her feet. The sugar in the pies must have given her a new burst of energy.

Brandon opened his mouth and looked from Presley back to Joy.

"How about I take her?" Anna asked as if sensing something in the air though she missed the near kiss. "I want some time to get to know my niece anyway."

Relief flooded Brandon's face, and he mouthed "thank you" to Anna, who smiled, looked at Presley with raised eyebrows, and then grabbed Joy's hand.

"Why aren't you coming Daddy?"

Her innocent question flustered him, and a smile formed on Presley's lips as she watched him struggle to come up with an excuse. "Well, um, Presley is going to give me a tour of the town to show me how much has changed."

Presley covered her mouth to hide the laugh bubbling in her throat. It was a good thing Joy was only five, or she would realize there wasn't much to this town and definitely not much that had changed in four short years.

"But I'll be back soon, okay?"

She nodded, accepting his lame excuse as gospel and headed out the door with Anna leaving Brandon and Presley staring at each other.

"So, a tour, huh?" Presley didn't even try to hide the humor in her voice.

"I wanted to have a chance to talk with you and with a five-year-old, that is often hard."

The gaze in his eyes was different, more serious. It sent her heart fluttering and the words running from her mind, so that all she could do was nod and smile.

She waved goodbye to Trudy who caught her eye as they walked toward the door. Her eyebrows raised, and she nodded knowingly. Warmth flooded Presley's cheeks once again.

CHAPTER 8

*G*lancing at Presley as he opened the door, Brandon wondered what he was doing. He didn't plan to stay in this town longer than he had to, but there was no denying the attraction building between Presley and himself. Maybe, if she felt the same way, she would come with him back to Dallas and wherever his job might lead.

The temperature had dropped while they were inside, and Presley burrowed into her coat. Her hat was pulled low over her ears, hiding her hair. Brandon adjusted his own hat, thankful for the beard that covered his face and provided an extra layer of warmth.

Presley's face turned up to the sky, revealing her perfectly smooth white neck, and Brandon had to force himself to refrain from pulling her into his arms right then. Her nose twitched. "The snow is coming," she said.

He used to tease her about this gift, but she was right more often than not, and he learned to take her word. "I don't mind a little snow, do you?"

She shook her head, a soft smile on her lips. How had he forgotten those perfectly pink lips?

"What happened with Morgan?" she asked, breaking the silence. Her eyes widened as the words tumbled out, as if she hadn't meant for them to pass her lips.

With a sigh, Brandon shoved his hands deeper in his pocket, sending his shoulders up near his ears as they continued down Main Street. "I don't really know. I thought we were happy, but she said she wanted more. She wasn't cut out for life in the small town."

Presley's eyes clouded with sympathy. "Is that why you moved?"

"Yeah, after Morgan left, I just couldn't stay, and I think I wanted more too. I wanted to see the world, to make a statement, get back to reality. Dallas seemed like a good first step."

"I'm sorry," she said, though her mouth opened again as if she wanted to say more, but nothing came out.

Brandon shrugged, no longer wanting to dwell on his past, but curious as to hers. "It is what it is. What about you? What really happened with the guy in France?"

Her shoulders rose as she took a deep breath, and her tongue darted out across her bottom lip. Brandon turned his head away as the desire to taste her lips ignited within him.

"He wasn't capable of seeing just me, and I just couldn't make myself stay, so I came home, to the last place I felt really comfortable."

His hand reached out, as if with a mind of its own, and grasped her arm, halting their forward movement. "Presley, I . . ."

The blue in her eyes brightened, like the clear ocean on a sunny day. "Yes?" Her voice was a whisper, choked back by emotion.

"Will you go to the dance with me tonight?"

She blinked, and he could tell that wasn't what she expected to hear. It wasn't what he expected to say either. He wanted to tell her that he'd missed her, that she was beautiful, and that just being near her was sending his heart into an overzealous beating.

A snowflake landed on her cheek, and her eyes widened. Another hit her nose, creating a tiny wet dot on the end. As Brandon looked up, one landed in his eye, causing him to blink and rub it out.

"I told you it would snow." Her laughter was pure happiness as she threw open her arms and spun in a slow circle. The snow picked up and surrounded her, creating the image of a figurine in a snow globe. She was exotic and hauntingly beautiful against the backdrop of white flakes, and before he knew it, his hand had reached out and grabbed hers.

Brandon couldn't feel her skin through their gloves, but the material didn't stop the heat generating between them. Her eyes, still dancing with delight, met his, and he knew there would be no stopping the kiss this time. He pulled her the few feet between them, closing the distance. His hand wound around her back, and though no words were said, everything was communicated in their locked gaze.

A tentative smile parted her lips, and that was all the permission Brandon needed. Pushing ever so slightly with his body, he leaned her back against his arm and placed his lips on hers. They were as soft as he expected, and he wondered how his beard felt against her cheek. He hoped it wasn't too scratchy.

Her arms reached up around his neck as her lips parted farther and the kiss deepened. His arm tightened, drawing her closer and for a moment Brandon cursed the snow. No, not the snow, just the cold temperature that had them bundled in heavy coats. The snow he loved as it fell softly around them. A stillness filled the air and imprinted the moment on his mind.

Her eyes were foggy as she opened them again, and Brandon hoped he hadn't overstepped.

"Well, that was better than I always dreamed it would be," she said.

He stood her back upright, but kept his arm close around her. "What do you mean always?"

Her eyes crinkled with kindness. "Brandon, I've wanted to kiss you since that Christmas we got the tree."

Now it was his turn to blink. He had no idea she'd had feelings for him back then. "Why didn't you ever tell me?"

Her gloved hand cradled his cheek, and her eyes caressed his face. "Because there was always someone else, Brandon."

He opened his mouth to protest but realized she was right. What she didn't know was that all those other women were his way of trying to mask his feelings for her. He knew within a few months of them becoming friends that he had feelings for her, but he was too afraid of ruining the friendship. Presley had always had a way of getting him to open up and relax that no one else had been able to do.

When Brandon had realized that, an unnatural fear of losing her friendship had covered him, and he had decided not to pursue his feelings for her, but now there was nothing stopping him. They hadn't spoken over the last five years, so there was nothing to lose, and his feelings were just as strong now as they had been then, so there was everything to gain.

"I never told you, but I had feelings for you back then too, but was too afraid of losing you. The irony is I ended up losing you anyway. I'm sorry, Presley."

Her finger moved to his lips, stilling them. "It's too late for regrets, but it's not too late for us."

As the snow continued to fall, Brandon pulled her in for another kiss, this one slow and lingering. He wanted to taste everything about her. The heat built between them, creating a shield between them and the snow, until his phone rang in his pocket.

Frustrated, he broke the connection and reached for the device.

Presley didn't seem upset. In fact, she smiled at his annoyance. "Hello?" Brandon punched the answer button without looking at the caller ID. He was expecting his assistant's voice, but the voice of his mother answered him.

"Brandon? They're releasing your father. Can you come help me bring him home? He's still very weak."

Instantly his demeanor changed, and Presley's eyes widened with questions. "Of course, Mom, I'll be right there."

"Is your dad okay?" Presley asked as he ended the call.

"Yeah." The word came out like a sigh though he hadn't realized he was holding his breath. "They're releasing him, but my mother needs help getting him home."

"I'll come with you."

"You don't have to. It won't be very interesting, and I may not make it back in time for the dance."

Her hand squeezed his arm. "Brandon, I want to come with you."

Inside, his heart soared. He didn't want to end their day so soon, and the hospital held no fond memories for him. "Thank you."

Hand in hand, they walked back down Main Street to Cooper Street and then up the road to his parent's house. As they entered the house, the sound of Joy and Anna in the kitchen carried to them. Brandon was glad Joy was in out of the cold.

Inside the kitchen, Joy's face was pressed against the back glass window, and Anna sat at the kitchen table nursing a coffee and coloring. She looked up as they entered and winked.

"Daddy, it's snowing." Joy squealed and turned from the window long enough jump up and down in an excited little dance.

"I know, Bug," he said to her before turning to Anna. "Dad is getting released, so Presley and I are going to help Mom. Can you watch Joy a little longer?"

"Sure." She took a sip of her coffee, which made him want to pour a mug of his own. He grabbed a travel mug from the cabinet and filled it up.

"You want any?" he asked Presley.

"Do you have any creamer? I never got used to drinking it black. I prefer my coffee tan."

Leave it to Presley to have to be unique. It was another thing that had always attracted Brandon to her. Though the chunk in her hair was not always purple, it was always a color different from her natural dirty blond. Her nails were typically painted in some sparkly polish, and even her clothes were often brighter than most people would choose to wear, but somehow on her it worked. Most people probably saw her as an oddity with her quiet nature yet sparkly exterior, but Brandon knew the real Presley who was somewhere in between the two.

Opening the fridge, he found some white chocolate creamer in the door. She nodded her approval as he held it up, and he rescued another travel mug from the counter and filled it up for her along with a healthy dash of the creamer. The coffee was indeed a light tan color when he handed it to her.

She took a long sip, closing her eyes in delight as she swallowed. The look on her face sent his heart pumping again. Images of morning coffee breaks following blissful nights flooded his mind.

He forced his eyes away from her soft pink lips though all he really wanted to do was cover them with his own again. A subtle head shake cleared his thoughts, and he grabbed his keys from the hook that hung on the wall. Then he grabbed his coffee, though the heat from his thoughts had chased away the cold.

"Back in a minute, Bug. Be good for Anna."

"Okay," she said, but her face was still pressed to the glass. It didn't snow in Dallas, but Joy had always been fascinated. Brandon hoped it snowed enough for her to play in it tomorrow.

Presley followed him out of the kitchen and to the car. Opening her door, he took a moment to steal another kiss. With her back pressed against the car, she grabbed his coat with her free hand and pulled him closer. Brandon could almost feel her heart beating through the thick fabric that separated them. Too soon, but for his own sanity, the kiss ended, and they climbed into the car.

Her hand found his as he started the car, and he shot her a smiling glance. It was nice having her in the car with him. Even after all the years apart, her presence still soothed and calmed him.

"Joy is amazing," she said as they pulled onto Main street. The snow was still falling, though lightly, and the street was empty. Everyone must be inside their homes bundled up.

"Yeah, she is."

"Do you want more?" The question was tentative and soft.

"More what? Kids?" His eyes flickered from the road to her face for a moment. She nodded, but her eyes were cast down on her lap as if she was afraid of his answer. "I honestly haven't thought about it." Though that was only half true. He had thought about how another child would impact his work and make it that much harder, but that was before Presley re-entered his life. Maybe if the situation were right, he would be open to another child.

They arrived at the hospital a few minutes later. His father's face was still shocking, and Brandon squeezed Presley's hand as he heard her soft gasp beside him. His left eye was now a faded purple, but still swollen. There were stitches across the back of his head where they'd had to drill a hole to relieve the initial pressure, and he was thinner. He looked as if he had lost twenty pounds as his shirt hung loosely on him, and his pants required a belt to stay up.

Brandon's mother's eyebrow raised at Presley's and his clasped hands, and a smile pulled across her lips.

"Mr. Scott, I'm so happy to hear you are coming home," Presley said.

His father turned his good eye to her. "Is that Presley Hays? Thank you for the treats."

"You are welcome, sir."

The orderly arrived a moment later and helped load his father into a wheelchair. He, of course, protested the whole time, declaring his ability to walk even as his legs shook against the foot petals.

When they reached the hospital entrance, Brandon and Presley stayed with him while his mother hurried to get her car. As she pulled up in front, his father attempted to stand and collapsed back in the chair. Brandon took one arm and Presley took the other. His father's face furrowed as if he was about to protest, but then his lips flattened into a line, and he shuffled forward.

It was a slow walk the ten or fifteen feet out of the hospital to where Brandon's mother had parked the car, but his father was out of breath when they arrived. With eyes full of concern, Brandon glanced at his mother. Though he knew his father had taken a nasty fall, he was not used to seeing him so weak and helpless.

She nodded once to let him know she was aware, and her smile assured him that everything would be alright.

Presley seemed to sense his unease on the drive home. Her hand landed on his arm. "Don't worry. He'll be okay. Sometimes it just takes a little longer to heal. I'll be praying for his speedy recovery."

Brandon knew she was trying to help, but at this moment, he wanted to do anything but think about his father. "After we help get him inside, how about we go to that dance after all? I could use a distraction."

Nodding, she squeezed his knee, and that simple gesture sent a flood of peace through his body. He had definitely missed having Presley in his life.

CHAPTER 9

*P*resley glanced in the mirror at the blue dress she had chosen. It was knee length, and had a line of flowers around the neckline. Simple, but dressy. She grabbed a cardigan in case it got chilly in the barn and threw her coat over her arm so she would be ready when Brandon arrived.

The knock sounded precisely at seven pm. Brandon had not lost his need to be punctual. A smile was already on her face as she opened the door, but it expanded at the sight of him. Though she could not tell what he was wearing underneath his heavy coat and hat, she could see his eyes and the smile behind his beard.

"You look beautiful." He took her hand and stepped into the apartment.

As he pulled her close, she could smell his cologne – a mixture of sandalwood and a clean scent like the ocean. Her hand pushed his hat back so she could run her fingers through his hair and then caressed his cheek. Presley wasn't sure she liked his beard, but it was softer than it looked. When her fingers touched his lips, he grabbed them and moved them over his heart before placing his lips against hers. Heat flamed through her body as the kiss deepened.

"We better get to the dance or we may never make it out of here." His voice was breathless and husky.

Recovering from the emotions flooding her body, Presley could only nod and slip into her coat. Being around Brandon was intoxicating, and she would have to be vigilant not to let it go too far.

The snow had stopped, but a layer of white lay about the town. Presley loved the snow like this, when the air was crisp and cold and everything looked pure and new. It wasn't quite enough snow to build a snowman with Joy as she had promised, but she was hopeful it would snow more. If her itchy nose was any indication, it would.

Brandon's fingers laced through hers as they began the walk to the barn. The town was quiet, and it looked different in the dark with few places lit up. Even Max's diner was dark as they neared it. Presley had a hunch that Layla had dragged him to the dance, though he would probably pretend to be annoyed by it.

Strings of white Christmas lights hung from the trees near the barn and several strands crisscrossed back and forth across the front of the building. Either someone had hung them since the festival or else Presley hadn't noticed them earlier.

Music carried on the still air – a lively teeny bopper tune that made Presley wonder if they had raided Justin's CD collection from a few years ago.

"Oh, dear, are we sure we want to do this?" Brandon asked, but the smile on his face belayed his amusement and softened his words.

The inside of the barn had been transformed again. The tables and the CD player were still on one side, but the other side had been cleared of the pop up tables, allowing for more dance floor space. Trudy waved from across the room and then raised her camera and snapped a shot.

Presley returned the wave as Brandon pulled her toward an empty table where they shed their coats. At the back wall, a row of potluck food lined a long table. As Presley's eyes took in the savory casseroles and bowls of salads, her stomach rumbled, and she realized she hadn't eaten in a few hours.

"Can we get some food?"

"Already ahead of you," he said laughing. "Why do you think I chose the table right by the food?" The old saying stated the fastest way to a man's heart was through his stomach, and whether that was true or not, Brandon had always enjoyed food.

As they joined the dozen other people in the line for food, Presley sneaked a look at Brandon. His green button-down shirt hugged his broad shoulders and tapered down to a narrow waist. It was tucked into a pair of black slacks that skimmed the curves of his lower body, hinting at what lay beneath.

After grabbing some salad and a casserole chunk which resembled lasagna, they returned to the table to see that Bert and Amelia, the quiet girl who ran the flower shop, had joined them. In traditional Bert flair, he was sporting a brown bow tie over a green checkered shirt. His hair was parted on the side and flattened down, but like Alfalfa, he had one finicky cowlick that stood on end at the back of his head.

Amelia's eyes were focused on her plate as she shifted a piece of salad back and forth across the plate. Her shyness was an odd contrast to Bert's outgoing persona. Her brown hair was curled into ringlets and pulled back with a white flowered headband.

"Presley, you might know. What would you think about me offering a taxi service for animals like Lyft?" Bert asked as he shoved a giant piece of bread in his mouth.

"I don't know much about Lyft, but where would animals need to go?" Presley asked, pursing her lips to keep from smiling.

"I would take dogs from their homes to daycare and back."

"Who would you drive? There is no dog daycare around here." Brandon rolled his eyes as he sat down.

Bert's head turned as he pondered this. "I could drive them out of town I suppose, but my sister's car is not very reliable."

Brandon and Presley shared an amused glance and continued eating their food. If nothing else, Bert's ideas were always good for a laugh.

When their plates were empty, Brandon grabbed her hand and pulled her to the dance floor. As his arms circled her, Presley's heart accelerated. She could feel the muscles in his arm through his thin shirt, and the chiseled features of his chest when he tightened his grip, pulling her closer. His eyes stared into hers, daring her to get lost in the chocolate pools that resided there.

Her throat closed making it hard to swallow. She could live here, safe in Brandon's arms. The feeling was natural, organic until his ringing phone interrupted it.

"Sorry, I have to take this."

And just like that, the mood was broken. His face hardened back into the stiff posture she saw the first day, and without a second glance, he left her on the dance floor and headed to the entrance of the barn. His phone was already attached to his ear as he wound through the dancing couples.

Trudy arrived at Presley's side moments later. "What happened?"

Presley shrugged, tears pricking her eyes. "Work, I think, but he didn't really say." She hoped it was just work, but her mind was thinking back to the last conversation she had with Pierre.

She sat on the small terrace, sipping a cup of tea and staring at the Eiffel Tower lit up in the distance. Tonight was her last night in Paris. It had been an amazing few years studying baking and then working in the city of lights, and she was going to miss it.

"I do not want you to go." Pierre joined her at the little table and handed

her a small cup of her favorite dessert, chocolate mousse. Breathing in the heavenly scent, she flashed him a warm smile.

They had met a year ago at a bistro. He had been reading the paper and watching her as she devoured her first chocolate mousse. After her second, he had come over to her table, explaining he had to meet the woman who so enjoyed her dessert. Though mortified, Presley allowed him to join her at the table, and it became the first of many dates. While she knew they would never marry, he had filled the hole in her heart that existed since leaving Brandon, at least until she had seen him with another woman.

"I know, but my time here is up." Scooping a delicate spoonful of the fluffy brown dessert, she closed her eyes as the spoon entered her mouth. She had never figured out why, but the chocolate mousse lit up her taste buds and set her pulse racing. One day, she hoped to be able to duplicate it in her own shop.

"What will I do without ma Cheri?" Pierre stood and crossed behind her. His hands landed on her shoulders and gently massaged them.

A shiver traveled down her spine. There were some things about Pierre she would miss, and the feel of his lips on her neck was one of them. "I'm sure you'll go back to all your other women," Presley said, trying to remain in control. Though she said the words lightly, they stung even as they left her mouth. It was only a suspicion, but perhaps if he thought she knew, he would admit it to her.

"But they will not be you," he whispered in her ear.

And there it was. The reason she could never stay with him. She had seen him with a buxom blond two weeks ago, but they hadn't appeared overly friendly. However, the next day her friend, Minuet, informed her that she saw him stealing kisses with a blond. Her description closely matched the woman Presley had seen him with, though she hadn't told Minuet about the sighting. She knew then it was time to leave. She put her notice in and began packing up.

"I have to go see my family again," she said softly, changing the subject. There was no reason to fight about the other woman. Pierre had never said they *were exclusive and somehow here in France, a woman or two on the side was more acceptable, though it was not acceptable to her. "It's been years, and I miss them." Another spoonful of mousse found its way to her mouth, and she sighed. Though Pierre was no longer one of them, there were things she would miss about France.*

"I could come with you." Pierre's breath tickled her ear.

The words snapped her eyes open. She did not want Pierre coming with her. "You would hate it, Pierre," she said trying to keep my voice even. "The food isn't nearly as good, and I'll have to live with my mom and younger brother for a while until I can get my own place again." Ryan wouldn't be there as he worked in Houston, but Pierre didn't need to know that.

His hands left her shoulders, and he circled the table and sat in the other seat. Placing his chin on folded hands, he stared into her eyes. Those eyes — they were Presley's weakness and he knew it. With his dark hair, he reminded her very much of Brandon, which was probably why she had fallen for him in the first place. His eyes were an arresting blue, the color of the ocean after a storm, and they were what kept her coming back. She would miss those eyes.

"I think you are trying to convince me not to come," he said in his lilting accent, "but I agree. I do not think I would like what you are describing. So, I suppose tonight is goodbye."

Though he stayed a little longer, he seemed anxious to leave now that their dating relationship was over. When he finally bid good night, Presley felt a flood of relief. After another longing look at the city that had been her home for the last few years, she stepped back inside the flat to finish packing. It was going to be a long flight home.

"I don't think I will be able to take it if there's another woman on the side."

Her hands were shaking as Trudy led her back over to the table. Thankfully Bert and Amelia were dancing, and they were alone.

"Oh, girl, that cheating Pierre affected you more than you're letting on, didn't he?"

Presley nodded; she had told Trudy just a little about what happened with Pierre.

"Well, I don't think Brandon is like that." Trudy's voice was soft as she placed a hand on Presley's arm. "Did he ever date multiple women in high school?"

She shook her head. Though she was worried about another woman, she was almost more worried that it wasn't. Because if it was his job, it would be even harder to compete with. "Work can be a mistress too."

Presley's voice was soft, but Trudy heard the words, and her eyes widened in understanding. Then her eyebrow arched, and she indicated something behind Presley with her head. Presley knew without even looking that Brandon had returned.

"Sorry about that," he said sliding in the chair next to her. "It was my assistant, but I think everything is worked out. She shouldn't bother us any more tonight."

He was trying to make her feel better. She could tell from his tone, and while she was still worried about her fragile heart, she decided to try and enjoy the rest of the evening. "Okay, shall we finish dancing then?"

"I thought you'd never ask."

He took her hand once again, and Presley shot a final glance at Trudy, who smiled and nodded. If she believed that it wouldn't overpower their relationship, then Presley guessed she could too.

As Brandon pulled her close on the dance floor, the fear began to abate, and she found herself once again wrapped up in his safe arms. Leaning her head against his shoulder, she enjoyed the solidity of it and the slight tickling of his beard on her forehead.

His phone did not ring the rest of the night, and Presley allowed herself to believe it was a one-time thing. When the dance ended, they gathered their coats and headed out into the cold night with the rest of the crowd.

"Oh, come on, Max, you know you had fun," Presley heard Layla say off to their right.

"Or how about a cat day care? You know like a dog one, only for cats?" Bert's voice carried from the left.

Giggling, Presley snuggled into the crook of Brandon's arm, and he pulled her closer. "I'll never get tired of that view. Bet you don't see that in Dallas." She pointed to the sky above, clear and filled with stars.

"That you don't," he said, "but we have other things that you can't get here."

Presley kicked herself as she heard his voice shift. She didn't want him thinking about what he was missing. It was clear she still had her work cut out for her.

CHAPTER 10

After church the next day, Presley stopped by Max's and grabbed sandwiches to take to Brandon's house. She didn't know if they had gone to a different church or even if they'd had lunch, but she felt the need to show up with something.

Max eyed her as he placed the wrapped sandwiches in a paper bag. There was something on his mind evident from his frownier than usual face and slightly pursed lips.

"What?" Presley asked with a sigh when he didn't offer his thoughts.

"I just wonder if you know what you're getting yourself into. I don't want you sitting in my corner table scaring the customers away again when he leaves."

It had only been two days, right after Brandon told her about Morgan, that she had sat in his corner table, eating ice cream and sketching, refusing to talk to anyone, but Max had let her know in no uncertain terms that she had affected his bottom line and should take her sulking elsewhere.

"I'm not getting into anything." Presley was trying to convince herself as much as Max. "It's just lunch with his family."

His eyebrow raised, but he said nothing more as he finished filling the paper bag and pushed it across the counter. Presley plopped down two twenties and picked up the bag.

"What about your change?" he asked as she headed toward the door.

"Put it on my tab for next time." She pushed the door open to the white wonderland outside. The snow was still falling lightly outside as she headed to Cooper Street.

Though not heavy, the bag was awkward, and she ended up shifting it several times from one hip to the other before reaching Brandon's house. He opened the door before her finger could hit the bell, and her eyes widened in surprise.

"I listened for the step." He grinned and took the bag from her. Presley stomped the snow off her boots before crossing the threshold into the house. After carefully removing her hat, coat, and scarf, she hung them on the rack and followed him into the kitchen.

"Presley brought lunch," Brandon said as they entered.

"Oh, good, I'm starving." Anna shut the book she had been reading and jumped up to search for paper plates.

"I want to build a snowman," Joy said.

Presley touched her head. "Let's eat, and I'll help you build a good one after lunch."

"You promise?"

The question caught Presley off guard, but it was the look in her eyes that really bothered her, as if Joy was often used to having promises broken. She sneaked a glance at Brandon, but he wasn't paying attention. He was busy emptying the bag and doling out the sandwiches.

"I promise." Presley dropped down to her knees to be on eye level with Joy. "Building snowmen is one of my favorite pastimes."

Her eyes sparkled and she leaned in as if sharing a secret. "Mine too, or at least I think it will be after I build my first one."

Laughing, Presley grabbed her hand and led her to the table where Brandon and Anna had laid out plates and sandwiches. Beverly arrived with two bags of chips and cups. Bruce, probably needing to feel useful, poured iced tea in each cup and passed it to his right.

After lunch, Presley helped Beverly clear the table as Brandon took Joy to add on layers. The snow was still falling, which meant the air was still cold outside.

Joy returned a few moments later, walking stiffly with her arms out and her legs straight. A scowl lined her face. "I can't move like this, Daddy."

"But you'll be warm which is more important." He was also bundled up, but only in a coat and hat.

"How many layers is she wearing?" Presley counted at least two from the different colored necklines protruding from her coat.

"Four. She doesn't have a heavy coat, and I don't want her to freeze."

Presley mashed her lips together to stifle the laugh. She didn't want Joy thinking she was laughing at her, but the situation was comical. "Maybe it will loosen up as you move." As she hurried into the living room, a giggle escaped her lips. She grabbed her coat, hat, scarf, and boots and hurried back to them.

Brandon held the coat for her as she shrugged her arms into the sleeves, and then he wrapped his arms around her, sneaking a quick peck on the cheek before letting go. Cheeks still aflame, Presley pulled her hat on and wrapped the scarf around her neck. Her gloves, tucked safely in her coat pockets, were the last item she added, and then they ventured into the backyard.

The snow, while light, had been falling almost steadily since it started the night before, and now a few inches coated the ground. Enough to build a snowman if it was the right kind of snow.

Joy squealed with delight and ran around in circles, stopping every few minutes to stick out her tongue and catch snowflakes. "It's so cold."

While Brandon watched Joy, Presley bent down and rolled up a ball of snow. She pelted him with it before he had time to turn around.

"Hey." His shout was more from surprise than annoyance, but the evil glint appeared in his eye. Squealing, she ran as he scooped up his own snowball.

His ammo hit the side of her leg, spraying her with cold pellets. Joy stopped to watch, and after realizing they were playing, she began scooping up her own balls and pelting Brandon.

Presley landed another one as he turned to deal with Joy.

"Hey, no fair," he shouted. "This is two against one."

"That's right." Presley dodged his next ball, a smile on her face.

Joy landed one on his hip and doubled over with laughter as he pretended to be angry and come after her. She didn't even try to get away, but allowed him to pick her up and swing her around.

"I'll get you later," he said. "Right now, we need to get Presley."

She agreed, and Presley sprinted toward the safety of some bushes, but not fast enough. Brandon's longer stride caught her, and as he grabbed for her coat, she lost her footing and fell to the soft snow.

Brandon, tripping over her flailing feet, landed on top of her, his face inches from hers. His arms, thankfully, caught his fall or else they might have smashed faces.

She could feel his breath on her face as his eyes stared into hers and began to close, his face lowering.

"What are you doing?" Joy asked.

Brandon's eyes snapped open, and he scrambled up. "Nothing, Presley and I both fell is all." He held out his hand and helped her up.

"Uh huh, sure." She eyed them both and Presley bit back her

smile. Joy was smart. Maybe too smart for her own good. Presley could tell Joy knew something was different, but she appeared unsure what to do with her information. "Can we build the snowman now?"

Presley took a deep breath to calm her racing heart. "Yes. Let's do this." Bending down, she began to push the snow into a ball shape. It was not quite as wet as it should be and pieces of snow kept falling off the ball, creating more of a lopsided circle.

Brandon pushed with her as the ball grew bigger, his eyes stealing furtive glances. When the base was made, they paused to catch their breath, and Joy brought snow over to patch the holes. A large winding trail of green grass where they had taken snow contrasted with the white of the rest of the backyard.

After the second ball was finished, Presley noticed Joy's teeth chattering. "Let's finish the head quickly," she whispered to Brandon. He looked up at her in surprise, and she nodded in Joy's direction. She was stalwartly still bringing snow over, but her nose was bright pink, and she couldn't keep her teeth locked together.

Brandon deftly rolled up the last smaller ball and placed it on the top before turning to Joy. "Okay, little one, let's get you inside and warmed up."

"I'm o. . .o. . .okay," she insisted, through teeth still snapping repeatedly together.

"No, you're not. You're freezing. We'll finish dressing the snowman later after you've warmed up."

Though she looked like she wanted to protest, the cold won and Joy nodded. Together, they trooped back into the house and peeled off their cold, wet layers.

Beverly, Anna, and Bruce were nowhere to be seen, so Brandon started a tea kettle warming on the stove for hot chocolate, and Presley took Joy into the living room and flicked on the electric fireplace.

As she sat, teeth still chattering, Presley grabbed a blanket from the back of the couch and wrapped it around both of their shoulders. "Is that better?" Joy nodded and curled into her. Unsure what to do, Presley opened her arm and allowed the girl to snuggle in.

Moments later, the tea kettle whistled, and Brandon entered bearing a tray with three steaming mugs of hot chocolate. He smiled at their pose before handing the smallest cup to Joy. "Be careful, it's hot."

"I know Daddy." Her nose was returning to its normal color, and she had warmed up enough that she could control her mouth. She pushed away from Presley and cupped the mug with both hands, holding it just under her chin and letting the steam float up to her eyes.

Brandon handed Presley a mug, holding her fingers longer than necessary. She flashed a warm smile up at him as he sat beside her. In silence, they sipped their hot chocolate and enjoyed the warmth, and it was easy for Presley to envision this as a regular occurrence for them. It felt like home for the first time in years.

When the hot chocolate was gone, and the trio was sufficiently warmed, Joy grabbed Presley's hand. "Do you want to put a puzzle together with me?"

Presley followed her over to a card table and was surprised to see a five-hundred-piece puzzle spread out over the table.

"She loves puzzles," Brandon said, coming behind her and placing his hands on her shoulders. It was an innocent gesture, but it sent a chill down her spine. It had been too long since anyone placed their hands on her shoulders in a show of possession, and it made her smile. With her left hand, she reached up and squeezed Brandon's hand, while her right searched for a puzzle piece to place.

An hour later the puzzle was finished, and they went off in search of the rest of the family. They had been mysteriously absent for the past few hours.

They were found in the family room, passed out in front of the television, which was playing the highlights of some football game. Putting her finger to her lips, Presley motioned them to follow her out of the room.

"Joy, are you warmed up enough?"

She nodded. "I'm toasty."

"How about we go get a tree?"

Her mouth opened, and Presley flung her finger back to her lips, sure Joy was about to squeal. She clapped a hand over her mouth and nodded, eyes wide and dancing.

"Fine, but you need another layer." Brandon steered Joy down the hall to the bedrooms.

Her sigh was audible down the hallway, and Presley smiled as she headed back for her own coat and hat. They were still a little wet from the romp earlier, but she figured they would be okay. They met back at the front door and headed into the cold.

The snow had stopped, which meant the air was slightly warmer, but only slightly. Brandon steered them to his father's pickup parked on the side; his city car would never be able to hold a tree.

He started the truck to warm up the engine and then headed into the shop, returning a moment later with a saw and some rope.

When the truck was sufficiently warmed up, he backed out of the drive slowly, partly because of the snow on the ground and partly because Joy wasn't in her usual car seat. The forest wasn't very far, and there was little traffic, but Brandon still drove cautiously. His shoulders hunched forward, and his hands gripped the wheel so hard that white erupted around the knuckles. Presley couldn't decide if he was more worried about the snow or the lack of a car seat.

Ten minutes later, he pulled the truck to a stop outside the forest. It was as she remembered it. Tall Virginia Pines filled the forest, like an army of green triangles ready to march into battle. They were accompanied by smaller scraggly trees and brush.

They piled out of the truck, and before the doors were shut, Joy took off running. "Daddy, look at all the trees."

"Find us a good one," he hollered back.

"She sure seems excited," Presley said meeting him at the back of the truck.

"Yeah, well there aren't many places to get a real tree in Dallas." The saw swung from his hand as they made their way to the forest.

Presley tried again to picture him in a big city, but couldn't do it. He fit so well here in this small town where he didn't have to try and impress anyone.

"Over here, Daddy. This one."

Joy's voice led them into the forest, where she stood pointing at a tall tree. It had to be nearly eight feet judging by how much taller it was than Brandon who stood at just over six feet.

"Will it fit?" Presley couldn't remember how tall the ceilings in his living room were, though she thought they were taller than eight feet.

"Yeah, but just barely." He walked slowly around the tree, perusing every branch and detail. Presley had forgotten what a tree connoisseur he was. The first year he brought her, he walked around for nearly half an hour before deciding on the perfect tree. "You sure this is the one?"

"Yes, this one." Joy jumped up and down, accentuating her words.

Smiling, Brandon crouched down and began to saw the thick trunk. The crunching noise of the saw ripping through the bark broke the stillness and Joy scurried to Presley's side. She put her arm around the girl and pulled her close.

"Here it comes."

The tree began to tilt their direction, and Presley moved Joy to the side a minute before the tree tumbled down. Brandon sawed the ragged edge at the bottom and then grabbed the trunk and began pulling the tree back toward the truck.

Remembering the last time and the slew of needles they lost as the tree dragged on the ground, Presley picked up the end. Joy, pretending to help, placed her little hands on the middle.

When they reached the truck, Presley placed her end in first and then Brandon shoved his end until the tree lay securely in the bed. Then he tied the tree down with the rope.

They repeated the procedure in reverse when they arrived back at the house, and Anna, who must have heard the commotion, opened the front door for them. Presley and Brandon shuffled down the hallway and into the living room.

"I'll go get the tree stand," Anna said and rushed off, a wide smile on her face.

"I'll get the ornaments," Beverly announced as she hurried off toward the attic.

"I'll just sit here, I guess," Bruce grumbled, the agitation at his inability to help clear in his voice.

Presley walked over to him, hoping to offer some words of encouragement. "You can help us make sure we don't have any holes once we're done decorating. I know it's hard right now, but at least you are home for Christmas."

He squeezed her hand and nodded.

Watching Presley with his father, Brandon couldn't help but picture the kind of wife and mother she would be. She always seemed to know exactly what people needed to hear and when they needed to hear it.

A tug on his pant leg broke his daydreaming, and he bent down to Joy, who motioned with her little finger. "I like her too Daddy. She's nice."

"Yes, she is, Pumpkin. Yes, she is."

"Are you going to marry her?"

Brandon glanced up to see if Presley had overheard, but she was still talking with his father. "I don't know, Joy, but I'd like to see her more. Would that be okay with you?"

She nodded, and her eyes lit up. "I know what to ask Santa for."

Before Brandon could say anything, she darted out of the room.

"What was that about?" Anna asked as she returned. She presented the tree stand to him like a gift.

"I have no idea." He unscrewed the tongs that held the tree in place, and then Anna and Presley joined in lifting the tree and guiding it into the hole. While they held it steady, Brandon crawled under the tree and screwed the tongs back in to hold the tree in place. "Can you get me some water while I'm down here?"

Anna's feet moved toward the kitchen and returned moments later. She handed down a plastic pitcher filled with water, and he slowly poured it into the base.

His mother returned with the lights and ornaments as he wiggled out from under the tree. She set the boxes on the couch and then grabbed the remote to turn on music. After a few clicks, cheerful Christmas music filled the air.

Brandon and Presley began untangling the lights and winding them around the tree. Joy returned a moment later, looking like the Cheshire cat with her silly grin, and watched.

After a few tries, the lights were on correctly and plugged in. Blue, green, white, and red colors burst forth from their plastic prisons.

"Oooh pretty." Joy smiled and clapped her hands.

With the lights on, they moved to the ornaments, taking turns picking one from the box and hanging it on the tree. Brandon's father shouted out directions from his chair. "No, a little higher. We need one to the right. There's a hole right by your hand."

It took a good hour, but finally the tree met everyone's approval. They stepped back and admired the lights as they reflected off the ornaments and reached into the corners of the room. Presley nudged Brandon with her elbow, a familiar gesture from high school, and he wrapped his arm around her and pulled her close.

As the smell of her strawberry scented shampoo hit his nose, desire coursed through his body. It was hard being this close to her and not being able to shower her with kisses. Her hand splayed across his chest, and it took all his strength not to tug her from the room for a private moment.

The grandfather clock on the wall bonged seven o'clock and

Presley jumped. "Oh, dear, I didn't realize it was getting so late. I need to go feed Niko."

Brandon's own stomach rumbled at the mention of food, but it could wait until he walked Presley home.

"I'm hungry too, Daddy."

"Why don't you come with me, Joy," his mother said, "and we'll figure out what we can rustle up for dinner."

After Presley bid goodnight to everyone and donned her coat once again, they stepped out into the chilly night air. Brandon's hand found hers, their fingers intertwining. He couldn't remember the last time he enjoyed holding hands, but he relished the moment now.

"Presley, are you happy here?" The air was still and quiet around them; their footsteps crunching in the snow the only sound.

"Yeah, I think so. It's nice to be home anyway."

Her words pierced his good mood. He'd been hoping she would say she missed the city life and wanted to return.

"You seem happy here too." She squeezed his hand.

"I'm happy with you." He wanted to believe it was just her and not the town working its magic on him again. He'd bought into that fairy tale once and it hadn't worked out well, but he couldn't deny there was a pull to the town. There was a simplicity and a friendliness that you didn't get in big cities, and a part of him not only missed that but wanted something similar for Joy growing up.

Before he had sorted out his thoughts, they reached Presley's apartment. As she turned to face him, he wanted to throw open her door and carry her into the bedroom, but Presley had always been adamant that she would wait for marriage. Brandon leaned into her, pushing her against the door, and took her face in his hands.

His eyes fixated on hers, an ocean of blue. Slowly, his thumb trailed down her cheek and across her lips, which parted at his touch. Her chest rose in anticipation, and he wrapped his hand around the back of her neck, pulling it to him.

The kiss was urgent in need. He had been teased with the sight and smell of her all day and unable to do anything to satisfy the desire, and the floodgates of passion opened. His hand moved from her cheek to the small of her back, pressing her deeper into him. Her body contoured against his, and his heart began to pound in his head.

Her hands ran up his chest, but instead of wrapping around his shoulders or his neck as he hoped, she pushed against his chest, breaking the kiss.

"We need a break." Her voice was throaty and breathless.

"Presley." Her name was almost a moan on his lips as he leaned in again, but she was resolute.

"Brandon, we need a break. I . . . I want to do this right."

Those were not the words he wanted to hear, but he respected Presley's wishes and backed off. "You're right," he said though his body was screaming otherwise. "Thank you for a wonderful day. Can Joy and I come see you tomorrow?"

"I'd like that." She placed a soft, quick peck on his lips before turning and opening her door. She stood in the doorway, an angel with a purple streak and waved goodbye.

As the door closed and he began the walk back home, his mind rehashed the day. His life felt so different with Presley in it, but he wondered if he was falling too fast, and he worried about Joy. What if Presley wouldn't come back with them? He might get over it, but he was not sure Joy would.

CHAPTER 12

Presley had just finished arranging the pastries in the display case when the overhead bell jingled.

"Hi, Presley, can I help you today and learn how to bake?" Joy's excited voice carried across the room before she even looked up.

"Well, hello Miss Joy."

"I'm sorry, but she really wanted to come see you today, and I need to help Mom around the house a bit. Is it okay if she stays for an hour or so? I'll come back before lunch, I promise." Brandon's face was apologetic and sincere.

"Of course, it's okay. Come here, Joy, and we'll make some cookies."

"Yay, cookies."

As Joy ran behind the display case to see the back, Brandon reached for Presley's hand. "Thank you for this." He brought her hand to his mouth and brushed the back of it with his lips.

"No problem. Joy is great, and I'm sure we'll be fine."

He held her eyes a moment longer before reminding Joy to be good and walking out of the shop.

Presley turned to the brunette angel beside her. "I started baking when I was about your age, so I guess it's time you learn. Okay, we need flour and sugar. Let's go to the back and get some from the pantry."

Her brown eyes, so like Brandon's, widened. "You have a pantry back there?"

"Of course." Presley chuckled. "Where else would I keep all the ingredients? I also have a big refrigerator and freezer for the cold ingredients."

Joy grabbed Presley's hand as they walked to the large pantry. Her hand was tiny in Presley's, but her grip was strong. It was obvious Joy was missing a mother figure. Presley had guessed it from the amount of time Joy spent with her yesterday, but every gesture of hers was confirming it.

"Wow, there's so much stuff in here." Joy's voice brought her back to the present, and she glanced around the pantry. It was rather large, the size of a large closet, with five shelves reaching from about knee height up to just beyond her head. Sugar, flour, baking soda, baking powder, salt, yeast, and many other dry ingredients lined the shelves.

Presley dropped Joy's hand long enough to grab flour, sugar, salt, brown sugar, and vanilla. She handed the vanilla and salt to the girl, and they headed to the mixing table and placed the ingredients down. Then it was back to the refrigerator for butter, eggs, and chocolate chips.

The refrigerator, also grand, earned another wide-eyed stare from Joy. Presley handed her the chocolate chips, and they journeyed back to the table. As they placed the ingredients down, the bell jingled. "Be right back," Presley said to the little helper and stepped into the main room.

Layla stood there with her daily order of muffins and bread for the inn. She was Presley's favorite customer as she kept her in business. Today she looked super smart in khaki pants and a pink flowered top. Her brown hair skimmed her shoulders.

"Presley, was that Brandon Scott I saw you with at the dance Saturday night?" Her voice held just a note of teasing laced with her interest.

"It was. He's back in town for a time to help out his father." Presley hoped Layla wouldn't say something unfortunate with Joy around.

"Oh, yes, I heard about that. Well, you two looked good together, but then again, I've thought that since you were in high school. Why did you never date?" Layla was managing the inn when they were in high school, but now she owned it. Though not typically a gossip, she had a pulse on everything that happened in the town.

Presley shrugged in answer to her question. "Timing was never right, I guess." As Layla handed over her list, Presley boxed up her muffins. Four chocolate, four blueberry, four flax, and one apple cinnamon which she was almost certain was Layla's personal choice.

"Ah, yes, timing. Well, as you know it took ten years for Max and me to come around. I hope your time is shorter."

"Me too." Presley chuckled a little because even back in high school, the romance between Layla and Max had been the talk of the town. They all knew Max had liked her – he kept a special seat reserved for her in the diner, yet she had seemed unaware. And there had been rumors she had feelings for him, but she had never told him. Presley would have to ask Trudy what finally brought them together as it had happened while she was in Paris.

She finished boxing the muffins and grabbed the loaves of bread Layla had requested as well. Two sourdough loaves and one cheddar bread – the bread changed day to day but there was always at least one sourdough. Layla slid her card across the counter, and

Presley handed her the merchandise. After signing her name, she waved, and the bell signaled her exit.

"Joy, are you still okay back there?" Presley was a little worried as it had been quiet, and while she didn't have kids, she had grown up with a younger brother and knew quiet usually meant disaster.

"Mmmhmm." Her reply was garbled as if her mouth was full of something. The chocolate chips. Slapping her head, Presley hurried back there to find half the bag gone and Joy's cheeks puffed out like a chipmunk.

"Oh, Joy. You are going to get a tummy ache from all that sugar, and your dad is going to have my hide."

Her big eyes filled with tears. Presley hadn't meant it seriously or at least not all seriously, but she forgot how literal young children were.

"Joy, don't cry. It's okay. Just spit it out, and I'm sure your tummy will be fine." She hoped that was the truth, but she had no idea how much Joy had shoved in her mouth before getting caught. The bag hadn't been full, but she could have sworn it had been three quarters full.

Presley steered Joy to the big silver basin sink, and she leaned over and opened her mouth. Chocolate chips cascaded like barrels over a waterfall out of her mouth. As they kept falling, Presley wondered how she stuffed that many in her mouth. She would have to keep a closer eye on her.

"There, that's better," she said when Joy was finally done.

"Please don't tell Daddy." Her soft, pleading voice pulled on Presley's heartstrings.

"I don't think he would be too mad, honey." She patted the girl's hair rhythmically. It was soft, like spun gold, but the color of chocolate. She buried her face in Presley's hip.

"But it will stress him out, and he's working so hard." Her voice hitched; tears wouldn't be far behind.

Presley's heart went out to her, and she wondered if Brandon had any idea the stress his need to succeed was having on his daughter. She guessed he didn't because she couldn't see him as the type of person who wouldn't care about that. "Okay, Joy, I won't tell him." She wouldn't tell him what happened, but she would be talking to him about the need to spend time with his daughter.

She had firsthand knowledge of this as her father left when she was four. He up and decided he no longer wanted to be a father. Her mother, who had been staying home with them, then had to find a job and since her father disappeared off the face of the Earth and paid no child support, she'd had to find two jobs. Though Presley loved her, she had rarely seen her, and it had caused her to withdraw into her art and baking. It was only meeting Brandon that had finally pulled her out of her shell.

Her younger brother had taken the opposite road; he had begun acting out as she tried to be a sister and a mother to him, so she had seen both sides of what could happen when kids didn't get enough attention, and she didn't want to see either of those happen to Joy.

"Do we still have enough to make cookies?" Joy wiped her eyes with her small hand and turned big doe eyes up at Presley.

"I think we do. I'll grab some peanut butter chips, and we'll add those to make sure. Chocolate and peanut butter make a great combination."

"Thank you, Presley." She let go of Presley's pant leg and hung her head. "I promise not to eat any more."

"Well, at least not until we're done cooking." Presley tipped up her face and gave her a smile.

After grabbing the peanut butter chips, they began mixing the ingredients and rolling out the dough. Joy reverted back to her sunny self, but Presley was still worried about her and why she shoved the chips in her mouth in the first place.

CHAPTER 13

"*B*randon Scott, what do you think you are doing?"

His mother's hands were akimbo on her hips as he stepped into the living room. He removed his coat and hat and hung them on the rack before turning back to her.

"I'm here to help you with Dad, Mom. What do you mean?" He thought they had covered this last night after he returned from walking Presley home. Was his mother going senile? Would he have to deal with that as well?

"That is not what I am talking about, Brandon. I'm talking about Presley."

His brow furrowed together. "Presley? What about Presley?" He felt like he'd just entered an episode of the Twilight Zone and that his mother had started this conversation with another him – a doppelganger or something.

"I'm talking about you leading that poor girl on. Unless you've changed your mind about staying." Her hazel eyes stared pointedly, and he was reminded of the feeling when he was five and caught with his hand in the cookie jar.

"You know I haven't, Mother. I'm still working on this promotion, but I'm not leading her on. I'm," he paused as the words that were about to come out of his mouth, he hadn't vocalized to anyone.

"If you break her heart again, Brandon, I may beat you myself."

"Again?" Her words halted the direction his mind was going and caused it to turn full circle. "When did I break her heart the first time? We never dated."

She stared at him, her anger softening to disbelief. "You mean you didn't know?"

"Didn't know what, Mother?" Brandon threw his hands up in exasperation. "I feel like you are speaking riddles to me."

"Brandon, you're the reason she went to Paris. She was finally going to tell you how she felt, but when she came to tell you, you told her Morgan was pregnant."

His mouth dropped open as his mind swam back to that day.

A knock sounded on the door. He was just about to text Presley to ask her over to share the good news, but it could wait. Opening the door, surprise and delight filled him. Presley stood on the other side in a flowered skirt, unusual for her, but he didn't ponder the reason for it.

"Presley, I was hoping you'd come by." He grabbed her hands and pulled her into the apartment, shutting the door behind them.

"I have something to tell you." Her words come out as a stutter, again a little odd, but he was so focused on his good news that he passed it off as excitement. Had someone already told her? She and Morgan weren't close, but he supposed it was possible.

Brandon propelled her to the hand-me-down couch. As they sat and the rusty springs squeaked, he remembered the day they bought it.

At the age of eighteen, he had decided to step out of his father's shadow and his money and try to make it on his own. After he had signed the lease, his first stop had been Presley's. He wanted her help in furnishing the apartment as she was not only his best friend but had a much better aesthetic eye than he did.

The first stop had been the local Goodwill in the next town for some furniture. This couch was the only one available that day, and though it had a few cringeworthy stains and wasn't very comfortable, the price tag of twenty dollars had been too good to turn down. They had loaded it, along with another chair and a few tables into the back of his black Chevy truck — the one thing he had kept from his parents.

After another stop at a store for kitchen items, plates, and bedding, they had returned to his new and very empty apartment and set the place up. Hours later, exhausted, they had collapsed for the first time on the couch. The resulting cacophony of squeaks had kept them laughing for a good ten minutes.

As the memory faded, he grabbed her hands, unable to contain his excitement any longer. "Morgan is pregnant. I'm going to be a father."

Her mouth dropped open, and her eyes blinked repeatedly. "That's" — *the words seemed stuck in her throat* — "That's wonderful, Brandon."

"I know. I'm so excited. Now, tell me your news."

She swallowed and bit the corner of her lip before pasting her own smile. "I'm going to France."

Suddenly the reason for her flowered skirt and stuttering words that he had dismissed as nothing on the day made sense. His mouth parted, and his hand raked across his beard.

"I didn't know, Mom."

She took a step toward him and touched his arm. "What happened then is in the past, but you have control over your future."

He nodded but was more confused than ever now. Should he stop seeing Presley? Should he just be open that he planned on leaving soon? But, she already knew that.

"Come on." His mother moved her hand to circle through his arm. "Your father needs to walk, and he's being stubborn about it."

She led Brandon through the living room and into the family room where his father was seated in the large recliner. His bruised eye had faded more today, and he was able to open it completely.

The scrapes he received stood out on his bald head, pink reminders of his bad decision. His feet were propped up on the reclining leg bar, and a walker stood to the side.

"Hey, Dad, you ready to go walking?" Brandon forced cheeriness he didn't feel into his voice; his mind was still focused on Presley.

"No." The word was short and almost snippy. His father, at least before Brandon left, had never been grumpy, so it was very different from the man Brandon was used to.

"He's still mad he has to use a walker," his mother explained.

"I don't need it. I just need to walk slower." He crossed his arms and stuck out his bottom lip like a petulant child.

Brandon's mother rolled her eyes and shook her head. "I'll leave you to deal with him." She patted his arm one more time before making her exit.

"Okay Dad, walker or no, let's take a walk."

His father flashed one more pout before closing the footrest and pushing against the chair arms to stand up. His legs wobbled beneath him, and Brandon grabbed his waist before he could fall.

"Dad, there's nothing wrong with needing some help from the walker for a bit. You fell, and you are going to need time to recover."

He glared, but finally agreed and took the walker. It was hard to see him like this, his father who had always been so strong now feeble and needing assistance. That was probably part of his reluctance as well; he didn't want to be weak.

Using the walker, they slowly traversed the house. His father was tired before they had gone completely around the bottom floor. When Brandon deposited him back in the recliner, his breath was labored and his legs shook. Brandon saw his week-long trip turning a lot longer.

His phone rang as soon as his father was situated. A quick glance at the caller ID confirmed it was his assistant. "Be right back, Dad." He punched the answer call button and headed to his room.

"Brandon, how much longer are you going to be gone?" Aubrey's irritated voice filled the other end, and Brandon cringed. It was never a good idea to make Aubrey mad. Though usually even-keeled, Aubrey was part Irish with fiery red hair and a temper to match.

"My father is worse off than I thought. I'm going to need at least another week, maybe a little longer. Why, what's happening?"

"Stewart is what's happening. He wants to see the presentation. I've told him you need a few more days, but he's getting antsy. He's threatening to go elsewhere if he doesn't see it by Friday."

Cursing the poor timing, Brandon raked a hand through his hair. He'd been working on this presentation for a month, and there was no way he was going to lose it. This could be his ticket to the big leagues and a secure future for Joy. "Okay, I'll book a flight to come home to do the presentation. Just stall him a little longer."

"What do you think I've been doing for the last few days?"

A sigh escaped his lips as he hung up the phone. He would have to get flowers or something for Aubrey to stay out of the dog house. Standing, he crossed to the desk that held his laptop and opened the screen. It was time to review the presentation and see if it was missing anything.

He was completely immersed in the slides when his mother entered later, and he jumped at the sound of her voice. "Where's Joy? It's past lunchtime."

Brandon's eyes jumped to the tiny clock in the bottom right of the computer. Crap. He should have picked her up an hour ago. "She's with Presley." Clicking the save button, he closed the screen again. He would have to finish it later.

"Still?"

"I know Mom, I lost track of time."

Her eyes narrowed, but before she could spout another lecture,

Brandon squeezed past her and down the hall. His coat was on before she entered the living room, and while she said nothing, he could feel her accusing eyes boring into his back. He grabbed his hat and threw open the door.

The cold blasted his face as he stepped onto the porch, and he pulled his coat tighter. He hadn't even buttoned it up in his haste to exit the house, and he fumbled with the buttons now. His breath created tiny puffs of smoke as he picked up the pace.

"I'm so sorry," he said pushing open the door to Presley's shop.

"Daddy." Joy ran to him, throwing her arms about his legs. "We made cookies, and I got to help serve people and then Presley made me lunch on this yummy bread."

As she rattled on, he looked to Presley. Her head was cocked, and her lips pursed, not exactly annoyed but he could tell something was on her mind. His luck with women was zero for two today.

"Thank you," he said, when Joy finished spilling every minute detail of her morning. Presley nodded. "See you tonight?"

She took a breath as if she wanted to say something, but her eyes fell to Joy. "Sure. Seven?"

Brandon nodded. He would have to pick up flowers for her too.

CHAPTER 14

$\mathcal{A}$s she stepped onto the porch at Brandon's, Presley was still pondering how to tell him what she wanted to say. Trudy had recommended being blunt, but "Hey, Brandon, your daughter is scared of you because you work so much," just didn't seem like the right words to say. Nor did, "She stuffed her face with chocolate chips in a cry for attention."

Sighing, she pressed the doorbell, hoping inspiration would strike or that God would send the right words to say. Brandon opened the door and held out a small bouquet of flowers.

Presley's forehead wrinkled. "What are these for?"

"For helping with Joy today, and for the favor I'm about to ask of you. Can we walk before dinner?"

The air was still cold. Another snow was expected for tonight, but as she was already bundled up, she agreed. She was curious as to what this favor entailed anyway.

He held out his arm, and she placed hers in his feeling a little like Ginger Rogers with Fred Astaire. "How was the rest of your day?"

"Fine." Presley's answer was slow and cautious as she had no idea what this favor might be.

He chuckled at her hesitation. "Don't worry, this favor isn't about your job. Well, not really anyway."

Her curiosity was piqued more than ever, but she didn't ask. He would tell her when he was ready. "How was your day?" She bantered the question back to him in hopes of eliciting more information.

"It was . . . challenging." He rubbed his free hand over his beard. She didn't remember him making the gesture when his face had been clean shaven in high school, but it seemed to have become a trademark nervous gesture for him. "My dad is still really weak, and he got tired just walking around the house, so I'll probably be staying a little longer than I originally thought."

"Well, that doesn't sound so bad." She nuzzled into him. It sounded a little like heaven to her, though she had no idea why she was allowing herself to fall for him knowing he planned to leave soon. Did she really think she could get him to stay?

"Yeah, that part's not so bad, but my assistant called and the buyer for this presentation I'm working on wants to see the presentation by Friday."

He paused as if this should mean something to her, but Presley had little knowledge of his job and none of this presentation.

"Anyway, it means I need to head back to Dallas for a few days to finish it up, and I know it's a lot to ask, but I was hoping you could help Mom and Anna with Joy. She seems to really like and relate to you."

There it was. Her opening. She couldn't have asked for a better lead in. "Of course I will, Brandon, but are you sure you need to do this? I think Joy would benefit more from having you around. She seemed terrified of disappointing you today."

His body stiffened, and he dropped her arm. "I'm trying to make the best life I can for Joy, and right now, that means this presentation. Once I get established, then I can worry about spending more time at home."

"But Brandon, what if that takes longer than you think? You remember how hard it was for my brother and me with my mother never around? She only has you, and she needs you."

"Presley, no offense, but you don't know what it's like. Morgan left because we didn't have a stable life, and I don't want Joy to feel the same."

His words hit like a slap in the face. "I may not know your situation exactly, but I know what it's like to be Joy, and I'm telling you she doesn't care about the money; she just wants her daddy home more."

His hand raked across his beard again. "Let's agree to disagree on this. I don't want to ruin what little time we have left."

Too late. Presley was irritated he wouldn't listen and annoyed he couldn't see what he was doing to Joy. The walk back was quiet, strained. Even when the snow began falling again, it didn't lighten the mood. Instead, it seemed to melt before it hit either one of them, as if their tension was creating an unseen heat force.

"Don't say anything about my trip yet," Brandon said as they returned to his house. "I haven't told anyone else."

Presley nodded. As much as she didn't agree, it was not her place to say anything.

As they stepped inside, the heat rolled over her, and she gratefully peeled off her coat and hat. After hanging them on the hat rack, she followed Brandon to the kitchen where everyone was sitting down for dinner.

"Ooh, pretty flowers." Anna winked at Brandon and smiled at Presley. If only she knew they were more of a bribe than a token of affection. "Do you want to put them in water?"

Presley nodded, and Anna rifled through a few cabinets until she found a glass vase. She filled it with water from the tap and placed it on the bar. As Presley unwrapped the flowers, her anger dissipated a little. The bright colors of the flowers really were pretty, a combination of red roses, pink carnations, baby's breath, and some purple flower she didn't know. He didn't have to buy them for her. He knew she would have helped without the bribe.

"Dinner is served." Beverly turned from the stove with a giant pot of spaghetti. Her "kiss the cook" apron was splattered with old stains. Presley had gotten her the apron the first Christmas she spent with the family because Beverly was always complaining about staining her clothes. Presley couldn't believe it had lasted this long.

"Sit by me, Presley." Joy grabbed her arm and pulled her to the chair next to hers. Brandon took her right and Anna took Brandon's left. Bruce was already sitting at the table, but he folded his paper and put it away. Though improving every day, he still looked weak and frail.

Beverly placed the pot in the middle of the table before taking her seat. Her spaghetti was the best. Presley wasn't sure what she did differently, but something about the meat and sauce combination she used always made it taste better.

As she scooted her chair in, the group joined hands and Bruce prayed over the food. Presley added a silent prayer for Bruce's health and for Brandon to open his eyes.

"So, I need to head back to Dallas for a few days," Brandon said as he scooped spaghetti on his plate. Presley was surprised he would bring it up at dinner.

"We're leaving already?" Joy's voice was laced with sadness as she turned her head up to Brandon.

"No, you're staying. Just me. I just need to do a presentation and then I'll be back."

"But why can't you stay?" she asked. "All you ever do is work, and I thought we'd get to spend some time together on this trip."

Presley shot a pointed look at Brandon; this was exactly what she had been trying to tell him. The rest of his family remained quiet, watching the exchange unfold. An air of tension settled on the table.

"We will spend more time together, but this presentation could lead to a promotion that could set us up for life."

"That's what you always say." Her soft voice was aimed at her plate. Presley wasn't even sure Brandon had heard it, but she had.

"Hey, it's snowing again. Maybe we can build another snowman tomorrow." Presley nudged Joy's arm and offered a smile, hoping to cheer the girl up.

She shrugged her small shoulders and twirled her spaghetti. "Okay."

Presley didn't dare look at Brandon again. She might be tempted to shout 'I told you so' at him. The rest of dinner was quiet, as if no one could think of anything to say. Only the sounds of chewing and forks scraping across porcelain plates filled the air.

When dinner ended, Brandon's cell rang and he excused himself. Joy's eyes drooped as she watched him go. Presley tapped her shoulder. "Hey, do you want to work a puzzle?"

She shook her head. "Nah, that's okay. I'll just go read." Her posture was so dejected as she shuffled to the couch that Presley's heart broke.

"Why can't he see what he's doing to her?" Presley asked Beverly and Anna as they cleared the plates.

"Because he's stubborn and a man," Anna answered.

"Hey, I take offense to that," Bruce spoke up from the end of the table. He'd been so quiet that Presley had forgotten he was even there.

"You're stubborn too," Beverly said pointing her finger at Bruce, "or else you'd be using that walker more."

He crossed his arms and scowled at her.

Beverly turned to Presley, her eyes sincere. "I know it doesn't seem like it now, but he is better around you. I'm hopeful that your influence will show him what really matters."

Presley sighed. "I tried talking to him today before dinner, but he didn't want to hear it. I'm afraid you might be putting too much stock in his feelings for me."

Beverly placed her hand on Presley's arm. "His feelings are deeper than he knows. Give him time."

Presley glanced to Joy, slumped on the couch with a book in her lap. A vein of fear gripped her heart as she realized she was not only falling in love with Brandon, but also with Joy.

CHAPTER 15

"Thank goodness you're here." Aubrey accosted Brandon as he entered the office. "Stewart is getting antsy." Her red hair was piled on her head though a few stray hairs escaped, and her jacket had been removed, displaying a white shell tucked into her blue pencil skirt.

Brandon took a deep breath to keep from snapping at her. He hadn't even been home, and he was sticky from the airplane ride. Plus, he was still recovering from Joy's snub this morning. She wouldn't say goodbye or look him in the eye, and her hug the night before had been apathetic as well.

All through the plane ride, Presley's words had haunted his mind. Was he pushing this promotion for the wrong reasons? Maybe he was, but Joy was only five. She didn't understand the intricacies of life.

He shook his head to clear the invading thoughts away. Once he got this promotion, he would be able to spend more time with Joy. It would all work out. "Okay." He sighed and dropped his overnight bag on the plush tan carpet. "What do we need to do?"

She smiled and motioned him to the conference table where she had a laptop set up. "Well, we've set up the preliminary on what the lodge should become, but we need to find pictures to represent what we want, and we need to finish the cost analysis."

His head swam with her onslaught of words, and he rubbed his hand across his forehead as he sank into one of the chairs. "Right, where are we on the cost analysis anyway?"

"We've figured out how much the renovations will cost, but we need to estimate the return over the next few years."

As the time they would need added up in his head, Brandon wondered why he'd ever thought leaving in the middle of this proposal would be okay. He and Aubrey would have to work nearly non-stop to be ready for Friday. "I'll take the money aspect. Why don't you work on the visual aspect?"

She nodded and pivoted back to her desk to begin working. Brandon stared at the screen, willing his mind to focus. Instead, Joy's doe eyes filled his mind. The sight of her sitting on the couch, shoulders slumped flooded his vision. He rubbed his eyes to clear the image. If he could focus, perhaps he could present before Friday and return sooner.

Two hours later, they called it a day. Brandon needed a shower and Aubrey needed to get home to her cat. As Brandon had left his car at his parents' house in Star Lake, Aubrey offered to drive him home and pick him up the next morning.

The apartment was quiet, tomblike, as he entered. It was odd, being there without Joy. Usually, she came bounding up to him, threw her arms around his legs, and rattled off everything that had happened in her day, from what she ate for breakfast to what the characters on her favorite show did.

Brandon would nod, having no idea what she was talking about, but not wanting to let on, and then, when he could peel her off, he would get a rundown from the nanny, bid her goodnight, and sit Joy down for dinner.

After dinner, they would play for a bit or read and then it was her bath and bed time. It wasn't much time with her during the week, but he always tried to make up for the fact on weekends.

Brandon shut the door and leaned against it, taking in the apartment. It was eclectic, decorated in whatever he could afford after Morgan left and he had to pay for a nanny and work. The couch was a faded brown squishy thing picked up from Goodwill and scrubbed thoroughly. The pictures on the wall were a mixture of pictures of Joy and odd landscape pictures he had picked up from thrift stores. Not exactly his style, but he couldn't afford the van Gogh's he would like to own. That was partly why he was working so hard.

Beyond the living room lay the kitchen, still glaringly white and green. He had never bothered to paint the walls, but he was no longer sure if it was from lack of time or lack of caring.

Dropping his bag onto the kitchen table, he flicked the light switch on and opened the fridge, hoping for something to jump out at him. He hadn't eaten since lunch at the airport, and it hadn't been very filling.

Unfortunately, since they'd been gone, Amber, the nanny, hadn't been making dinner, so there wasn't much to choose from. He resorted to an old high school favorite and pulled out a few eggs, butter, and the bread.

As he started the eggs cooking, he put the bread in the toaster and waited for it to pop up. A fried egg sandwich was going to feel like a pauper's meal compared to the food his mother had been cooking, but it was better than starving.

When the bread was buttered, and the egg was nestled securely inside, he took out his phone. It was nearly eight but surely Joy would still be awake. His fingers flew across the keys, inputting his mother's number from memory.

She answered on the second ring. "Hey, Mom, can you put Joy on? I want to wish her good night at least." The pause was so long on the other side that Brandon looked at the phone display to make sure it was still connected. "Mom?"

"Hang on. I'm trying to convince her to take your call."

"Daddy?" Joy's voice was not full of the laughter he was used to. It was quiet and subdued, and it sounded more like a statement than a question.

"Hey, Bug, how was your day?" He tried to inject an extra dose of happiness in his voice to cheer her up, but it ended up sounding fake even in his ears.

"Fine."

Her monosyllabic words hurt his heart, and he wondered again if he was doing the right thing. He wanted to hug her and have her tell him about her day, but he could tell she didn't want to, so he decided to cut the call short and end both their misery.

"Okay, honey, well, I hope you have a good night, and I'll call again tomorrow."

"Okay."

And then, before he could say goodbye, the line went dead. He hoped his mother was gently informing Joy that hanging up on her father, even when she was angry, was not the polite thing to do.

He stared at the phone a moment longer and then tapped in a different, less familiar number.

"Hello?"

Presley's voice was a soothing aloe on the other end. He couldn't believe how quickly she had re-entered and bettered his life. "Hey, Presley. Did you see Joy today?" His finger traced a circle on the dining room table as he waited for her answer.

"Yeah, we built a snowman this afternoon. I closed the shop for a few hours and played with her. She misses you Brandon."

"I know, but I'll be done in a few days, and then I'll be back."

"Until you leave again." Her voice was soft, but there was no denying the sadness in it. Though not sorry he called, Brandon wished the conversations had been happier. After she filled him in on the rest of her day, and he bored her with details of his presentation, they ended the conversation.

As he put the phone down, the silence crept in again, and he wished Presley were here with him. Hearing her voice had helped, but he missed her face and her lips. What he wouldn't give to curl up on the couch with her right now and breathe in her scent.

It was still early, but the empty apartment held nothing for him, so he changed into shorts and crawled into bed. Though tired, Presley's voice reminding him that Joy missed him ran circles through his brain, and doubt sneaked in again.

$\sim$

*A*ubrey arrived at seven the next morning, and after a stop at a coffee shop for a morning pick-me-up, they were back at the office and plugging away.

"Do you think we could finish today?" Brandon lifted the coffee to his mouth and took a sip. The warm liquid flowed down his throat, but it did nothing to ease the ache he felt.

Her green eyes flashed as she laid her pen down on the table. It was a deliberate controlled movement, one that showed the anger building inside her. "You want to finish the presentation today?"

Swallowing, he plowed ahead, knowing she might blow up at him but taking the chance anyway. "Yes, Aubrey. I miss Joy, and want to spend more time with her while I can. I promised her."

Her eyes bored into his, but her shoulders relaxed. She didn't have kids, but she had a soft spot for Joy. "Okay, it will mean a busy day today, but I'm almost done with the video aspect if you are close on the cost analysis."

"I am. I think I can finish today."

"Well, we better buckle down then."

She turned the laptop screen toward him and started the slide show she had assembled. It was good, exciting. He offered a few suggestions and then turned his screen to her, so she could see the cost analysis. She pointed out a few items he had forgotten, and they continued working.

When lunch rolled around, she ordered in and they ate while they worked. At six pm, they finished. "Can you call Stewart and ask him to meet us tomorrow instead of Friday?"

She nodded and headed to the phone, and Brandon began practicing the presentation in his head. But he wasn't feeling it. He was worried about Joy, and he wanted to hear Presley's voice.

Aubrey returned a minute later. "Okay, he can meet us at eight am tomorrow morning, and I took the liberty of booking you a return flight for late morning."

"Thank you, Aubrey." She really was an amazing assistant.

When Brandon returned to his apartment, his first order of business was to order a pizza. The he dialed his mother. The phone rang four times before going to the answering machine. His parents had not embraced voice mail and while they each had a cell phone, they almost never answered it.

When the beep sounded, he left a message, trying to sound cheerful, though loneliness was all he felt. "Hi guys. I hope everyone is well. I'm almost finished here and should be home tomorrow. I can't wait to see you, Joy. I miss you."

He ended that call and dialed Presley's number. Chances were she was with them wherever they were.

"Hi, you've reached Presley, but I can't answer the phone right now. Leave a message at the beep."

His heart ached even more at the sound of her sweet voice and the fact it was only a recording. He hung up without leaving a message. Not talking to them compounded the loneliness, but perhaps it would allow him to focus on practicing for the presentation.

CHAPTER 16

"What do you want to do today?" Presley asked Joy. She had shut the shop down early again to have some time to spend with her. Hopefully her customers would understand. She couldn't really afford to lose any business right now.

"Can we build another snowman?" Her eyes danced at the prospect, and she folded her hands together in a pleading gesture. Her lip fell out in a perfect pout, a trait she must have gotten from Brandon as he too had perfected the gesture on Presley in high school.

She glanced into the backyard, but they had used most of its snow yesterday and Sunday, and there hadn't been any new snowfall. "How about we go to the lake and see if there's enough there to build a snowman."

"Yes." The word was squealed in delight, and she bounded off to get her coat and hat.

"You want to come, Anna?"

Anna and Beverly both sat at the kitchen table. Beverly was

working a book of crossword puzzles, and Anna was reading a book.

"Sure," she sighed. "This isn't catching my interest anyway." She closed the book and pushed back her chair.

After bundling up, they stepped out into the cold air and began the short trek to the lake. Joy ran ahead, stopping every now and then to pick up a stick or a stray leaf. The snow was thinner here on the sidewalks due to the foot traffic.

Presley shoved her hands in her pockets and voiced the words that had been parading through her head. "Do you think he'll ever stay here?"

Anna shrugged and sighed. "I don't know, Presley. Morgan really did a number on him. I think his avoidance of this place has more to do with her than with the place itself."

It was what she had expected, but it didn't make her feel any better.

"Do you think you would ever move to be with him? I know Joy has really taken to you. She could use a good mother figure."

It was Presley's turn to sigh. "I'm not sure. I love Joy, and care deeply for Brandon, but I did the big city in Paris, and it wasn't all I thought it would be. There's something about a small town where everyone knows you that is welcoming."

"Yeah, I missed that this year." Her head dropped, and her eyes focused on the ground. Her shoulders rolled forward from the invisible weight she was carrying on them.

"What happened, Anna?"

"Nothing, really, but it was so big that I didn't make any close friends. It just felt lonely, and after being here — well it was a shock."

Presley could relate. She had always been more of an introvert, and the move to Paris had been a shock. If it hadn't have been for Pierre — as much as she loathed him for cheating on her at the end — she didn't think she would have lasted as long as she did. Anna wasn't as quiet, but Presley could imagine the shock of a big college campus. "Will you go back?" They reached the lake and sat down on the green park bench.

Anna plucked a leaf off a bush that sat next to the bench. "I don't know. I do want to get my nursing degree, but I might consider a closer school for next year. My dad falling really affected me too. My parents are both getting older, and I want to be closer to them in case something happens again."

Presley understood that. Her mother and brother were all she had, and even though she lived in an apartment attached to her mother's house, Presley rarely saw her. But, she would be close by if anything happened.

"Presley?"

The male voice grabbed Presley's attention, and for a moment her heart believed it was Brandon. She turned to the approaching figure, but the proportions were not right to be Brandon. The figure was taller and a little thicker. "Ryan?" She jumped up from the bench and ran to embrace her brother. He had graduated from college this last summer, but she hadn't seen him since then. He'd been working as an architect in a firm in Houston.

He picked her up and twirled her around. Even though he was younger, he had always been bigger than Presley, at least since he turned thirteen and shot up like a weed. "What are you doing here?"

"I came to spend Christmas with my mom and sister. I took a week off work."

"But how did you know where to find me?"

He rolled his eyes. "I was accosted by Paula on my way in. She told me you had been hanging out with Brandon Scott and that if I couldn't find you at the bakery, then to check his house." He shuddered and rubbed his arms. "I wish she would just use words and not her hands so much."

Presley laughed as the mental picture appeared in her mind. She could almost see Paula's hand gliding up Ryan's muscular arm as she shared her gossip.

"When did you start hanging out with Brandon again? I thought that was over."

Presley shook her head. "It's a long story."

Ryan's eyes shifted from her face to something over her right shoulder. Presley turned to see Anna approaching them.

"Anna Scott?"

"Hi Ryan. You look good." Anna's hands were clasped in front of her, and as she twirled the ring on her right hand, Presley remembered Ryan telling her they had dated for a time in high school, after her move to Paris.

Presley stepped back to the bench to give them a moment.

"Can we build the snowman now?" Joy asked as she ran up to the bench. Presley had forgotten that was their purpose in coming here, but she smiled and started rolling snow for her.

Ryan and Anna soon joined in, and between the three of them, they managed to put together a snowman taller than Presley. In fact, he was almost Ryan's height. Joy scurried toward the lake and returned with two sticks for arms and two rocks for eyes. Ryan lifted her up so she could place the eyes herself.

"It's too bad we didn't bring a carrot," she said as she stepped back and admired their work.

"I think he looks wonderful anyway," Presley said squeezing Joy's shoulder.

"I agree," Anna said, smiling shyly at Ryan. "I know, who's up for a movie? I think they are playing a Christmas movie."

"Me, me; I love movies." Joy jumped up and down and pumped her arm in the air.

Presley shrugged. "Fine with me. I have nothing better to do." Her phone had been too silent all day.

"Ryan?"

He shrugged as well. "Sure, I love a good Christmas movie, but can we get something to eat first? I'm starving."

At the words, Presley's stomach joined in with a rumbling chorus. "All right, to Max's."

Presley and Joy led the way, so Anna and Ryan could have a little privacy behind them.

The Diner was busier than Presley had seen it in a while, and they had to squeeze into a small table near the kitchen. Max dropped off menus without a word as he maneuvered plates of food to another table. After placing their plates down, he came back their direction.

"What'll you have?"

"What's going on Max? Why is it so busy?"

He rolled his eyes. "Barnard thought it would be a good idea to drum up business for the local shops by offering sales. Today is evidently half price burger day. Course he never told me about it." Max raised his voice and glared across the room. Barnard waved before shoving a burger in his mouth.

"Oh dear, I better find out what he has planned for me. I'll take a burger by the way." As Max finished taking orders, Presley eased out of her chair and weaved through the crowded chairs to Barnard. "What is going to be the sale at the bakery? I need to have some warning as I'm helping out with Joy while Brandon is gone."

He motioned her to lean down. "There is no sale for the other businesses. I just wanted a half price burger today, but maybe it's not a bad idea looking at this crowd, huh?"

Presley shook her head at Barnard. The man certainly had guts. If Max ever found out, all Hades was going to break loose.

"So, what does he have planned for you?" Ryan asked as she returned to the table.

"Nothing," she whispered. "He just wanted a half price burger."

Anna and Ryan stifled their laughter as Max returned with the drinks.

"What's so funny?" he asked, his eyes flitting from one person to the next.

"Nothing, nothing at all." Presley clapped a hand over her mouth as another giggle took over.

"Barnard!" Max's voice turned from frustration into an angry growl as he marched over to Barnard, who paled, shrank back, then turned red and puffed up. Max led Barnard out of the building and the two proceeded to have an angry spat in front of the store. Presley couldn't hear the words, but their angry gesticulations said a lot.

Ryan whistled through his teeth. "I would not want to be Barnard right now."

Moments later, the two returned. Max stomped into the kitchen and Barnard stopped at the door and raised his hands. "Excuse me, folks, can I get your attention? I'm afraid there was a mix up and there is no half price burger day."

The crowd groaned and booed.

"But, but," he continued, "to make up for it, I am offering a free scoop of ice cream to everyone in this restaurant." The words looked as if they physically pained him to say.

"Score one for Max," Presley whispered as the crowd grumbled and returned to their food.

Max appeared a moment later and plopped the plates down on the table. He might have won, but it had done nothing to soften his mood.

After the food was finished and the tab was paid, the group headed down the street to the cinema. Miracle on 34th Street was playing, and after purchasing tickets, they entered the one theater.

The old chairs were worn and a faded brown color from the eighties where they weren't patched, but they worked. A few other people sat in the theater, but they had their choice of seats. Joy led them down the aisle to about ten rows from the screen and smack dab in the middle of the row. It was closer than Presley usually sat, but as she didn't have to crane her neck, she agreed. Anna sat next to her and Ryan on the other side of Anna. Presley doubted either one of them would really be paying close attention to the movie.

When Presley returned home from watching the movie, she noticed a missed call from Brandon on her cell phone. She clicked on the voicemail button, but there was nothing waiting. Why hadn't he left a message?

She considered calling him back, but it was nearly ten. If he was working, she didn't want to bother him, and if he was sleeping, she didn't want to wake him. Perhaps it was better this way anyway. If he still planned on leaving, she should probably begin distancing herself, if that was even possible.

An exasperated sigh escaped her lips, and Niko looked up from his dish on the counter where he had been crunching his dry cat food.

"I don't know what I'm doing Niko. I'm just going to get my heart broken again."

Niko wandered over rubbed against her hand. At least he understood; he always understood.

Flicking off the kitchen light, Presley headed down the hall to her bedroom. It was late and five am came early. The nice thing about owning her own store was being able to set her hours, but owning a cupcake shop/bakery meant people expected to get their breakfasts there and that meant opening by seven am.

As she changed into shorts and a tank top, Presley wondered if she could move with him. Could she close the shop and reopen somewhere with him if he asked her to? She found no easy answer as she brushed her teeth and climbed into bed, so she handed it over to the Lord in prayer.

~

*T*he next morning, the answer was no clearer, but she had faith that He would show her the answer when He was ready.

The day was slow, and Presley found herself whipping out her cell phone between customers to check for a message from Brandon, but it was always empty.

After the lunch rush, she took out a rag and began wiping down the tables. The bell jingled and Joy rushed in.

"Presley, did you hear? Daddy's coming back tonight."

"Sorry, she just had to tell you," Anna said, shaking her head.

"That's okay," Presley said to Anna before turning her attention to Joy, who was patting her hip excitedly. "No, I hadn't heard, but I didn't get to talk to your daddy last night. That is good news though." Why hadn't he left a message telling her that? The thought sent tiny tendrils of doubt into her heart.

"He said he'd be home tonight. You'll come, won't you?"

"Of course I will." Though Presley wondered if the reason he hadn't told her he was coming home was because he didn't want her there. Joy hugged her legs before dashing over to the pastry case and pressing her nose and hands against the freshly wiped glass.

"Dinner will be at seven," Anna said. "Will that give you enough time?"

"Yeah, it gives me plenty of time." Presley had tried staying open later than six in case people wanted dessert after dinner, but very few people had shown up. So, she had left closing hours at six, which gave her some time to unwind in the evenings.

"Great, we'll see you then. We have to go expend some energy." Anna nodded at Joy, who was tapping at the glass as if trying to convince the pastries to come out. "Come on, Joy. Let's let Presley get back to work."

Joy smiled and waved as she bounded out of the shop, and Presley returned to wiping tables. She had just finished re-wiping the glass case when the bell sounded again and Paula sauntered in, a black knit dress clinging to her large frame. A white fur coat covered most of her top half.

"Well, hello Paula, what can I get for you today?"

Her bright red lips pursed as she perused the offerings in the case. "I'll have that." She pointed an equally red fingernail at a mini chocolate pie, and Presley bent down to snag it from the case. "Where is that handsome man of yours?" she asked, peering behind the counter as if she hoped to find him stashed back there.

"He had to take a trip back to his job, but he'll be back soon." Presley placed the pie in a little brown box and closed the flaps.

"It's not another woman, is it?" Her voice was low and conspiratorial as if they were sharing a secret. Presley didn't bite.

"No, just work, Paula. Here you go. That will be two fifty."

She handed over the money, looking disappointed that Presley had no gossip to share with her. After a final look toward the back of the shop, she rolled her eyes and left.

At six pm, Presley bundled up, locked the door, and headed home to change. Her stomach was a wad of knots at seeing Brandon again and hearing how his presentation went. She didn't want to hope it hadn't gone well, but she couldn't stop the thought.

Changing into a blue sweater that brought out her eyes, she ran a brush through her hair, checked Niko's food and water, and then headed back out into the cold.

CHAPTER 17

*A*s the taxi pulled up to the house, Brandon took a deep breath before throwing open the door. This was not going to be easy, and though he'd been practicing the words to say the whole way here, nothing sounded right.

The driver popped the trunk, and he removed his bag and placed a tip in the driver's hand. He tapped his head and got back in the car, leaving Brandon staring at the house.

Another deep breath gave him the strength to climb the first step. The door was unlocked, and he entered quietly, hoping to surprise Joy. Somehow, he doubted she would be enthused by the news, and he wanted to see her happy for a moment before facing the tears he knew would come.

Noise from the kitchen drew him that direction, and he turned the corner to see his entire family, Presley included, gathered around the table. The happy picture struck him, and he wondered again if he was making the right decision.

"Daddy." Joy saw him first and scrambled off her chair. Her hug was so forceful it sent him back a step.

"Hi, Bug. I missed you too." He bent down to give her a proper hug. His eye caught Presley's over Joy's shoulder, and she smiled and flicked a small wave.

"How was your trip?" his mother asked.

It was his opening, but he was too scared to take it right now. He would save his news for later. "It was good, but I am famished. There was no food in my place, well no real food anyway. Please tell me you're cooking something amazing."

"Roast and potatoes and salad."

His mouth watered at the words and the scent of roasting meat he could now smell. Joy tugged his hand to the table, and as he sat, she told him everything they had done over the last two days. Presley took the chair to his left, and her hand found his under the table and squeezed. He hoped she would feel the same way after she heard his news.

After dinner, Brandon decided he couldn't wait any longer. "Can everyone join me in the living room?" Their faces were a series of questions, but they headed that direction. His father even used his walker without complaining, which helped Brandon feel a little better about leaving.

"So, you guys all know that I was doing this presentation the last few days. Stewart really liked it, and he offered me a job working for his company."

"That's wonderful," his mother said, but her voice relayed her true feelings. She didn't find it wonderful at all.

"Where is the job?" Presley's voice was soft, and her blue eyes filled with sadness as they met Brandon's.

"New York."

"Where's New York?" Joy asked. The somber mood had hit her, and her voice was full of fear.

"It's up north, honey, but it will be fun. We'll get to live in a big building, and they have lots of fun places to see."

"I don't wanna go." She crossed her arms and stomped her foot.

"I wanna stay here with family and with Presley. I like it here." This was exactly the reaction Brandon had expected.

"I know you do, Bug, but this is a great opportunity for Daddy. One that will set us up for a good life."

"It's always about you," she said, water filling up her eyes. "How come you never ask me what I want?"

"Because I'm trying to do what's best for both of us."

"No, you're doing what's best for you, like you always do. I hate you, and I don't want to go." With that she ran from the room. His mother rose to go after her, but Brandon held up his hand.

"Just let her go. She needs to cool off a little." The tension in the room pressed down, and he shifted uncomfortably in his chair. He had known this would be hard but had been hoping for some happiness or heartfelt congratulations at least.

"When do you leave?" Presley asked.

"Next Friday." There was so much more he wanted to say to her. He wanted to ask her to come with him, but it would have to wait until they could be alone.

"You're leaving before Christmas?" This time the shocked voice was his mother's.

"I know the timing is bad, but Dad is looking better, and I pushed for as late as I could." Brandon had tried to push the start date back to the New Year, but Stewart was adamant Brandon be in place before the end of the year.

"I can't believe you, Brandon. The one Christmas we would get to spend with our granddaughter and you leave early. Have you even thought about how much this will upset her?"

Brandon's anger boiled over, and he lashed out at his mother. "Of course I have, Mom. I tried to push it back, but this is a once in a lifetime opportunity, and I can't let it pass me. I'll finally get to have everything you and Dad did before you moved here."

His mother's jaw dropped open, and his father, who had been

sitting quietly, cleared his throat. "Do you not remember why we moved here, Brandon?"

"You retired, and we needed a smaller place."

He shook his head. "No, I retired because I didn't like what the money was doing to us. Your mother was hung up on all the latest fashions and spending more on shoes than food each month. You and Anna were quickly following in her footsteps. I didn't want to lose my family to money, so I took an early retirement and moved us here, so we could start over and focus on what really matters."

"I won't get like that again, Dad. I know how to avoid it now, but I need to do this for Joy."

"For Joy or for you?" His face was as serious as his voice as they locked eyes. He could tell himself it was for Joy, but as he held his father's stare, he was no longer sure.

"Well, this sounds like a family affair, so I think I'll be going," Presley said, rising from the couch.

"Wait, Presley, I need to talk with you. Let me walk you home." She shrugged but didn't say no, so he took that as a yes.

When they stepped outside, he reached for her hand, and while she allowed it to be held, she did not return the grip. "Presley, I want you to come with me. I can't imagine going without you, and Joy adores you. You always talked about working in a big city. You could open a shop there and live your dream too."

Her shoulders rose with her breaths. "I have a life here, Brandon, and my own shop. I'll have to think about it."

It was not the answer he had hoped for, but it wasn't a firm no, which gave him hope. "Please do." When they arrived at her doorstep, he leaned in to kiss her, but she turned her head, and his lips landed on her cheek.

"Just give me time," she said, and before he could say anything else, she had entered her apartment and shut the door. He stood staring at the white door and wondering how everything got so messy.

CHAPTER 18

*A*fter Brandon left, Presley entered the main house, looking for Ryan. He was not normally her confidant, but she needed to process. He was parked in front of the TV watching sports.

"Can you turn that off a moment?"

Without questioning, he flicked the remote and turned his attention to her. He would make some woman very happy one day. Presley sat on the other side of the couch from him.

"Brandon just told us he's taking a job in New York, and he wants me to go with him."

His eyebrow inched up his forehead. "Are you going to go?"

"That's the thing, I don't know." She grabbed a piece of hair and twirled it in her fingers. "I want to be with him, but I like it here. I like the slower pace and the people are friendly. Weird, but friendly. It's home, you know?"

"I do now," he said, nodding. "I've been thinking about coming back myself."

"Before or after you saw Anna?" Presley punched his leg.

"Before," he smiled, "but I certainly wouldn't say no to being closer to Anna."

"Why did the two of you break up anyway?"

He shook his head. "I don't even remember. Something stupid would be my guess. That's usually why people break up. I haven't seen you with Brandon, but I know how much you cared about him in high school. Are you sure you want to lose that?"

Presley shrugged. She wasn't sure of anything except how unsure of everything she was. "Thanks, Ryan. I guess I have some thinking to do."

"And some praying." He rose from the couch with her and offered a hug before flicking the remote back on.

Presley walked back to her apartment, more confused than when she came over. With a sigh, she got ready for bed, hoping everything would be clearer in the morning. Crawling into bed, she gave it over to God.

～

The next morning, Paula was waiting outside the door to the shop when Presley arrived.

"Am I late, Paula?" She checked her watch, but it showed five till seven.

"No, I just wanted to see how you were doing. I heard Brandon is moving to New York."

Presley blinked at her. How on earth had she heard that information so quickly? She was like some kind of super magnet for gossip. "He is, but I'm fine. Thank you for asking." She shouldered past Paula to insert the key in the door.

Paula followed her inside. "Not that we want you to leave, but are you thinking about going with him?" She was fishing now. Maybe this was how she received her information.

"I don't know, Paula. I haven't decided." Presley flicked the lights on and headed to the back.

"Oh, well, while I'm here, perhaps I'll see what you are offering today." She sidled up to the counter.

"Right, give me a second." Presley hurried into the back and grabbed the left-over pastries. Paula waited patiently while Presley unwrapped them and placed them on the trays. She would have to do some cooking today as the inventory was running low.

Paula selected her pastries and waved goodbye. When the door closed, Presley headed to the back to grab the ingredients needed to make some new desserts. She spent the day whipping up new batches of muffins, brownies, and cookies in between the customers that walked in the door, asking the same questions Paula had. By the time it was closing time, Presley was exhausted both from cooking and from answering questions, but she finally had her answer.

She nearly lost her nerve as she stepped onto Brandon's porch, but it had to be done. Her breath came out in a giant sigh as she pressed the doorbell. Brandon opened the door, and his eyes, so full of hope, nearly change her mind.

"I was hoping you would come by tonight," he said, opening the door for her to come in. He leaned in to kiss her, and because she knew it would probably be the last one, she savored the feel of his lips on hers.

She must have done something differently though because she could see in his eyes when he pulled back that he knew something was off. "Can we talk somewhere?"

He nodded, and taking her hand, led the way to his room. As the door shut, Presley took a deep breath. "Brandon, I adore you and Joy, but I realized today that I love this town and the people in this town. I've never been to New York, but if it's like Paris, you don't get customers like that, people who care about you and come in to ask you how you are."

"Maybe it will be different than Paris." The hope in his voice pulled at her heart.

"I can't go, Brandon. It's not just that. You are different when you work that job. You're so relaxed and kind here, but whenever your phone rings, you change. You become this stiff, focused, almost angry man, and I wouldn't be able to bear seeing you like that every day. I would resent you and the move. It wouldn't be good for anyone."

She could tell she'd struck a nerve as he bristled and took a step away from her. "Fine, Presley. I shouldn't have asked you to come anyway, but I thought you wanted a chance to realize your dream."

Presley let the harsh words slide. She knew his ego was bruised, and he didn't really mean them. "I'd like to say goodbye to Joy, and then I think it would be best if I don't come back before you leave. I don't want to make it any harder on Joy." The words scraped like a razor blade against her heart as they poured out of her mouth.

"That's probably best."

There was a wall between them now, an invisible field of tension that saddened her. This was not the way she had wanted it to go at all. Nodding, she opened the door and headed down the hallway to the living room. The family was gathered there watching a movie.

Joy looked up at the sound of footsteps and came running. Presley caught her in a hug, and the tears she had been holding back so well threatened to pour down her cheeks.

"Presley, I wondered when you would get here. Come watch with us." She twirled her hands in Presley's hair.

"I can't, Joy. I came to say good bye."

"Good bye? Where are you going?" Her face scrunched in confusion.

"I'm not going anywhere, honey, but I'm not coming to New York with you either, and since I'm not," *and since Brandon and I just broke up,* "I thought it would be best if I didn't come back around. I don't want to make it harder on you when it's time to go."

Her blue eyes shimmered as they filled with tears. "No, you have to keep coming, Presley. I don't want you not to come back."

"I know, Joy, but one day, I think you'll thank me for this."

She threw her arms around Presley's neck one more time and sobbed into her shoulder. The sound broke the last wall Presley had built around her heart and her tears joined Joy's.

When Joy pulled back, she flashed her eyes at Brandon. "This is your fault," she said. "I hate this move, and I hate you." As she ran from the room, the rest of the family stared after her, unsure what to say or do.

The uncomfortable weight settled on Presley's shoulders, and she stood, wiping the tears from her eyes. "Bruce, I'm glad to see you improving. Beverly, thank you for a wonderful few days. Anna, I'm sure I'll be seeing more of you." She turned to Brandon who was leaning against the wall with his arms crossed. "Brandon, I . . ." She wanted to tell him she loved him, but this didn't seem the time or the place. "I had a wonderful time, and I will miss you incredibly. Most of all, I'm sorry."

He said nothing, but his hand rubbed his beard again, and his eyes pulled to the right. She could tell he was fighting emotion too. Before she became a blubbering mess, Presley exited the room and showed herself out of the house.

The tears hit full force as the front door closed behind her, and a loud sob escaped her lips. Pain like she'd never felt before ripped through her body, shattering her heart into a million pieces. Head down, she hurried home and threw herself onto her bed. Niko jumped up beside her, but even his purring and butting her with his head couldn't change her mood. She felt broken and empty and immediately wondered if she'd made the right decision.

CHAPTER 19

The taxi pulled up in front of the high-rise apartment building, and Joy's eyes widened. "We're going to live here?"

"Only for a month or so. The company is putting us up in their suite until we decide where we want to live." Though she was not entirely on board, it was good to see Joy finding some happiness in the move. Leaving the family had certainly been tough.

The day Presley said she wasn't coming had been the worst. Brandon had expected she wouldn't leave. Star Lake was her home and she fit there, but hearing the words had created a pain he hadn't known could exist. Joy had taken it even harder, clinging to Presley and then spewing hatred at Brandon. She had spent the rest of the day in her room, not even coming out for meals.

Brandon couldn't fault Presley. He knew she was trying to make it easier on Joy, but it sure had been harder the next few days. Joy had been nearly mute, only answering when directly spoken to. Even on the airplane ride, which she normally loved, she had been stony silent.

The company had offered to pack up their apartment and ship the car, and Brandon had taken them up on it. He and Joy had only packed a few changes of clothes and her favorite toys of course.

As Joy stepped onto the sidewalk, her head swiveled from one high rise to the next. Her mouth opened in a nearly perfect "oh" shape. Brandon grabbed the bags from the trunk and tipped the driver. Then the taxi pulled away from the curb and joined the flood of traffic. Brandon wanted to hold Joy's hand, afraid to lose her in the sea of people, but his arms were full of luggage.

"Come on, grab my pocket," he said. The crowd was much larger here, and his fear of losing Joy in a car accident was quickly being replaced by her being abducted or shuffled away in the throng of busy New Yorkers who had their phones attached to their ears and their eyes on their watches. He'd forgotten how impersonal busy executives could be.

The door of the apartment building opened as they approached, and a man in a maroon suit greeted them. "Welcome to the Stratton apartments. Please come in." After a little perfunctory bow, he spanned his arm out and stepped back, holding the door open and allowing their entrance.

The lobby of the apartment was like an expensive hotel, decorated in reds and golds. Brandon's eyes were nearly as wide as Joy's as he took in the opulence. Large, golden chandeliers hung from gold-plated ceilings, creating a stunning visual display. Four red couches created a large square around a glass-topped coffee table, and an enormous white marble desk occupied the right corner, a colorless distraction from the stimulating room.

A petite brunette with her hair pulled tightly on her head manned the counter. Brandon sidled her direction, making sure Joy was still firmly grasping his pocket.

"Hi, I'm Brandon Scott. Stewart said to check in with you. We'll be staying in the company suite."

Her head nodded, just once, proficiently. "Absolutely, Mr.

Scott." She punched the keys on her computer. "There you are. I just need you to sign this. It's a listing of the rules and the responsibility clause."

A printer whirred to life behind her, and she turned, grabbed the sheet, and placed it before him. It read like a small contract. No loud noise after eight pm, all visitors after six pm had to be approved by the front desk, no pets – good thing he didn't have any. Nothing seemed out of order, so after juggling the luggage so he could grasp a pen, he initialed and signed at the bottom before handing it back to her.

Her eyes scanned the paper. "Very good, sir. One moment."

As she reached for the phone beside her, Brandon glanced down at Joy. Her eyes were still wide, and her hands clutched her bunny in a death grip.

"Don't worry, Bug, it gets easier once you get used to it."

A moment later, another man in a maroon suit appeared at their side. His nose was long and hawkish above a neatly trimmed brown mustache that matched his eyebrows and the sideburns peeking out from under his hat.

"I'll take those, Sir, and show you to your apartment."

Grateful, Brandon handed over two of the bags, keeping his laptop bag over his shoulder. With his now free hand, he grasped Joy's, and they followed the man whose name tag read Mark. He led them down a marble floored hallway where the red and gold décor followed. Elegant abstract paintings hung at interspersed intervals along the wall.

Mark stopped in front of an elevator with ornate gold doors. The button chimed and lit up as his finger pressed it. Instead of the normal digital display of floors, there was an old timey arc of numbers and an arrow that pointed to each one as it passed that floor.

When the arrow touched down on the number one, the elevator dinged and the door slid open. The inside had a gold and white interior and a dark red carpet. A golden panel with rows of buttons from one to thirty lined one side, and as they stepped in, Mark punched button thirty.

The doors closed, and the elevator ascended, but the movement was so smooth it was barely noticeable. At the top of the doors was the little black panel that illuminated the number of each floor as they passed. When the elevator hit thirty, another chime sounded, and the doors opened.

The deep red carpet carried into the hallway. Mark turned to the right and led them to the single white door at the end. As he slid the key into the door, Brandon looked behind them. There was only one other door on this floor at the other end of the hallway.

"Who lives in the other apartment?" he asked, hoping it was perhaps a large family with children for Joy to play with.

"The head of the company." Mark's reply was short and succinct. Brandon would be getting no more information from him.

He swung open the door to the apartment, and Brandon's jaw dropped. The place was huge. A wall of windows greeted them, staring into the heart of New York. Two plush leather couches faced a giant television mounted on the wall. To the left was a kitchen and dining room done all in black and white.

"The bedrooms are to the right. There are four, so you have your choice. Does it meet your approval?"

Brandon could only nod, awestruck by the immensity of the apartment. He knew the company had money, but he wasn't expecting anything this extreme.

Mark set down the suitcases and stood patiently waiting. Brandon cocked his head at him before it dawned that he was waiting for a tip. After extricating his wallet, Brandon handed over two bills, and Mark nodded and exited the room.

"Shall we go pick our rooms?" Brandon asked Joy.

"It's so big." Her voice tremored with fear. This place must seem even larger to her. Their apartment back in Dallas had been a modest two-bedroom. Nothing fancy, but enough for the two of them.

"It will be okay. It's only for a little bit. When we get our new place, it will be much smaller." Even on his new larger salary, he would never be able to afford a place like this.

The floors in the apartment were hardwood, and their feet plopped softly on the wood as they headed down the hallway. The first room on the right opened to a large guest bathroom decorated in beige and crème. Across from it was the first bedroom, which held a full bed, dresser, and small desk. The room was blue and white.

The next door revealed a similar room only done in pink and white, and the third door opened to a crème and beige one. At the end of the hall was the last door. Brandon assumed it was the master bedroom.

It opened to reveal an enormous room with a king canopied bed. A rose-colored lounging couch sat near the window. A massive maple dresser filled the wall across from the bed and above it was another large television. A roll-top desk was in another corner next to a door he was sure led to the bathroom and closets.

"Can I just sleep in here with you?" Joy asked. "You can lay a mattress on the floor."

"For tonight," Brandon replied and patted her head. "We'll see if we can get a smaller bed for the pink room tomorrow if you think that one's too big."

❧

The next morning, he rolled over to find Joy curled up in the bed beside him, bunny snuggled under her chin. Her little pink lips were slightly parted, and a soft snore escaped with each breath.

Quietly, he crawled out of the bed and padded to the kitchen to start some coffee. The hardwood floors were cold in the morning, sending a shiver through his body, even though he was relatively warm in his flannel pants and t-shirt.

He began opening random cabinets in search of coffee mugs and grounds. The first cabinet revealed plates and bowls, all solid black. The second held glasses of all kinds. The third cabinet revealed mugs, and he grabbed a black one with the words "I need a coffee break" emblazoned in white lettering across it.

Mug in hand, he scanned the room for a pantry. That was where he would keep coffee. Two white recessed doors caught his eye, and upon opening them, he found a completely stocked pantry with cereal boxes, canned goods, and coffee.

After grabbing the grounds and a filter, he set the coffee pot up and pressed the button to start the brewing. The small machine whirred to life with a few clicks, and the smell of coffee began to fill the air, followed by the soft dripping of liquid magic into the mug.

When the final hiss ended, he grabbed the mug and looked up to see Joy standing at the end of the bar. Her eyes were still heavy with sleep.

"Hey, Bug. Do you want some cereal? I saw some in the pantry. The good kind." He wiggled his eyebrows at her in hopes of earning a smile.

"Okay," she said. Not quite the reaction he was hoping for, but he grabbed her a bowl and filled it up with one of the sugary cereals and placed it on the table in front of her.

The doorbell rang as he was replacing the milk in the also well-stocked refrigerator. His brows knit together as he wondered who could be on the other side. Almost no one knew they were here besides Stewart, and he had agreed to give Brandon a few days to find a nanny for Joy before calling him into work.

"Stay here, Bug," Brandon said to Joy as he headed to the door. His eyes darted around for anything he could use as a weapon, but while this apartment was fully stocked, there was no baseball bat or crow bar lying around anywhere.

At the door, he peered through the peephole and his heart stopped. It couldn't be. He couldn't keep the trembling from his fingers as he turned the lock on the door.

CHAPTER 20

Though the sun shonr brightly through the pale curtains covering the window, it did not bring cheer. It had been nearly a week since the last time Presley saw Brandon and Joy, and her mood had been sour every day.

She kicked back the covers and stumbled to the shower. Even the warm water and lavender scented soap, which usually awakened her senses, made no dent on her mood today. She grabbed a pair of pants and a shirt from the closet without even looking to see if they matched and then sauntered into the kitchen for some coffee.

Twenty minutes later, she was opening the bakery, oblivious to the white wonderland that still covered the town. As the door closed and she flipped the sign to open, she forced a smile to her face. She refused to lose customers simply because she was heartbroken over a boy yet again.

Presley rescued the left-over pastries from the freezer and began heating them up. Her stomach grumbled at the smell, and she realized she had forgotten to eat or maybe she had skipped it on purpose. Food held no flavor lately.

The bell jingled, and she greeted her first customer of the day. Though not a heavy onslaught, the customers continued steadily for the next few hours.

After the breakfast rush and another grumble from her stomach, Presley took a break and nibbled a scone. When the bell jingled, she nearly dropped her scone until she realized it was just Trudy.

"Sit down and take a break like a normal person," Trudy said in her no-nonsense voice. Her finger wagged with each word. "Stop hiding in the corner, sneaking food. It makes you seem like you're doing something wrong."

Trudy had this brusque way about her that Presley loved, but it also made her feel sheepish sometimes. Pastry in hand, she walked out from behind the counter and joined Trudy at a table. Today, she was in her overalls but free from paint.

"Are you not painting today?" Presley asked before taking a bite of the scone. The hungry monster in her stomach demanded more, and she forced her hand to the table to stop it from shoving the entire pastry in her mouth.

"Not yet. I had to check in on my grandmother." Trudy's grandmother lived in the Star Lake nursing home on the outskirts of town. Presley had never met her, but Trudy had shared stories. She sounded like an amazing and interesting woman until dementia set in. Now, it seemed she hardly even remembered Trudy.

"How is she doing?"

Trudy shrugged, and her eyes dropped to the tabletop. "She's okay, I guess. She knew me for a bit today, and she kept asking about Jacob. He was her husband, but he died ages ago. It got me thinking though." Her brown eyes pulled back to Presley's. "Maybe there is something to this love thing."

Presley's head dropped forward in surprise, and she nearly

choked on the morsel in her mouth. "Trudy, are you going soft on me?"

Her face scrunched in alarm. "No, not for me. I'm too set in my ways. I mean for you. You and Brandon. The two of you could have a love like my Bethel and Jacob did. I saw it in the way you looked at each other."

"I don't know," Presley said shaking her head. "He took the job and moved to New York. He asked me to go with him, but I just couldn't do it. My home is here, and it didn't go well the last time I saw him."

Her hand reached across the table and grabbed Presley's arm. It was two shades darker due to Trudy's ability to tan every time she was in the sun. Presley envied that about her. She was the type of person who burned and then peeled, no matter how much sun she got.

"I don't want you to go," she said, "but what if this is a once in a lifetime love? Would you give that up just to stay here in Podunk Star Lake?"

"I like it here." Trudy shot a pointed stare. "Okay, I've been praying about what to do, but my last venture into the big city didn't go so well. Remember?"

She flicked her hand and leaned back, dismissing the concern. "Yeah, but that wasn't with Brandon. You know him. Would he do that?"

Presley wanted to say no, but he had changed some since she knew him well in high school, and she was no longer confident in her answer. The Brandon she knew hadn't been obsessed with money, and she'd like to think he would have stayed where his daughter was most comfortable. She certainly couldn't imagine the Brandon from high school dragging his daughter off to a big city where she knew no one right before Christmas.

The image of Joy clinging to Presley's neck as they said

goodbye still pulled on her heartstrings, and she was no longer sure whether she loved the girl or the man more.

"Why don't you at least go visit? Check out the place and see if you could live there?" Trudy glanced at her watch. "Plus, if you hurry, you could get there by Christmas."

Presley gestured at the empty store. "Who would run the store? I can't just close it for a week."

Trudy tipped her head to the side and her eyes scanned the room. "You could. In this town, it would be fine, but what if I run it for you?"

"You? You hate even helping me clean." Who was this woman in front of her?

"I do, but I love you, and want the best for you."

Presley stared at her, trying to decide if she was serious and if she could take Trudy up on it. It would only be for a few days, and it would be nice to spend Christmas with Joy. She knew Joy was upset having to leave, and with a new job, Brandon was probably distracted, but did she want to butt in her life again if she was not going to stay? She didn't want to make it harder on the poor girl.

"I'll think about it," she told Trudy, but in her mind, she was already packing her bags.

CHAPTER 21

*B*randon had thought he was imagining things, but as the door opened, it was clear the woman in front of him was indeed Morgan. Her face hadn't aged a day. It was still chiseled to perfection with high cheekbones, a classic upturned nose, and flawless skin. Her dark hair cascaded around her shoulders, which were hidden under a tight white blazer that narrowed at her thin waist before flaring out at her hips. A black shirt with a cowl neck lay under the blazer.

"Morgan?"

Her eyes widened in surprise. "Brandon? What on earth are you doing here? I thought you were still in Star Lake."

She really had been out of touch. "I moved to Dallas after you left. I've been working for an ad firm there, but I just got hired by Bling Inc., and they moved us up here."

If his barb about her leaving affected her, she didn't show it. "That's wonderful, Brandon. I always knew you could do great things if you put your mind to it."

Her words bothered him, though he was not exactly sure why.

More pressing on his mind was why she was here. "Thanks, Morgan, but what are you doing here?"

"Oh, right," she flicked her hand, "I live across the way, and I wondered if I could borrow some creamer for my coffee. I forgot to pick some up on my way home yesterday. You know how I like my coffee with a little bit of sweet."

Brandon narrowed his eyes at her. Why was she being so friendly? "I know how you used to like your coffee, but that was four years ago before you up and left Joy and me. I don't know anything about you now."

Her perfectly manicured hand touched his arm. The red on her nails matched the color on her lips. "Don't be like that, Brandon. We're going to be neighbors, at least for a while; we might as well be neighborly." She tried to poke her head around him. "Speaking of Joy, where is she?"

He pulled the door closer, blocking the view of Joy behind him. "She's here, but I'm not sure I want you seeing her. You put her through hell when you left the first time. I don't want to put her through that again."

A cold gleam flickered in her eye for a moment, and then it was gone. Her hand left his arm to flick a dark strand behind her ear. "She's my daughter, Brandon. You can't keep her from me forever."

Icy fear trickled through his body, stirring a cold anger. She better not be trying to take Joy. "You didn't want to be a mother when you left."

Her weight shifted from one foot to the other. "I know, but I was wrong. I've had a lot of time to think about it."

He pulled the door completely closed behind him and crossed his arms. "You never even bothered to contact us. Not for birthdays or holidays."

Her full lips pushed out into a pout. "I'm not trying to take her, Brandon. I just thought since we're living right across from each that maybe I could get to know my daughter."

"We'll see," he said. "For now, wait here, and I'll get your creamer."

Without letting her in, he opened the door and slipped inside, closing it after him.

"Who is it, Daddy?" Joy asked. Thankfully, she was still working on her cereal, or she would have probably run to the door to check the visitor out. He hadn't spoken of Morgan since she left, and he had no idea if Joy would remember her or not, but he was unwilling to chance it right now.

"Just a neighbor looking to borrow some creamer." He opened the large black fridge and scanned the door. There was a bottle of Peppermint creamer situated snugly between some strawberry jelly and a bottle of ketchup. Plucking it from the shelf, he closed the fridge and crossed back to the front door.

Morgan still waited on the other side. He shoved the creamer into her hands, anxious to be rid of her for now, until he could sort out his feelings. "I have to get back to her, but we'll talk later." Without waiting to hear an excuse from her, he stepped back in the apartment and closed the door.

Brandon leaned against the closed door and ran his hand over his face. Morgan. Back in his life. He was not expecting this, and he had no idea how to feel about it.

The clatter of the bowl falling into the sink broke his thoughts. Joy smiled sheepishly from the sink. "Sorry, Daddy."

"It's okay, Bug. How about we get dressed and see what there is to do around here, huh?"

"Okay." She shrugged, and her voice was flatter than normal.

He had been hoping for more enthusiasm, but he was sure the city would grow on her.

After they were both dressed, he peeked out the hole in the door. Morgan no longer stood in the hallway, but he wondered if she would be watching for them to leave. He opened the door slowly and scanned the hallway before pulling Joy out the door and locking it behind them.

As he pressed the elevator button, he worried that Morgan would be in the car when it opened, but no one was inside. His heart resumed its normal beating.

Five minutes later, they exited the lobby into the cold New York air. Dirty snow lined the sidewalks from a previous storm, creating a cloudy white atmosphere. They joined the steady stream of people heading right. Joy clasped his hands tightly as people pushed past them. Smells from the neighboring restaurants competed against each other as they passed their doors.

After a few blocks, Joy began slowing down. Brandon slowed his pace to match hers, sure there was a park nearby. It finally appeared after another block, a small play structure surrounded by patches of white left-over snow.

A gaggle of women he assumed were nannies surrounded one bench. One or two pushed strollers back and forth with one hand. A few children Joy's age and younger played on the playground, in careful view of the nannies.

"Can I play for a little bit, Daddy?" Joy's energy suddenly returned as she bounced up and down and tugged on his hand.

"Of course, Bug, that's why we're here."

She dropped his hand and took off like a rocket. Within minutes, she had found a friend on the playground and was running around playing hide and seek with the girl. Brandon wandered to the other unoccupied park bench and took a seat.

While he watched Joy play, he slipped his phone out, hoping to see a message from Presley, but there was nothing. He knew he had been awful the day she came to say she wasn't coming, but he had hoped that she would change her mind and at least come see if she liked New York. But Presley was stubborn. Probably as stubborn as Brandon.

Before he could stop them, his fingers flew across the keyboard with a mind of their own. "I wanted to say I'm sorry, and I miss you. We made it. We're staying at the Stratton apartments if you change your mind. Thirtieth floor, number two. I know Joy would love to see you, as would I." His fingers paused for a moment and then hit the send button. His eyes were glued to the phone as he waited for the little white circle with a check mark to turn blue. It did, but no reply came.

With a sigh, Brandon leaned over to shove the phone back in his pocket when it rang. "Hello?" He hadn't dared look at the caller ID. Could he be so lucky as to think about Presley and make her call?

"Brandon? It's Stewart." His heart fell. "I need you to come in tomorrow for a few hours to get familiarized and get the paperwork in order."

Brandon glanced over at Joy. "I don't have a nanny yet, Stewart. Can it wait a few days?"

"I'm sorry. It can't. Isn't there someone who could watch her for a few hours?"

His mind flicked to Morgan. Could he trust her for a few hours with Joy? She was Joy's mother, and she had seemed interested in getting to know her, but what if she told Joy? It had taken a long time to get Joy to stop asking about her mother, and he didn't know what it would do to her five-year old psyche to come face to face with the woman who left her. Maybe. Let me check, and I'll call you back later."

He ended the call and tucked the phone back in his pocket. Then he shivered. The air here was colder than he expected, and he hadn't dressed for warmth. Joy hadn't either, and a few minutes later she returned, cheeks and nose red with cold.

"Daddy, can we go home? I'm cold."

"Of course, Bug."

~

*T*hat night, after laying Joy down, he ventured across the hall and knocked on the other door. Morgan swung the door open, a smile lighting her face as she saw him. She had changed out of her white suit into a pair of pink sweats that hugged her slim hips and a cropped tee. Her stomach showed no signs of ever birthing a child. He pulled his eyes from her toned abs to find a bemused look on her face.

"What can I do for you, Brandon?"

"Were you serious earlier when you said you wanted to get to know Joy?"

"Absolutely."

He took a deep breath. Every fiber in his body screamed this was a bad idea, but he saw no other choice. "I have to go into work for a few hours tomorrow, and I haven't found a nanny for Joy yet. Would you be available to watch her?"

Her mouth opened, but before she could answer, he held up his hand. "There are a few things you'd have to promise me. You can't tell her who you are yet. I will tell her, but I need to figure out the best way, and you have to stay in the apartment."

"I can do that. What time do you need me?"

He had set the meeting time for during Joy's nap. She didn't nap long anymore, but she almost always laid down for thirty to forty-five minutes right after lunch. "Twelve-thirty pm. I should only be a few hours, and she should nap at least a little of that."

"Don't worry." Her hand found his arm again. "I have been around kids before. It will be fine."

Her words did nothing to soften the unease developing in his stomach, but he nodded, extricated her hand, and thanked her. As he walked back to his apartment, he couldn't help but feel as if he'd just made a deal with the devil.

CHAPTER 22

*P*resley's stomach was a bundle of nerves as she took her seat on the airplane. She had given Trudy a crash course in how to run the shop while she was gone, and though she knew nothing terrible would happen, she couldn't help but feel as if she'd forgotten to tell Trudy something important.

Presley ran through the list in her head. She had given her a copy of the key; told her about wrapping up the pastries each night; and even left a few recipes in case she was forced to make more, though Presley doubted she would be gone that long. She had showed Trudy where the price list was and how to use the register.

"Where are you headed, dearie?" The woman beside her was older with white hair and a kind face.

"New York." Presley slid her bag under the seat and buckled her belt. "How about you?"

"The same. My granddaughter is graduating from design school."

"Oh, that's wonderful. Congratulations." Presley's fingers tapped on her leg, and she reached down to pull a book from her bag. She rarely had time to read anymore, but long flights were always good for that.

"You seem nervous." The older woman smiled. "You must be going to see a man."

Presley swiveled to her, eyes wide. "How could you possibly know that?"

She laughed, and the sound was a pleasant throaty chuckle. "I raised four girls. I can always tell when it's a man. Do you love him?"

A heat flared across her cheeks. "I do, at least I think I do. I love him when he's himself, but he took this job, and this side of him – I'm not so sure." Her hands clenched the book, folding it into a cylindrical shape.

The woman nodded as if she understood the incoherent babble. Maybe she did after raising four girls. "And you're going to find out?"

"I am. He asked me to come and gave me his apartment name, but I didn't tell him I was coming. I wanted to surprise him and Joy. That's his daughter." She had no idea why she was sharing all of this with a complete stranger, but her mouth seemed incapable of shutting.

"Ah, there's a child involved," the woman said, her eyebrow arching. "That makes it even harder." The way she looked at Presley made her wonder if the woman had experience in this area too.

As the plane took off, she found herself sharing the whole story with the woman. She listened, nodding at all the right places, and interjecting her opinion when Presley paused. Then she told Presley about her daughters, and before she knew it, the plane was landing. Her book remained closed on her lap. *Oh well, another time.*

"I'll be thinking about you tomorrow," they woman said as they gathered their bags. "I hope everything works out for you."

"Me too."

As she navigated through the crowded airport, Presley's heart began to pull tighter. Should she call him and let him know she was in town? She had no idea what his work schedule was; he hadn't said in the text, but she was afraid to call him. Afraid he would have changed his mind and tell her not to come, and she'd already traveled all this way.

She weaved through the throng of people over to the transportation desk. A frazzled woman with a pair of black glasses that kept sliding down her petite nose was behind the giant desk.

As she stood in the line, Presley scanned the surroundings. A board advertising local hotels with a phone in the center caught her eye. Stepping out of the line, she moved closer and realized she could use this phone to call for a van to her hotel. She was glad she had thought to book one ahead of time.

She picked up the phone and dialed *63 for the Marriott Hotel. It was the closest one to Brandon's apartment building, and since she was unfamiliar with New York, she didn't want to tempt getting lost on her way there.

"Marriott Hotel, how may I help you?"

"Hello, my name is Presley Hays. I have a reservation for tonight. I just arrived at the airport and was hoping a shuttle could come and get me."

"Of course, what kiosk are you at?"

Kiosk? She scanned the area for a number. "Um, I'm not sure. I'm calling from the phone by baggage claim three."

"Is there a number and letter combination on the phone you're holding?" The woman's voice was patient. She must deal with clueless people all the time.

Presley held the phone out and there was indeed a white strip on the back with G7 typed in black letters. "G7. I'm at G7."

"Wonderful. I'll tell the shuttle driver. It's a black van with the Marriott logo on the side. Please go out and wait by the post with G7 on it. He should be there momentarily."

"Thank you." Presley replaced the phone and grabbed the handle of her wheeled suitcase.

The air was cold as she exited the airport. She pulled her coat tighter and wished she had put on her gloves and hat before exiting the building.

Concrete posts lined the area, and she made her way to the one with G7 in big blue letters. Four lanes of traffic lay in front of her, and her mind boggled at the sheer number of cars jockeying for position. If traffic was bad here, she was not sure she wanted to see it on the city streets.

A few minutes later, the black van pulled up, and she flashed a small wave at the driver. He put the van in park and came around to open the door and help with luggage. He was a squat man with thinning brown hair, and his white top stretched across his belly, the buttons nearly bursting at the seams. A black vest with the Marriott logo covered some of his shirt but had no chance of meeting in the middle.

Presley climbed into the van and squeezed down between two other passengers. "Hi, thank you," she said, but received only grunts in response. New York was certainly different from Star Lake.

The traffic was just as bad as she had imagined, and it took over an hour to get to her destination. While the people beside her were glued to their smart phones, her eyes were focused on the world outside. There were so many lights and even this late in the evening, a sea of people swarmed the sidewalks. How could Brandon want to live here?

When the van parked in front of the hotel, she waited for the other people to disembark before grabbing her bag and stepping down. "Thank you very much," she said to the driver, placing a tip in his hand.

His other hand covered hers. "Don't lose yourself here." The seriousness in his brown eyes chilled her soul, but she nodded. He released her hand, handed her the luggage, and climbed back in the driver's seat leaving Presley standing on the sidewalk as the people parted around her, either ignoring her entirely or shooting glares her direction.

When the tide slowed, she skirted into the hotel door, which was opened by a tall thin man in a smart burgundy uniform. "Welcome to the Marriott, miss."

"Thank you." The lobby unfolded before her, and her eyes widened. Two white candelabras hung from the ceiling. A fountain issuing crystal blue water took up one corner. A white couch and a few lounging chairs sat around a glass coffee table under one chandelier. Towards the back, a row of computers lined a table. On the right, a gleaming gold and white desk filled most of the real estate. A man and a woman stood behind it, serving the customers in the line.

Presley joined the queue, her eyes still large as she took in the rest of the opulent surroundings.

"Can I help you?"

Startled, she turned to the woman behind the counter. Her auburn hair was pulled back in a tight bun and her skin was flawless except for a dusting of freckles across her nose. The tiny typed tag on her fitted jacket read Kaya.

"Hi, yes, I'm Presley Hays, and I have a reservation for tonight."

She nodded and began tapping away on her keyboard. "Will you be staying with us just one night, Ms. Hays?"

Presley hesitated. She had no idea how long she would be staying. Her hope was that it would be more than one night, but what if Brandon had changed his mind or what if she hated it here and changed her mind? "I'm not sure."

Kaya smiled and ignored the indecision. "That's fine. We're not booked right now, so if you decide to stay longer, it should be no problem."

"Thank you."

She nodded and finished checking Presley in before printing off a contract sheet, which Presley signed and handed back to her. After processing the payment, Kaya handed over the key card and pointed the way to the elevator.

Presley's shoes echoed on the marble flooring, making her feel conspicuous as she made her way to the elevator. She punched the round button to go up, and a moment later, the bell dinged. The cab inside was lavish with dark carpet and a white and gold wallpaper on the walls. Presley admired the artistic design but wondered why they felt the need to wallpaper an elevator. Stepping in, she punched the button for twenty-one, and the door closed.

When it opened again, she stepped out on the twenty-first floor where the dark carpet continued into the hallway. A gold-plated sign pointed her to the right for room 2103.

After inserting the key, she pushed open the door to a large hotel room. The queen bed didn't even fill half of the room. A large mahogany dresser sat across from it and above the dresser hung a big screen TV. Next to the bed was a matching dresser that held an ornate lamp, and against the window, a matching table.

To her right, a door opened to a large bathroom and to the left was a large closet. After wheeling the suitcase in, she hefted it onto the chair at the table and pulled out her sleepwear and toothbrush. She'd never been able to sleep at night without brushing her teeth. The one time she'd tried, the fuzzy feeling on her teeth kept her awake all night long.

It was still early, but having not slept well the last few nights, Presley changed and brushed her teeth. Plus, she wanted to make sure she was up early to do some shopping for Brandon and Joy.

She pulled back the comforter on the bed and climbed in. The sheets were like heaven, and her eyes closed as soon as her head hit the pillow.

~

The sun shining in the window woke Presley the next morning, Yawning, she stretched her stiff back and sore shoulders. The cramped seats of airplanes always wreaked havoc on her the next day.

She padded into the bathroom and turned the shower on. The warm water erased the last remnant of sleep from her eyes, and when it was over, she felt refreshed and ready, though still nervous.

After a quick breakfast, she pushed open the doors and joined the crowd on the sidewalk. The chilly wind nipped at her face, and she slunk further down in her coat, wishing she had brought a scarf. Perhaps she would add that to her list.

She had a map in her pocket of how to get to Brandon's apartment building that she had printed at one of the computers in the hotel lobby before embarking, but she wanted to stop and get their Christmas gifts as well. The map had showed a few shops along the route, and Presley was hopeful one would have what she was looking for.

The toy shop appeared on her right first, and with a quick maneuver, she ducked inside. A gust of warm heater air hit her as the doors closed, and she unzipped her coat. Rows and rows of shelves lined the store with colorful toys and games. She scanned the aisle headings that hung on square signs suspended from the ceiling.

As she entered the correct aisle, her eyes widened at the sheer number of puzzles. They lined the shelves on either side from floor to about eight feet. A myriad of colors and picture options stared back at her, but she knew exactly what she would love to find. Slowly, she sauntered down the aisle, head swiveling from left to right and top to bottom until her eyes landed on it. It was perfect, and though it was a thousand pieces – bigger than any she had done so far – Presley knew that Joy would love it.

She grasped it like a cherished doll as she returned to the front check out and joined the long line. Evidently, other people had the same idea. When she reached the front of the queue, she passed the box to the young red-headed man who was running the register.

"Is there any chance I can get it gift wrapped?"

He flicked agitated green eyes up at her and sighed. "Yes, I'll add in the charge, and you can take it to Patrice near the back. She's wrapping."

"Thank you." Presley handed over her credit card, and after signing, she took the box the direction he had pointed. The line here was shorter, and she was in front of Patrice within five minutes.

"Hi," she said with a smile. "Do you have a paper preference?" Her smile was warm, but her brown eyes looked tired.

Presley held out the box. "It's for a girl."

Nodding, she turned in her chair and grabbed a roll of silver paper with pink trees. She held it up for approval, and Presley nodded. "Fill out a tag, and pick a bow," she said, pointing to a bin of both beside her at the table.

After selecting a pink bow, Presley grabbed a white tag with snowflakes on it and filled out "To Joy, From Presley."

Minutes later, she was walking back out into the frigid air, her newly wrapped package beneath her arm. Brandon's gift would be a little harder, but she was hopeful a store with a Christmas section would have what she had in mind.

Another block up on the right, a Christmas outlet store appeared. Surely, they would have something similar to the picture in her head.

The store was large and full of everything Christmas you could wish for. There were trees, ornaments, stockings, lights, hats, and more. Presley found herself wandering up and down the aisles looking at all the intricate ornaments. Christmas had long been her favorite time of year.

Near the end of the third aisle, she saw it. A glass ornament with a boy and girl kissing inside as snow fell on them. It reminded her of their first kiss in Star Lake, and it was perfect. The couple even resembled them a little.

She took the ornament to the counter and repeated the process of paying for it and getting it wrapped. The lady was nice enough to hand her a tote bag to carry both Brandon's and Joy's present.

Presley's stomach rumbled as she hit the sidewalk again, letting her know that too much time had passed, and lunch was now in order.

She stopped at a bistro just down the street from Brandon's apartment building, and as she ate her turkey and ham on sourdough, she gathered the courage to finish the journey. Her heart told her he would be happy to see her, but her head was insisting she should have responded to his text.

She swallowed the last bite of sandwich down with a helpful swig of iced tea and then gathered her trash and her bag. A few minutes later, she stood in front of Brandon's apartment building.

A man in a maroon suit, like the one at the hotel she was staying at opened the door for her. The inside was as impressive as the lobby of her hotel, but she had no time to admire the view. Her heart pounded in her chest as she bypassed the front desk and followed the signs to the elevator. She had no idea if she was supposed to check in, but she hoped if she just looked like she belonged that no one would stop her.

As the elevator door opened on his floor, she turned right down the hallway. With each step toward the white door, the pounding in her head grew louder. Sweat broke out on her hands, and a solitary bead rolled down her spine.

Her hand rapped the door three times, and she waited. When it swung open, the bag nearly tumbled from her hand.

"Morgan?" The words came out as a tortured whisper. She couldn't believe her eyes, and she fought the urge to rub them and hope the nightmare disappeared.

"Why, hello Presley." Her voice sounded sweet but her blue eyes were cold as ice. A tight t-shirt and pants accentuated her perfect figure, and her dark hair was perfectly curled and lay seductively across her shoulder.

"What are you doing here, Morgan?" The words were a little more forceful this time, but Presley's entire body was shaking with the strain of not punching Morgan's perfect nose.

"I could ask you the same thing." Her voice was smug, and she leaned against the door as if the apartment was hers.

"I'm here to see Brandon and Joy." Anger boiled up inside Presley, threatening to spill over any moment.

Her eyes widened in false regret. "Oh, now's not a good time. We are having some family time. You see, now that we're back in the same city, we've decided to reunite our family."

Her words knocked the air out of Presley, and her hand reached for the wall to steady her weak knees. Why wouldn't Brandon have told her? Why would he ask her to come? The logical part of her brain insisted that something wasn't right, but the emotional side saw Morgan in his apartment. Why else would she be here? The need to vomit burned in her throat.

Presley held out the bag, unable to remain in the hallway any longer. "Tell him I said hi then and give him these, will you?"

"Of course." Her smile was like a predator's before it devours its prey.

Numb, Presley turned and walked back down the hallway, barely registering the click of the closing door behind her. Her hand pressed the elevator button with no conscious thought, and the walk back to her hotel was a blur.

Why would he be back together with Morgan? Had she meant so little to him? It didn't matter. She shouldn't have come, and this must be the sign that she should have stayed back in Star Lake and moved on.

When the door to her hotel room opened, she entered, letting the force of the door close it behind her. She threw herself on the bed. She would need to schedule her return tickets for tomorrow, but first she needed another good cry. She curled into a ball and let the tears flow silently down her cheeks.

CHAPTER 23

"How was your day, Bug?" Brandon asked Joy after Morgan had gone.

"It was okay." Her words were nonchalant, but the accompanying shrug told him it wasn't the best day.

"Did you not like Morgan?"

"She was all right, but not like Presley. She didn't play with me or talk to me like Presley does."

With a sigh, Brandon sank down on the couch, which looked much more comfortable than it was, and took Joy in his arms. "I know, honey. I thought Presley would at least come and see us, but I think I messed it up too badly."

Joy leaned her head against his shoulder. "Me too. I should have told her I wanted her to be my mom."

Her words pricked like a thorn in Brandon's heart. *If this job is so good, then why are we both so sad?*

He put Joy to bed and then returned to the couch where he flicked on the television. He had just gotten comfortable when a knock sounded at the door. Tossing the remote on the couch beside him, he crossed to the door and peeked out the spyhole.

He sighed at the sight of Morgan on the other side. "What can I do for you, Morgan?" he asked as he opened the door.

She smiled and held out a basket full of muffins. "I wanted to say thank you for letting me watch Joy this afternoon. I thought maybe we could talk?" Her attire was more casual today, just an oversized t-shirt over a pair of leggings. Perhaps she had changed, at least a little.

He stepped back and held the door open. Hearing her out wouldn't hurt anything. Joy was asleep, and it wasn't like he had anything else to do. She closed the door behind her and followed him to the living room, where he resumed his position on the couch.

Morgan sat at the other end and held the basket out to him. He surveyed the contents and selected a muffin. After peeling back the paper, he took a bite. It was good, but it was not the same as Presley's homemade muffins, and it just made him miss her more.

"So, I wanted to apologize again for leaving four years ago," Morgan said as she unwrapped her own muffin. "I was selfish, and I shouldn't have done that to you or to Joy." She plucked off a tiny morsel from her muffin and put it in her mouth.

Brandon wanted to tell her 'no kidding,' but she did appear to be trying, so he swallowed the spiteful words and tried again. "It was hard, Morgan. Harder than you'll probably ever know. Joy cried for months after you left, but finally she got over it and seems to have either forgotten or moved on. That's why I don't want you saying anything yet. It needs to be done right."

"Of course, you're right." She folded the rest of her muffin back up in the wrapper and set it beside her. "I wouldn't want to do anything to damage her further. Is there any way I can make it up to her? Or to you?" She shifted closer with those words, and her hand touched his knee.

"Morgan, don't."

"Don't what?" She batted her eyes, as if pretending not to know what he was talking about.

Brandon shot her a pointed stare and then looked down at her hand. "You know what."

"Don't you think we owe it to ourselves to see if we could be a family again? I mean, I've changed, and you're successful now."

Her words struck a chord in him, and he pushed her hand away. "And what if I lose this job? Would you walk out on us again?" The irritation quickly shifted to full-blown anger.

"You wouldn't."

"You can't know that Morgan." His voice came out as a hiss as he tried to keep the volume down so as not to wake Joy. "You can't control what might happen, and I can't take the chance of you deciding our life doesn't suit yours anymore and leaving again. However, since it is what you seem to do best, I think it's time you leave now." He stood and waited for her to follow suit.

Her mouth opened as if she had more to say, though what she could possibly say now was beyond him. With a sigh, she shut her mouth and stood up. "I'm sorry. I'm saying everything wrong, but I'll keep working Brandon. I want us to be a family again." She touched his arm again on her way out, and it took all his reserve not to shake it off.

After closing the door behind her, he pulled out his phone and stared at it. He missed Presley more now than ever, and more than just her, he missed being able to tell her whatever was on his mind. Morgan reappearing had affected him, and he wished he could discuss it with Presley. She would know what to do.

Brandon hadn't ended it well, but Presley had never said he couldn't call her. His teeth raked across his bottom lip as he entered the bedroom and sat on the big bed. A swipe of the screen showed no new calls or messages, but he desperately missed his friend. He'd forgotten how much until she'd walked back into his life.

Swallowing his pride, he dialed the number, hoping she would pick up. It was not to be. His heart dropped as her voice mail kicked on. *Do I leave a message? I can't say anything about Morgan on a message, but maybe she'll call me back.* "Hey, Presley, it's me, Brandon. I left you a text, but never heard back from you. We miss you. Joy and me. We'd love to see you if you get a chance. Okay, well you know where we are."

He punched the end call button feeling like an idiot and wishing there was a way to delete the idiotic message, but he knew it had already gone through the airwaves.

~

*T*he next morning, the nanny search began. Stewart had given him until the day after Christmas to get one hired, and then he had to return to work. Leaving Joy with anyone made him uneasy. It had taken him ages to find Amber, and he couldn't imagine how long it would take here in New York where people were much more uptight and hard to read.

The first knock came at eight am. A nice-looking woman in a tie-dyed shirt stood on the other side. "I'm Amelia, and I'm totally stoked to meet you."

As she stuck out her hand, the smell of weed carried over. No way was he leaving his daughter with someone who showed up stoned to an interview.

"Sorry, we're no longer looking." He shut the door before she had a chance to respond and shook his head. Marijuana wasn't even legal in New York, but ever since Washington and Colorado had made it legal, people had been bolder everywhere.

"You didn't like that one?" Joy asked, looking up from her cereal.

"Not even a little." He ruffled her hair and grabbed his coffee mug for a quick sip before the next knock.

This time the woman was severe looking with her hair pulled back in a tight bun and angry lines filling her face.

"I don't do laundry or cook or change diapers," she said as she shoved her resume at him.

"Good thing Joy is five then." She didn't catch the humor or else she simply ignored it as her eyes focused on Joy over his shoulder. The disapproving stare she gave his daughter was enough to end the interview. "We'll be in touch."

"What was wrong with that one?" Joy had finished her cereal and was washing her bowl in the sink. Brandon was taken aback by how grown up she seemed sometimes.

"I didn't like the look she gave you, like she wanted to change you. You are perfect just the way you are."

She rolled her eyes. "Da-ad." The word was drawn out to two syllables the way she said it.

"I'm sorry. I'm going to be picky because you are the most important thing to me."

"That's not true." Her words surprised him. "If I was, we would have stayed in Star Lake with Presley."

"Joy – " He was interrupted by another knock at the door. Sighing, he held up a finger to tell her the discussion was not done and crossed to the front door. A blond woman with the surprised expression of too many Botox injections stood on the other side, dressed impeccably in some ridiculous designer jumpsuit.

"Hi, I'm Alex. I'm here about the nanny job." She extended a slender hand with a French manicure.

She was too perfect for his choice, but he had yet to interview anyone. He might as well give her a whirl. "Brandon." He shook her hand and nearly laughed when she grimaced at his grip. "Come in." Holding the door open, he stepped back.

Her kitten heels clicked on the floor as she entered the apartment. Her eyes scanned the room appreciatively. "Nice place."

"It's only on loan for a few weeks until our stuff arrives and we get settled."

"I see, and where will you be locating to?" Her voice held just the smallest hint of disgust that this wasn't their permanent home.

"I'm not sure. I guess I should start looking."

Her slender eyebrow shot up her forehead. "If you want a good place, you should."

Brandon didn't like the way she appeared to judge him, but after glancing at her resume, she seemed solid. The Botox made her look younger than her experience showed, but she had evidently nannied for some high-profile people in the city, at least if her resume was truthful.

"Right, well why don't you tell me what a day would look like in your book?"

She folded her hands together. "I believe in schedules, so your child would eat breakfast at eight am. Then we would spend an hour reading or doing school work. I believe exercise is important, so we would walk to the nearest park for an hour. Lunch would be after that, and then the child would nap. If you allow television, they would get an hour after lunch. Then there is free play time and crafts."

Brandon's mind was dizzy trying to keep up with her schedule, but there could be worse things.

"My resume has references you can call. I'm very dedicated."

"Why did you leave your last job?" Everything on paper seemed right, but if she were so perfect, why was she free?

"My last family just moved. As you can see, I was with them for three years." She pointed to the bottom of the resume, the last job entry.

"Well, Alex, everything looks good. I'd like to contact your references, and of course, I'm sure there will still be more interviews today. Can I call you tomorrow?"

"Of course. I'll be at my mother's house in Brooklyn for

Christmas Eve and Christmas, but I'm not leaving until late on the twenty-third."

The twenty-third? Was it that close to Christmas already? He hadn't decorated the apartment at all for Christmas. He shook hands with Alex and walked her to the door, making an impromptu decision that she would do. He wanted to take Joy out to get a tree and some decorations. There was no way he would let her first Christmas in New York be un-Christmassy.

When the door closed behind Alex, he dialed the agency he had called for nannies and asked them not to send any more prospects out. "Joy, bundle up. We're going to get a tree."

Joy looked up from the dolls she had been playing with on the living room floor. "We're getting a tree?"

"Yes, hopefully we can find a lot that still has one. Hurry up."

"A lot? You mean we can't cut one down like we did at Nana's." Her face scrunched in confusion.

"Sorry, bug, there are no forests around here, but we'll find a good one at a lot."

She looked unsure, but hurried to her room to get her coat and hat. Brandon grabbed his off the rack, and by the time he had it on, she had returned. He grabbed her hand and locked the door behind them.

"Well, hello there."

Brandon froze at the sound of Morgan's voice. He had been hoping not to run into her. He was still frustrated by her insinuation the previous night, and he didn't want Joy finding out who she was yet. He also still wasn't certain she wasn't trying to take Joy away.

"Hi, Morgan." He kept his eyes on the floor in hopes she would get the hint, but she didn't. As she sidled up to him at the elevator, he could smell her perfume. Something strong and heavy. His eyes flicked her direction long enough to take in her tight shirt with a low cowl neck and her skin tight white pants.

She was still beautiful, but it no longer affected him. She seemed too done up, and he missed Presley's easy going way. She could be ready in ten minutes for whatever they wanted to do, and she would never be caught dead in skin tight white pants.

"Where are you guys headed?" She took another step closer, so that her arm was touching his.

"We're going to get a tree," Joy piped up. Brandon stifled a sigh. He had been hoping she would keep that information to herself.

The elevator dinged, and they stepped inside. Brandon punched the button for the lobby, hoping Morgan was getting off elsewhere.

"What a coincidence," Morgan said, "I was just going out to find a tree too. I know of a wonderful lot. They have the best trees. Maybe we can go together." Her hand found Brandon's arm, and she batted her eyes at him.

He didn't want to say yes, but it would be incredibly rude to say no now, and he had no idea where to go. "Sure, Morgan, that sounds nice."

She squeezed his arm, but instead of a lover's touch, it felt like claws digging into his skin. He had a hard time believing he had fallen in love with this woman six years ago, but he couldn't hate her too much because she had given him Joy.

When the doors opened to the lobby, Morgan led the way out of the elevator cab. The swiveling of her hips was meant for Brandon, and while he could appreciate the view, it did nothing for him.

"Mark," she called, "be a dear and fetch me my coat."

Mark tipped his hat and exited the room, returning a moment later with a long blue Burberry hooded trench coat. A ring of fur surrounded the inside of the hood. He held it out for her, and she slipped her arms in.

As Brandon watched the display, a bubble of nausea developed in his stomach. Was she always this spoiled? He tried to think back to when they first met, but the memories were hazy.

"Shall we?"

Nodding, he gestured for her to lead the way. Joy clutched his hand tightly as if it was a life line as they followed Morgan and Mark out of the hotel. Brandon wondered why Mark was still with them until he saw the man hailing a cab on their behalf. *Of course, heaven forbid she hail her own cab.* After Morgan climbed in, Brandon sent Joy in before climbing in himself. His hope was that Joy's presence would be a buffer and keep Morgan's hands off him.

Joy's eyes were wide as they buckled up, and they grow wider still as the cab weaved in and out of traffic. A few minutes later, they stopped in front of a tree lot situated snugly between two buildings. The lot was half empty, but the selection left appeared worthy.

Morgan paid the cabbie, and they climbed out of the car. Joy pulled on Brandon's hand, excited to see the trees. Laughing, he allowed her to lead him to the lot. She perused each tree carefully as if judging them in a contest.

"They aren't as nice as the ones in the woods, are they?"

Though serious, her question made him laugh. "No, I guess not quite."

She nodded like she expected that answer and continued her critiquing.

"I didn't get a chance to ask you last night, but how have you been?" Morgan asked. Joy had dropped Brandon's hand in order to examine the trees, but he kept her close in his sight.

"You mean since you left?" His voice was barely above a whisper as he didn't want Joy to hear.

Morgan rolled her eyes. "Sure, if you want to go back that far."

"Well, let's see. After you left, I couldn't bear to stay in Star Lake, so I packed up my one-year-old daughter and moved to Dallas. I got a job at a promotions firm and had to hire a nanny to watch her while I worked all day. Something I always thought her mother would do or at least help with.

"My father fell off a ladder, and I had to return to Star Lake. I ran into Presley Hays, remember her?" Morgan's face pinched into a tight smile, and she nodded. There was no love lost between those two, though Brandon had never understood why until now. "Then I returned to Dallas to do the presentation for Stewart, and he offered me the job, and here we are."

"Are you ever going to forgive me for leaving?" Morgan asked. "I really am trying to be better." Her claws once again found his arm, and he shook them off.

"I'm sure you are, Morgan, but I need someone stable for Joy, someone I know will be there for the long haul."

Her lips formed a tight smile. "I've changed, Brandon. You should really consider giving me a chance."

Her words felt more like a threat than a promise, but thankfully, Brandon was saved from answering by Joy's call. "I think this is the best one, Daddy." Relieved, he caught up to her and appraised the tree. It was not as nice as the one they cut down in the woods, but it was decent for a lot tree.

"Okay, this one it is." He grabbed the tag, blinking at the price of one hundred dollars. Things were certainly expensive in New York. Hoisting the tree, he took it to the checkout table. After charging the card, the man twined it up, and Brandon threw it back over his shoulder.

Morgan plucked a tag off a tree, not even bothering to check it out and handed it to the man who got the tree and wrapped it up for her. Then he passed the tree to an associate who carried it out for Morgan as they strolled back to the sidewalk to hail a cab home.

The tree man helped secure the trees on the roof of the cab, and Morgan slipped him a bill for his trouble. Then she whipped out her phone and tapped off a text. As they pulled up to the apartments, Brandon realized she had texted Mark as he stood waiting for them. He took Morgan's tree as Brandon grabbed his and the stand he had purchased from the lot. He shook his head at Morgan's inability to do anything for herself as he led the way to the elevator.

They parted ways at the thirtieth floor – Mark taking Morgan's tree to the left, and Brandon taking his tree to the right. Brandon had never been so glad to be rid of someone.

He drug the tree into the living room and set it up. When it was secure, he and Joy began cutting off the twine. With a few snips, the tree expanded, sending a shower of pine needles across the floor.

"Well, what do you think?"

She stared at the tree, her finger tapping her chin. "It needs ornaments."

He agreed but didn't dare chance another meeting with Morgan. "We'll go tomorrow."

CHAPTER 24

"Oh, no, what happened?" Trudy's face was a canvas of empathy.

Presley's was still red and splotchy from all the tears it had shed the last few days. She shook her head. "I'm so stupid. I flew all the way across the country, but he had already moved on."

"What are you talking about? He may be an idiot for taking that job, but the man was clearly in love with you." She wrapped an arm about Presley's shoulders as they walked to the exit.

"Morgan answered the door."

"Morgan?"

"Yeah, Joy's mother. She said they found each other and now they're working on reuniting as a family."

"Well, I don't know about you, but she didn't seem exactly trustworthy from what I remember." Trudy dropped her arm to punch the elevator button.

"It doesn't matter." Presley shrugged as they stepped inside the silver box. "Even if she was lying, I lost him once to her. Why would I stand a chance living over fifteen hundred miles away while she is right in the city with her perfect hair and her perfect figure?"

"Stop being so hard on yourself. You're beautiful too."

Trudy was trying to cheer her up, so Presley tried not to roll her eyes too hard. "He made his choice. I'll just have to deal with it and move on." The elevator door opened, and they continue down the short hallway to the parking garage. It was nearly devoid of cars, but a few other vehicles dotted the cement structure.

The hour ride from the airport was quiet. Presley spent most of the time staring at the lack of scenery out the window, and she was sure Trudy was spending it trying to come up with words to mend her thrice broken heart.

She offered a hug at the driveway which Presley took before heading into her apartment alone. When the door closed behind her, she pulled her phone from her pocket and played Brandon's message again.

He had called the previous night when she was pigging out on ice cream in her hotel room. She hadn't had the courage to take the call, in case he was calling to tell her about Morgan, but she had listened to it after. Again and again. His voice had sounded sincere, but he'd said nothing about Morgan. Could it be then that Morgan had lied? That they weren't together? If so, though, why had she been in his apartment?

Frustrated and confused, Presley punched the end button on her phone and hauled her bag into her room. After hoisting it on the bed, she began unpacking it. The clothes had barely had time to get wrinkled as she had just packed them two days ago. She shook her head, still unable to believe she had hopped on a plane to see a man only to hop on the next one out. What a waste of time and money.

Her sleep was restless that night, just as it had been the previous night. Presley wondered if she would ever sleep well again. She grabbed the phone from the nightstand where it was charging and listened to Brandon's voicemail again.

Her hand hovered over the call back button, but in the end, she decided to replace the phone on the nightstand without calling or texting him. Maybe it was her stubborn pride, but after traveling across the country, she felt that the next move should be his.

~

She woke before the alarm the next day, and in a daze, she sauntered into the bathroom to get dressed for the day. After a cup of coffee, she threw on her coat and walked into town.

"Ah, Presley, you're back. How did it go?" Max was sweeping a light snow off the sidewalk in front of his door. His flannel today was a green and white plaid, but his ball cap was the same blue one he wore every day.

"Not well." She forced a smile. "Maybe I'm just meant to be single."

He motioned her inside. The diner was quiet with only the two of them inside. The chairs were still up on the tables. He flipped two over and motioned for her to sit.

"Look," he said, "I know we aren't the same age, and this whole topic makes me uncomfortable, but I used to feel that way too. I'm sure you know that I pined after Layla for years."

"That's an understatement," Presley said under her breath.

His face pulled into a glare, wrinkling his forehead. "All I'm saying is, give Brandon time. He'll come around. Love has a way of working things out."

"And if that doesn't work, I'm always available."

Max and Presley both jumped as Bert popped out from a booth.

"Bert, what are you doing there?" Max's face was red with anger or exasperation. It was hard to tell.

"Well, I came in early for the first pot of coffee. The first pot is always the best before it sticks to the bottom and gets metallic tasting, but you weren't here yet, so I curled up in this booth to catch a little more sleep until you arrived."

"How did you get in here? Never mind, I don't want to know." Max rolled his eyes and shook his head.

"I appreciate the offer, Bert," Presley said as he turned his eyes on her, "but my heart just got broken again. It's going to need some time to mend, so I think I'm swearing off men for a while."

His brown eyes reminded her of the commercials to help fund animal shelters, and she had to fight the urge not to change her mind. Not because she wanted to date him, but because she wanted him to stop making those eyes.

"I should get going; I need to open the bakery. Thanks for the advice Max."

She ducked out before either of them could say another word and crossed the street to the bakery. Though she'd only been gone two days, it felt like a lifetime had passed.

After fumbling with the keys, she managed to open the door and flick the light switch. *Well, Trudy didn't destroy the place. I guess that's good.* The pastry case was empty, so at least she had remembered to take them out. Hopefully, she remembered to put them in the fridge.

Presley dropped her purse off in the small office in back and headed to the fridge. The pastries were individually wrapped and filled the top shelf. Sighing, she grabbed them, stacking them in her left arm and headed back to the front. One at a time, she peeled the saran wrap off and put the pastry back in the case.

The bell jingled as she placed the last one. Layla entered, swinging a basket and bearing a smile.

"Oh, good, you're back. Don't get me wrong, I love Trudy, but she had no idea what all the items on my list were. I really missed you." She placed the basket on the counter and pulled out a piece of paper – her list.

"At least someone did," Presley muttered.

"Uh oh, it didn't go well?" Her voice shifted to an empathetic tone.

Presley shook her head as the tears began to prick her eyes. There would be no crying at work.

"Well, you know it took Max and I years to find each other. Maybe Brandon will come around, and until then, you have all of us."

The thought brought a small smile to Presley's face, not because she found friendships fulfilling but because this town was full of quite a cast of characters that pretty much assured there would never be a dull moment.

"Thanks, Layla." Presley finished packing her bread and pastries in the basket.

"Anytime, kid." With a small wave, Layla picked the basket back up and exited the building. In true Layla fashion, the room felt darker once she was gone. She had the uncanny ability to light up a room whenever she was in it.

As Presley waited for the next customer, she pulled her phone from her pocket. A picture of Brandon, Joy, and herself with the tree they had cut down stared back at her, but there was no message or missed call from Brandon. She should probably change the picture, but she just didn't have the heart to take it down. Not yet.

The bell jingled again, and she shoved the phone back in her pocket.

"No word yet?" Anna asked. Presley hadn't been quick enough to hide her guilty gesture.

She shook her head. "Nothing since the first night. Do you think I should call him back?"

Anna shrugged. "I honestly don't know anymore. I thought he was going to stay, and you guys would become the couple we all expected. His leaving caught all of us off guard too. Anyway, that's not why I'm here. I know his leaving was hard, but we'd like your family to join us for Christmas. We'd love to have you, and you can bring some chocolate eclairs if you'd like."

Her eyebrows danced as she made the suggestion, and Presley couldn't help but smile. "Deal. Although I'm not sure if Mom will be working or not," Unfortunately for her mother, she and Ryan had both gone to college, so she was still working two jobs to help pay the expenses. Presley hoped one day to be able to repay her some, or at least lighten her load. "but I know Ryan will be free."

Anna blushed and dropped her eyes. "Wonderful. I'll tell Mom, and maybe my brother will come to his senses and come home by then."

As Christmas was only two days away, Presley highly doubted it, but she didn't say anything to Anna. There was no sense spoiling her hope.

The rest of the day was a slow blur, and Presley was glad when six hit and she could pack up and go home. Right now, all she wanted was some chocolate ice cream and Niko on her lap, though she had better find another consolation item soon. Her pants were already feeling snugger from her ice cream binges the last few days.

CHAPTER 25

"*D*addy, when did Presley come by?" Joy asked.

Brandon looked up from his phone. "What do you mean, honey? Presley hasn't been here."

"Well, then where did these come from?" She held out two gifts, a large rectangular box obviously for her with its pink trees and a smaller square box wrapped in green and white striped paper, which Brandon assumed was for him.

"Where did you get these?"

"In the closet. I was playing hide and seek with Bunny, and they were there buried under some blankets." She handed him the smaller package. "Can we open them?"

Brandon's heart ached at the familiar curve of Presley's letters. It was not Christmas until tomorrow, but he was curious as to what these were as well. "Yeah, bug, let's see if she left a note with them."

He watched as she tore the paper off the present. Her eyes widened, and a smile lit up her face. "It's perfect." She turned the box to him, and Brandon saw the picture of the Eiffel Tower on the puzzle box. A perfect combination of Presley and Joy. The ache grew a little bigger. "Open yours, Daddy."

He pulled open the paper to reveal a small white box. Lifting the lid, he peeled back the tissue paper and emotion welled inside him. His fingers grasped the tip of the ornament, and he pulled it out. The happy couple, so reminiscent of him and Presley stared back, and with a flick of his wrist, snow swirled about. It was an image of their first kiss, and it was nearly perfect. His throat constricted with sadness and anger and love. "Where did you say you found these?"

She pointed behind her. "In the hall closet under some blankets."

Presley had to have come by some time while he was at work and Joy was napping for neither of them to see her, but the only day he'd been at work so far was . . . "Morgan." The word came out more as a growl than a name. "Be right back, Bug."

He stormed through the door, slamming it behind him, and down the hall to the other end. His knuckles pounded on the door before he had his words all figured out. It swung open, and Morgan blinked at him.

"Well, hello Brandon, did you change your mind?" She leaned seductively against the doorframe, her red lips curved in a predatory smile.

"When did Presley stop by?"

Her eyes blanked for a moment, and her posture shifted. "What do you mean?" Her voice had lost its lusty lilt and now held an essence of fear.

"I mean we found the presents you hid in the closet. What did you think you were doing?"

She rolled her eyes. "I was protecting you. Presley has always held you back. You're finally doing it right this time; you're in the big leagues. You don't need some small-town girl riding your coattails."

Anger surged through his veins. "What did you tell her?"

Morgan shrugged. "Just that we were working on being a family again."

His hands clenched into fists at his side. "Morgan, that's not true. You had no right."

"I had every right. I'm the reason you're even here." Her eyes widened, and her hand flew to her mouth.

"What do you mean you're the reason I'm here?" Brandon's voice trailed off as Mark's words from the first day came back to him. "You're the owner of the company?" The pieces began to fall into place. "What did you do, Morgan?"

She took a deep breath, and her arms folded across her chest. "When I left, it was because I wanted you to see that you could do more. You had gotten used to that sleepy town and you were willing to settle there. I wasn't. I hoped if I left, it would spur you into action, and it did. I followed your move to Dallas and then began working behind the scenes here to get Stewart to meet with you."

"So, my whole career is just because of you." Brandon shook his head at her, not believing she could stoop so low.

"Not your whole career. You still did the work; I just got the connections in front of you."

He ran his hand through his hair as he rolled his eyes. "It's the same thing, Morgan. I can't believe you thought this would work."

He turned to leave, but her claws reached out and snagged his arm. "You can't leave now. If you quit Bling, Inc, your reputation will be ruined."

Slowly, Brandon turned to face her again. "I don't really care, Morgan. My heart isn't here anyway. It's back in Star Lake. With Presley." The truth of his words hit like an anvil over the head. How could he have been so stupid?

After prying her nails off, he left Morgan, face gaping in her doorway, and headed back to his apartment.

"Joy, how would you feel about getting out of here?"

"Like to the park?" she asked, looking up from her puzzle.

"No," he shook his head, smiling, "I mean home. To Star Lake."

She scrambled up and ran to him, throwing her arms around his legs. "Do you mean it, Daddy?"

He crouched down to wrap his arms around her. "I do, bug. Let's go home."

As she began packing up her things, Brandon jumped on the phone. First to Stewart.

"I'm sorry Stewart, but I can't take the job after all."

"I don't understand. What happened?" His voice was utterly confused on the other end.

"Morgan did, and it's not your fault, but I went down that road once, and I'm not doing it again. Can you give me the name of the moving company, so I can call them to get them to turn around? I'll pay the return trip."

Brandon jotted the number down as he rattled it off and thanked him before hanging up. The moving company was the next call, and he reached the manager on the second ring.

"I know this is unusual, but I need the drivers to turn around. I need them to go to 812 Cooper Street, Star Lake Texas."

The woman on the other end chuckled. "You'd be surprised. This happens more often than you think. I'll let the driver know right away, but can I ask you one question?"

"Sure." Brandon had no idea what she wanted, but the fact that she was so willing to accommodate him made him more comfortable answering her question.

"Is it for love?"

A smile broke out on his face, and though he knew she couldn't see it, he was sure she could hear it in his voice. When Brandon first started sales, that was one of the tricks they taught him. Always smile on the phone because people could hear it in your voice. "Yeah, it is."

"I knew it. It's almost always for love. Good luck."

He thanked her and hung up. One more call. After looking up the number on his phone, Brandon dialed the airport.

"Customer service, how can I help you?"

"I need to get tickets for the first flight you have to East Texas Regional Airport, and please say it's soon."

"One moment, sir, let me check." He could hear the tapping of keys through the phone. "It looks like there are only two flights a day sir. I can get you on a late flight tonight that leaves at eight pm and would get you into East Texas at eight am. There are two stops, but you won't have to de-plane. Or there is a flight first thing tomorrow at five am that will get you there at four pm. You'd have to change planes once."

Brandon looked down at his watch. It was just past noon. There should be plenty of time for them to pack and get to the airport, although there was one more stop he wanted to make. "I'll take tonight. Two tickets please." He tried not to cringe at the price she read off, and rattled off his credit card. He would have to find a job quickly in Star Lake, but it would be worth it.

"Okay, you'll need to pick them up at the check in gate, but here's your confirmation number."

After jotting down the number, Brandon ended the call and helped Joy finish packing. They filled up the suitcases they had brought and managed to squeeze in the presents from Presley, but as he looked over at the tree, Brandon realized all those presents wouldn't fit.

"We'll have to mail them back, Bug. Is that okay?"

"Of course, daddy. None of those hold what I really wanted for Christmas anyway."

"What did you want for Christmas, bug?" He had gotten her the set of books she asked for and a new Barbie.

"I wanted to spend Christmas in Star Lake with Nana and Poppy and Presley."

Brandon scooped her up in a hug and twirled her around the room. "This is going to be the best Christmas ever."

She giggled and squealed as they turned in circles.

"Okay, let me see if I can get a box and have someone take this to the post office. Should we take the ornaments we bought?" They hadn't found many original ones, so they were mainly the colorful balls and a few that looked like icicles.

Her face scrunched, and she shook her head. "Nah, we can get new ones with Presley."

Brandon sighed. "Bug, we're going back to Star Lake, but I can't guarantee Presley will take me back. You have to be prepared for that."

Joy shook her head, a knowing smile on her face. She looked so much older than her almost six years. "Daddy, she loves you, and she brought us these presents. She'll take you back."

In his heart, he hoped she was right. When he explained what Morgan did, surely Presley would forgive him. "Okay, let me get these presents taken care of then, and we'll head to the airport. We'll have to sleep on the flight, but we'll make it home in time for Christmas."

She smiled and sat on the couch, reading one of her books while he contacted Mark and asked him to bring up a box. The knock sounded a moment later. Mark stood on the other side of the door with a large cardboard box in hand.

"Ah, thank you Mark. Can you come in for a minute while I box these up?"

"Of course." He stepped inside and closed the door behind him. He stood with his hands behind his back as Brandon packed up the few presents under the sparsely decorated tree. "You're going somewhere for Christmas?"

"We're leaving for good, actually. Going back home."

He blinked in surprise. "Oh, I'm sorry to hear that. Have we done something wrong?"

"Oh, no, it's not you. We're going home for love."

A smile broke Mark's normally stoic face. "Well, in that case, let me know how I can help."

"Can you drop this at the post office for us when I'm done and call us a cab for the airport?"

"Absolutely," Mark nodded. "It would be my pleasure to."

Brandon smiled up at him as he finished packing the box. When it was done, he took the roll of tape and Sharpe marker that Mark produced and held out. Brandon didn't know how he had known, but he had come prepared. He was like a male Mary Poppins, only he was pulling things out of his jacket instead of a purse.

After the box was packed, Mark tucked it under his arm and Brandon checked his watch. It was only two pm, but with traffic in New York, he would rather be safe than sorry. "Ready, Joy?"

She slammed her book shut and tucked it in her suitcase. "Ready."

Mark opened the door and led the way to the elevator. As they waited for it to open, Brandon heard Morgan's door open.

"What are you doing?" Her heels clomped so hard as she stomped toward them that he could hear the sound even through the soft plush carpet.

"We're leaving, Morgan, and there's nothing you can do to stop us. You shouldn't have tried to control me." He placed his hands on Joy's shoulder, pulling her closer.

Morgan saw the gesture and smiled. It was a vicious predatory smile that sent a chill down his spine. "I'll tell her who her mother is."

Brandon was about to respond when Joy piped up. "I don't care who my birth mother is because she left me. Mothers don't do that. Presley is what a mother should be. She hugs me and reads me stories and plays with me."

Morgan's mouth dropped open, but before she could reply, the elevator dinged and they stepped inside, leaving Morgan standing in the hall catching flies.

"That was awesome, Miss Joy," Mark said softly, a smile tugging at his lips. "No one speaks to Miss Warner like that, but they should."

Brandon's own smile played across his lips. Evidently Joy got more than just his hair. In the lobby, Mark gave Joy a high five and wished Brandon luck. After thanking him, they stepped outside. A yellow cab waited at the curb.

Brandon held tight to Joy's hand as they marched through the current of people to the edge of the sidewalk. Within minutes, their luggage was in the trunk, and they climbed inside.

"Where to?" The man was foreign with a long scraggly beard, and his accent was hard to understand.

"The airport, please. American Airlines."

"You bet," he said, and the car pulled into traffic.

"Wait, can we make one stop first?" Brandon gave him the name of where he wanted to go, and the cabbie smiled in the mirror and nodded.

Though his watch still showed plenty of time, the nerves had started taking root in Brandon's stomach, twisting and turning into a tightly coiled knot. His head was focused on Presley and what he was going to say to her.

The car stopped, and he glanced around. They were stuck in the middle of traffic. He realized he hated traffic, yet another reason to get out of this city.

"Are we going to make it, Daddy?" Joy's face was pressed against the glass, and her voice was full of worry.

"We left early for a reason. We'll have plenty of time," he reassured her, but his own nerves balled even tighter at the delay.

CHAPTER 26

"hanks for coming with us, Mom." Presley gave her mother a hug before they threw on their coats to make the short trek to Brandon's parents' house.

"I'm just glad I could get the day off to spend with you guys," she said, returning the hug. There were tears in her tired eyes and more wrinkles than Presley remembered on her face. Even her hair was grayer than it had been six years ago. "I'm sorry I didn't get to spend more time with you children when you were younger."

"Don't be sorry, Mother. Yes, we would have loved to have you around more, but we understood the sacrifices that you made for us, and we love you even more because of it. I hope one day I'll get to be as great a mom as you were to us."

Ryan nodded his agreement.

Her mother smiled. "I have no doubt that you will my dear. If not Brandon, then some man will come along and make you a very happy woman."

Presley had her doubts in this small town, but she didn't want to ruin the mood. Yesterday had been lonely as her mother had to work. She had kept the bakery open but only had two or three visitors all day. The evening was spent watching sappy romantic Christmas movies on the screen with Ryan and wishing her life could be like theirs. She was looking forward to some festivities and people today.

They didn't speak much on the short walk there, each lost in their own thoughts, but Anna made up for it as they were ushered into the house.

"Here let me get your coats. Mom made gingerbread cookies, and they are delicious. Plus, she has a ham with all the fixings baking for lunch."

Presley's smile was genuine as she handed over her coat. Part of it was based on Anna's verbal outpouring and part of it was based on the food. She remembered missing that aspect in Paris. Though they had amazing food, it was often small portions and delicate dimensions, nothing like 'all the fixings' in Texas, which usually meant bread, potatoes, green bean casseroles, sweet potato pies, and more.

They followed Anna into the living room where Bruce was situated in the recliner in front of the television. The Cowboys were playing the Eagles today, and as he was a diehard fan, he would be parked in front of the set until the game was over. For his sake, Presley hoped the Cowboys won. She remembered a few rough Christmases spent with Brandon when they lost, and everyone was in a sour mood for the rest of the night.

"Helena, Ryan, we're so glad you could join us," Beverly said, addressing Presley's mother and brother as she entered the living room. The two women hugged like long lost friends while Ryan waved and then planted himself on the couch to watch the game with Bruce.

"Thank you for inviting me. It seems I miss more of these gatherings every year, but now that Ryan has graduated, and I've started to pay down debts, I think I'll be taking more breaks."

"You'll have to promise to stop working so hard."

"You won't have to tell me twice. Is there anything I can do to help?"

The two women headed into the kitchen leaving Presley staring at Bruce and Ryan and wondering what she should do.

"Presley, come help me finish wrapping some gifts," Anna called from the family room.

Glad to have something to do, Presley joined her. She was wrapping a large black box on the floor.

"Who is this for?"

"Dad," she answered, looking up just a second before returning her concentration to the paper that kept falling off one side while she held the other. Her sigh of exasperation sent her bangs flying into the hair before falling back to her forehead. "It's a tool box."

"Isn't it a little early for that?" Presley wasn't trying to be rude, but Bruce was still using the walker to get around. She couldn't see him picking up this tool box anytime soon, but she dropped to her knees and held the side for Anna.

She shot a grateful look. "Yeah, that's what Mom said too, but I know Dad, and he's going to want to do something as soon as he feels normal again. This way it will be ready when he is."

"Sounds good." With Presley's help, Anna finished the job quickly, though the wrapping job itself left a lot to be desired. Some of that was caused by the odd shape of the box though. It took both of them to push it under the tree. As they did, Presley's eyes landed on a present addressed to Brandon.

"Is Brandon coming?" she asked Anna, hoping she would say yes, even though she knew the answer was probably no.

"No, that was just one we forgot to give him before they left."

"Oh."

"If it's any consolation," she said, reading the emotion on Presley's face, "Brandon can be pretty dumb sometimes, but he almost always comes around."

Presley flashed an appreciative smile, and then Beverly's voice carried down the hallway. "Girls, lunch is ready."

As they gathered around the table, Beverly and Presley's mother placed the food on the table. Anna hurried to the living room to help Bruce join everyone around the table, and Presley grabbed the cups and placed them at the settings.

They had just sat down at the table when a knock sounded at the door.

"Who could that be?" Beverly asked, looking up.

"I'll go see." Anna bounded out of her chair to the front door.

Beverly started the procession of food by scooping some potatoes onto her plate and then passing them to her right. She followed this with the ham and had just started the rolls when she gasped. Presley glanced up to see her wide eyes staring at something behind her. She twisted in her chair to see Brandon and Joy both smiling like loons. Anna stood beside them, as bewildered as her mother.

"Merry Christmas everyone. We're home." Brandon threw out his arms as if he was expecting everyone to rush in for a hug.

"Well, I'll be," Beverly said. She dropped the biscuit she had in her hand and rushed around the table to embrace them both. "What happened?"

"It's a long story," Brandon said with a shake of his head, "but we have Presley to thank."

"Me?" *What had I done?*

"Yes, if you hadn't shown up and left those presents, we would never have known."

Presley stood and crossed to him. "I don't understand. If you saw them that day, why didn't you call me to come back?"

He shook his head. "We didn't see them that day. Morgan hid them and didn't tell us you stopped by. Joy found them just yesterday, and I confronted Morgan. It seems she set the whole thing up – the promotion and everything."

"Oh, Brandon, I'm so sorry." As her words faded, she realized the rest of the family was watching in rapt silence. A blush spread across her face.

"So, will you forgive us?" Joy asked.

"Of course I will. I should have known better. I never trusted Morgan."

Joy dropped Brandon's hand and ran into Presley's arms. Then the commotion commenced. Beverly and Anna surrounded Brandon lavishing hugs and talking over each other. Even Bruce used his walker to stand from the table and give Brandon a hug. Ryan stood, though he seemed unsure what part to play – whether to be supportive or pull the brother card. Presley looked up at Brandon over Joy's shoulder and smiled.

After lunch, everyone gathered around the tree. Brandon nodded at the couch as he looked at Presley, the silent question evident in his raised eyebrow. Stifling a grin, she agreed, and the two parked on the couch, each taking one end. Joy climbed up between them, grabbing one of their hands with each of her own.

"Who's going to hand out?" Beverly asked. Anna finished helping Bruce to the recliner and then sat in a chair beside him.

"I will."

Joy jumped up from the couch and pulled Presley's hand so that she was forced to slide closer to Brandon. Laughing, he opened his arm, and she snuggled into it. His cologne wafted to her nose, woodsy and familiar. She had missed the smell of him and definitely the feeling of his arm around her. Her mother smiled from across the room where she was sitting and Presley smiled back.

Joy delivered the first present to Bruce, who opened it to reveal a new necktie. Beverly was next. She opened her gift to find a new pair of gloves. Joy delivered a gift to Helena next.

"Oh, you guys didn't have to do this," she said, but smiled as she opened the gift to find a beautiful scarf.

"Bug, get the one from my bag," Brandon said as Joy reached

under the tree. She paused, then her eyes lit up as she realized what he meant, and she hurried to the hallway where they must have left their suitcases. She returned bearing a small black box.

Brandon took the box and slid from the couch to his knees in front of Presley. Her eyes widened as she realized what he was about to do. "Presley Elizabeth Hays, I've loved you from almost the first moment we met, but I let my fear of losing you keep me from telling you. I didn't realize how much you meant to me until you came back into my life. I was a fool for not realizing the strength of what we have, and those few days apart from you in New York were the longest days of my life. The thought of losing you again ate me up inside, and I don't want to go through that again. I love you, and I'm asking if you will make Joy and I the happiest pair on Earth."

"Please Presley," Joy added.

Presley's eyes teared up, and her voice stuck in her throat, but she managed to nod. Brandon opened the box to showcase a beautiful diamond ring with a large carat in the middle and three smaller stones on either side. He slid it on her finger and then leaned forward placing his lips on hers. The rest of the family erupted in clapping, and as Brandon pulled back, Presley saw pink on his face as well, at least what could be seen above his beard.

The rest of the present opening flew by, a blur to Presley as her mind was focused partly on the ring on her finger and partly on the man beside her. She was still having trouble believing this was real as just yesterday she had resigned herself to possibly never seeing him again. When the presents were all opened, Brandon grabbed her hand pulling her up beside him.

"Take a walk with me?" His voice was low and throaty in her ear. The vibration of his whisper sent a shiver down her spine. She nodded and followed him to the front door to grab their coats.

"I'm so glad you found it in your heart to forgive me," Brandon said as they stepped onto the porch.

"I wasn't mad, more confused. Seeing Morgan was a shock. I'm sorry I didn't call you back that night, but I couldn't figure out why you didn't say anything about her on the message. I guess I know now." Brandon's fingers intertwined with hers. It was a fit that felt like perfection.

He shook his head. "That woman has some nerve. I can't believe she didn't think I'd find out or that I'd be okay with her trying to dictate my life."

"Is she gone out of your life for good?" Presley wasn't afraid of Morgan anymore, but that didn't mean she wanted to have to deal with custody battles or her coming into their life.

"Yeah, I think so. Joy kind of told her off. I don't think she was used to that."

Presley's eyes widened. "She did what?"

He laughed and turned toward the park. "I'll tell you about it sometime. It was amazing."

"So, what are you going to do now? You're out of a job, right?"

The large intake of his breath told her he didn't have it all figured out. "I don't know for sure, but I thought maybe I could use some of my promotion skills to put Sweet Treats on the map."

Presley stopped in her tracks, pulling his arm so he was forced to stop as well. "Are you serious?"

His brows knitted together in confusion. "Well, yeah. I think you could get online. Have orders to go, that sort of thing."

Her eyes filled with water, and her lips pursed together. "That would be amazing. I've been hanging on by a thread, and if I don't get some new customers soon, I'm not sure how much longer Sweet Treats will last."

"Why didn't you say anything?" He wrapped his arms around her and pulled her closer. "I could have helped sooner."

Presley rolled her eyes at him. He must have no idea how focused he was on his job. "You wouldn't have listened Brandon. You were too ready to get out of here."

His eyes clouded for a minute, and his teeth pulled on his bottom lip. She hadn't meant for the words to hurt him. "You're right. I was. I had tunnel vision and was only thinking about myself. Promise me that you'll help me keep from doing that in the future."

"I'll try, but you're a stubborn man, Brandon Scott." Her hand brushed through his curly hair and trailed down his beard.

"You're stubborn too, Presley Hays, but I'm glad of it."

As his hands tightened against her lower back and pulled her forward, her arms slid behind his neck. His lips were soft and warm against hers. She had always thought people who said they saw fireworks when they kissed someone were full of it, but she could almost hear the explosions as his lips explored hers.

"Are you planning to stay here?" she asked when they parted.

"Of course. In fact, I was hoping you'd go house hunting with me this week. I know you have your place until we get married, but I'd like to only buy one house and it makes more sense to have your input on it."

"I'd love that."

"Good, it's a date."

CHAPTER 27

The parade of visitors began promptly at seven the next morning as Presley opened the shop. Paula, true to form, was the first one there.

"Is it true?" she squealed. "You must let me see it."

Presley held out the ring as Paula oohed and aahed over it. "Paula, one day you will have to tell me how you always have the information before everyone else."

She smiled. "I can't tell you that sweetie. It's a secret that will have to die with me, but I wonder if it will turn into a double wedding. I hear your brother and Anna are getting quite close as well."

Presley laughed and shook her head. "Whatever will you do when we all get married off?"

"Oh, there will be new people. Don't worry. If you succeed in getting this place noticed, I see many newcomers in our future. By the way, Shane at the realtor office asked me to drop these flyers off. He thinks some of these might be exactly what the two of you are looking for."

She placed the papers on the counter and then headed for the exit, passing Brandon on his way in and issuing her congratulations to him as well.

"How does she know?" he asked as he set his laptop bag on a table. He had offered to take pictures of the shop and begin working up a promotional website.

"I have no idea, but she even dropped these by." Presley handed him the flyers as they traded a quick kiss over the counter. She would love for it to be longer, but she had a lot of baking to do today. Brandon wanted pictures of all the pastries she could make for the website and some of them were out of stock.

Shaking his head, he skimmed the papers, nodding at a few and frowning at others. She left him to his work and began grabbing the ingredients she would need from the back. The bell jingled as she returned, arms laden with sacks and Tupperware containers.

"I'm so happy for you guys." Layla's voice carried in the small room.

"Thank you," Brandon said, and though he meant it, Presley could hear the discomfort in his voice at being the center of everyone's attention.

"What's on your list today, Layla?" After freeing her arms from the load, she turned to the counter to get the list.

"Same as yesterday except for one thing. I want to see the ring."

Presley held out her hand and enjoyed the light that danced in Layla's eyes.

"It's a good one," she said with a wink.

"He's a good one," Presley said winking back. She filled up Layla's order and waved goodbye as she exited.

"Is it like this every day?" Brandon asked from his chair.

"No, but it's not every day I get engaged either. You better get used to it. By my calculations, we have at least four more intrusions and that's not counting the non-regular patrons."

He sighed and rolled his eyes before turning back to his screen.

Her estimations were nearly correct as by the end of the day Trudy, Max, Bert, Barnard, and Pastor Robert had all stopped in. She sank down in the chair next to Brandon, exhausted but happy.

"Let me show you what I've done." He pivoted the screen, so she could see it better and showed the webpage he had built. It was colorful and sweet and exactly what she would have wanted if I knew how to ask for what she wanted.

"It's amazing."

"Yeah, and here's the best part." He clicked off the webpage to some sheet filled with numbers. "If we can drive one hundred people to your site every month, and that's pretty small, you should see double the income you have coming in now."

The words and numbers on this page meant nothing to Presley, but she smiled and nodded as this obviously meant something to him. His entire face lit up as he talked about the numbers, and she could see why he had done so well in this job.

"So, shall we?"

"Shall we what?" Her mind had zoned off as he was talking, and she had missed his last question.

"Shall we go and check out this house?" He placed the page in front of her. The picture showed a quaint rambler with a wraparound porch. The siding was painted a pale blue and trimmed in white. A white rocker sat on the porch. She scanned the details. 2200 square feet, four bedrooms, two and a half baths.

"It's amazing, but do we need something so large? There are only three of us."

His smile was mischievous as it stretched across his face. "For now, but you once asked me if I wanted more kids, and I can honestly say with you Presley that I hope we have a dozen."

She didn't know whether to laugh or blush, so she did both. "Yes, let's go see it then."

They bundled up, and after locking the door, headed home to grab Joy. After all, this house would be hers as well and they wanted her input. The house was a little farther from the shop, but still a walkable distance.

The yard was large and fenced in with a white picket fence. "Daddy, look, there's a swing set in the back." Joy's voice rose in excitement as she dropped their hands and ran to get a closer look.

Brandon's hand filled the void left from Joy's, and he smiled over at her.

The front door opened as they approached, and Shane, the local agent stepped out on the porch. He was older than Brandon and Presley with a Friar Tuck hairline but kind brown eyes. His long brown trench coat covered up whatever suit he was wearing underneath. Shane always dressed to impress. "Brandon, Presley, good to see you. Come on inside, and I'll show you around."

The front room was large and homey, painted a soft tan color that complemented the brown in the hard wood flooring. A large cream-colored couch sat against one wall underneath a colorful painting. An overhead fan held three light bulbs surrounded in frosted glass casings. Two ornate chairs sat on the other side of the room with a brown table between them. At the far end of the room was a large fireplace with a brick mantle.

"The furniture doesn't come with the place," Shane said, "but it helps you get the idea."

He led the way out of the front room and into the kitchen. The colors were bright and airy, soft beige and cream. A travertine floor in a soft brown with silver specks ran throughout the room. The appliances were stainless steel, and a glass door opened to a large backyard. A slide and swing set stood in the yard.

"See, Daddy? See the swing set?"

"I see it, Bug."

The dining room sat next to the kitchen and down the hall lay the bedroom and a hall bath as well as another living room. At the very back of the house was the master bedroom, painted a soft rose color with beige carpet. A queen four poster bed took up a large part of the real estate in the room, but there was still room for a dresser and two nightstands. A large walk in closet and a master bathroom with a soaking tub completed the room.

"It's beautiful." Presley squeezed Brandon's hand.

"Yes, it is, but I'm afraid I need to get some money coming in first before going farther into debt. How long do you think it will stay on the market Shane?"

Shane pursed his lips and scratched his balding head. "Don't rightly know. It's been up for a month, and I've only shown it twice. Best guess'd be another couple of months."

"Wonderful. I'll start crunching some numbers and looking for work, and we'll let you know."

The two men shook hands and they made their way back to the front door.

"Daddy, are we going to buy this house?" Joy asked, once again grabbing each of their hands.

"I hope to Joy, but we have to get some money coming in first. Now that I've quit my job, I'll have to find something here."

He was quiet as they walked back to his house to drop off Joy, and Presley knew that not being able to provide for his family was weighing on him. She sent a quick prayer heavenward for something to materialize for him soon.

CHAPTER 28

*B*randon closed his eyes and then opened them on the screen again. It couldn't be true. It just wasn't possible. "Presley, when you get a second, can you come here?" He leaned back in his chair which sat just under the Eiffel Tower picture covering one wall in Presley's store.

"What is it?" she asked as she appeared around the corner. Her hair was piled loosely on her head, and her purple streak – that adorable purple streak – had once again fallen out of place and hovered over her right eye. She blew it off her face and tucked it behind her ear as she approached.

"I want to show you something." He turned the computer to face her, and she sat down in the other chair. Her eyes scanned back and forth across the page, but when she glanced up, he could tell she didn't understand what she was seeing.

"Those are the orders that came in on your website this morning."

Her eyes returned to the screen and widened as she took in the page of emails. Her lips parted, and her hand – nails painted a sparkly purple today – touched her mouth. "There's so many of them."

Brandon laughed. "Yeah, thirty to be exact. You're only seeing the first twenty-five. There is another page."

"Thirty orders? How on earth am I going to bake that much?"

"Well, you have me, but I have the feeling you are going to need some help as well. If the orders keep coming in like this, and I have a good feeling they will, you are going to need a full-time helper."

"Brandon, this is incredible. I don't know what to say." The shock was evident in her voice as she struggled to find the words, a rare trait for Presley.

"For right now, I suggest we start baking. I'll be your help today. Just tell me what we need to do."

A laugh escaped her lips. "Okay, let's get you an apron, and we'll start mixing."

While she headed to the back to grab an apron, Brandon took the laptop and set it up on the table behind the counter, so they could see the orders while working. They spent the rest of the afternoon that way, mixing and baking and cooling and boxing up orders. Every once in a while, she left him to man the counter, but the customers were slow today, at least the in-store ones. The online orders continued to fly into the inbox faster than they could fill them.

"Do you think Anna would help? I know she's only home till school starts again, but we could sure use her help." Presley wiped her forehead with the back of her hand leaving a white mark of flour in its wake.

Brandon smiled at her exhausted appearance and complete lack of knowledge of the smudge. She was so beautiful. "I'm sure she will as long as Mother can handle Joy alone."

Presley sighed. "Oh, that's right. I forgot she was helping your mom out during the day. I'd ask Ryan, but he burns toast. I suppose I better put out signs or take out an ad."

"I'm sure Bert could help you with that." It was meant as a joke, and Presley caught it, joining in laughter as the image of Bert either baking with her or going door to door to find her a helper filled their heads.

"I'll talk to Rita at the Gazette tomorrow," Presley said when she managed to calm her laughter. The Star Lake Gazette was not a big newspaper, but Rita was a perfectionist and always put out an amazing copy, and since it was the only newspaper in town, many of the residents still read it.

"That's a good idea. For now, I'm starving, so can we call it a night?" The clock on her wall read six fifteen, past closing time, but he hadn't had the heart to stop her in the middle of a batch of cookies. The oven timer dinged, signaling the last batch was ready.

"Let's box these up and get out of here," Presley said and while Brandon took the cookies out of the oven, she locked the front door and turned the sign to closed. They finished packing up the cookies, performed a quick cleaning of the kitchen, and headed over to his mother's house for a late dinner.

Ryan met them at the corner of Cooper Street. He and Anna had begun hanging out together quite regularly and while they were not officially dating, Brandon would give his blessing. He had always liked Ryan, not only because he was related to Presley, but because he always seemed genuine. It would be interesting to see how their story worked out.

As they reached the porch, Joy came out hollering. "Daddy, Presley, come see. Come see."

Unsure of what had her so excited, they followed her into the living room to see his father slowly walking circles around the room, using only a cane. He looked up and smiled. "I've been practicing."

They hurried to embrace him, and Brandon heard Presley whisper, "Praise Jesus" as her arms encircled his father. Brandon had never been as big of a believer as she was, but he was starting to wonder if there was something to it all. The bakery, his father, even his coming back all seem precipitated by prayers.

He asked Presley about her faith on the walk back to her apartment after dinner that night. She smiled and squeezed his hand as she told him the entire story he only knew bits and pieces of.

"I don't think I was doing the best I could," she said, "I wasn't practicing faith, but when you left, I knew I had to give it to God. Then I prayed for your father and for your job. I know you like to see things in person, but for me just seeing the things I prayed for come true is enough to make me a believer. I think if you would truly give your life to God, you would see amazing things happen as well."

Her words continued to rattle around in his head that night as he laid in bed staring at the white ceiling. He had nothing to lose and everything to gain, and he found himself whispering his own prayer before his eyes closed for the night.

～

*A*nna accompanied him to the bakery the next morning. With his father able to walk more using his cane, his mother was freed up to watch Joy and insisted that Anna help. As it was New Year's Eve, Brandon knew Presley would want to close early and would probably stay closed the next day, so today was their shot to get as many of the orders taken care of as they could.

Presley was just opening the door as they arrived. "Oh, Anna, I'm so happy to see you. Not that Brandon wasn't a big help yesterday, but I kept having to differentiate between the flour, sugar, and salt for him." She smiled and winked at him.

He pretended to look shocked. "It's not my fault. I never claimed to be a chef."

"Baker," Presley said laughing. "Now, come on, we have work to do."

After a quick stealthy kiss, he released her and flipped the sign on the window to open. The girls got the ingredients ready, and he set up the computer. As he clicked on the website, his jaw fell open. There were another fifty orders waiting.

"Presley, did you talk to Rita yet?" His voice shook with enthusiasm as he scanned the page.

"Briefly, she said she'd come by this morning. Why?" Her voice carried down the hall from the back pantry.

"Because we're going to need that help soon."

The girls returned, arms laden with ingredients.

"Holy cow, what is that?" Anna said as she set down her Tupperware containers. Her eyes had found the computer screen.

"**That** is why you're here. We have another fifty orders."

Presley dropped the bag she was holding, which thankfully was sealed though it landed with a thud on the table. "Fifty? We didn't even finish the orders from yesterday."

"Don't worry. I'll send emails to everyone letting them know there will be a slight delay due to New Years. You two just get to baking."

The girls mixed the ingredients as Brandon responded to each email. When that task was finished, he donned an apron to help with the baking. With each jingle of the bell, Presley stopped to help the customer, and Brandon worried they wouldn't finish.

"Stop worrying," Anna said, poking his arm.

"I'm not." He laid out dough and began running the rolling pin over it.

"You are too. Your forehead gets these frowny lines whenever you worry." She pointed at his forehead with her brown mixing spoon. The metal mixing bowl in which she was stirring cookie dough was cradled in her left arm.

Brandon always wondered how she knew. Anna, like Presley,

had always been able to read his moods. Perhaps it was because of some tell he didn't even know he had. He reached up to feel his forehead, but it felt the same way it always had. "Okay, so I am, a little. I just want this to go well for Presley." He wanted it to go well for another reason as well. If this took off, they could afford the house and start putting money away for a nice wedding.

"It will. We're doing really well, and I have a few more days until I have to go back, so I can help out." She set the bowl on the counter and cracked two eggs into it before stirring again.

"You're a good sister." He smiled at her and reached for the raisins to sprinkle them into the cinnamon roll batter he had rolled out.

Presley returned a moment later, a smile on her face. "Well, Rita has agreed to run an ad for us, but until it gets filled, her niece has just graduated and is looking for a job. I told her we'd try her out for a week, and if it works then we'll talk a full-time job."

"That's wonderful." Brandon crossed to Presley, gathered her in his arms, and spun her around. She laughed as her loose hair flew about her head.

When they stopped, his hands slid down to sit on her hips. Her eyes stared into his, and her breath caught. Every fiber in his body wanted to kiss her, but they were in her shop and Anna was only a few feet away.

"Ahem," she said, clearing her throat, "I hate to interrupt you two lovebirds, but we still need to do some baking over here."

A soft pink blush, the color of carnations, spread across Presley's nose and cheeks. With great reluctance, Brandon removed his hands and returned to the cinnamon rolls. Presley began boxing up the completed orders. By four in the afternoon, they had finished all but ten orders.

"Come on, Presley. We can always come back tomorrow to finish. Let's get ready for the dance," Anna said as she removed her apron.

Presley stared a moment longer at the order screen, sighed, and removed her apron as well. "Okay, I guess one more day won't hurt."

After she locked up, Anna and Brandon walked Presley to her apartment before continuing back to their parent's house to change and get Joy. Brandon felt like he hadn't seen his daughter the last few days, but she wasn't angry about it. It had to be this town and having family close.

"Daddy, is the dance tonight?" Joy asked as they entered the house.

"Sure is, Bug. In a few hours. How was your day?"

"It was great. Come see what I did." She grabbed his hand and pulled him into the living room where her little card table was set up. Finished, and taking up a good part of the table, was the puzzle Presley had gotten her for Christmas.

"Wow, Joy, did you do this all yourself?" Anna asked as she spied the puzzle.

"Well, mostly. Nana helped a little." Joy's voice was full of pride as she beamed in front of the table.

"I guess it's time to get you an even bigger puzzle," Brandon said as he ruffled Joy's hair.

Her eyes widened. "They get bigger?"

A small chuckle escaped his lips. "Yeah, they can get a lot bigger. I've seen a five-thousand-piece puzzle before."

"Five thousand pieces?" Her voice was barely louder than a whisper and dripping with awe.

"Yeah, maybe one day when we move into our house, we'll get a big puzzle and put it together. We'll need lots of floor space."

Brandon left her beaming and dancing to check on his father, who looked even stronger today. He was still using the cane, but not as much. Then he headed to the shower to get ready for the dance.

CHAPTER 29

*A*s the warm water sprayed on her back, Presley rehashed the events of the day. It was amazing to be baking again, though a little daunting. She couldn't believe how much business had picked up just from Brandon's webpage and whatever advertising he had done.

She lathered the strawberry scented shampoo into her hair and smiled. She would never have imagined a year ago when she moved back that Brandon would re-enter her life or that he'd propose, but she couldn't be happier. He was so much more relaxed working here than with the promotional company in Dallas, and Joy completed a part of Presley's life she hadn't even known was missing. Though the non-stop orders coming in were tough to complete now, her hope was they would allow her and Brandon to purchase the house they toured and maybe put away a little for the wedding.

She hadn't even begun planning it, but she hoped that Brandon would be okay with it being a simple affair. Presley wanted to get a dress and a cake from out of town, but her hope was that Trudy would help decorate and Max would cater. Other than that, she had no grand plans. Just marrying him would be enough for her.

After washing the shampoo out, she turned the water off and stepped out amid a cloud of steam. She had always liked her showers short but hot. The steamy air always seemed to clear her head, and she liked to think it helped her skin. Though that might just be wishful thinking.

She grabbed the purple terry cloth towel off the rack and dried off, wrapping it around her head when she was done to soak up some of the excess water still in her hair. The dance tonight was going to be more lowkey, so she picked a long-flowered skirt and matching shirt to wear.

With the clothing on, she dried her hair one more time and applied just a dab of makeup. Eye liner to brighten her eyes, a tiny stroke of eye shadow across the lids, and a shimmery pink gloss. The image looking back from the mirror met her approval, and she clicked off the light and headed to the other part of the house for Ryan. They had agreed to walk together to meet up with Brandon, Joy, and Anna.

He was sitting at their mother's small kitchen table finishing a sandwich when she entered.

"You know, they're going to have food there." Presley pulled up a chair beside him and snagged a chip off his plate.

"I know, but I'm starving, and this way I can focus more on Anna than filling my bottomless pit."

It was true. He had eaten several large meals a day since the time he was thirteen. Presley had always thought it would taper off when he stopped growing, but evidently it hadn't. "Well, that was thoughtful of you. How are things with you and Anna anyway?"

His forehead wrinkled as his eyes clouded over. "They're good, I think, but I have to head back to Houston tomorrow. I don't know what the future holds for us."

"My suggestion is just to enjoy tonight and don't worry too

much about the next few months. If it's meant to be, it will work out."

"Yeah, though as you know," he pointed a finger at her, "that is easier said than done." He finished the last bite of burger and rinsed his plate in the sink. "Shall we?" He held out his arm and, with a smile, she placed her arm in his.

They stopped just long enough to grab coats, and then made their way toward Brandon's. He, Anna, and Joy met them halfway, and they turned toward the barn. Along the way, they were joined by Max, who seemed less grumpy today, and Layla, who was smiling in her naturally happy way.

The air was crisp and cold and the sky was clear, giving them a clear view of the stars' brilliance. Presley squeezed Brandon's hand as they approached the barn. Music spilled out of the open door, some country tune she didn't recognize, but as this dance was for the whole family, she knew there would be other songs coming soon.

As they stepped inside, she was surprised to see the barn divided. To the right, Justin was doing his DJ routine and blasting out the country music. A few couples, including Bert and Amelia were dancing. Bert's lime green suit elicited a small giggle, and she shook her head at his eccentricity. To the left, a pull down white screen was set up and an animated movie was playing for the younger kids. They were spread out on bean bag chairs and munching handfuls of popcorn. Across the back hot dogs, hamburgers, chips, salads, and desserts lined a buffet table. Just inside the door was a movable metal rack filled with coats and hangers. Everyone shrugged off their coats and added them to the group.

"I'll be by the food if you need me," Max said from behind, but before he could make it to the table, Layla snagged his arm, turning him back.

"No, you won't. You're going to dance with me." She wound her arms around his neck, and a slow smile crossed Max's lips. His arms encircled her waist, and he allowed himself to be pulled to the dance floor.

"That looks like fun. Ryan, will you join me?" Anna held out her hand, and Ryan, looking like he had just won the lottery, put his hand in hers and followed her to the dance floor. Anna's dark blue dress flared out as he spun her around before pulling her close.

"What about you Joy?" Brandon bent down to Joy's level. "You want to dance with us or go watch the movie?"

Joy's lips pursed, and she looked from right to left and back again. "I guess one dance with you, and then I'll watch the movie."

"Sounds like a plan." Brandon winked at Presley before leading Joy onto the dance floor.

"I hope he plans on saving you one."

Presley turned to see Trudy behind her, though she had to blink a few times to make sure it was her. Her dark hair fell down in soft curls at her shoulders. Her denim overalls had been exchanged for a denim skirt and bright red shirt that fell off one shoulder, revealing smooth brown skin underneath.

"Who are you? And what have you done with my friend Trudy?" Presley had never seen her in a dress, and the teasing jab escaped her mouth before she could stop it.

"Shut up. I just thought I'd see what all the fuss is about." She punched Presley's arm lightly before folding her arms across her chest.

"Well, you look wonderful. You should do it more often. You could have the kind of love your grandmother had too, you know." She wiggled her eyebrow to emphasize her point.

Trudy shrugged and they went back to watching the dancers. Brandon's face radiated pure happiness as he spun Joy around the floor. Anna's and Ryan's faces were nearly identical – the dopey starry-eyed faces of young love. Even Max's face, though serious, was focused on Layla, and the love between them was evident in his stare. Presley smiled as she took them all in. This was the reason she loved this town. These crazy characters who somehow still managed to find love and happiness in this small town.

"Would you look at that." Trudy's voice was quiet, but Presley turned to see what she was looking at. Paula was entering the barn on the arm of Barnard. She wore a tight black dress and he had on a white suit with a black tie. They looked more like they belonged at a formal dance than a small town one, but it was more surprising to see them together. Was it a new romance, just a friendly date, or something that had been going on in secret for some time?

"I guess there's someone out there for everyone. See, that means there's hope for you too." Trudy rolled her eyes, but there was a smirk on her face that led Presley to believe that maybe, just maybe, she was rethinking her self-imposed ban on love.

"Sorry to interrupt," Brandon said, returning, "but may I have this dance?"

Presley looked to Trudy to make sure it's okay. She didn't want to leave her alone when she was all dressed up and feeling vulnerable.

"Go, go." She motioned with a wave of her hand. "I'll go watch whatever is playing with Miss Joy for a bit."

As she took Joy's hand and led her to the left, Brandon led Presley to the dance floor. The music switched from an upbeat song to a slow ballad, and he pressed his right arm against her lower back, pulling her closer to him. She could feel the beat of his heart through his shirt. Her left arm glided up his shoulder, stopping just behind his neck.

"Did you ever think we would end up here?" His brown eyes stared into her soul, and the words swam in her head again.

"Not really, though I often dreamed about it."

"Me too." He spun them slowly around. "I'm so glad you didn't give up on me."

"I'm glad you gave me a reason not to."

As the music slowed, he leaned down just brushing his lips against hers. "More later," he whispered in her ear. Presley nodded, but it took every bit of effort not to return the kiss now. Her lips tingled and craved another taste. "Let's get some food."

He steered them to the buffet table, and they piled their plates and then a plate for Joy. Walking carefully, to avoid spilling food, they made their way to the kids' side and found her snuggled in a blue bean bag chair. They delivered her plate, which she barely acknowledged, as she was engrossed in the movie, and then returned to the other side where a few tables were set up around the dance floor. ·

Anna and Ryan joined them, their own plates brimming as well. Presley shook her head at Ryan's plate, which was filled from one end to the other as if he hadn't just eaten a few hours ago.

"Did Max do the food?" Anna asked, glancing around to see if he was close by.

Brandon took a bite of his burger and shook his head. "No, these aren't his burgers. Too dry. They must have had someone else bring the food in."

"Huh, wonder why?"

"Maybe Max didn't want to cook for all these people. It is a pretty big crowd." As Presley looked around, it appeared most of the town was there. Even Pastor Robert had shown up, though he was already dozing in the corner. Trudy was talking to a handsome man Presley couldn't remember ever seeing before. His black leather jacket gave him the air of a visitor. She would have to ask her about him later.

"Maybe Bert brought the food over in his Lyft service," Brandon said, chuckling at the thought.

"His what?" Ryan asked.

Presley pulled her gaze from Trudy and the unknown man. "You would have had to have been here, but at the winter festival dance, Bert said he wanted to start a Lyft service and taxi dogs around in his sister's car."

Anna's fingertips touched her forehead as she shook it back and forth. "Ah, Bert, I'm gonna miss him when I go back to school."

"I'm going to miss a lot of things." Ryan's words were said solely in the direction of Anna, and as their gazes locked, Presley felt conspicuously like a third wheel, even though Brandon was sitting right next to her.

"Are we that bad?" she whispered to him.

"Worse," Anna said with a smile.

After dinner, they checked on Joy, who had passed out in her bean bag chair. Trudy had wandered over to the adult side and was chatting with Mr. Baker, the school principal. He was too old for her, but the fact that she was chatting with a man at all gave hope that one day she would take a chance on love.

Feeling the need to take a break from dancing, Brandon and Presley found a deserted bean bag chair and plopped down in it. It wasn't exactly made for two, and neither of them got a very comfortable piece on the first try. After a little bit of shifting and a few different positions, they found one that worked, and she curled into his arm.

As his arm circled her shoulder, she found her eyelids slowly falling. It had been a long and busy day, and before she knew it, she could barely lift them anymore. Hoping that Brandon wouldn't be offended, she allowed them to close and the world to go dark.

"Presley, wake up." Brandon's voice reached into her dream, and a hand shook her shoulder. Still heavy with sleep, she forced her eyes open to look up at him.

"What is it?" Her voice was slurry, and her throat felt fuzzy.

"It's nearly midnight," he stroked her cheek, "and there's no way I'm not kissing you on midnight."

His words pushed the invading sleep from her eyes, and she sat up. There was no way she wanted to miss midnight either. "How much time do we have?"

"Five minutes. Everyone is gathering to get some champagne."

"Then what are we waiting for?" She pushed herself up and held out her hand to help him. Hand in hand, they strolled back to the adult side where Paula was ushering everyone to a table filled with fluted glasses. Joining the crowd, they snagged a glass and made their way to a more deserted part of the room to wait for the count to begin.

"Okay, everyone," Justin said into the microphone, "Happy New Year in ten, nine, eight…."

"Seven, six, five," they joined in the count, "four, three, two, one. Happy New Year." Auld Lang Syne began playing through the speakers, and after a quick sip of champagne, Brandon took Presley's glass and set it beside his on a nearby table.

"Presley Hays, I just know this is going to be the happiest year of my life. I love you." He folded his arms around her.

She smiled and wrapped hers around his neck. "Brandon Scott, I have waited for this moment for seven years, and I can't wait to spend the next year with you. I love you more."

His lips formed a smile before they parted and pressed against hers. Heat flared through her as the passion between them ignited. This moment, this feeling was better than she ever could have imagined, and as the kiss continued, her heart warmed at the knowledge that she would get to do this every day with the man she loved for the rest of her life.

he End

WOULD YOU LEAVE A REVIEW?

As an author, I highly appreciate the feedback I get from my readers. It helps others make an informed decision before buying my book. If you enjoyed this book, please review at your retailer.

Do you like free books? I'm offering a free sample of my next book Free Sample!

ONCE UPON A STAR

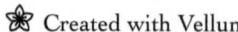

CHAPTER 1

*A*udrey stared at the nurses leaning over the silver table, obscuring the view of the thing she wanted to see most.

"Are you ready, Mom?" The head nurse turned to Audrey, a tiny blue package in her arms.

Mom. The word had never applied to her, and she wasn't sure it fit. Was she ready? Probably not. Would she ever be completely ready? Probably not. But that didn't change reality. She tucked a strand of blond hair behind her ear and nodded.

"Here's your son." The nurse held the swaddled bundle out to her. Audrey opened her hands, unsure of what the nurse wanted her to do. The nurse's face softened and her warm brown eyes sparkled. With one hand, she adjusted Audrey's arms to place the tiny bundle in them. "Hold him like this." She demonstrated the proper technique. "You always want to support his head."

Audrey nodded, trying to keep her arms from shaking. She was afraid to breathe, afraid to move, but mostly afraid she'd drop the infant, so she kept her eyes glued to him. Would he shatter like a piece of glass? The image sent a shiver down her spine. She didn't want to find out.

The nurse's eyes twinkled as she watched Audrey adjust and readjust her holding position. "There is a bassinet here." The nurse pointed at a clear plastic tub that looked like a large shoe box on top of a wheeled table. It didn't look comfortable to Audrey, and she wondered how a baby slept in it. "If you want to take him walking, you need to put him in the bassinet, okay?"

"Do I hold him the rest of the time?" As much as she was enjoying the baby in her arms, what happened when she needed to sleep or use the bathroom?

The woman chuckled. "You hold him as much as you want and put him down when you need a break. We'll come in every few hours to check on you, and we'll show you how to change his diaper and dress him. You'll be a pro before you know it. Don't worry." She patted Audrey's arm like her grandmother used to when she asked a silly question, and then the nurse walked out of the room, still smiling and shaking her head.

Audrey's eyes dropped to the sleeping baby. His shock of dark hair reminded her of his father, the olive-skinned Italian who had charmed her with his fast tongue. She hoped it was the only trait Cayden would get from him. The world didn't need another heartbreaker. "I have no idea what we'll do, Cayden, but we'll figure something out."

∼

Blake turned the glass on the countertop and glanced up at Max who leaned against the back counter, arms folded across his chest as if he were waiting for the answer to a question. The green of his plaid shirt matched the faded ball cap turned backwards on his head. "Sorry, did you say something? I'm distracted; it's just getting close to Christmas, and I miss Connie." A vision of the day she left popped into his head.

Blake opened the door, expecting to see Connie on the other side in her Sunday best. The church service started in half an hour. Though Connie stood there, his smile faded as he took in her jeans and t-shirt. There was no requirement of the patrons to dress up, but Connie always wore a dress or skirt. "What's going on?" Blake asked.

Connie bit her lip and her eyes fell to the ground. "I wanted to say goodbye."

"Goodbye?"

"I can't stay any longer, Blake." Her eyes lifted to meet his, and he saw the shimmer of liquid in them. "I hoped I could make a life here, but I'm a city girl. I miss the lights and night life. I miss the excitement."

"But, we were discussing marriage last week." Blake struggled to make her words compute in his brain.

"I know," she nodded, "and that's what got me thinking. The thought of living the rest of my life here is depressing, so though I love you, I have to say goodbye." She leaned in and pecked his cheek before flashing a sad smile and walking back to her car.

With a heavy heart, Blake watched her drive away before shutting the door and leaning against it. His brain tried to make sense of her departure.

"I get it," Max said, leaning forward and dispersing Blake's memory. "It's not the same, but you're welcome to spend Christmas with Layla and me.

Blake offered a half smile. "I'll consider it, but it's your first Christmas together. You've been in love with that woman since I've known you and I don't want to be a third wheel. Besides, I'll probably hit the Christmas Eve service at church and spend the day with my mom. She's been lonely without my father around."

Max shrugged and turned back to the kitchen to finish serving the lunch crowd.

Blake took a bite of his hamburger, but while he knew it was delicious—Max was known for his burgers—it held no taste in his current mood. He fished a few dollars out of his wallet, laid the money on the counter, picked up his coat, and walked out the door.

The McAllister development where he worked sat a mile up the road, but as he still had fifteen minutes remaining on his lunch break, he decided to walk through downtown. His own house resided on the quiet outskirts of town, so other than hanging out with Max at The Diner, he didn't spend much time in the downtown area.

Blake pulled his coat tighter as the winter air bit through the heavy wool. Star Lake generally received one or two good snowfalls every winter, and though Christmas was still a few weeks away, the chill in the air made him believe the first snow was coming.

He didn't mind the snow, but he enjoyed it more when he had someone to share the experience with. Curling in front of the fireplace alone held little appeal.

~

*A*udrey shoved the last item in her suitcase and pushed down on the bulging bag as she tugged on the zipper.

"Where are you going to go?" Desiree asked, leaning against the doorframe.

Desiree was Audrey's roommate, and the two were about as different as night and day. Where Audrey was pale and blond, Desiree had darker skin and long dark hair.

"The only place I can," Audrey said with a sighing. "Home."

The thought held little appeal. Her wealthy parents had given her access to her trust fund at eighteen, and Audrey had opted to move to LA to try her hand at acting. At first, it had been fun. She'd found a few jobs and been in a few commercials, but then the jobs had become fewer and farther between, and after she ended up pregnant, they had dried up completely. Now all the money she had saved was almost gone.

Desiree's nose scrunched in disgust. "You'd go back to that tiny town, why?"

"I haven't had a job in months Dez, my savings have run out, and I can't go to work without someone to watch Cayden. If I go home, I can get help from my parents until I get back on my feet."

At least she hoped they would help. They hadn't been too happy when she decided not to go to college, but she didn't think they would turn their grandson away, even if they didn't want to help her.

Desiree shrugged and flicked her hair behind her bony shoulder. "Nothing in the world would make me return to my crappy hometown."

Audrey knew Desiree's home life had been rough, but while she hadn't wanted to grow up under her mother's thumb, it hadn't been a bad childhood. "I don't know if I'll ever be back, but I wish you luck."

After a quick hug, Audrey picked up Cayden's car seat, slung her bag over her shoulder, and left the apartment she had called home for the last few years.

CHAPTER 2

*A*udrey stood outside the mansion, her heart a lead anchor in her chest. She ran the possible options one more time, desperate for a new solution, but nothing came to mind. Her last five hundred dollars had paid for the flight and the rental car, so even if another way had existed before, it was gone now.

Her finger trembled as she pressed the ornate gold doorbell.

A young woman in a pale pink uniform answered the door. Though her face was unfamiliar, her position was not. Audrey's mother had always insisted on help.

"Can I help you?" The woman's even and friendly tone didn't mask the sadness in her eyes. Audrey knew that expression too well. Though she loved her mother, Evelyn's overbearing personality and her obsession with money and status often left those around her feeling drained and empty.

"I'm Audrey. Is Evelyn home?"

The woman's eyes widened at Audrey's name. Her mother must have informed even the newest help of her wayward daughter, but the woman said nothing, just nodded politely and motioned Audrey to follow her.

Audrey stared at the threshold. If she stepped over the line, there would be no turning back, and the anchor on her heart pulled ever tighter. Was this the only way? Audrey hadn't even spoken with her mother yet, and still she felt the imaginary noose tighten around her neck. Her throat dried up, and she closed her eyes to calm the beating of her erratic heart.

"Are you all right?"

Audrey's eyes flicked open. The young woman stared at her as if she were crazy, which perhaps she was. This was her mother for goodness sake, not an ax murderer. After another deep breath, Audrey forced her foot into the grand foyer.

It was exactly as she remembered it. The wooden floor gleamed a bright amber color, and the white marble columns sparkled as if they had just been cleaned—which, considering Evelyn's hatred of dust and clutter, they probably had been. A glass chandelier sent reflections of rainbows across the room though they didn't lighten the oppressive mood that filled the room. Over the marble fireplace, a portrait of the family done ten years ago stared back at her.

The sullen girl in the portrait sent shivers down her spine. She had looked so petulant. Getting away from her parents had been good for her. The freedom of the past years had erased the scowl from her face and straightened her shoulders. If only she could have stayed away.

"Wait here." The woman pointed to the white leather couch Audrey had once considered spilling grape juice on just to spite her mother. "I'll go get Mrs. McAllister."

The family in the picture continued to rain judgement on Audrey as she perched on the edge of the couch feeling like a schoolgirl waiting to see the principal. She glanced at the car seat on the floor beside her, thankful Cayden had fallen asleep before she pulled up to the house. Evelyn wouldn't tolerate his noise well.

The clickity-clack of heels on the hardwood floor sent an icy tremor through her body. Audrey drug her eyes from the sleeping infant to the hallway entrance. Her mother, with her brown hair perfectly in place and a string of pearls accenting her immaculate beige suit, stepped into the room.

"To what do I owe this pleasure?" she asked. The words sounded polite, but the cool inflection behind them told the real story.

Audrey stood, blocking the car seat with her legs. Evelyn hadn't appeared to have noticed it yet. "Please sit, Mother, I need to ask you a question."

Evelyn's lips pursed, and her eyebrow arched on her forehead, but she smoothed her skirt and sat in the straight-backed chair across from the couch. "What is it? It must be important. We haven't seen you here in what three years?"

Four. Audrey had come back for Elliana's wedding four years ago, but there was no need to point that out. Ignoring the dig, Audrey cleared her throat and proceeded with her rehearsed script. "I know you didn't approve of my going to Hollywood to pursue acting, but I needed to follow my dream."

"It must have gone well if you're back here." The sarcasm dripped from her mother's voice.

"Please let me finish. LA was amazing, but I made a mistake when I fell for a man who I thought loved me. I ended up pregnant, but he left me." Audrey stepped to the side, clearing the view of Cayden's car seat. "I kept Cayden, but I couldn't continue working."

Evelyn blinked but remained silent, waiting for the question.

Audrey gritted her teeth and took a deep breath. "I'm wondering if I can borrow money to hire childcare until I get back on my feet."

"Let me get this straight," Evelyn began once Audrey finished.

"You've been gone for nearly ten years, and now you're only here because you need money?"

Audrey swallowed the irritation threatening to bubble over and answered through clenched teeth. "I wouldn't be here at all if it weren't for Cayden, but I've had no jobs the last few months and therefore no money to pay for help, so yes I am asking for money."

"No," Evelyn said, folding her hands on her lap.

"No?" Audrey narrowed her eyes, sure she heard her mother wrong.

"That's right, no. You were given money, which you squandered when you ran away to Hollywood."

"I was there for ten years."

Evelyn held up her hand, cutting off Audrey's protest. "If I give you the money, you learn nothing, but I can't have that baby going hungry either, so here's what I'm offering. I will give you enough to get a place as I'm assuming you would not accept my offer to live here, but then you will work for your father."

Audrey's head shook before Evelyn had finished. "Mother, no. I can find a job." Her father owned a development company, and Audrey knew nothing about it. Her passion had always been the stage.

"It's my money, so I get to set the conditions. Take it or leave it." Evelyn stared evenly at Audrey.

There were no options. Audrey needed the money and maybe working for her father wouldn't be too bad for a short time. Once she saved up enough money, she could always find something else. "Fine, Mother, is there anything else?" She didn't want to ask, but she feared a secret condition could come back to bite her.

"You have dinner here once a month."

Audrey bit the inside of her lip and closed her eyes. Once a month. She could handle once a month. "Fine, Mother," she said, opening her eyes. "You win."

"Very well. Julie?" The blond woman reappeared in the entryway.

"Yes ma'am?"

"Get me my purse."

Julie nodded and hurried away.

"I expect to see you at dinner next Friday," her mother said as Julie returned with her purse. Evelyn pulled out her pocketbook, and after rifling through it for cash, which she handed to Audrey, she filled out a check, tearing it from the register with an exaggerated slowness. "I assume you don't have a bank account here yet, so the cash is to help get that started. The check should cover your first month's rent, deposit, and household necessities."

Audrey mumbled a quiet thank you as she took the money. It felt like dirty, blood money in her hand, but she had no other choice.

"We'll give you the rest of the week to get settled, but your father will expect you at work at eight a.m. Monday morning."

"Yes, Mother."

Evelyn had never been a hugger, but she tilted her left cheek up in expectance of her obligatory kiss. Audrey planted a quick one, her lips stinging as if she had just made a deal with the devil.

The money burned in her pocket as she gathered up Cayden's car seat and headed back to her car.

CHAPTER 3

"*D*id you hear the news?"

Paula leaned over Layla's table three spots away, but her loud voice carried across the interior of the small eatery. The Diner was known for two things: Max's amazing food and being the hub of gossip, though Max hated that everyone congregated in his establishment to share news.

"No, but everyone will now, Paula," Max said with a raised voice from the front where he was wiping the bar counter after the lunch rush.

Paula shot him a dirty look before turning back to Layla. "Audrey McCallister is back in town."

Blake's pulse stopped at the mention of Audrey's name. He placed his coffee on the table top and leaned forward to eavesdrop on the conversation.

"And she has a baby," Paula continued.

As quickly as it flourished, the happiness in his heart fizzled as if doused with water. If Audrey had a baby, then a husband probably existed as well.

"That's nice," Layla responded. "I'm glad she's happy."

Paula's eyebrow arched up her face, and she jammed her hands on her thick waist as she shook her head. "I didn't say she was happy. The rumor is her man dumped her, and she came home for financial assistance."

Blake's heart lifted with the news Audrey was free, but a twinge of sadness remained for the hardships she must have faced.

"Well, the past is the past," the ever-enigmatic Layla said as she smiled up at Paula. She often avoided conflict and chose the higher road. "I say we welcome her with open arms and remind her what a great town Star Lake is."

Paula had the decency to look abashed as she squared her shoulders. Her nose tilted in the air and her dark hair swirled with the flick of her head. "Of course we will. I'm sure we'll see her around as the word is she rented a place in town and will be working for her father."

Blake's eyes dropped to his coffee to conceal his excitement. Audrey McCallister was not only back in town, but she would be working at her father's office, the same office he entered every day. Though he had been too shy to tell her his feelings in high school, perhaps now he would find the courage.

～

Audrey set Cayden's car seat on the living room carpet and glanced around the small house. The odor of paint still hung in the air, along with the scent of carpet cleaner. Though not huge, the two-bedroom house was in good shape though bland with tan wall to wall carpet and white walls. The kitchen continued the theme with white laminate flooring and brown cabinets.

"Well, Cayden, it isn't much, but this is home for now," she whispered down to the sleeping infant.

Tomorrow, she would have to get furniture—a crib for sure, a bed for her, some chairs and a table, but tonight they would sleep on the blankets she had brought from her old apartment. Blankets, clothes, and baby necessities were about all she had been able to bring on the plane.

She added furniture and groceries to her mental to-do list, along with a cheap car. Audrey had sold hers to help pay for plane tickets. The sheer enormity of the growing list elicited a sigh from her as Cayden continued to sleep. Jealous of his lack of responsibility, she tiptoed out of the house to grab the blankets and clothes from the car.

When the bags were all inside, exhaustion settled on her shoulders and Audrey yawned. She wanted to curl into a ball and sleep for a week, but she knew it wasn't a possibility. Her internal sensor told her Cayden would be up soon to eat, and after that, she was sure sleep would be slow in coming as sleeping on the floor had never worked well for her.

~

The morning light peeked in the open windows early the next morning. Curtains or blinds. She would need those too. Audrey tried to squint her eyes shut, but it was no use. Her stomach growled in frustration; she'd have to get up soon to feed it. At least she had thought to make a quick stop at the market downtown yesterday, and coffee and cereal waited for her in the kitchen.

Stretching her arms, she tried to work the kinks out of her neck. The hard floor had taken a toll on her body, and every joint crackled in agony.

Cayden laid spread eagle beside her. He had woken like clockwork every two hours to eat, but thankfully he'd fallen back asleep quickly each time.

With as little noise as possible, Audrey struggled to her feet. A shooting pain spiraled down her back as she tried to stand upright, and she leaned back to stretch the knot out. When her shoulders returned to their normal position, she tiptoed into the kitchen to make her breakfast before Cayden awoke.

The bright white of the kitchen hurt her tired eyes, and she squinted them shut as she rummaged through the bag from the market. She hadn't picked up much, but small plastic bowls, a mug, and spoons had been at the top of her list. Cereal and coffee were staples in her life.

She ran the bowl under hot water to clean it, wishing she had remembered soap yesterday at the store. Another item she would have to add to the list for today's trip. Along with paper towels, she realized as she turned off the water and waved the bowl in the air to dry it off.

Coffee. That was what she needed. A nice, steaming mug of the hot liquid would kick her brain back into gear, but as she turned around, she realized she hadn't picked up a coffee maker either. With a sigh, she grabbed the cereal from the bag and filled the bowl before adding the milk from the very bare fridge. She'd have to make a caffeine stop, or she wouldn't make it the rest of the day.

Cayden woke as Audrey placed the rinsed-out bowl in the sink. After feeding him, she ran a quick brush through her long blond hair before piling it onto her head in a loose ponytail. She needed a shower in the worst way, but she had to tackle this list first.

After changing out of last night's clothes into a sweater and a pair of jeans—the temperature was much cooler here than in California—she loaded Cayden up in the car.

Her first stop was the Goodwill on the outskirts of town. Most of the groceries she could get at the general store in Star Lake, but they wouldn't have the furniture she needed. Luck was with her as she found a sturdy crib, a comfortable couch and bedframe, a decent dining room table, and a few scratched tables. The store even agreed to deliver the items later that afternoon for a nominal fee and gave her the name of someone they knew selling a gently used mattress.

After buckling Cayden in again, she pointed the car back to Star Lake's downtown. The Diner was sure to have coffee. Whether it would taste good was another matter, but she doubted Star Lake had built a Starbucks or any other coffee joint for that matter. In fact, she doubted much had changed about the downtown at all. Star Lake seemed to live in its own bubble, away from time and passing trends.

Few cars lined the street as she pulled into a spot in front of The Diner. As she grabbed Cayden's car seat from the back, she noticed a new shop across the way. Sweet Treats Bakery. *Hmm, maybe a few things have changed. If The Diner's coffee is terrible, perhaps this new place will have a decent cup.*

The bell chimed overhead as she pushed open the front door. A man with slicked brown hair and a checkered shirt sat reading a newspaper at the back booth while Max filled ketchup bottles at the front. Though five or six years older than she, Audrey had harbored a secret crush on the broody owner through high school.

Max glanced up as she approached the counter. "Well, I'll be. Audrey McCallister. The rumor mill said you were back in town." A growth of stubble gave him a rugged look, and Audrey's heart fluttered in her chest.

She placed Cayden's car seat on the tile floor beside her before climbing into the barstool. "Hey, Max. It's good to see you. Let me guess, Paula?" She had taken a few dance classes with Paula in high school, and she remembered the busty woman often sharing tidbits of gossip.

"Who else?" he asked with a crooked half-grin. Audrey had never seen Max's actual smile. "Can I get you something? The breakfast rush just ended, but I could whip something up for you."

Audrey waved her hand, not wanting him to make a fuss for her. "I had cereal, but I could go for a cup of coffee."

With a swift nod, Max grabbed a mug from under the counter and poured in the murky black liquid. "I don't have any fancy creamer, if you wanted that. Presley, across the street, does more of the frou-frou coffee." He placed a cup of milk and a canister of sugar on the counter.

"Is she the owner of the bakery?" Audrey asked, looking over her shoulder in the direction.

"Yep, she moved back a few months ago. Evidently, she studied in Paris for a time, but it didn't work out. She makes good pastries too."

"Moved back? So, she lived here before?" Curiosity at meeting anyone else who had left town and come back burgeoned inside her. Perhaps it would help her feel less like a failure.

"Yeah, Layla said she was a few years behind us in school, so she'd have been a few years ahead of you I guess. I don't really remember her." Max shrugged and returned to filling the ketchup bottles.

"You still keep in touch with Layla?" Audrey tried to keep her voice even. She had known, even back in high school, that one reason Max was still single was that he adored the pretty Layla Matthews.

"Actually, Layla and I are together now." His hazel eyes pierced hers, and one side of his lip pulled up in a crooked smile—probably the closest thing he could do to a real one.

There was no mistaking the pride in his voice, and Audrey swallowed her disappointment. "That's wonderful, Max. I'm thrilled for you." As she turned her attention to the coffee to hide her reaction, he finished filling the bottles and took them out to the tables.

When her coffee was empty, and she felt a little more awake, Audrey plunked down a five-dollar bill, grabbed Cayden's car seat, and walked back to her car. He woke just as she snapped him in, so she climbed in the back seat next to him, pulled a bottle from her bag, and fed him. She had never gotten him to nurse and had been forced to settle on bottles.

After Cayden finished, Audrey climbed into the front seat. Though it would be a quick walk to the market, the heavy carrier made driving more appealing.

The general store parking lot was also mostly empty as most people were at work. Audrey was glad. If Max and Layla had stayed in town, then peers she went to school with might have as well, and she wasn't ready to face them yet.

After grabbing a cart and placing Cayden's carrier in it, Audrey entered the store. A young freckled-face checker greeted her as she passed, and she flashed a small wave before continuing to the produce section.

She piled bags of apples, oranges, lettuce, and peppers in her cart. She might no longer be in health-conscious Los Angeles, but she still wanted to regain her pre-baby figure. The extra twenty pounds she carried around now was a source of embarrassment and a hindrance on her outfits. Not to mention it was a constant reminder of why Tony—Cayden's father—had left her. As Audrey reached for a bunch of bananas, she heard a male voice speak her name.

Turning, she spied a sandy haired man with chiseled features and warm brown eyes. Though he looked vaguely familiar, she could not place how she knew him.

"Audrey McCallister, is that you?" His deep, rich voice flowed over her ears like silk.

"Yes, it's me." She paused, racking her brain one more time for a name. "I'm sorry, I feel I should know you, but—" she shrugged, letting the sentence trail off without an ending.

The corner of his lip twitched, forming a playful smile and highlighting a dimple in his left cheek. "Blake Dalton. We went to school together though I doubt you would remember me."

She wrinkled her forehead, running through the boys she knew in school. The name didn't belong to anyone who had run in her immediate circle, but an image of the skinny class president in glasses flashed in her mind. Her eyes widened as she made the connection. He looked so different, so. . . handsome.

Blake laughed at her reaction. "Yeah, I get that a lot. I worked out in college and put on some muscle. My job helps too."

"Oh, what do you do?" Audrey asked, visions of him modeling parading through her mind.

He blinked at her and tilted his head. "You don't know? I work for your father; I'm on his construction crew."

"Oh, I haven't spoken to my father yet. I just got into town two days ago."

A twinkle lit Blake's eyes as he nodded. "Yes, I heard that. . ."

"From Paula," they finished together and exchanged smiles before the awkward silence descended.

"Well, I'll let you get back to your shopping. I have to get back, but I'd love to catch up sometime." He nodded at her.

"I'd love that too."

As she watched him walk away, she couldn't help but admire how the years had treated him.

CHAPTER 4

"Good morning, sunshine," Audrey said, picking Cayden up out of his crib. She rubbed the sleep from her eyes with one hand, holding Cayden on her left hip. His wails lessened as he wriggled in her arms. Though she had assembled the crib, he had not enjoyed sleeping in it and had been up longer than normal between feedings.

"Let's get you fed, huh? It's only been"–she blinked at her watch, trying to make her tired eyes focus on the blurry image - "two hours. All right, you must be hungry."

She shuffled to the kitchen, flicking on the hall light as she went, and opened the fridge, grabbing a pre-made bottle. After shaking it up to mix the contents again, she popped it in the bottle warmer.

"It'll be ready in a minute," she said to Cayden. When the warmer dinged, she stuck the bottle in his mouth. Then she grabbed a k-cup pod from the cabinet she had stocked after her grocery run. With a quick flick, she loaded it in the new coffeemaker and punched the button, watching Cayden drain the bottle as the melodious dripping of coffee began.

The drip slowed like the end to a beautiful symphony before stopping. Yawning, she grabbed the mug and stumbled into the living room to the couch. After placing the mug on the end table, she plopped down on the couch with Cayden on her lap. As she reached for the aromatic liquid, a knock at the door sounded, and Audrey sighed and stared longingly at her drink.

"Now who could that be?" she asked Cayden as she stood and crossed the carpeted floor. Though his blue eyes considered hers, he continued to suck on his bottle oblivious to her question. She shifted him in her arms and opened the door.

A petite blond with her hair pulled back in a severe bun stood on the other side. Her grey suit rivaled many of Audrey's mother's. "Hello, I'm here for the nanny position." She held out a white sheet of paper, presumably her resume, with one hand. The other held a small black satchel.

"Excuse me?" Audrey blinked at her.

"The nanny position. My company said an order existed for nanny candidates to come to this address today at eight, so here I am."

Audrey sighed. It had to be her mother. Even when she wasn't helping, she was meddling. Audrey doubtless couldn't afford a true nanny, but interviewing them would at least allow her to see what was out there. "My mother didn't tell me what time she set these up," she said, playing along. Her face flamed as she glanced at her checkered flannel pajama pants and t-shirt. "I'm sorry. I haven't even dressed."

"That is fine," the woman said in perfectly proper English. "I assumed I would take care of the child in the morning while you got ready for work. May I come in?"

"Of course, I'm so sorry. Please come inside." Audrey stepped back, allowing the polished woman to enter.

Her heels sank into the carpet as she crossed the living room, and though she said nothing, her nose wrinkled slightly in displeasure.

The modest room was neat, but it was no fifth avenue penthouse. The furniture from the Goodwill was clean, but mismatched. No television sat featured in the room as Audrey hadn't found one at the Goodwill, and no art adorned the stark white walls. Audrey surveyed the room from the lens of the woman and swallowed her embarrassment. She must look atrocious and poor to this woman, who worked for wealthy families.

The woman eyed each furniture piece, deciding on the beige recliner. She perched on the edge of it as if afraid of catching something if she sat all the way back and set the satchel on her lap.

Audrey stifled a grin at her obvious discomfort. If this woman avoided a used chair, how on earth would she deal with a baby who spat up multiple times a day?

With perfectly manicured fingers, the woman opened the satchel and pulled out another white sheet and passed them both to Audrey, who took them before returning to the couch.

"My name is Tess Fairchild. As you can see, I have impeccable references. I believe in a strict schedule as I find it helps the child adjust easier. I arrive at seven to allow you to get ready for work, and I need to leave precisely at six. Though I clean up after children, I do not do other housework." She folded her hands in her lap. "Now, do you have questions for me?"

So many questions spawned in Audrey's head. Where did she even begin? "I should have questions, shouldn't I?"

Tess's head tilted to the right, and her right eyebrow arched, but she said nothing, just stared with an unwavering gaze.

"Okay, um, would you play with Cayden?" The image of this poised and proper woman crawling on the floor with a baby was laughable.

"I will make sure he has adequate play time."

That hadn't been her question, but it was probably the best this woman would give. "I guess that's it then." Audrey stood, signaling the end of the interview.

"Very well. I look forward to hearing from you." Tess smoothed her skirt as she rose from the chair and crossed the floor, stepping with her toes to keep her heels out of the carpet.

As Audrey closed the door behind her, Cayden finished the bottle. "Hungry, were we?" After setting Cayden on the floor for his tummy time, Audrey rinsed the bottle in the kitchen sink and placed it in the drainer.

On the way back, she spied her mug still steaming on the end table. With a relieved sigh, she picked it up and managed one glorious sip before another knock sounded at the door. Audrey rolled her eyes, placed the mug back on the table, and opened the door again.

A thick, elderly woman returned her gaze from the other side.

"Hello, I am Helga, and I am nanny." Her German accent made the words hard to understand.

"Of course you are," Audrey said under her breath, but Helga hadn't heard her as she had muscled her way past Audrey and into the living room.

"It is small. This is it?" she asked.

Audrey assumed she meant the house and nodded. "Cayden's room is down the hall. This is the living room, dining room, and kitchen space."

"Good, easier to keep clean. I do only light housework. Here are my resume and references."

Two more white pieces of paper appeared under Audrey's nose. Similar to the previous woman, the references on the resume were impeccable, but impersonal. Helga rattled off her rules, never bothering to sit down. Instead she paced like a predator stalking a prey. Her heavy footsteps sent shudders along Audrey's spine. She could not imagine Cayden spending all day with this large, fear-invoking woman.

He must have had the same idea because as Helga leaned over him, he let out a loud wail and flailed his tiny fists. Audrey picked him up, and as soon as she could, she ended the interview.

"Okay little one, let's change your diaper and lay you down for a nap."

After grabbing a diaper and some wipes from the nearby stash, Audrey laid Cayden on the carpet and unzipped his sleeper. Before she had gotten his legs out, another knock sounded.

"You've got to be kidding me," she whispered to Cayden. "Come on in, the door's unlocked."

"That's a good way to get robbed," Elliana, her older sister, said, poking her head in.

"Ellie!"

Elliana was three years older than Audrey, but the two had grown up close friends. After Elliana married and stopped coming around as often, Audrey was the only one for her mother to focus on. It was then Audrey became disillusioned with her parents' money and wanted a way out.

Audrey finished the changing and hugged her sister. "Sorry I didn't open the door for you; I figured it was another nanny."

"Yes, mother told me she lined candidates up for you."

The snort escaped Audrey's mouth before she could stop it. "Yeah, candidates I can't afford. She refused to lend me money to help pay for one."

Elliana crossed to the kitchen and placed her bag on the bar. With her dark hair, she was the antithesis to Audrey. Growing up, people had often asked if they were related. Audrey had taken after their mother's fair complexion, while Elliana had gotten their father's darker hair and skin. "Hand me my nephew."

"Ugh, I don't think I can handle more interviews," Audrey said as she handed the baby over. "Want to stay and help?"

Elliana pursed her lips, pretending to think before smiling and shaking her head. "Sure, why don't you go get dressed, and I'll get the next one." She pointed to the pajama pants and grinned. "I'm surprised they haven't gone running after getting a look at you."

"Ha Ha," Audrey said, but the smile remained on her lips. Though she hadn't missed her parents much, she had missed her sister.

As she reached her room, she heard Elliana open the door and greet the next nanny hopeful. The blissful silence in the room comforted Audrey, and she took her time changing clothes, relishing the momentary break from nannies and Cayden's crying. From her drawer, she pulled out a pair of jeans, tugging them up over hips still puffy with baby weight. An oversized grey t-shirt went next to cover the jeans. Then she brushed her teeth and ran a brush through her hair before exiting the sanctuary.

"Thank you. We'll be in touch," Ellie's voice carried down the hall.

"But I was told to meet with Ms. Audrey McCallister," a woman protested. Audrey pressed herself against the wall so as not to draw attention.

"Well, Audrey was a little busy, but I assure you I will relay your information." There was a forcefulness in Ellie's voice that Audrey remembered from childhood. She had always envied that fortitude because Ellie had been better about standing up for herself, even against their mother. When the front door closed, she pushed herself off the wall and continued down the carpeted hallway.

"That was fast," she said as she rounded the corner.

"Eh, she wasn't the right one. Too stiff."

"They've all been too stiff so far. Mother put them together, remember?"

"And who could deign to deny Evelyn McCallister, right?" Ellie's chin tilted up in the air as she uttered the mocking statement.

"What am I going to do, Ellie? I can't afford any of these women." Audrey picked up the mug of coffee, hoping to swallow a little of the comforting nectar, but the cold liquid crawled back up her throat. With a shake of her head, she popped the mug in the microwave to warm it again. Before it finished the minute reheat, another knock echoed through the room. A frustrated sigh escaped Audrey's throat. Would she ever be able to finish this cup of coffee?

"Want me to send them all away?"

"I'd love that, but then what do I do?"

"Leave that to me." A playful smile curled Ellie's lips up at the corner and she crossed to the door. "Sorry, the nanny position is filled. You can all go home."

"What are you doing?" Audrey asked. "I told you I need someone to watch Cayden."

"Yes, but you have another option you haven't explored." Ellie's brown eyes twinkled with whatever secret she was toying with.

Audrey was too tired to play this game. "What other option, Ellie?"

The playful smile spread into a wide grin. "You have me." She held her hand up as Audrey's mouth opened. "Now, wait, hear me out. Phillip and I have no children yet. I live right outside town, and I want to get to know my nephew."

Though Audrey liked the idea, she worried about infringing on her sister. "I can't pay you much, at least not at first. I need to purchase a car, so I can return the rental, and it will be a bit before I get paid."

"That's fine. Phillip makes plenty of money, and I still have my trust fund. I don't need the money, and I want to help you out. I'm so tired of staying in the house, but a rich debutante with no skills isn't exactly in high demand these days."

Audrey opened her mouth to agree, but Ellie cut her off.

"Please, you know I'm good with kids. Let me try for a week, and if you hate me after that, you can call one of these cardboard cutouts." She flicked her hand at the stack of white papers.

"Of course I'll let you watch him," Audrey replied. "I can't think of anyone I'd rather have. I'm just worried about Mother finding out."

"You leave Mother to me if she finds out." Ellie flashed a conspiratorial wink, and Audrey smiled. Just like old times.

CHAPTER 5

*B*utterflies raced around Blake's stomach as he dressed for the day. The thought of seeing Audrey again had kept him awake all night, and he splashed water on his face to diminish the visible rings under his eyes.

The McAllisters had moved to Star Lake when Blake was a Sophomore, and his attraction to Audrey's beauty had been immediate. With her long blond hair and bright blue eyes, she was the epitome of cheerleader stereotypes, but even though she was wealthy and hung out with the richer kids, she was never mean to anyone, at least not that Blake witnessed. However, she'd also never tried to get to know those outside her social class, and so Blake had pined for her from afar.

Blake had known he'd had no chance with her back then–the skinny, geeky kid with coke bottle glasses and checkered alligator shirts, but when he'd gone to college, he'd packed on some weight. When he'd found weightlifting, that weight had changed into muscles. His first girlfriend in college also set his fashion straight, throwing out his pocketed shirts and Levi jeans for the more popular variety and cutting his curls to make a manageable hair style. The dramatic effect had started a chain reaction. While the two of them hadn't lasted, he was forever grateful to her.

With a final glance in the mirror, Blake flicked off the light, grabbed his keys and lunch, and loaded up in his red Chevy truck.

Twenty minutes later, Blake pulled into the parking lot of McAllister development and parked in his usual spot. After locking the truck, he gathered his courage, pulled back his shoulders, and sauntered in the front entrance.

Audrey sat at the front desk, her lips pinched into a tight line. Her jaw clenched as the phone rang and she brought it to her ear. Though he could tell she was frustrated, she looked like an angel to him with her blond hair skimming her shoulders like spun gold. He wanted to say hello, to bring a smile to her face, but she was on the phone, and he had no real reason to stay in the lobby. His shoulders dropped as he drug his feet across the floor, hoping the caller on the phone would be quicker than his slow pace.

No such luck. The phone was still against her ear as he entered the door to the employee lounge where the check-in resided, but then inspiration hit, and a smile lit his face. A small coffee bar had been installed next to the cafeteria the previous month. Blake had never frequented it because he liked his coffee black and coffee from home was cheaper, but Audrey didn't appear a black coffee type of person. He didn't even know if she drank coffee, but he thought she would appreciate the gesture.

"Hey, good morning Blake," Wes, a fellow contractor, waved to him as he punched his card.

"Morning, Wes."

"Where are you hurrying off to?"

"I was going to try the new coffee bar. Is it any good?"

Wes's forehead wrinkled in confusion. "Yeah, but don't you bring coffee?"

"I figured I'd get a coffee for Audrey. She looks a little frazzled out there."

Wes' lips curled into an understanding smile, and he nodded, one eyebrow raised. "You hoping to impress the boss, huh?"

Impressing Audrey's father had never crossed his mind, but he preferred others thinking that rather than knowing his true reason of trying to win Audrey's favor. "It's not like that. I just want to welcome the new girl."

"Sure, whatever you say, man." Wes' laugh followed him out of the room as he made his way to the cafeteria. The lunch area was not a large room as many of the workers took their lunch elsewhere, but the open room housed several tables and a buffet line right near the kitchen. The coffee shop sat on the far end, closest to the outdoor entrance.

A mousy brunette glanced up at him from behind large glasses as he approached, reminding him of himself in high school. "What can I get you?" Her voice was so soft that he leaned in over the counter to hear her.

"What's the best drink for someone who may not like a strong coffee flavor?" he asked as his eyes scanned the menu. Mocha, frappe, latte–the words were all Greek to him.

"Um," the girl's face scrunched in confusion. "Well, I like my coffee sweeter, so I prefer either a mocha or a macchiato, but everyone's different."

"Which has fewer calories?" He wasn't sure if Audrey was watching them or not, but if she was, he wanted to be prepared.

"A caramel macchiato is lower in calories."

"Great, I'll take that one please in a medium size."

"You mean a Grande?"

"Is that medium?" he asked, confused.

"Yeah," the woman nodded, a 'what rock have you been living under' expression on her face.

"Then, that one."

A few moments later, she placed a cup on the counter. "It's four dollars," she said.

Ah, yes, this was why he brought his coffee from home. How did people afford specialty coffee?

"Aren't you going to taste it?" she asked as he picked up the cup after forking over his money.

"It's not for me. It's for a friend." He flashed her a small smile and strolled back to the front entrance.

Audrey was off the phone, but her gaze was focused on the computer screen in front of her.

"I thought you could use a little pick me up," Blake said, tapping the top of her desk.

She glanced up at him, dark shadows circling her eyes. "Thank you. I told my father I did not know how to be a secretary, but he and my mother insisted I learn a skill. They don't consider acting a skill."

"Well, that's because they never watched you on stage." Blake flashed a smile, wishing he could bring one to her face. The memory of her playing Juliet their senior year still popped into his mind occasionally. He had never been a fan of Shakespeare but watching her on stage had made it tolerable.

A sad smile played across her lips. "Yeah maybe. Well thank you anyway. I gotta get back to this."

"Of course, I hope it gets better." He had hoped to ask her out, but now did not seem the right time. He would just keep praying for an opening to become clear.

CHAPTER 6

"How was the first day?" Ellie asked as Audrey dropped her purse on the floor and collapsed into the couch.

Audrey exhaled a giant sigh. "I don't think I'm cut out for secretarial work. Everything went wrong. The only positive part of the entire day was lunch and the coffee Blake brought me this morning."

Ellie's eyebrow lifted, and she crossed her arms. "Who's Blake?"

Audrey shook her head. "A peer from high school. He said I looked as if I could use a pick me up, and he brought me a coffee."

"Yeah, I'm sure he's just a guy from high school," her sister stated sarcastically. "Sounds like he has a soft spot for you."

"Stop it. I'm a single mom still struggling to lose baby weight. I'm not what one might call a hot commodity." Self-esteem had never been Audrey's strongest suit. It was probably why she had fallen for Cayden's father in the first place. She had known Tony hadn't been the marrying kind, but she had let herself believe she could change him.

"You are incredible, little sis. Don't sell yourself short." Ellie patted Audrey on the shoulder before grabbing her bag. "Cayden was perfect today. He laid down for nap an hour ago. I'd stay and chat, but I promised Philip I'd make dinner tonight."

"Thanks, Sis. See you tomorrow." Audrey pushed herself off the couch to give Ellie a hug before shutting the door behind her.

As the silence descended, her mind rehashed Eliana's remarks. Could Blake be attracted to her? Or was he being nice because she was the boss's daughter? Before she could reach a conclusion, Cayden's cry pierced the air.

With a sigh, she pushed the prospect of romance from her mind and headed to Cayden's room.

~

*A*udrey arrived at work the next morning eager to try out her new idea. After taking care of Cayden the night before, her mind had wandered back to the possibility of Blake's attraction, and while she wasn't sure she was ready to date yet, she could use companionship. So, she had decided to ask him to dinner. If he declined, then he had brought the coffee to be nice. If he said yes, either he liked her or at least wanted to become better friends. It wasn't a foolproof system, but it was better than waiting and wondering.

After straightening the desk from the disarray she left it in yesterday, Audrey sat in the chair and began the task of reviewing documents for the day while keeping one eye peeled for Blake. He entered a moment later, smiling her direction.

"Morning, better day today?"

"Well, we'll see," she answered with a slight laugh. "Thank you for the coffee yesterday. It was the highlight of the day."

"You're welcome. Any time."

"Um, so I was wondering." A bout of shyness descended on

Audrey, tying her tongue and forcing her eyes to the desk. "I wanted to invite you to dinner." She glanced up from lowered lids. "As a thank you."

The dimple appeared in his cheek as he returned the smile. "While no further thanks is needed, I'd love to have dinner with you. In fact, I wanted to ask you out, but you beat me to the punch."

Audrey's cheeks heated. "Sorry, I didn't mean to steal your thunder."

"I don't care who asks," Blake said, his eyes twinkling. "I'm looking forward to dinner with you."

An odd stirring sensation fluttered through Audrey's heart. "Here is the address," she said, holding out the paper she had written her address on moments earlier. "I'll make spaghetti tonight if you want to come by around seven?"

"I wouldn't miss it for the world."

The ringing phone halted any further conversation, and he flashed a wave as she picked up the handset. Though her attention should have been on the caller, she couldn't help but watch Blake exit the room.

~

*W*hen work ended, Audrey hurried out of the office and to the general store. Not sure if she had everything she'd need at home, she decided to just purchase all the needed ingredients. The dinner had to be perfect.

The sky outside was darkening as she parked the car. Was it possible it might snow tonight? Audrey hoped it would hold off at least long enough for her to get home. As the chill permeated her coat, she ducked into the store and grabbed a basket. Pasta, sauce, meat, and bread found their way into her basket, and then onto the checkout conveyor belt. With the bill paid, and the groceries tucked in the front seat, she sped home.

"Can you stay a little longer tonight?" she asked Ellie as she muscled the bags into the house.

"Why? What is all this?" Ellie asked, her forehead wrinkling in confusion.

"I'm fixing dinner for Blake."

A sly smile crossed Ellie's face, and her left brow arched. "Just friends, huh?"

"It's a reciprocal gesture for yesterday," Audrey said. *And a test to see if my feelings are more than surface attraction.*

"Unh huh, a simple thank you wouldn't suffice? You had to cook the man dinner?"

Audrey set the bags on the counter and turned to her sister. "Okay, he's cute, and I'm not sure I'm ready to date yet, but it couldn't hurt to see if something's there, right?"

"Of course not, and I don't think it's too early to date either. You said Tony left when he found out you were pregnant right?"

Audrey nodded, not wanting to correct her sister and share that Tony stayed until she gained weight and started wearing stretchy pants.

"Then I think it's time you forgot him and looked forward to the future, and this Blake sounds like a nice change. Now, go shower and clean up. I'll start the spaghetti."

"Thanks, Ellie."

Elliana nodded before shooing Audrey out of the kitchen.

After a quick shower and a change of clothes, Audrey returned to the kitchen to take over, but Cayden had woken, and Ellie shoved the bottle in her hand and ushered her to the living room instead.

Gratitude flooded Audrey. It had been hard being away from Cayden all day, and she relished holding him and watching him eat, but a small part of her felt guilty that Ellie was slaving away in the kitchen making a dinner she promised to someone else. It was spaghetti, which wasn't rocket science, but still, Ellie had her own husband to cook for.

The doorbell rang as Cayden finished his bottle. After setting it on the table, Audrey stood and opened the door for Blake who had changed as well. His dark green shirt brought out tiny tan flecks in his eyes, but it was the flowers in his hand that captured her attention. The small bouquet held six delicate orange roses, and she wondered if he understood their meaning of bridging a friendship into a romance.

"You look beautiful," he said, holding them out to her.

"Thank you. You do too. I mean handsome. You're handsome."

He smiled as she stumbled over the words. Dropping her eyes, she took the roses with her free hand and waved him inside. He followed her into the kitchen where Ellie was putting the finishing touches on dinner. "This is my sister, Elliana. She's been watching Cayden for me while I work, and she made dinner tonight."

"But only because you needed time with your son," Ellie said, jumping in and smoothing Audrey's awkward statement. "Hi, I'm Ellie," she added, sticking out her hand.

"Blake," he responded, returning the shake.

Ellie wiggled her eyebrows at Audrey in approval before turning back to the stove.

"And this is my son, Cayden," Audrey said, thankful that Blake hadn't seemed to catch Ellie's gesture. "He's the reason I'm back in town."

"He has your smile."

"And he's going to go lay down and give you guys dinner time," Ellie said as she took Cayden from Audrey's arm.

"Ellie, you don't have to. You've already been with him all day."

"Nonsense, I already checked in with Philip, and he has to work late, so I have nowhere to be. This way, I can keep him entertained and you two can have a nice dinner as adults."

Before Audrey could protest, Ellie fled with Cayden, leaving Audrey and Blake staring awkwardly at each other.

Blake broke the ice first. "Your sister is amazing."

"Yes, she is." Audrey laughed, easing the nervous tension in the room.

"And the dinner smells marvelous. It would be a shame to let it get cold, so shall we?"

"Of course, yes, let's eat." Audrey grabbed two plates from her small collection and handed him one. She scooped a portion of spaghetti and added a slice of bread to the plate in her hand and then traded plates with Blake and filled the second one. Two glasses of water sat on the table waiting for them.

"To a nice dinner with an old friend," Audrey said, raising her glass in a toast.

"To new possibilities," Blake added as he clinked her glass.

The words sent a tingle through Audrey's body. Did that mean he liked her?

"Would you mind if I prayed before we eat?"

Her daydream crashed down at his words. He was religious? She had never been one for religion herself; it held too many rules that reminded her of her overbearing mother, but as Blake was a guest in the house, she kept her opinion to herself and nodded her head. One little prayer wouldn't hurt anything, but the flames she had felt fanning inside her now smoked as if doused with water.

When he finished, an uncomfortable silence fell across the table and Audrey wondered if she should just end the date, but a voice inside her head wanted to know why.

"Why do you pray?"

The question seemed to catch Blake off guard, and he blinked at her. "You mean you don't?"

Audrey shook her head. "I was never religious. My parents never saw the need, but I tried praying in Hollywood. God didn't answer." She picked up a piece of garlic bread and took a bite.

"What were you praying for?" he asked. "If you don't mind me asking."

Audrey shrugged. "I prayed to find work, and I received enough roles to pay the rent. Then I met Tony and things improved until I got pregnant. I prayed not to be pregnant, but that one wasn't answered. When Tony left me, I prayed for work, but God didn't answer that one either."

Blake's lip folded in as if he were biting the inside of them. After a long pause, he spoke, "I'm not God, and I can't explain why it sometimes seems as if he says 'no' to our requests, but I think you might want to try praying in a different way."

Audrey's eyes flicked to his. "There's a wrong way to pray?"

"No," - he shook his head - "but a different way of praying. Jesus said we are to pray 'Thy will be done' yet many of us pray just like you did for our will to be done."

"I never knew that." Even though her words were audible, they were quiet, meant more for herself than his benefit.

Another silence descended between them, but it wasn't an uncomfortable one this time. Audrey wracked her brain for something to say when Blake sucked in his breath and pointed outside.

"Oh my goodness, it's snowing!"

Audrey whipped her head around, excitement filling her. "I love the snow, but I haven't seen it in years. LA doesn't get snow."

"Then let's go enjoy it." Blake pushed back his chair and held out his hand.

"But our dinner..."

"Will be here when we return. Come on."

With a laugh that tinkled like a bell and set her eyes sparkling, Audrey accepted his hand and the two ran to the living room to grab their coats before stepping outside.

Though chilly, the air was not biting cold yet.

"I'd forgotten how pretty it was," Audrey said with a sigh, throwing her arms out and twirling in a small circle.

"It's not as pretty as you are right now." Blake held her gaze as she paused and turned to him. A pink color tinted her lips and a tingle of embarrassment traveled through her veins.

"I'm not where I'd like to be. This baby weight is stubborn." Her eyes dropped to the ground as her self-consciousness took over.

With one large step, Blake covered the distance between them and grabbed her hands. "You are beautiful, Audrey McAllister. I've thought so since the day I first saw you in high school."

"But this isn't high school," Audrey began, glancing up at him from the corner of her eye.

"I'm glad it's not," he said with a smile. "I wouldn't have the nerve to do this if it were."

With his right hand, he tilted her face up until their eyes met. The intensity radiating from his eyes caused her to take a breath and part her lips. As if in slow motion, his head lowered until his lips gently brushed hers. The kiss was over in an instant, but the heat from his lips flamed across hers long after he had pulled back.

"I've wanted to kiss you like that for years."

"Blake, I don't know if I'm ready to jump into a relationship again," Audrey said. Though her body screamed yes, her head kept flashing a yield sign.

"That's okay, Audrey. I don't mind waiting for you. I'll wait as long as it takes."

~

Blake smiled as he left Audrey's house. Kissing her had been better than he'd imagined, and even though she said she wasn't ready for a relationship, he believed she was more open than she admitted.

He wanted to share his good news with someone, and he pointed his car toward The Diner. Max was locking the door as he approached.

"Well, someone looks like the cat who ate the canary," Max said, opening the door to let him in. "I guess you had a good night."

"It was amazing," Blake said, brushing the snow off his jacket.

"That's good." Max picked up the chairs, turning them upside down on the tables.

"But?" Though he hadn't said it, Blake felt the unsaid word.

"Nothing, I just don't want to see you hurt again. I don't know Audrey well, but she left once. How do you know she'll stick around this time?"

"I don't," Blake said, trying to hold on to the elated feeling he had walked in with. "I guess I'll just have to trust that God brought her back into my life for a reason."

Max shook his head. "I don't understand your faith, but for your sake, I'll hope so too."

CHAPTER 7

*W*hen Friday night rolled around, Audrey clocked out
right at five o'clock and headed to the parking lot.
The last few days, she had been waiting to walk out with Blake,
but tonight was her dinner with her parents and she couldn't
be late.

"Oh good, you're back. Mother called and said Philip and I
have to attend this dinner too, so I have to run home and change,"
Elliana said as Audrey entered the house.

"Ellie, I'm sorry. Is she requesting you attend once a month like
me or just this once?"

"I'm not sure. I hope it's just this once, but now my nerves are
all bunched up. Why does she always make me feel like I've been
called to the principal's office when she makes me come over?"

Audrey smiled as she took Cayden from her sister's arms. "I feel
the same way." She turned her attention to the baby. "How are you,
little man?"

"Cayden was an angel today. I wonder how Mother will deal
with a baby."

"Is it awful that I kind of hope he throws a fit and makes a big enough mess that she won't make us come back?"

"I don't think so," Ellie said with a laugh. "I'd have the same thoughts. Okay, I have to run and change, but I'll see you there."

∼

*E*llie's car wasn't at the mansion when Audrey arrived. She stifled the sigh threatening to escape. Seeing her mother again would be a lot easier with Ellie to act as mediator. A check of the clock revealed only a few minutes before seven, so surely she would arrive soon.

After turning off the engine, Audrey grabbed Cayden's car seat from the back and drug her feet up the walkway to the front door. It was just dinner, so why did it feel like impending doom?

Julie answered the door before the bell had finished ringing. "She's waiting for you in the dining room," she said in a clipped tone. Audrey knew she had been cutting it close, but she wasn't late, unless her watch was off.

Audrey followed Julie into the spacious dining room decorated in creams and golds to make it appear more opulent. A large table filled the middle of the room though Audrey could never remember having people at dinner.

Her father, Bruce, sat at the head of the table, a newspaper open in his hands. Though he had the money to buy whatever technology he wanted, he had never given up the paper newspaper, claiming reading it online just wasn't the same.

"Ah, finally. I thought perhaps you were breaking our deal," Evelyn said, rising from the chair next to her father. "Please come sit down and join us so we can eat before the food is ice cold."

"I'm not late, Mother. My clock said it was 6:57 when I pulled in." Audrey worked hard to keep the irritation out of her voice.

With an exaggerated gesture, Evelyn glanced at the diamond

encrusted watch on her wrist and pursed her lips. "Perhaps it is time you obtain a new watch. Mine shows ten after seven, and I highly doubt you took ten minutes to get here from the atrium."

This would be harder than Audrey thought. Where was her sister to help out? After placing Cayden's carrier on the floor next to her father, Audrey pulled out the chair across from her mother and sat down. "Are we waiting for Ellie?"

"Elliana called and said Philip is sick, so they will not be making it tonight."

Dread settled in Audrey's stomach.

"Ah, Audrey," her father said, lowering his newspaper. "Good to see you again. How are you enjoying work?"

"The position is challenging to be sure, but I think I'm getting a better hang on it."

"Good, good."

"Can we eat now?" The vein of contempt was ripe in Evelyn's voice

"Of course." Bruce folded his newspaper and placed it under the plate.

Evelyn picked up the dainty silver bell at the end of the table and rang it. Audrey closed her eyes and took a deep breath. How did her parents justify this? They didn't need anyone to wait on them hand and foot.

Julie appeared a moment later pushing a cart laden with small china bowls. Without a word, she placed one before Evelyn, Bruce, and Audrey and then stepped back and waited.

"Thank you, Julie, that will be all," Evelyn said, and Julie curtsied and left.

Not thinking, Audrey lowered her head and closed her eyes. After their dinner on Tuesday, she and Blake had eaten lunch together the rest of the week, and though she still wasn't sure she was ready to be religious, she had shown respect and bowed her head each time.

"What are you doing?" Evelyn asked.

Audrey's head popped up, a faint heat searing across her cheeks. "Sorry, I've been seeing Blake Dalton, and he prays before every meal. Bowing my head was just habit."

"Blake Dalton," her father said, rubbing his chin, "why does that name sound familiar?"

"Because he works for you Dad. He's on the construction crew." Audrey shook her head, wondering how he could not know one of his own employees.

"You've been seeing one of your father's employees?" Evelyn asked.

"Well, we only had one real date, but we've been having lunch together. I like him. He's nice."

"You can't keep seeing him," her mother said, lowering her head and dipping her spoon into the bowl as if the discussion were over.

"What do you mean I can't keep seeing him?" White hot anger bubbled in Audrey's stomach. "I'm a grown woman. You can't tell me who I can and can't see."

"Maybe not, but you are a McAllister. We marry higher than common construction workers."

The anger grew so intense that red flashed across Audrey's eyes. "That is horrible, Mother. Just because he's a construction worker doesn't make him less of a person. And no one said anything about marriage. I'm not ready to marry. We had one date for goodness sakes." It took all of Audrey's strength to keep her voice even as Cayden was sleeping in the carrier beside her, and she didn't want to wake him. "Dad, tell her that Blake is a good guy."

While Bruce rarely stood up to Evelyn, he was more level headed and not as obsessed with status. "Blake is a good guy, but..."

"I can't believe you two. This is the reason I moved away to LA," she said emphasizing each word. "I didn't want to end up like you guys, so obsessed with money."

"Why can't you find someone like Phillip?" Her mother asked.

"Stop it. You've always compared me to Elliana. I was never smart enough or pretty enough for you. Now I can't even date the right guy? You know what? Fire me if you want. I'll pay back what I borrowed as soon as I can, but I'm going to keep seeing Blake."

Evelyn's mouth dropped open, but before she could say anything, Audrey leaned down and grabbed Cayden's carrier. "I'll show myself out."

Her anger didn't fade as she stomped out of the front door and climbed into her car though as she closed the door, the fear set in.

If she lost her job, how would she pay her rent? Without thinking, words spilled out of her mouth in a prayer.

"Lord, I don't know what to do without help. Please show me what to do."

CHAPTER 8

"What's the matter?" Blake asked as Audrey opened the door Sunday morning.

Audrey shook her head. "It was a rough weekend. When I came to town, I had no money, so I had to ask my parents for help. They agreed, but only if I worked for my father and attended a dinner with them once a month. Friday was the first dinner and needless to say, it didn't go well."

"I'm sorry," he said, touching her arm. "What happened?"

She bit her lip as she glanced up at him, wondering if she should tell him. She didn't want to hurt him, but if they were going to have a relationship—and she thought that's where they were heading—then she wanted to share everything with him. "My parents forbade me from seeing you because you don't meet their idea of what I should be dating. I left, but not before telling them I didn't need their money, but in reality, I do."

The news that her parents didn't approve of Blake didn't appear to faze him in the least. Instead, he opened his arms and Audrey stepped into them, enjoying the warmth and security they provided.

"It will be okay," he said, patting her hair. The simple touch felt like home, and she buried her face further in his chest.

"How? I even prayed on the way home, but I haven't had any bright idea come to me." Her voice was muffled against his shirt, but he seemed to understand her anyway.

"We'll figure something out."

Audrey pulled back and looked up at him. "Unless it's the fact that you're a secret millionaire, I doubt it will change their mind."

Blake said nothing, but a small smile pulled at the corner of his mouth.

Audrey's eyes narrowed at him. "Are you a secret millionaire?"

"Maybe not a millionaire," Blake laughed, "but I do have quite a bit of money to my name."

"But, if you have so much money, why are you working for my father?"

Blake brushed a strand of her blond hair back behind her ear. "I work because I like it, and because I don't want to end up one of those people who becomes attached to money and looks down on everyone else."

Audrey snorted. "It's like you've met my mother."

"I have," - Blake said - "at the Christmas party last year, but I don't think your mother is bad. She's just missing something in her life."

"What?" Audrey asked, her brow furrowing. Her mother was lacking for nothing except for maybe decent civility.

"God. All the money in the world means nothing if I don't have two things—God being the first."

"What's the second?"

Blake's hazel eyes stared into hers. "Love," he said as his thumb caressed her cheek. "First Corinthians says, 'three things will last forever—faith, hope, and love—and the greatest of these is love.' But if you don't have Jesus in your heart, it's hard to understand love."

Suddenly, Audrey wanted to know Jesus the way Blake seemed to. She wanted the peace he exuded. "Will you teach me about love?"

There was a double meaning in her words, and Blake didn't miss it. His eyes glistened as he nodded. "I would love to teach you about love." Then his eyes closed, and his head lowered to hers, sending a tremor of emotion through her body as his lips pressed against hers. Her hands wound around his neck, her fingers locking in his hair. As his hands lowered to her low back, he pulled her closer to him and the kiss deepened until the cry from Cayden broke them apart.

"I think he might be jealous," Blake said, brushing a finger across Audrey's lips. "But we need to get going anyway or we won't make it to church."

Audrey nodded. Any words she might have been able to respond with had left her head when his lips seared hers.

Ten minutes later, they were pulling into the parking lot of the small white church. A large white steeple that held a bell rose from the left side of the building and a single cross sat in the middle of the roof. Stained glass windows dotted the building, adding bursts of color to the plain white siding.

Blake grabbed Cayden's car seat from the back and slung it over his left arm, leaving his right hand free to clasp Audrey's hand. When his fingers entwined with hers, she couldn't stop the smile that spread across her face.

"Hello, Blake, good to see you." A young man with dark hair and a bright smile greeted them as they approached the entrance.

"Hello, Pastor Tom. It's good to see you again too. Are you teaching today?"

"Yes sir. Pastor Robert is taking a few weeks off."

"This is my friend Audrey McAllister. Audrey, this is Pastor Tom."

Tom's eyes widened at the name, and Audrey smirked. "Yep,

Bruce McAllister is my father. I'm sort of the black sheep of the family I guess."

"Well, sheep of all color are welcome here," Tom said with a laugh. "We will have to try to get your parents to join us."

Audrey rolled her eyes. "Good luck with that. Religion isn't their thing."

"But it wasn't yours either, remember?" Blake said, squeezing her hand.

"That's true, but I think I was an easier sell than they will be."

"We'll keep praying regardless," Tom said. "And we're glad to have you here today."

Audrey followed Blake into the sanctuary, feeling out of her element. She couldn't remember the last time she had been in a church. Rows of chairs filled the open room, and a stage at the front held a piano, a drum set, and a few guitars. One large white screen hung on the wall at the very back of the stage.

As Cayden was awake, Audrey rescued him from the carrier after they sat down and held him on her lap. His eyes flicked back and forth as if taking the new environment in.

The room filled quickly, and those who knew Blake came by and greeted him. Blake was careful to introduce her each time, but she knew she would never remember all the names. Perhaps after she had been coming a few weeks, they would stick in her memory. She paused at that thought. She had never planned to stay when she came home, but the idea didn't sound so bad now.

When the music started, Audrey found herself swaying to the beat, though she didn't know most of the words. Blake sang beside her, his voice a clear, strong tenor. She'd had no idea he could sing, but she found she wouldn't mind hearing his voice every Sunday.

After the songs ended, Pastor Tom took the stage. Audrey had no Bible, but Blake held his out, so they could look at it together. When the words 'but the greatest of these is love' hit her ears, Audrey glanced up. Was it just an odd coincidence that the pastor was speaking on the very verse Blake had said to her this morning or was this God speaking to her? She turned to Blake, who smiled and nodded at her.

As the pastor continued to speak, Audrey's heart called out to God asking him to lead her, to change her, and to show her love.

When the service ended, Blake took her to The Diner for lunch. It appeared to be the hangout place after church on Sunday as several other church goers ended up there as well. Audrey was glad Blake didn't call them over or ask them to join their table though. It wasn't that she didn't want to get to know everyone soon, but she wanted a little time with Blake to decompress and discuss his plan for the next day.

"I'm so glad I got to know you," Audrey said as they opened the menus. "I know it hasn't been long, but I feel like a different person now."

"Well, it's been a lot longer for me," Blake said with a smile. "I've been waiting to be with you for years."

Heat climbed up Audrey's face at the compliment. She couldn't believe this wonderful man had been in front of her all those years ago and she had been too blind to see it.

"But you are a different person now. Accepting God into your heart changes you. Now we just need to get your parents and your sister together, so we can see about changing their hearts too."

"Do you think it will work?" Audrey asked. "I can't see my mother ever giving up her money and leaning on Jesus."

"Well, she doesn't necessarily have to give up her money, but as for leaning on Jesus, I've seen tougher cases than your mother come around. Never doubt what God can do. Christmas is next week, and that seems to help with people's spirits too. We'll figure something out."

Audrey nodded, but the doubt still rumbled around in her head. She wanted him to be right. No, she needed him to be right, but it would take a miracle to turn her mother around.

CHAPTER 9

*A*udrey applied the last dab of lipstick and leaned forward to inspect the finished product in the mirror. Not bad, if she did say so herself.

When the knock sounded at the door, her heart fluttered in her chest. She hadn't expected to fall for someone in Star Lake and certainly not so fast.

With a smile, she flung the door open to greet Blake, but it wasn't Blake who stared back at her from the front stoop.

"Tony? What are you doing here?" On the other side stood the man she thought she'd never see again, the dark-haired Italian who had left her six months ago.

"I came for you and my son. Audrey, I'm sorry I wasn't there. I should have been."

"How did you even find me?" Confusion covered Audrey, clouding her thoughts. She and Tony had never spoken of her hometown; he had never appeared interested.

"Dez told me you came home for money. I had no idea you were from such a small town, but once I arrived, it was easy to follow the gossip train to your house. You don't have to stay any longer. Return to LA with me and let's create a life together."

Audrey opened her mouth to say no, but indecision flooded her. She wanted to go back to LA, didn't she? It's what she had told herself when she first moved back, but now Blake was in the picture, and she was no longer sure.

"I'm not positive I want to go back. I mean I want to act again but there's something magical about this town."

Tony blinked at her. "This town? This town has one stoplight and no Starbucks. Why would you live in the middle of nowhere when you aren't forced to?"

Audrey shrugged. "I don't know. There's something about the small-town vibe I like. It's kind of growing on me again."

Cayden's cry interrupted the discussion and Audrey turned to get him.

"Is that him? I want to see him." Tony followed her into the house and to Cayden's room.

As Audrey picked Cayden up out of the crib, Tony reached for him. "Please, let me hold my son."

After a moment's hesitation, Audrey held the bundle out, adjusting his arms the way the nurse had showed her that first day in the hospital. Though sweet, the image triggered the memory that Tony hadn't been there, that he had left her when she started gaining weight to have the baby alone.

"I need to get his bottle. Can you hold him without dropping him?"

"I think I can manage," Tony said with a narrowed look.

Audrey wasn't so sure, but she exited the room anyway. She filled the bottle quickly and returned, afraid to leave Cayden too long. "Here let me take him," she said, holding out her arms.

"I can feed him. Just hand over the bottle."

Audrey bit her lip, but before she could argue, a knock sounded at the door. *Blake. Oh no, this will not be good.*

"Who's that?" Tony's eyes shifted to the door and he moved that direction.

"A friend of mine," Audrey said. "I'll get the door. You sit in the chair and feed Cayden."

With heavy feet, Audrey walked to the door, playing different scenarios over in her head. She could tell Blake Tony was here, but how would he react? The other option involved lying, which brought a different kind of unease and Blake would see right through the lie and want an explanation.

"Evening," he said, as the door opened.

"Hi." He leaned in for a kiss, but she placed a hand on his chest, stopping the motion. "Um, Tony's here."

Blake's face blanked for a moment as if trying to place the name, and then he nodded, but his face remained devoid of emotion.

Audrey hated hurting him. "I didn't invite him," she continued hoping to ease the evident tension in the air. "He found out where I lived from my old roommate and just showed up. I wanted to throw him out, but Cayden is his son."

"I understand. Do you want me to stay?" His voice held no emotion and tugged at Audrey's heartstrings.

Though she wanted him to stay, with no idea what Tony would do, she worried his staying would make the situation worse. "Can we take a rain check and talk at work tomorrow?"

Blake took a deep breath and nodded, sadness manifesting across his handsome features. "Okay, I'll talk to you tomorrow."

Audrey couldn't let him leave without trying to make him understand her conundrum, but as she reached out to touch his arm, Tony's voice sounded from behind her. "Who is this?"

"This is my friend Blake. We had planned to hang out tonight before you showed up." Audrey fought to keep her voice calm.

Cayden was still in Tony's arms, and fear at what he might do if challenged coursed through her veins.

"Well, I'm in town now to take care of Audrey and Cayden, so thanks for stopping by Brad, but..."

"Blake. The name is Blake." Blake's shoulders tensed as his eyes narrowed.

Audrey took a step toward Tony, hoping to extricate Cayden from his arms in case blows were about to rain down.

"Whatever. We're good, so you can leave."

Audrey reached out for Cayden, but Tony turned away, clutching the baby in his large hands.

Blake's eyes flashed. "I'll leave, but only because Audrey asked, and I'll be checking in with her again."

As the door closed behind Blake, the anger bubbling in Audrey rose to the surface. "That was rude, Tony. Blake is a friend."

"Looks like he wants to be more than friends."

"Maybe he does. Maybe I do. After all, you left me when I was five months pregnant because I gained too much weight. He knows I have a kid, and he doesn't care about my weight."

"I'm sorry I left, Audrey. I wasn't sure I could be a dad, but, I want my son in my life." Tony crossed to the couch and sat down, still cradling Cayden in the crook of his arm.

Audrey crossed her arms, angry at Tony's leaving and then showing up unannounced, but the ire fizzled the longer she watched him. Tony held Cayden and gazed at him as if he wanted to be a father. How often had she dreamed about him coming back and raising their son with her? And shouldn't she want Cayden to be around his real father? But then there was Blake. Audrey felt closer to Blake in one week than she could remember being to Tony the whole time they had been together. Audrey sighed as she sat in the chair across from him. What was she going to do now?

∽

*T*he snow crunched under Blake's feet on the journey back to his truck. This was an unexpected turn of events. Not only was he having to overcome Audrey's parents' objection to him, but now Cayden's father was in the picture.

Max was busy behind the counter when Blake stepped into The Diner. He chose the last empty seat at the counter, next to Bert.

"Hello, Blake. Where is your pretty friend tonight?" Bert asked, closing his book and turning his attention on Blake.

Blake shook his head, not wanting to drudge through the issue with Bert, whom he rarely spoke to. "Something came up."

Max, overhearing the exchange, shot Blake a questioning look.

"Just a burger for now," Blake said, knowing Max would want the full story later.

Max nodded and put the order in, and when the burger arrived, Blake tried to eat it, but couldn't muster the desire to finish it.

An hour later, the last customer left. After locking the door and flipping the sign to 'Closed,' Max walked back to the counter and sat next to Blake.

"Okay, spill it. What's going on?"

A long, deep sigh spilled out. "We were supposed to meet tonight and brainstorm ways to smooth the issue with her parents, but when I got there, Tony was there."

Max's brow furrowed. "Who's Tony again?"

"Cayden's father. Evidently he just showed up unannounced, and she seemed unsure of what to do. I think I love her, but I don't want to keep a child from his father. I don't know what to do." Blake dropped his head into his hands.

Max clapped a hand on his shoulder. "Hey, I know I'm not as religious as you, but don't you always say God knows best? I think the best thing you can do is wait. Let her know you're there, but wait and see what happens."

Blake raised his head to regard his friend. "I wasn't sure you had been listening, but I'm glad some of my advice wore off on you. It's nice to hear it back, but it doesn't make it any easier to follow."

"It never does, my friend," Max said.

CHAPTER 10

"*H*ow long do you plan on staying, Tony?" Audrey asked as she cleaned the dinner dishes. After Blake's exit, Audrey had whipped up dinner hoping Tony would eat and leave, but he appeared in no hurry to leave.

"Leave? I'm not leaving. This is my son, and I'm taking you both back to California."

Audrey sighed and turned off the water. "Tony, you didn't understand. I'm not going back. I'm enjoying being home."

A sneer crossed Tony's face as he stood and closed the distance between them. "Are you sure you're not enjoying your new boyfriend?"

Audrey stepped back as fear flooded her body. Tony had never been violent, but she didn't like the vibe he was emitting. "It's not like that. Blake is a Christian who hasn't pressured me to do anything, unlike someone else from my past."

While Audrey had been interested in Tony, things had moved at a faster pace because Tony had pushed. Perhaps if Audrey had been stronger, she would have noticed some of the less desirable traits Tony possessed, and run instead of jumping into bed with him.

"I never had to pressure you," Tony said with a sadistic laugh. "You would have done anything to get ahead and land a starring role."

Anger replaced the fear as the realization he had never cared for her sunk in. "You took advantage of me."

Tony snorted. "It's Hollywood, baby, what did you expect? You do what you must to get ahead and succeed. If you plan to make it there, you better learn that lesson."

"Then I guess it's good I don't plan on going back." The words surprised even Audrey as they exited her mouth. She had planned on returning one day, when the money grew, and Cayden was a little older, but seeing Tony now opened her eyes. Audrey reflected on the other things done to get roles and cringed. A tiny ember of self-loathing flickered within her.

Tony's voice softened. "Look, Audrey, let's sleep on it. You'll change your mind in the morning after I've reminded you how much fun we have."

Audrey shook her head in repulsion. How had she fallen for this hardened, insensitive man? Had fame been so blinding she had convinced herself of his charm? "I'm not spending the night with you, and you're not staying here. Go home, Tony. I don't know why you're really here, but you don't want to be a father."

"You have no idea what I want," Tony said, narrowing his eyes. "I'll leave tonight, but this isn't over."

When the door shut, Audrey rushed to lock it before sinking to the carpet, her back against the door. "Lord, I don't know what to do. Help me get Tony out of my life."

～

*a*udrey filled Elliana in on the previous night's events when she arrived the following morning.

"Should I worry this guy will show up here?" Fear threaded Elliana's normally bold voice.

"I don't expect he will, but I honestly have no idea. If he does, call me and then drive to Mother's. If anything can scare him away, Evelyn might be it."

The girls exchanged tentative smiles laced with apprehension. Audrey didn't want to leave Cayden, and she hated placing Elliana in an awkward situation, but she had to get to work.

Blake was waiting at the front desk when she arrived. "I wanted to check and make sure everything was okay."

His words, meant to uplift, only reinforced the fear, and she began shaking. "I'm not sure if it will be okay. Tony left last night, but says he won't go back to California without Cayden. Elliana is home with Cayden now, but what if Tony returns?"

"Have Elliana take Cayden somewhere safe. Maybe to your mother's?"

Audrey nodded. "I told her to go there if Tony showed up."

"No, now, before Tony shows up. At least that way Evelyn is there to help, and she's forceful enough to be convincing. I will call Sergeant Powell and see if there's any information on Tony's past we can use as leverage."

Blake's words sent Audrey's head spinning, and she gaped at him unsure of where to start.

"What's Tony's last name?"

"Bachetti," Audrey managed through the cloud of uncertainty.

"Good, call Elliana. I'll be right back." Blake's tone was firm and pushed Audrey into gear.

She picked up the desk phone as he pulled out his cell.

~

*W*ithin minutes, Blake and Audrey were in his car on the way to her house. Audrey clutched a fax in her hand, surprised at the information it contained. She'd had no idea Tony had a record, but hoped it would be enough to get him to leave.

Tony's car was in the driveway when they pulled up, but thankfully Ellie's wasn't.

"You ready?" Blake asked, squeezing her hand after turning off the engine.

Audrey nodded, though her nerves were wound as tight as a drum. After a final deep breath, she opened the car door and stepped out.

"Where's my son?" Tony asked approaching her. An aggressive wave rolled off his demeanor halting Audrey's steps until Blake's hand landed on her back, a reassuring gesture.

"Cayden's not here," Audrey said after flashing a look of gratitude Blake's direction. "You didn't come here seeking to be Cayden's father. You came here in hopes of money, but you won't get any."

"What are you talking about?"

"This!" Audrey held out the paper and Tony snatched it, his eyes widening at the information. "You shouldn't even be here, Tony. According to this, you are violating parole, and I'm sure the LAPD would love to obtain that information."

Tony's eyes narrowed into slits.

"Or you can go back to LA and forget about Audrey and Cayden and we can tear this paper up," Blake said, taking a step forward.

"You haven't seen the last of me." Tony scowled before crumpling the paper and stomping to his car.

As the black Mercedes Benz roared to life, and the tires

squealed out of the driveway, Audrey sagged against Blake, the adrenaline leaving her knees weak.

"Everything will be okay," Blake said, wrapping both arms around her. "We'll get a lawyer and get you full custody, so he can't do this again."

Audrey turned to Blake. "Thank you. I couldn't have done this without you."

Instead of a verbal response, his arms tightened around her, and he lowered his head to mark her lips with his own.

"I want to make sure Cayden's okay," Audrey said as the kiss ended. The desire to remain in Blake's chiseled arms was strong, but so was the maternal instinct to check on her son. Blake nodded and ten minutes later they pulled into the estate.

Elliana opened the door instead of Julie, sending alarm bells ringing in Audrey's head.

"Where's Cayden? Is he okay?" Audrey asked. Her eyes darted behind Elliana in search of her son.

"Relax, he's fine. He's with Mother. Tony never even showed up here."

"That's because we met him first. I hope he won't be back," Audrey said.

"If he does, we'll figure something out," Blake said, squeezing her shoulder.

"I need to see Cayden."

Ellie led the way to the formal living room where Evelyn sat with Cayden on her lap.

The change in Evelyn stopped Audrey in her tracks. Not only was Evelyn not in a pantsuit, but no pearls adorned her neck. "Mother?"

Evelyn looked up and smiled, sending another shock of disbelief down Audrey's spine. When was the last time her mother had smiled like that?

"Ah, Audrey, Blake, welcome."

Audrey glanced at Blake who shrugged and then she turned her attention to Ellie. With a raise of her eyebrows, she asked the silent question, knowing Ellie would understand.

"You got me," Ellie said with a laugh. "She's been like this for about an hour. After Cayden spit up on her white Nina McLemore suit, she changed into this and her whole attitude shifted. You should have seen her laying on the floor with him."

"I can relax on occasion," Evelyn said, feigning mock hurt.

"No, you can't Mother," Audrey said. She wanted to scoop up Cayden to make sure he was okay, but shock kept her rooted in place.

"Ah, Blake," her father's voice grabbed everyone's attention as he entered the living room, "I want to say thank you for your calm head today."

"You're welcome, Sir. I'm glad I could help."

"You should all stay for dinner," Evelyn said, "though with all the hubbub today, I'm not sure Maurice cooked anything, but there is always pizza."

"Pizza? Mother are you feeling all right?" Audrey moved to a chair and sat down, the complete and utter change in Evelyn too much to deal with.

Evelyn shot a pointed look and sighed. "I'm fine. Look, when I heard Tony was trying to take Cayden away, I realized more important things in life exist than money, but if you'd like me to go back..."

"No," Audrey and Ellie shouted simultaneously and then laughed. "No, Mother," Audrey said, "We like this new you. It's just going to take some getting used to, but I hope you've also changed your mind about Blake." She smiled up at him and reached for his hand. "Because I expect he will be in my life for the foreseeable future." He squeezed her hand and grinned.

"I think we may have been too hasty in our earlier judgment," Bruce said, clearing his throat. "Anyone who can conduct himself the way Blake did today is welcome in my house and to date my daughter."

"Thank you, Bruce, and while I don't think it matters, I can support Audrey financially. My father was very wealthy, and when he died, he left me a small fortune.

"I'm glad to hear it, but I agree with Evelyn. Money has been our bane for far too long. Family is what really matters."

Audrey and Ellie shared another glance, and Audrey knew Ellie was wondering the same thing: Was this for real and would it last?

～

"I think you should stay here," Evelyn said as the family retired into the living room after dinner. "At least until we know Tony has left town."

Audrey shook her head. "I can't, Mother. All of Cayden's stuff is at my house. I need to go back."

"Evelyn might be right," Blake said. "I'm not comfortable with you staying there alone either," he raised his hand as Audrey opened her mouth to object, "but I know you need to be at home, so I was wondering if anyone would object to my staying on her couch at least for tonight."

"I could agree to that," Evelyn said. "It sounds like you proved yourself today."

"I can't say I'm a fan of you two being in the house alone together," Bruce said.

"I understand your concern Bruce," Blake said. "But I'm a God-fearing man. While I care for your daughter, my love for God is even greater. I assure you I will do nothing to harm that relationship or your daughter's virtue."

Bruce leaned back and regarded Blake. "I don't know about this God thing, but not many men today would say what you did, so I will accept it as well."

A handshake sealed the deal, and after a round of hugs—another thing that never happened in the McAllister household—Audrey and Blake headed out to the car.

"That might just have been the weirdest day of my life," Audrey said as Blake strapped Cayden in the car seat.

"I thought it was nice," Blake said.

"No, it was nice," Audrey said as she buckled her seatbelt. "But you met my mother before. Is it natural for someone to make such a drastic change in so short a time?"

Blake smiled. "I'm no expert, but the threat of loss can cause drastic changes. Couple that with the fact we've been praying for them, and I'm not surprised at all."

"I hope you're right. They invited us over for Christmas on Friday. Feel up to it?"

He squeezed her hand before starting the car and turning his attention to the road. "I wouldn't miss it for the world. Do you think they would mind if I brought my mother?"

Audrey chuckled and shook her head. "Yesterday, I wouldn't have even believed they would invite you, but after tonight, I don't think they'd mind."

CHAPTER 11

*A*udrey glanced around the room and marveled at the difference. Years ago, when she left, she would never have pictured a happy gathering at her parent's house.

Blake had told her the Christmas party was often held at work, but Evelyn had hired a last-minute decorator to adorn the house, so it would exude a welcoming and Christmassy air for the party. No expense had been spared. A twelve-foot tree complete with lights and decorations sat near the fireplace and twinkle lights hung from the beams in the ceiling. Garland draped across nearly every surface and fake snowflakes hung from invisible threads.

Even more surprising was that half the town had showed up at the McAllister's invite. Max and Layla stood by the long table sipping eggnog or cider. Bert and Amelia sat on one of the white couches looking like uncomfortable statues afraid to touch anything. Only their eyes moved back and forth as they watched the crowd. Paula had cornered Barnard near the tree and the two were arguing over whether white lights or colored lights looked better on trees.

Evelyn and Bruce sat in the chairs nearest the fireplace with Cayden asleep on Evelyn's lap. She had scooped him up as soon as Audrey arrived and carried him around the room showing him off to everyone. Audrey couldn't remember seeing her mother so happy.

Blake's mother, Irene, stood near Evelyn smiling down at Cayden's dark head. She had spent most of the night by Evelyn's side, probably to be by the baby, but now the two appeared to be fast friends. Audrey shook her head at the image. She would never have believed it if she wasn't seeing it with her own eyes.

Last but certainly not least, Philip and Elliana stood near the refreshments sharing a quiet conversation. Audrey smiled as she watched Elliana touch Philip's arm and laugh. It was obvious her sister was still very much in love with her husband.

"Come here." Blake grabbed Audrey's hand and pulled her out of the living room.

"Where are we going?" Audrey asked, laughing.

"I want a moment alone with you," Blake said. His eyes scanned the doorways as he pulled her from one room to another. "Ah, there we go."

Audrey looked up and felt the heat sear across her face. Hanging from the door jamb was a bright green sprig of mistletoe.

"You needed a mistletoe to kiss me?" Audrey laughed.

"No, but it makes it more romantic at Christmastime, don't you think?" His arms circled her waist as he pulled her closer.

Her arms wound around his neck, and she smiled. "I can't imagine anything more romantic." As she closed her eyes, her lips parted expecting his, but nothing came. She opened her eyes, confused.

Blake's grin reached from ear to ear. "I wanted to tell you before I kissed you that I had one thing even more romantic than Mistletoe."

Audrey couldn't imagine anything more romantic than being under the mistletoe with Blake. "What's that?"

"I heard from the LA police today. Tony was back at work today, so you can relax and enjoy the holiday. I asked a friend of mine to keep a tab on him and let me know if he disappears again."

"That may be the best Christmas present ever," Audrey said with a smile. Though she'd miss having Blake on her couch, she was relieved she could stop worrying about Tony showing up and stealing Cayden in the night.

"No, the best Christmas present ever is you," Blake said. "I love you Audrey McAllister."

"I love you too, Blake Dalton."

Electricity crackled between them as he lowered his face to hers. When his lips touched hers, heat flooded her body. She couldn't believe how much her life had changed in such a short time, but she wouldn't trade it for the world.

The End!

WOULD YOU LEAVE A REVIEW?

As an author, I highly appreciate the feedback I get from my readers. It helps others make an informed decision before buying my book. If you enjoyed this book, please leave a review at your retailer.

Do you like free books? I'm offering a free sample of my next book Free Sample!

LOVE CONQUERS ALL

For my family - Thank you for letting me write the stories that fill my head. For my friends - Thank you for your support and allowing me to watch you for inspiration.

CHAPTER 1

*L*anie Hall's footsteps echoed in the now half empty house. True to his word, Denny had cleared out his half of the furniture. The rusty orange recliner she had always hated? Gone. The glass topped coffee table she had always imagined children breaking and cutting themselves on? It was gone too. The fact they had never had kids to break the coffee table hadn't deterred her fears over the years.

All that remained of the living room furniture now was the couch her parents had given her when she first moved out. Faded and slightly stained, but otherwise in decent shape, it had lasted through college, and without kids, had held up well over the years as well.

Lanie wandered into the kitchen. Most of the appliances remained on the counter, but she did note the absence of the coffee pot. She might have to replace that as Denny's morning coffee habit had rubbed off on her some time in their ten years together.

With a heavy heart, Lanie followed the hallway into the bedroom which had felt empty for the last few years anyway.

Somewhere around their fifth year of marriage, she and Denny had stopped touching and kissing. Forget sleeping in the same room at the same time. She would turn in and read a new book or get lost in a TV show until she fell asleep. He would fall asleep in the living room and leave for work without even saying goodbye. And that's how the last few years had passed.

Lanie crossed to the closet and opened the door. The small room had once been bursting with both their clothes, but now only hers hung on one side, creating a haphazard effect like a sinking ship. With a sigh she thought back to the last conversation she'd had with Denny.

"*I can't do this anymore, Lanie. We hardly talk, and when we do, it's short and curt. I want to experience something again.*"

"*Let's try counseling, Denny,*" Lanie said, curling her hands against her legs. "*I don't like feeling like roommates either.*"

"*We could.*" Denny nodded and ran a hand through his short brown hair, "*but I don't expect it would help. Neither of us is getting anything out of this marriage any longer. I think it best we go our separate ways.*"

Lanie blinked at him but nodded. A part of her had hoped he would fight, that he would agree to counseling or something else, but his adamant stance informed her he no longer cared to try. It saddened her a little, but she didn't have the energy to fight for them both.

She shut the closet door, hating the reminder of her failed marriage. Though the divorce wasn't official yet, it was only a matter of time. Denny was gone, and the paperwork was filed. As they hadn't wanted any of the same things and they planned on selling the house and splitting the profits, the smooth process had taken no time, and now she was simply playing the waiting game.

Suddenly, the house felt too empty, too condemning, and Lanie needed a break. She retraced her steps, grabbing her keys at the door, and hurried to her car. With no idea of where to go, she let her mind wander and her hands do the steering, but it wasn't much of a surprise when she pulled into Mic's, the radio station hang out.

It had been where she had spent many Friday nights, belting out karaoke until Denny decided he no longer wanted to go out. He had never insisted she not go, but there had been a silent request coupled with a heaping of guilt, and she had eventually stopped showing up.

Lanie paused with her hand on the door handle. What if this was no longer the hangout? What if she stepped inside and recognized no one there? Squaring her shoulders, she decided she didn't care. It couldn't be any worse or feel any lonelier than her empty house.

The darkened club looked exactly as she remembered if a little emptier, but a check of her wristwatch revealed the hour was still early. She sidled up to the bar for a drink, not because she was much of a drinker, but because she needed something to do.

"What'll you have?" the bartender asked. His bald pate contrasted with a full, thick beard, which formed an interesting contrast. Large gauges created gaping holes in his ears, but his kind smile softened the hard image.

"Can I have a Sprite please?"

The bartender raised one eyebrow at her, but turned and grabbed a glass.

"Lanie? Lanie Hall?"

Lanie looked to the left where the voice had come from, and her breath caught. Azarius Jacobson, a blast from her past, stood there dapper as ever in grey jeans and a darker grey shirt that accentuated his finely-toned arms.

They had once worked together at the radio station, though he had quit and done something else shortly after her marriage to Denny.

"Azarius? How have you been?" she asked before throwing her arms around him. They hadn't been close when he worked at the station years ago, but he was a familiar face on a day she needed one.

He chuckled as her weight knocked him a step backwards, and his arms surrounded her to keep them both from falling over.

Though purely innocent, she hadn't had a man's arms around her in so long that it ignited a flame deep inside her, and a heated flush crawled up her face as she registered his touch. "Sorry, I'm just excited to see someone I know, and I haven't seen you for what? Six years?"

"Eight," he said, dropping his arms. "You look fantastic. Just as I remembered."

Just as he remembered? The flush climbed higher up her face. She had only a vague memory of him from when he worked at the radio station, but he appeared to have a much better recollection of her.

"You look great too. Why don't you get a drink and join me? I'd love to hear what you've been up to." Why did the simple thought of him joining her send her heart racing?

"Sure, I'd love to catch up with you."

He ordered a Vodka Tonic and led the way to an empty table.

"When did you get back to town?" she asked as they sat. The light above bounced off his dark skin, creating a glittering caramel effect.

"About six months ago," he said. "I'm not working for the radio station this time though."

She smiled as she sipped her soda. "I figured you weren't. I'm still there, and I would have noticed if you were back."

"Would you have?" His dark brown eyes bored into her soul, and she dropped her eyes and bit her lip.

"Honestly, I don't know," she said, stirring her straw in a circle. "Things have been crazy."

"Oh yeah? What's been going on?"

His gaze never wavered from her, and the intensity of it sent a shiver down her spine. When was the last time someone had looked at her like that? As if he really saw her? Years, she decided. It had been years, and the simple act not only made her feel beautiful but lowered her emotional walls.

"My marriage fell apart," she sighed. "I guess it had been going that direction for awhile, but we finally decided to stop fighting the lack of feelings and call it quits."

"I'm sorry to hear that," he said, but something about his expression made her wonder if he really were sorry.

"So, what about you?" she asked, changing the subject. Her failed marriage was a topic she wanted to forget, not rehash. "How has life been for you?"

He shrugged. "It's been okay. I re-enlisted for awhile. You knew I was National Guard, right?"

Lanie blinked and shook her head. She'd had no idea he was in the service. Wow, she really had been clueless about him. That was a pretty big piece of information to miss about someone.

"Oh, well I needed a change, so I re-enlisted for a few years. My time just ended, so I'm back here as a civilian again, doing some contract work."

The shifting of his eyes led her to believe there was more to the story, but she didn't press the issue. It felt like prying and that seemed rude after not having seen him for so long.

"Do you sing?" she asked, gesturing at the karaoke book on the table in an attempt to change the conversation.

A small smile pulled at the corner of his lips. "No, but I'd love to hear you sing. I always enjoyed watching you belting it out in the booth."

Unsure how to respond to that tidbit of information, Lanie felt her face flush again. Had Azarius had a crush on her? If so, did he still? And did she want him to? These questions circled through her brain, but all she could manage was, "You watched me?"

"Only a few times," he said. "You always looked like you were having fun, so go ahead and pick something. I'll cheer you on."

❧

*A*zarius kicked himself as Lanie's auburn head dropped to scan the binder of songs. He had almost spilled how attracted he was to her. He had been for years. In fact, her marriage was what drove him from the station and to re-enlist. Though he'd never gotten up the nerve to tell her how he felt, seeing her married to another had been unbearable.

Now here they were back in the same town and both single. He finally had the chance to show her how he felt, if he didn't mess it up too badly.

"Okay, I think I'll try this one." Lanie pointed to a song in the book.

He smiled and nodded at her as she scribbled the choice on a piece of paper. Azarius didn't care what she sang; she had the voice of an angel any time she opened her mouth.

Lanie stood and made her way to the stage, handing over the piece of paper to the DJ. He scanned it and motioned for her to take the mic on the small raised platform that served as a stage. Looking a little timid, she stood in front of the microphone and offered him a small smile.

Azarius flashed her a thumbs up and smiled as the music started. She probably had no idea the Duran Duran song she chose reminded him of her. He thought back to the day he had accidentally stumbled upon her singing it in the booth.

• • •

"*A*zarius, can you look at the board in control room three?" the station manager asked. "It's been frizzing out again."

"Of course, sir," Azarius said. He grabbed the tool box from the closet that housed it and headed downstairs to the control booths. Lanie was on in control room three, which made the job even more appealing. Azarius didn't believe in love at first sight, but from the moment he had met Lanie, she had affected him in a way no other woman had. Now if he could just get up the courage to tell her.

Duran Duran's "Come Undone" was billowing out of the room as he approached. He knocked on the door, but when the music didn't lower, he assumed she hadn't heard his knock, and he pushed the door open slowly.

Lanie stood behind the board in a pair of cutoff denim shorts and a red tank top. Her auburn hair flowed freely down her shoulders and bounced with the movement of her head from side to side.

Her beautiful soprano voice belted out the lyrics, mesmerizing Azarius. He could have stood there all day watching her. "Can I believe you're taking my... Oh!" Her voice stopped as she turned and spied him standing there. "I'm sorry, I didn't hear you come in."

"That's okay." He smiled and held up the tool box, so she would realize he wasn't being voyeuristic. "I knocked but ..." he shrugged. "I need to check out the control panel."

She lowered the music and stepped back. "Of course. You have about two minutes until this song ends though."

"I'll be quick."

"I love singing," she said as if trying to explain her actions. "And since the booth is soundproof, I often test my range since no one can hear me. My singing doesn't go out over the radio."

Azarius bit his lip to hide his smile at her nervousness. "Even if it did, no one would mind," he said. "You have a beautiful voice." He watched the soft pink color climb her face before turning back to the control panel.

• • •

"*W*as it okay?" Lanie asked as she finished the song and returned to the table.

"It was amazing," Azarius said.

A rose color flooded Lanie's cheeks, and she dropped her eyes. "You don't have to say that."

"No, I don't, but you are an amazing singer." Her eyes lifted, and he felt himself falling into the hazel depths. "Lanie, I'd love to hang out with you again," he began. "Are you into eighties music?"

Lanie blinked at him. "Am I into what?"

"Eighties music. I know it sounds silly, but I love to watch old music videos, and I thought maybe you'd like to hang out and watch them with me."

"Like a date?" she asked, one eyebrow arched in the air.

Azarius realized how silly that sounded. Yeah, come hang out and watch videos with me, but it was who he was. "Like two old friends reconnecting," he said. "With the possibility of more."

She smiled at him and placed her hand on his, sending tingles down his arm. "I'd like that. I could use an old friend right about now."

CHAPTER 2

*A*zarius walked through his two-bedroom apartment looking for any mess he may have missed. He was generally a neat person, but on laundry day he had a habit of throwing the clothes in his oversized chair where they stayed until the sight bothered him enough he put them away. Thankfully, today hadn't been laundry day and everything appeared to be put away and neat.

A knock sounded at the door moments later. Lanie stood on the other side in a brown sweater and jeans. Her hands were shoved in her jean pockets as if nervous.

"Hey, come on in." Azarius stepped back and opened the door for her.

"Thanks." As she stepped over the threshold, her eyes darted left and right, taking in the small living room. "Nice place."

Azarius shrugged. "It's nothing much, but it works for me. Would you like something to drink?"

"Sure, I'll take water."

As she wandered around the room, taking in the pictures on his walls, he darted into the small kitchen to fill her a glass. When he returned, she was staring at a picture of his mother and her family.

"That's my mother, her husband, and my sisters." Azarius laughed when Lanie's eyebrows knitted together at the difference in their skin color. "My adopted mother."

"I had no idea you were adopted," she said.

"Yeah, my mama was taken from me way too young, but my mother and I are close." He hoped she wouldn't ask about his mama. Though he might tell her one day, it was not a story he shared often.

"I always considered adoption special anyway because you know your parents really wanted you."

Azarius had never thought about it like that, but it did make sense, and while his memories of his mama were hazy, he was close to his mother.

"Yeah, I guess you're right. Here's your water. You wanna have a seat?"

Lanie nodded and chose an edge of the couch. He opted for the opposite edge, leaving enough space between them they weren't immediately touching though he longed to feel her warmth against him. Reaching behind him, he grabbed the remote and flicked on the TV.

"Now you get to see how I spend my nights," he said with a laugh. "YouTube," he said into the remote and his video log popped up.

"Your remote is voice activated?" Lanie asked, her eyes wide.

He nodded. "You got a favorite eighties song?"

"Um." She pursed her lips and closed her eyes, creating just the tiniest of wrinkles across her forehead. "'The Wild Wild West' by Escape Club."

Azarius had never heard of the song, but he repeated the name into the remote and a video lit up the screen.

"Oh my gosh, that is so weird," Lanie said as a pair of lips filled the screen.

"You've never seen this before?"

Lanie shook her head, a smile on her face. "We never had cable growing up, so I only heard it on the radio. I don't think I would have liked it as much if I had seen the video," she laughed.

"Well, then close your eyes," he said.

Lanie shut her lids and began singing along with the video. Azarius's attention shifted from the TV to Lanie. He could listen to her sing all day. The movement of her lips garnered his attention, and he fought the urge to kiss her. As her head moved slightly to the music and her voice filled his ears, he realized he wanted more moments like this with her.

~

*L*anie couldn't believe how much fun she was having watching old music videos with Azarius. His taste in music matched hers to a T, at least when it came to old songs, and there was something comforting about hanging out with him.

"You hungry?" he asked. "We could go get dinner."

Her stomach rumbled in answer. "Yeah, I guess I am."

Azarius stood and held out his hand to help Lanie up from the couch. She placed her hand in his, enjoying the soft feel of his skin against hers. As he pulled her up, she lost her footing and fell into his chest, her hands splaying across his muscles. She had deduced he worked out, but his chest was solid and well-formed. His arms wrapped around her waist to steady her, and for a moment Lanie thought he might kiss her.

She found the thought exciting and terrifying at the same time. Though she couldn't deny she was beginning to feel something for Azarius, she wasn't sure it was appropriate. After all, Denny had moved out only a few days ago, but it had been much longer since there had been romantic feelings between them. In fact, she couldn't remember the last time she had been in Denny's arms like this.

"Sorry," Lanie said, dropping her eyes.

"Don't be."

Azarius removed his arms, and Lanie immediately missed the warmth of his touch and then felt guilty for it. *What is going on with me?*

"Shall we take my car?" Azarius asked.

Lanie nodded, curious about his Mustang and not trusting her voice. Did he see the effect he was having on her?

She followed him through the kitchen to the small garage where his lime green Mustang took up most of the footage. A washer and dryer and some shelves filled the rest of it.

Azarius opened the passenger door for her and Lanie slid into the black leather seat. She'd never been in his car, but she had seen plenty of posts of it on Instagram.

He slid into the driver's side beside her and punched the garage door opener.

"You ready?" he asked, flashing her a smile as he donned a pair of large grey shades. They resembled old cop glasses, but they didn't look silly on his face.

"Ready for what?" Lanie asked as she fastened her seatbelt.

"This is a turbo," he said with a mischievous smile, "and I like to go fast."

The engine hummed to life and Azarius backed the car out. As soon as he shifted into drive though, the car zoomed forward and Lanie shot back against the seat. Her hand flew to the handle above the door, and she held on for dear life.

A few minutes later, she was thrown forward as Azarius parked.

"Do you always drive like that?" Lanie asked, trying to calm her racing heart. Her hand was still firmly fastened around the "oh crud" handle.

Azarius laughed as he plucked the key from the ignition and opened the driver door.

Before Lanie could open her door, he had come around the side, opened it for her, and held his hand out to help her up.

Lanie took his hand, thankful for the support as she stood on wobbly legs. He didn't drop her hand as she expected, but instead laced his fingers through hers. Something about the clash of his dark skin against her fair skin caused her heart to flutter.

"This is my favorite sandwich shop," he said, holding the door open for her. His eyes danced like a kid's at Christmas time, eliciting a small laugh from Lanie as they entered the quaint establishment.

An elder teen stood below an enlarged menu and behind the cash register. "Welcome to Johnie's, what can I get you?" The monotonous timbre of his voice matched his expressionless face.

"I recommend the number two." Azarius focused on Lanie, ignoring the boy behind the counter, "but you order what you want."

Lanie smiled at the employee, whose name tag read Brad, and scanned the large menu. She had been hoping to start eating healthier - she'd packed on a few extra pounds in the last year from lack of exercise and feeling undesired. Ordering a salad felt wrong somehow though, and the number two did look delicious if they could hold the onions.

"I'll take his recommendation, but can I get it without the onions?" Cooked onions were fine, but raw ones never agreed with her stomach. Plus, she didn't like the spicy taste in her mouth or the way her breath smelled afterwards.

"Sure." Blank-faced Brad punched a button in the register and shifted his eyes to Azarius.

"You don't know what you're missing," Azarius said, dropping her hand as he crossed his arms and leaned back. "Am I right, man?"

Brad shrugged, and Lanie bit her lip together to keep from laughing.

"Well, I think the onions make the sandwich," Azarius said. "So you can add her onions to mine."

"That's not the way it works," Brad said with a minute shake of his head.

"It's okay, he's only kidding," Lanie smirked.

"No, I'm not. They can smother mine with onions," Azarius continued. "And I'll take a big bowl of the chili. It's delicious here. In fact, you can throw more onions on the chili."

"But we don't..." Brad began.

"Don't worry about it," Lanie said, trying to keep from busting out laughing. "He's giving you a hard time." She'd never seen this playful side of Azarius. "Behave; he doesn't get paid enough to deal with you," she said.

Brad punched another few buttons and glanced up. "Will that be all?" His voice finally registered emotion - an impatient desire to be done with them.

"I'm good," Lanie said.

"Yep, I guess we're good," Azarius said, reaching for his wallet.

"That will be $21.43 then."

"Oh, I can pay for mine," Lanie said, patting her pocket.

Azarius fished two bills out and placed them on the counter. "No, I got this, but you're an expensive date," he said, winking at Lanie.

"Hah, I only ordered a sandwich. The rest was all you," she said, swatting at his arm.

He caught her hand and held it to his chest, sending a shiver up her arm. Time seemed to slow as their eyes locked. Did this mean he had feelings for her too?

"Ahem," Brad cleared his throat, breaking the connection. "Your change."

"Oh, right, thank you." Azarius scooped up the bills and stuffed them back in his wallet. The small amount of change he dropped in a glass jar on the counter that sported a "give a penny, take a penny" sign.

Lanie's hand tingled from the recent touch, and she wandered over to a window to process her feelings.

It felt wrong to be having romantic feelings for Azarius, but it had been ages since she had felt anything romantic for Denny, and he had never looked at her the way Azarius did - as if she were the most beautiful woman in the world.

"You ready?" Azarius asked, holding the bag of food up. It was an innocuous question, but the look in his eyes made her wonder if a second meaning existed in the innocent question.

Lanie nodded and followed him out to the car.

CHAPTER 3

*A*zarius shut the door after Lanie left and sighed with relief. Spending the evening with her was even better than he had imagined it would be. She hadn't laughed at his video watching habit, and she had enjoyed his favorite dinner, even if she did ruin it by leaving the onions off. Best of all, she had agreed to come back again. It had taken eight years, but Azarius finally felt as if he'd be able to show her his true feelings.

As he collapsed on the couch and flicked the television on for a reminder of the evening – "Wild Wild West" would now forever remind him of her - his phone rang.

"Hello?" he asked, punching the button. It couldn't be Lanie as they hadn't exchanged numbers yet. He preferred his privacy and didn't share his number with most people though he figured he would share it with Lanie soon.

"Az?"

Azarius stifled a sigh as he recognized his friend, Greg's voice. He liked Greg; after all he'd been there for Azarius when Krista left, but Greg didn't always have his life together. If he was calling, it was probably because he wanted something.

"Hey, Greg, what's up?"

"Not much man, just checking in to see how life is treating you."

Azarius knew this was a soft opening to see what mood he was in before Greg laid out his request, but spending the evening with Lanie left him so elated he decided to play along. "Life is good. I spent the evening with a lovely woman."

"Alright, Az," Greg said.

"Not like that, man. We just hung out. This girl's special."

"Special, huh? I can't remember the last time you called a girl special."

"Yeah, it's been a while." Azarius didn't want to ask the question, but he knew it was coming whether he asked or not. "So, how is life for you?"

"It's not bad, but uh, my sister's baby is due in a few weeks and she needs me to find another place to stay. I hate to ask, but it'll probably only be for a few weeks. I'll find another place as soon as I can. So, can I come stay with you?"

And there it was! Azarius wanted to say no. The last thing he needed was Greg hanging around cramping his style or scaring Lanie away, but he had been there for Azarius when he was at his lowest. Azarius owed him.

"Sure, man. I mean if it's only for a few weeks. You know I like my space."

"Awesome. Yeah, a few weeks, a month or two at the most."

Azarius rolled his eyes. This would probably end in disaster, but he'd already agreed. "Can you wait another week at least?" That would give him time to see Lanie a few more times before introducing Greg.

"Yeah, Cheryl will probably give me a week. I appreciate this man, more than you know."

Azarius doubted that, but the wheels were already set in motion.

~

"*W*hat's up?" Lanie asked, touching Azarius' shoulder. "You've seemed distracted all night."

He tapped his index finger against his lips. "Are you having fun hanging out with me?"

"Of course I am," she said. She hadn't told him how much she was enjoying it, but she couldn't imagine not seeing him once or twice a week.

"Would you still enjoy it if there was someone else here?"

Lanie furrowed her brow, not understanding his cryptic question. "What do you mean? Like hanging out with us or just sitting here staring at us?"

"Not really hanging out with us, but here. I have a friend I owe a favor to who needs a place to stay. He's moving in at the end of the week."

"Well, that's nice of you," Lanie said. "Are you going to be okay with a full-time roommate?" It was a question that had plagued her the last few days. Azarius seemed set in his ways and a fan of routines just so, which made her wonder if he'd ever be ready for a real relationship. Not that she was ready to jump into anything full-time, but eventually she wanted to marry again and that meant living together and sharing a space.

The corner of his lip pulled into a small smile. "I honestly don't know. I haven't lived with anyone in ages. I'm pretty happy having my own space."

"Yeah, I figured that about you, but I still think it's nice of you to help your friend out." Plus, maybe it would let Lanie know if he'd ever be able to marry. Marriage? She wasn't looking for marriage. Her own divorce wasn't even final yet. What was wrong with her?

"So, it won't bother you? We could always hang out upstairs if he gets too annoying or lock him in his room."

Lanie chuckled and batted his arm. "Any friend of yours is a friend of mine. It will be fine." *Kind of like having a chaperone*, she added to herself. Nothing other than holding hands had occurred, but if she kept coming over, she knew something might.

"Good. Now let's jam some."

He turned up the television, stood, and held out a hand to her. West End Girls blared out of the big screen. Not the best song to dance to, but Lanie didn't mind.

Azarius twirled her around as if they were waltzing, smiling as he did. Lanie leaned her head back and laughed. She couldn't remember the last time she felt so free or so comfortable.

~

*L*anie stared at the silent phone and bit her thumbnail. It had been days since she'd heard from Azarius. She knew he was probably busy with his roommate, but his lack of communication reignited old fears. Maybe she had misread him and he didn't have feelings for her. Maybe he just needed a friend and now that he had a roommate, she was no longer needed.

Lanie hated this insecurity that plagued her. Growing up in an ice cream parlor with a sweet tooth had kept her from being a skinny kid. While she had managed to lose most of the weight when she got to college, she still often felt like the fat little girl. It was one reason she believed she had accepted Denny's marriage proposal when she did. Sure, she thought she had loved him, but she also feared there might not be another proposal, and so she'd said yes even though there had been a few moments of doubt early in their relationship.

Now, she was facing the same doubt but for different reasons. Azarius was an enigma. He hadn't asked for her number, nor had he offered his own, saying he preferred to chat through instant messenger. Lanie hadn't minded at first, but now she wondered if it was so he could ignore her when he wanted.

After all, it was harder to ignore a ringing phone than a text message.

She didn't want to be the one texting him again, but she did want to see him. The indecision plagued her another few minutes before she swallowed her pride and tapped out a message to him. -*Just saying hi and wondering how your day went.*- Yeah, that seemed innocent enough. If he didn't respond, she would know he was no longer interested.

Lanie hit the send button and stared at the blue box of text, willing a reply to come through. She had almost given up hope when the phone vibrated in her hand.

-*Hey you, my day was good. Where have you been?*-

Where had she been? She'd sent the last text a few days ago and then nothing. Shaking her head, she texted out a reply. -*I've been okay. Wondering where you were since I sent the last text.*-

She bit her thumbnail again as she waited for his reply.

-*I'm sorry. My phone has been messing up lately, and I haven't been getting all my texts.*-

His answer soothed her ego though it didn't calm all of her old fears. -*Want to hang out tonight?*- He was always easier to read in person.

-*Yeah, but the roommate will be here.*-

The corners of Lanie's lips pulled into a smile. She didn't care if the roommate was there as long as she got to see Azarius. "See you about eight."

~

There was no new car in the driveway when she pulled in that night, which made Lanie wonder if perhaps the roommate was out after all.

She rang the bell, expecting Azarius to be on the other side, but when it swung open, a skinny white man with a goatee stood facing her. His stare caught Lanie off guard slightly and she rocked back on her heels.

"Hi, I'm Lanie. Is Azarius home?"

The man stepped back. "He's upstairs."

Lanie had expected an introduction in return, but the man shut the door behind her and plopped back down on the couch where he must have been when she knocked. With a slight shake of her head, she mounted the stairs. Azarius was the one she was here to see anyway.

His door was shut, and she knocked gently before pushing it open. Azarius lay on his bed in the dark. The only light was from the television, which was of course playing music videos.

"Hey, come join me," he said, patting the bed beside him.

Lanie hesitated momentarily. Though they had yet to even kiss, she knew accidents often happened when beds were involved, but he looked so out of sorts that she threw caution to the wind and climbed in beside him, leaving a small sliver of space in between them.

"What's up? You look miserable," Lanie said.

"He's so loud," Azarius said.

"Who?"

"Greg, my roommate. I thought I could handle having someone else here, but he's driving me crazy."

Lanie chuckled. "It's only been a few days, Az, I'm sure you'll get used to it."

"I don't know. I like being able to do my own thing, and he's crimping my style."

His words reminded Lanie of a fear she had been battling. "Do you think you'd ever be able to live with a woman then, a wife?"

"I don't know," he said, leveling his gaze at her. "I might have to have my own house, a getaway."

"Wouldn't that defeat the purpose though?"

He shrugged. "Maybe if it were the right woman, it wouldn't matter."

Lanie tried to tell herself it didn't matter if she weren't the right woman. They were just friends after all, weren't they? She was no longer sure. Though she had tried to quash her feelings for him, every time she was around him, they grew stronger.

He opened his arm and pulled her against him. Lanie could feel his heart beat beneath her palm. "When is your birthday?"

"Why?" he asked.

"Because I'm curious," Lanie asked. In reality, she wanted some piece of him. So far, everything he had shared had been superficial. She knew he liked eighties music and working out. She knew where he lived and what he drove, but she didn't know much else about him, and it was starting to worry her.

"It doesn't matter," he said. His eyes stayed glued to the television but his arm tightened around her.

"It does to me," she said, reaching up and turning his face to hers. "I want to know you, Azarius, like really know you."

He returned her gaze, but instead of answering with words, he leaned closer and placed his lips on hers. Fire burned through her at his touch, and for the moment, it didn't matter.

CHAPTER 4

*A*s the weeks continued to fly by, winter's icy talons faded to the first buds of spring. Though Lanie always felt connected to Azarius when they were together, doubts would creep in when they were apart. If only he would open up to her, then perhaps she could quell the thoughts that haunted her when her phone remained silent.

On the way to his house that evening, Lanie realized he had never been to her house. Though she didn't mind hanging at his place - there were no memories of a failed marriage there - she did wonder why he'd never even asked to come to her house, especially with Greg at his place. Not that Greg ever bothered them. Most of the time he excused himself and went upstairs as soon as Lanie arrived.

The lights in the house were dark when Lanie pulled into the drive. She checked her watch. 8:05, five minutes later than she said she'd be there. Lanie fired off an instant message, but no reply came. Perhaps he was resting upstairs. Azarius had often told her to come on in if the door was unlocked.

With the engine off, the surrounding stillness blanketed her. Would the neighbors think she was breaking in? She'd never spoken with any of them, but surely they would recognize her car by now.

She rang the bell, feeling more conspicuous as the seconds ticked by. When no lights came on, she tried the knob. It turned in her hand, and she ventured inside. The living room was completely dark, and Lanie wasn't sure where the light switch was.

As she fumbled with the flashlight feature on her phone, a light in the kitchen flicked on. Lanie jumped, nearly dropping her phone, before she realized it was Greg. He stood against the far counter, a bottle of milk in between his feet.

"Greg, it's me Lanie," she said when he made no motion to greet her.

"Lanie?" Though not slurred, it was clear he had been drinking by the way he said her name.

"Yeah, is Azarius home?"

Greg shook his head as he bent over and retrieved the milk container from the floor. "I don't know where he's at, but you're welcome to wait."

Lanie bit her lip as the refrigerator door opened and closed. She did want to see Azarius, but she had never been alone with Greg, and she wasn't sure she trusted him. "Um, maybe I'll just see if he answers a call." She punched in his number, but as it rang in her ear, a light flashed on the back of the couch and she realized his phone sat there charging. Well, at least that explained why he hadn't responded to her text.

"He gave you his number?" Greg asked as he entered the living room. Dark circles ringed his eyes and the wrinkled t-shirt and sweats he wore appeared as if he'd slept in them all day.

"Um, yeah, finally," Lanie said, ending the call. "Why is he so secretive about it anyway?"

Greg shrugged and sat down on the end of the couch. "He just is. I won't talk bad about my brother. I mean he's not my real brother, but you know what I mean."

Lanie nodded and sat at the other end of the couch. "I wasn't asking you to speak ill of him."

"He likes you though." Greg's tone was so nonchalant Lanie almost missed the words, and rather than look at her, he flicked on the television.

"How do you know?" Lanie asked, wishing she had his undivided attention, but determined to fish for whatever information she could get.

Another shrug. "I just know. He's different around you. I haven't seen him that way since..." He snapped his mouth shut, and Lanie knew there was more to the story.

"Why doesn't he ever tell me then?"

Greg shook his head, keeping his lips sealed.

With a small sigh, Lanie turned her attention to the television, hoping Greg would open up again. "Does he talk about me?" she asked.

"A little. I know you're still married."

"Only on paper," Lanie said. "Denny's moved out, and I haven't even heard from him since he left. The paperwork should be finalized any day now."

"How serious are you?"

The intensity of the question caught Lanie off guard and she paused before answering. She believed she loved Azarius, but the secrecy he held kept her from falling completely. There were times she could imagine a life with him and other times she believed he would change his mind one day and she would be left alone, again.

"I could be serious," she said. "If I knew he was."

"What makes you think he's not?" Greg asked.

"He never asks me over," Lanie said, dropping her eyes to her hands. She had never voiced that insecurity out loud, and she couldn't believe she had told Greg, a near stranger. "I always have to ask him if he wants to see me. I just want to know he wants me. I told him that the other night and you know what he did?"

"No, what?"

"He sent me a Nine Inch Nails video. No explanation, just this video. Then he told me to listen to it."

"Which one?" Greg asked, sitting up straighter.

"'Dead Souls.' It's from the movie The Crow. He asked me if I got it, and I tried but I didn't see how the words applied to us. I told him I liked the movie, how The Crow would do anything for the woman he loved, and he just replied with 'It means everything.' Why can't he just tell me how he feels?"

"Az marches to a different drum," Greg said with a smile, "but don't give up on him. It's not my place to say anything, but there's a reason he's the way he is and believe it or not, him telling you 'It means everything' is his way of telling you he cares."

The whir of the garage door ended the conversation.

"This conversation never happened," Greg said and Lanie nodded. Telling Azarius of the conversation wouldn't help her position anyway.

She stood as the door to the garage opened and Azarius appeared in the kitchen. "You stayed. I was so afraid I would miss you," he said, stepping toward Lanie.

"Where were you?" Lanie crossed her arms to keep from running into his. "I told you I was coming."

"I know," he sighed. "A friend called asking for help to set some things up. I thought I would be done in time, but traffic was bad and my friend was very talkative. I'm sorry."

His eyes looked sincere, and though his answer was vague, Lanie weighed it with Greg's words and figured it was as good as she was going to get. He took another step toward her, asking permission to touch her with his eyes. At least he recognized she was angry.

Sighing, she closed the distance and felt his arms wrap around her. If only she could stay here, in his arms where she felt warm and loved.

~

*A*zarius wasn't expecting the knock that came at six that night. He had just gotten home and was hoping to change clothes and hit the gym before Lanie came by.

When he opened the front door, Lanie stood on the other side with wild eyes and a dazed expression. "Sorry I didn't call first. Can I come in?"

"Of course. You know you're always welcome."

He closed the door behind her and grabbed her upper arms. The look on her face scared him. He'd never seen her so frazzled.

"It's official," she said and then laughed or snorted; he wasn't sure which.

"What's official?" He felt like he had missed some crucial piece of information.

"My divorce." She held up a paper he hadn't even seen clutched tightly in her hand.

"Ah." He knew this feeling. Even though he and Krista had been separated for years before she filed, the final proclamation that his marriage was over had hit him similarly. "It's going to be okay," he said, moving his arms to the back of her waist.

Before he could say another word, she leaned up and covered her lips with his own. He responded, enjoying the soft feel of her mouth, until the intensity changed. Emotions he had never experienced from Lanie poured into him and with all his energy, he pushed her back.

"Lanie, not like this. You're hurting, and you're not thinking straight." Though he wanted to be intimate with her, she had often said she wouldn't have sex outside of marriage. It was one reason he didn't kiss her as much as he wanted to because he was afraid if he started, he might not be able to honor her wishes.

Instead of words, her reply was another fevered kiss. Her hands locked around his neck, and though he knew they'd probably both regret it in the morning, he let her lead him up the stairs and to his bed.

~

*W*hen Azarius woke the next morning, he sensed something was missing before he even opened his eyes. His hand reached out, but the place where Lanie should have been was empty and cold.

He forced his eyes open, but the room was empty. On the other pillow lay a white piece of paper. 'I'm sorry' was all it said, but somehow Azarius knew it was more than an apology for last night. In the pit of his stomach he suspected he had lost her for good, and a darkness descended upon him.

CHAPTER 5

*L*anie Perkins Hall stared at the two-story house she had once called home and sighed. Coming home felt like a failure and not at all how she imagined her life at thirty. At this point, she was supposed to be married with three kids - two boys and a girl or two girls and a boy. Instead, she found herself divorced, childless, alone, and back in Star Lake where single men were as prevalent as four-leaf clovers, but she hadn't known where to turn after last night.

She had spent the morning avoiding Azarius's calls while she hired a moving company and a realtor to sell the house. Her final stop before making the trip home was the radio station where she requested a leave of absence. It wasn't normally done, but Lanie had been such a staple at the station for so long that the manager had agreed to give her six months to sort her life out and decide what she wanted to do.

With that chapter of her life mostly closed - she'd have to deal with Azarius at some point - she packed a few bags, threw them in her car, and pointed it to the last place she had felt grounded: Star Lake.

With a sigh, she turned the engine off and popped the trunk. Inside was a small suitcase with some clothes and toiletries, her tablet, and a few books. The rest of her furniture and clothes would arrive later.

"Lanie, you're here!" Her mother's voice carried from the porch where she stood waving. Lanie shut the trunk and grabbed her purse from the passenger side before mounting the few steps to join her mother, an older, plumper version of herself.

"Hi, Mom. Thanks for letting me crash here a few days while I find a place."

"We couldn't leave you on the street, honey, and don't worry about a place." She held the door open for Lanie to enter. "You can stay here as long as you'd like."

Lanie forced a smile and swallowed her reply. If she had anywhere else to go, she wouldn't be crashing with her parents. Though she loved them, they were easier to tolerate in smaller doses like at Christmas or Thanksgiving. If she'd planned better, she could have rented a room at the inn, but spring was Layla's busiest time, and Lanie didn't want to be an inconvenience.

"Dad is watching TV if you want to stop in and say hi."

"Can I drop my bag off first?" Lanie asked. Elaine, her mother, was easy to get along with, but her father was another matter. Ex-military, Bob had always been strict, and he hadn't jumped for joy when she moved away or when she married Denny. He'd be even more disappointed if he learned about her latest indiscretion, but she hoped never to have that discussion with him.

Her mother seemed to understand the hesitation as she nodded and ran her hands over the faded apron across her front. "I'll be in the kitchen. When you get settled in, come and join me."

"Thanks, Mother." Lanie continued down the familiar hallway

to her old bedroom. A faded patch stood out in the middle of the door where her "Danger! Moody Teenager" sign used to hang. The door opened, revealing a room decorated in pink and beige. That hadn't been the way it had looked in high school, but after she moved out, her mother had removed the posters, re-painted the walls, and mellowed the color scheme. Lanie couldn't blame her. While John Stamos had aged well, he was no longer the teen heartthrob he had been at one time.   Lanie set her suitcase on the floor and plopped down on the full-size bed. It wasn't as comfortable as her own bed, but it would do for the few days she planned to be here. House hunting was in her immediate future.

She lay back and regarded the ceiling, wishing she didn't have to greet her father. Not that she didn't love him, but he was a ritualistic Christian who didn't believe in divorce. While she didn't either, sometimes life didn't turn out as planned. She certainly hadn't planned last night, and she'd asked repeatedly for forgiveness. Still, she wondered if the guilt would ever leave her. With a sigh, she pushed herself off the bed and prepared to face the music.   True to form, her father occupied the old recliner and faced the television. A home improvement show blared back at him. For as long as memory served her, this was how he spent his evenings. Elaine would cook, they would eat, and then her father would retire to the living room. Lanie wondered if her parents loved each other any longer or if they had decided being roommates was enough after such a long time together.

"Hi, Dad." Lanie perched on the tan couch, ready to flee if he became too disagreeable.

"Hello, Lanie." An eye flick her direction, but words cool as ice. "You couldn't try counseling, huh?"

"It wasn't all my decision, Dad. Denny didn't want to try counseling. What was I supposed to do, beg?"

"Pray, for one."

"I prayed, Dad, but it didn't work out." Lanie tried to hide her exasperation at her father not hearing her words.

"What are you planning for employment?" he asked, changing the subject.

"I'm not sure yet. Being a disc jockey was fun, but no radio station exists around here, and even if one did, I doubt the pay would be enough." Lanie had thought little about work, but the question gave her pause. There weren't many skills in her arsenal. Radio had been her passion in college and had become her career. A few odd jobs existed in her past, but nothing boasting much talent.

"Work at the store," he suggested. "I'm getting older and would like to spend more time at home. I'd always hoped you would take it over."

This was not new information. Her father had been pushing for her to run the shop since she was sixteen, and while it wasn't where she wanted to end up permanently, it would solve her immediate employment issues and give her a steady income while she decided what she wanted to do with the rest of her life. "I can do that, Dad. I can't guarantee I'll take it over, but I'll help until I decide what I want to do next."

His sniff showed his annoyance that she was still not following his footsteps, but he kept the thought to himself. "Fine then," was all he said.

Lanie rolled her eyes, wondering if she and her father would ever have a better relationship. "I wonder if Mom needs any help," she said, standing and moving toward the exit.

Her father nodded as she exited the room and made her way to the kitchen where her mother was finishing cleaning. A neatnik, her mother never retired for the night until the kitchen was spotless.

"Up for a game?" Elaine asked.

Lanie and her mother had often passed the time playing card games when Lanie was growing up.

"Sure, how about some Yahtzee?" Lanie pulled out a barstool and sat down across from her mother. Though she hadn't played in ages–Denny had never been interested–Lanie enjoyed the challenge.

~

*L*anie woke the next morning as the first rays of light peeked in her window. A visit to Layla, her high school chum, was on her docket before approaching the realtor to see what was available. After pulling on a pair of jeans and a shirt, she ran a brush through her hair and headed to the kitchen for some coffee and cereal.

Her father sat at the table, a mug on his right and his Bible open in front of him. He read it every morning before work without fail. Lanie wished she had his passion for studying the important book, but some days, even though she knew she should, she couldn't get into it. Her lack of being in the word probably had a lot to do with her slip as well.

"Will you be able to work the evening shift tonight?" he asked without looking up.

Lanie stifled a sigh as she pulled a mug from the cupboard. Couldn't he have started with a 'good morning' at least? "Yeah, Dad, I should be able to. I'm visiting the realtor today hoping to find a house to rent, but I should finish by four. Will that work?"

"We close at eight," he said, looking up at her. "That's a short shift."

Lanie bit her lip as she poured the coffee. She didn't want to start the morning by fighting with her father. "It's just for today, Dad. Once I have a place rented, I can start earlier, okay?"

His hazel eyes regarded her, and just like when she was

younger, she shrunk under the gaze. How did he make her feel small even at age thirty?

"I suppose it will have to do," he said, as his eyes dropped back to the Bible.

With a shake of her head, Lanie took a sip of her coffee and decided to get breakfast out. She no longer felt like sitting even for a bowl of cereal.

Another few large gulps of coffee sent enough caffeine through her system she assumed she could make it until she found more. Max served coffee at The Diner, and she had seen a new bakery on her drive in which might have an even better option. She rinsed the cup in the sink and placed it in the dish rack.

"Tell Mom I'll be back later," Lanie called as she headed for the front door, grabbing a light jacket on the way. Without even bothering to pull it on, she opened the door and stepped outside.

Though nearing summer, an unusual chill nipped at her light jacket, sending a shiver down her spine as she closed the door behind her. She jammed her hands in the sleeves and snuggled down into the jacket as she zipped it up. The keys jingled in her right pocket, and she retrieved them as she walked to the car. It wasn't a long walk into town, but it was a little too cold for the jaunt today, especially since she had left without her scarf and gloves.

The cold leather seats had barely warmed up when she parked the car in front of the Star Lake Inn.

"Lanie," Layla shrieked as she entered the foyer.   Lanie smiled as her high school friend came around the desk and enveloped her in a hug. "Hey, Layla. You look great." Layla always looked good. With her long dark hair and blue eyes, she had been the focus of the boys in high school, though her eyes had only been on Max and the rumor was they had finally gotten together.

"You do too," Layla said, stepping back to inspect Lanie.

"I'm okay," Lanie said, rolling her eyes. "I need to increase my gym time."

"Oh pooh, you look amazing. Now you need a man."

Lanie shook her head, remembering the last night before she left. It wasn't an awful experience, but it was a mistake that should never have happened. "I'm in no hurry to jump back into a relationship, but it looks great on you. When did you and Max get together?"

"A few months ago," Layla said, returning to the desk. "He finally gathered the nerve to tell me how he felt. Of course, true to Max form, it wasn't the most romantic revealing. He blurted it out one evening as he was closing, and all I could say was 'what took you so long?'" Layla chuckled as she arranged things on the desk.

"Well, better late than never," Lanie said. "I'm glad you two got it together. Will there be a wedding soon?"

"I don't know," Layla said with a shake of her head. "Maybe after another decade, but a wedding is happening soon."

"Oh yeah? Who's getting married?" Lanie wasn't a fan of gossip, but in a small town where everyone knew everybody, it was hard not to be curious. "Presley Hays and Brandon Scott. Remember them?"

Lanie searched her memory. "Behind us in school, right?"

"Yep. Presley moved back about nine months ago, and Brandon came home early December to help his father out. I guess sparks rekindled, and the rest is history as they say."

Lanie longed for a love story like that. Having always been a hopeless romantic growing up, she had pined for her wedding day, probably so much that she had put expectations on her relationship with Denny that he would never have been able to fulfill. "Well, that's great," she said, swallowing her own disappointment and faking happiness for the couple. "I should run to the realtor soon, but I wanted to ask, is The Diner the best place for coffee or have we gotten anything better?"

Layla chuckled. "I'm a bit biased, but I think Max's coffee is fine. However, if you're looking for something other than black, Presley opened Sweet Treats across the way and makes a decent cup too."

"Thanks, I'll try it. I'm working for my father until something better comes along, but we should get together soon."

"You bet," Layla said, as the phone rang. She waved goodbye as she picked up the receiver. "Thank you for calling The Star Lake Inn, how can I help you?"

Lanie exited the way she had come and climbed back in her car. Though she desperately wanted a cup of coffee, with no idea how long the house search would take, she figured she should hit the realtor first.

A petite blond woman was opening the office as Lanie pulled in. Since she didn't recognize the woman and the name of the building wasn't what she remembered, Lanie assumed she was newer to town.

After locking the car doors, Lanie dropped her keys in her pocket and pushed open the door to the realtor office.

"Hello," the woman said, greeting her as she walked in. "I just opened, but I'll be happy to help you in a minute. Would you like coffee?" She pointed to a Keurig and Lanie smiled, nodded, and walked to the table.

A silver metal tree-like apparatus sat next to the dispenser holding a variety of pods. Lanie grabbed a caramel mocha one and popped it in the coffee maker. When the coffee had filled, she held it to her nose, sniffing in the wonderful aroma before taking a sip. The warm beverage flowed down her throat, warming her from the inside out.

"Okay, I'm ready now," the woman said. "Have a seat." She pointed to the chairs across from the desk, and Lanie sat down in the one closest to her. "I'm Annie Goodman," she said, reaching her hand across the desk for a shake. "What can I do for you today?"

"I'm looking to rent a house. One or two bedrooms. Something in town if possible."

Annie's pink lips pursed as she turned to the computer on the right side of her desk. "Hmm, I rented the last two-bedroom house in town a few weeks ago, but let me see if there is a one bedroom available."

Lanie wasn't surprised at the lack of real estate. Few people moved to Star Lake unless they were moving back to be near family, like she was.

"Well, I have two. I'm sorry that's not much selection, but would you like to see them?

"Yes, please." Large selection or not, Lanie needed a place that wasn't her old room in her parent's house.

Annie led the way, flipping the open sign over so it now read 'be back soon.'

"Aren't you going to lock the front door?" Lanie asked.

"No need," Annie said. "There's nothing here to steal and besides, it's warmer in here than waiting outside if someone else comes by. Shall we take my car?"

Lanie nodded and climbed in the passenger side, curious how Annie could stay warm in her knee-length pencil skirt and heels. Though she wore a long-sleeved shirt, she hadn't even grabbed a coat.

The first stop was a small brown and tan cottage on Earl street. It appeared in good shape from the outside with a little garden area and a single car garage. The inside was also in decent shape. A beige carpet lined the floors, and the kitchen and bathroom boasted a neutral color scheme. Though the bedroom was a little smaller than she was looking for, Lanie liked that the house was close to work, which meant she could walk and save on gas.   The second house was a little bigger, but farther on the outskirts of town, and though it was a little cheaper, it didn't have the homey feel the first house had presented.

"Well, have you decided?" Annie asked as Lanie finished the tour of the second house.

"Yes, I like the first place. I'll be working at my dad's ice cream shop, and I like that I could walk to work."

Annie's eyes lit up. "Oh, Mr. Perkins? I love his triple chocolate brownie sundae."

Lanie smirked as she remembered the day she created that dessert. Donald Preston, a boy from a neighboring town, had decided she was too mousy and ordinary to continue dating. Crushed, she'd wandered into the shop, looking for something chocolatey to drown her sorrows in. She'd dumped in brownies, Oreos, and chocolate chips. Then she'd topped it with chocolate ice cream, whip cream, chocolate sauce, and a cherry on the top for good measure. The dessert hadn't healed her broken heart, but it had tasted delicious, and she'd named it the Triple Chocolate Brownie Sundae and added it to the menu. "Yep, that's my favorite dessert too. I named it when I was sixteen."

"That's so sweet that your father kept it all these years. I shouldn't frequent the shop as much as I do," Annie said, leaning in as if sharing a juicy secret, "but with no real night life and few men around, a girl's gotta do something for fun, you know?"

"What brought you out here then?" Lanie asked. She knew how boring her town could be.

"My uncle owned the realtor office before me, but he retired to Florida. Having no kids of his own, he called me up to see if I was interested. I was working in a competitive agency in Atlanta, so I thought owning an office might be a good change of pace, but I failed to realize just how small this town is."

"It grows on you though," Lanie said, "and the town puts on great festivals near the holidays."

"I'll look forward to that then," Annie said with a laugh. "Well, shall we head back and get your paperwork in order?"

Lanie nodded and a few minutes later they were pulling into the office parking lot again.

~

*A*zarius lay in the middle of his bed watching the black netting sway back and forth from the gentle breeze blowing in the window. There was a chill in the air, but he didn't feel it. He was too numb. The smell of her shampoo, some strawberry vanilla concoction, still lingered on his pillow, and when he closed his eyes, he could see her auburn hair splayed across his pillow. It had only been one night, but it was a night burned in his memory.

When she had finally responded to his text that she thought their night together had been a mistake, he had understood. After all, he knew her religion was important to her, and she had reacted emotionally to her divorce finalization - his own had been finalized for over a year - but when a second message had come in that she was leaving town, he'd retired to his room. Though he knew he cared for Lanie, he hadn't expected her leaving to hit him so hard.

A knock sounded at his door, but he chose to ignore it, hoping his roommate would go away. Normally, Greg would never enter his room, but he hadn't spoken to him all day. Azarius had barely left his room for work, and as soon as he'd gotten home, he had retired up the stairs, not even flashing a wave or granting a mumble as he passed Greg.

"Az, you okay man?" The door swung in a few inches, and Greg's bearded face appeared in the small crack. "I've never seen you like this."

"I'm fine," Azarius said. He grabbed the remote and turned up the volume. Real Life's "Send Me An Angel" blared out of the big screen TV, reminding him of the first day he met her.

Azarius opened the glass door and stepped into the foyer of the radio station. A woman's voice echoed over the loudspeaker.

"That was Real Life's "Send Me an Angel," which was made famous by the movie The Wizard."

He looked around for the voice. An older woman manned a large desk in the middle of the room, but a phone was to her ear, so it wasn't her voice he had heard. To his left was a glass window, but an older gentleman stood in front of a mic. Azarius turned to his right, and his lips parted. Behind a similar glass window, a beautiful woman stood speaking into a mic.

"I always loved the beat in the middle. I know you can't see me jamming, but I have an air drum solo every time I play this song. Now I know why my mother never let take drum lessons."

The smile that stretched across her mouth lit up her whole face. She looked up, catching his eyes, and flashed another smile.

"I'm Lanie Wolffe, and you're listening to Mixx 98.6. Be sure to give me a call if there's something you want to hear. Duran Duran's "Come Undone" is coming up next, so don't go far."

The voice was replaced by the sound of commercials, and Azarius shook his head. He missed the angelic melody of the woman. She glanced his direction again, and seeing him still watching her, she raised her hand in a small wave. A playful smile resided on her lips, and she flashed a wink with her left eye.

Azarius returned the wave and then continued on to the desk. Whoever the redheaded beauty was, she was not the one he was supposed to be meeting, at least he didn't think she was.

The woman behind the desk hung up the phone and glanced up at him. "Can I help you?"

"Yes, ma'am. I'm Azarius Jacobson, and I'm here about the engineer

position." He pulled his resume out of the satchel he was carrying and slid it across the counter to her.

"Ah, yes. Wait here, and I'll call Mr. Johnson."

"You are not fine. What is going on? Talk to me man." Greg still didn't dare to enter fully into the room. Thankfully, he'd known Azarius long enough to know that his room was his sacred space.

"I don't feel like talking right now."

"Alright, brother, but I'm here if you need me." Greg wasn't his brother, but they had been friends for the last few years and Greg had helped Azarius through some very tough times.

Azarius mumbled and rolled his face into the pillow that still held her smell. A minute later, the door clicked closed, and the darkness descended once more. Closing his eyes, Azarius replayed the last few months with her in his mind, ending with the night that ended it all.

The raucous night had been at her prompting. Perhaps he should have tried harder to tell her no; maybe he should have demanded they wait, or maybe it wasn't even the night itself. Maybe it was his evasiveness. He thought back to the many times she asked him to open up and mentally kicked himself. Would he ever get the chance to show her his true feelings?

CHAPTER 6

*L*anie sighed as she donned the pink apron with a smiling ice cream cone on it a few days later. This certainly wasn't how she had seen her life going, but it was a minor setback. Once she figured out what she wanted to do next, she could start saving and move on from here. At least she had managed to find a small house to rent, so she no longer had to live with her parents, even if she did have to work for them.

She pulled out her phone and checked the screen for the umpteenth time. Even though she had been the one who said they shouldn't see each other again, she had expected he would reach out to her, but her phone remained silent. Perhaps Greg had been wrong about his feelings for her.

The bell above the door jingled, and Lanie pocketed the phone, hoping her visitor hadn't caught her slacking off.

"Whatever you're hiding, you don't have to hide it from me," Layla said with a laugh.

"Hey, what are you doing here?"

"I came for the ice cream of course," Layla said, swinging her slim hips onto the barstool across from Lanie. "I took a dinner break with Max and thought I'd stop in to see you. You all settled in?"

"Mostly, I still have a few boxes to unpack. I know coming home was the right thing to do, but I have to admit it's kind of quiet and lonely in the evenings."

Layla's lips pulled into a knowing smile. "I understand that. Even when Max and I hang out, he isn't the biggest conversationalist."

Lanie smirked, remembering many of her evenings with Azarius. He wasn't much for conversing either, preferring to watch videos and engage in small talk when necessary. Still, there had been a comfort with him, an ease she hadn't felt with Denny in a long time, and somehow being near him had been enough, until she ruined it.

"What are you thinking about?" Layla asked, narrowing her eyes and leaning across the counter.

"Nothing. What do you mean?" Lanie grabbed a rag and began wiping the counter, keeping her eyes away from Layla's penetrating gaze.

"You know what I mean. You were just thinking about something or should I say someone," Layla said with emphasis. "You got all moony faced."

Lanie sighed and stopped pretending to clean. "I was thinking about this man I left in Dallas.

"Denny?"

"No, not Denny." Layla's brow arched and Lanie knew there was no way she would drop the subject now.

"When Denny and I separated, I ran into an old friend I used to work with. We met years ago at the radio station - he was an engineer, though I don't remember him much from back then. He disappeared about the time I married Denny, but the day Denny left, I went to the old bar hangout and he was there. We started talking, realized we had a lot in common, and began hanging out."

Layla folded her hands and placed her chin on the top of them. "And?"

Lanie rolled her eyes. "It's not what you think. We watched eighties videos and made fun of them, but it was comfortable. Anyway, we began hanging out more often, once or twice a week."

"Don't you mean dating?" Layla asked.

A small snort escaped Lanie's lips. "I don't think you could call it dating. We didn't go anywhere together, just hung out at his house."

"That doesn't sound fun," Layla said slowly.

Lanie sighed. "It wasn't about what we did. It was just being together. We'd dance to old songs or watch old videos and sing. When he looked at me, I felt like he was seeing me, like he cared about my interests."

"Is he a good kisser?"

"What?" A blush spread across Lanie's cheeks, and she averted her eyes.

"You heard me. I refuse to believe you only watched old videos on television, so spill it."

Lanie bit the inside of her cheek, remembering the first time she and Azarius had kissed. While this kiss itself had been okay, it was the look in his eyes before their lips touched that had seared itself in her memory and kept her coming back for more. "Fine, yes, he's a good kisser, but he doesn't kiss much."

"What do you mean?" Layla leaned back and folded her arms across her chest.

"I don't know; it's weird. I love kissing, but he didn't initiate it much."

"Was that why it didn't last?"

Lanie shook her head. "No, while I would have preferred more, there was something about the way he looked at me that made the kissing or lack thereof not as important."

Layla leaned forward and splayed her hands across the counter. "Okay, what happened then?"

"It just didn't work out," Lanie said, skirting the question. "I think I was looking for more than he was, and I realized it would never work in the long run."

"Well, it's good you found out now," Layla said. "You know what you want now, so why mess around?"

Lanie nodded, glad that Layla wasn't pushing further. She was embarrassed she had let the last night happen, and she didn't feel like airing that laundry yet.

The overhead bell jingled again, and both women looked to the door. A man in a checkered shirt and drab brown coat entered. His hair was perfectly slicked down except for a cowlick in the back that resembled Alfalfa.

"Hello, Bert," Layla said, "What are you doing here?"

"Oh, hello, Layla, I wasn't expecting to see you here. I heard a familiar face was back in town, and I thought I'd come and say hello to Lanie. Hello, Lanie." He raised his hand in a wave.

Lanie pasted a smile on her face. "Hello, Bert."

"Why didn't you bring Amelia?" Layla asked.

A red blush spread across Bert's cheeks. "Oh, Amelia had to work late, but I'll probably bring her next time. Well, nice to see you again, Lanie." Bert executed an awkward bow before turning and scooting out the door.

"What was that about?" Lanie asked.

A small chuckle escaped Layla's mouth. "I'm pretty sure he was coming here to check you out. Though he has been seeing Amelia, I don't think it's as serious as he would like, and you are the new commodity in town. You're welcome."

It took a moment, but when Layla's meaning clarified in Lanie's head, she laughed as well. "You don't think he'd try to ask me out, do you?"

"I wouldn't put anything past Bert. I stopped trying to understand him years ago." Layla's dark locks bounced as she shook her head. "Well, I better get back to the inn."

"Wait, will you go to church with me on Sunday?"

Layla hesitated. "I don't know, Lanie. Church isn't really my thing."

"I know, but it's my first week back, and I wasn't very dedicated back in Dallas. I want to try to recommit, but I don't really remember everyone, and there are some new faces."

Layla looked unconvinced.

"Please, don't make me have to sit with my parents." Lanie knew she was begging, and while she was perfectly capable of sitting alone, the thought held no appeal.

"Alright," Layla said with a sigh. "I'll go with you this week, but don't get used to it."

Lanie smiled. If she could get Layla in the door, there was hope she could get her to see religion wasn't bad. Lanie had never pushed Layla, but she had always prayed for her and now that she was back in town, it seemed the perfect time to motivate her more closely.

～

It was dark when Lanie left the store that night. The air was still crisp and cold, and Lanie hunched her shoulders against the chill. Few people lined the streets as most of Star Lake retired indoors when the sun set, but a few shop owners were locking their doors or just setting home as she passed them.

"Well, well, well. I wondered when I would see you, Lanie Perkins."

Paula's unmistakable boisterous voice sounded behind her and Lanie turned, forcing a tight smile across her lips. It wasn't that she disliked Paula, but the woman had to be at the center of everything and was a hopeless gossip, not of the malicious kind usually, but Lanie had been hoping to avoid being the center of Paula's attention.

"I'm so sorry. I've been meaning to come and see you sooner, but you know how it gets before a recital." She flicked a scarf as red as her lipstick over her left shoulder. "We are working hard for the summer program, though it certainly doesn't feel like summer right now, does it? Will you be coming?"

Paula's question appeared innocent, but Lanie knew ulterior motives threaded her carefully chosen words.

"I don't know, Paula. It depends on if my father needs me to work the shop that night."

"Of course, but I wanted to let you know that boyfriends are not required. You don't have to be part of a couple to come."

Ah, there it was. The dig. Even though Paula had never married that Lanie knew of, she had long been obsessed with men and often resented those who were in relationships. She was probably getting some sick pleasure out of Lanie's divorce.

"I mean, I heard about your divorce." Paula leaned forward as she spoke, whispering the last word as if it were a dirty secret. "We're all sorry for you, dear, but don't let that keep you from enjoying the festivities of the town."

"Don't worry, Paula, I won't." Lanie wanted to add a snippy remark about Paula never having a man either, but she chose to be the bigger person and keep the thoughts in her head. "It was good to see you." Before Paula could continue, Lanie twirled around and continued her walk to Earl Street. She had certainly not missed this aspect of small town life.

The dark house elicited a sigh from her as she rummaged in her pocket for the keys. Not for the first time, she wondered if she should have stayed in Dallas. There she had Azarius and his roommate Greg, whom she had gotten to know the last few times she had stopped by. Perhaps she and Azarius could have discussed their mistake and started over, but then she remembered the frustrating nights she had spent wondering why he wouldn't share information with her and the days she had spent waiting for a message from him asking her to come over, only to never get it and have to ask him if he wanted to see her. No, if she had stayed she would have been settling again, just like she had with Denny. She wanted someone to want her, to fight for her attention, and to share his life with her - the good and the bad.

With a sigh, Lanie flicked on the living room light and shut the door behind her. She was not going to settle this time even though it was tempting. At least she had her books and her television shows to keep her company until the perfect man came along. She might never have a chance with Jensen Ackles but he would do until her Romeo arrived.

~

*A*zarius scowled as Greg changed the channel. "Hey, I was watching that."

"No, you weren't," Greg said, muting the television. "You were staring off into space, thinking about whatever you've been obsessing over lately, and I can't hear this song one more time. What does it even mean?"

"It means everything," Azarius said.

Greg shook his head. "Dude, sometimes your riddles are too hard to figure out. Is this about Lanie?"

The name sliced Azarius like a dagger, and his eyes darted to Greg, but he said nothing.

"Look, I wasn't going to pry, but she hasn't been around this week, and you've been in a dark place the last few days, and I know dark places, so I just figured they were connected. Tell me what happened."

Azarius shook his head and folded his arms. "It doesn't matter."

"Yeah, it does man. I can't keep seeing you like this, especially because I know how much she cared about you."

Azarius's eyes narrowed. "How do you know how she felt?"

Greg sighed. "Because she told me man. You remember that day you were helping my sister out, and you came home late?"

The evening flashed to the front of Azarius's mind. He had made plans with Lanie when Cheryl had called, wanting help in moving furniture to set up a surprise party for Greg that weekend. Thinking he would have time to help before his date with Lanie, he had agreed, but the traffic along with Cheryl's indecisiveness had led to him arriving home over an hour later than he planned. Lanie had waited, but she hadn't been too happy with him. "Yeah, I remember. What about it?"

"I never told you, but Lanie came in that night at eight. I had left the door unlocked, and I guess she thought maybe you fell asleep waiting for her, so she tried the lock and came in when it opened. Scared me half to death," he laughed, "because I was sitting in the kitchen in the dark nursing a headache. It was a day my depression hit hard, so I hadn't been sleeping much."

Azarius motioned for him to continue, trying to urge him to get to the meat of his story.

"She asked if I knew where you were, and I didn't at the time, but I told her she could wait for you. Anyway, we got to talking, and I asked her how serious she was because you know, I wanted to look out for you and avoid another Krista. She told me she could be serious if she knew you were serious."

"I was serious," Azarius said, leaning forward.

Greg held up his hand. "I know you were, but she didn't. She said she was confused by you; she wanted you to open up to her more, to show her you wanted her."

"I sent her that song."

"What song?" Greg asked, confused. "That Nine Inch Nails song you keep playing? That's hardly romantic."

"But I told her she means everything."

"Yeah, but then you never ask her over," Greg continued.

"I told her she was always welcome," Azarius protested.

"That's not the same thing," Greg said. "She wanted you to want her to come over. She wanted to know that you wanted her around and not just that you didn't mind if she were here."

"How do you know that?" Azarius asked. While Lanie had told him she wanted him to want her, it had always been through texts.

"Because we texted a few times after that night," Greg said. "I didn't tell you because I didn't want you to think I was trying to pick her up, but she was confused and looking for answers. I never said much to reassure her though because I didn't want to cross you. Is that why she stopped coming around?"

The words bounced around his head. He had been sure she left solely because of the incident, but maybe it had been a combination of factors. "She stopped coming around because she moved," Azarius said.

Greg blinked. "She moved?"

"Yeah, when she came last time, she was emotional because her divorce had been finalized. I was elated because it meant we could be together, but we let our guard slip and we," he shrugged, "you know."

"Was it bad?" Greg asked.

"No, it was amazing," Azarius said with a smile, "but I shouldn't have let it happen. I knew she didn't believe in intimacy outside of marriage, but I didn't stop it. The next day she texted that it had been a mistake and she wanted to step back. I was fine with that, but then I got a message that she was moving back to her hometown."

"You think it was just because you guys crossed the line?" Greg asked.

"I did, but after what you said, I'm wondering if I drove her away before that. Maybe the incident wouldn't have been that upsetting if I hadn't kept her at arm's length before that."

"So, what are you going to do?"

Azarius shrugged. "What can I do?"

Greg's head dropped forward as his brow arched. "What do you mean what can you do? You go and get her."

"She probably wouldn't come back anyway."

"That's not the point. Do you miss her?"

Azarius nodded.

"Do you love her?"

"I," Azarius opened his mouth and paused. Did he love her? He enjoyed having her around, and he always felt better when she was in the room, but was that love? "I don't know," he said. "All I know is that everything feels more complete when she's here."

"Then you have to tell her," Greg said. "Where is her hometown?"

"I don't know, some small town. Sun City? Star Shore? Star Lake," Azarius said, snapping his fingers.

Greg whipped out his phone and tapped the screen. "Star Lake isn't far from here. You could take some time off and go woo her."

"I can't take time off. I just started this new job."

"Then go on the weekend, man, but don't let her get away. I know you are scared, but I think you guys are perfect for each other, and I know you are going to regret it if you don't at least tell her." Greg tossed the remote back to Azarius and headed up the stairs to his room.

Azarius held his finger over the volume button, but didn't press it. Maybe Greg was right. Could he open his heart again and let

Lanie fully in? More importantly, could he live with himself if he didn't try? He definitely didn't like the way he had been feeling the last few days, but would it get better? His friends called him a gambler, but he was no longer sure which would be the bigger gamble.

CHAPTER 7

*L*anie's doorbell rang at nine am on the button. Layla stood on the other side, nervously brushing her slacks.

"You made it," Lanie said.

"I feel silly. Do I look alright?" Layla tucked a dark strand behind her ear, and Lanie smiled at the nervous gesture. Layla was normally so collected; it was funny to see her struggling.

"You look wonderful, and it's church, not a dinner engagement. We're there to worship and reflect, not win pageants."

"I'm sorry. I told you I was no good at this," Layla said.

"You'll be fine. Want to walk or drive?"

"Drive. I want to get it over with."

"It's not a death march you know," Lanie laughed, grabbing her jacket and Bible before stepping out and locking the door behind her.

"Maybe not for you. Religion was never big at my house."

"It shouldn't be about religion anyway. It's about a relationship with Jesus." Something Lanie had forgotten lately.

Layla shook her head as she climbed in the passenger seat. "I don't see the difference, but that's okay."

Lanie smiled and put the car in gear. The church was just a few minutes down the road, a small building with beautiful stained-glass windows.

"I thought it would be bigger," Layla said as she exited the car.

Lanie chuckled. "Star Lake is a small town; why would we need a bigger building?"

"I guess that's true," Layla agreed. "I just think of the churches on movies I suppose. They are always big and imposing."

"My church in Dallas was a lot bigger, but I rather like the smaller, homier feel."

"Welcome to Star Lake Church." An elderly woman in a long dress smiled and handed them a thin bulletin.

Lanie couldn't remember her name, but she was fairly certain this same woman had been a greeter ten years ago before she left for college. "Thank you," she said, scanning the bulletin as she led Layla inside.

The layout of the service hadn't changed much either, it seemed. There was still music to open with, a prayer time, the service, and then closing music. What had changed was the pastor's name. She didn't think it had been Tom when she left though she couldn't remember what it had been. Also, the sanctuary had been updated.

The red velvet pews had been removed and replaced with rows of grey chairs. Lanie assumed the change had come about to offer more versatility to the space.

A white screen now hung at the back of the stage as well for the words to be projected on and several more instruments filled the stage area. All Lanie remembered was a piano before she left, but now there was a drum set and at least two guitars as well.

The room was not yet full as she led Layla to a seat near the front; however, before they even sat down, they were approached by several elderly women.

"Lanie Perkins, is that you?" one woman with a slightly blue tint to her hair asked. "I haven't seen you in ages. Are you home for good?"

"For now," Lanie said.

"We were so sorry to hear about your divorce," the other woman added, "but I bet your mother is so pleased to have you home."

"I'm sure she is," Lanie said with a tight smile. An awkward silence descended until finally the women pretended to see someone else to talk to and scurried away.

"Ugh, that is the one thing I didn't miss while I was gone," Lanie said to Layla. "I hate that everyone knows everything about you in small towns."

Layla nodded. "Definitely hard to keep secrets, that's for sure."

The musicians came out then and the worship began. Lanie enjoyed the familiar songs, and though her life was not where she wanted it to be, she felt a small measure of peace as the music flowed around her. The new pastor was a good speaker as well though Lanie was surprised by how young he seemed.

When the service ended, she turned to Layla. "Well, was it as bad as you thought it would be?"

With a slow shake of her head, Layla responded, "No, it was actually kind of nice. I might even consider coming back sometime."

Lanie smiled as a feeling of joy for her friend coursed through her. "Good, well how about some lunch? I'll treat you to one of Max's famous cheeseburgers."

Layla laughed as she stood and filed out of the row. "You do know I get my food for free now that we're dating, right?"

"Now that you're dating? I bet you never paid for food," Lanie teased.

"Yeah, I guess you're right."

The girls' laughter was cut short as Lanie's parents appeared in the exit doorway.

"Lanie, we're so glad to see you made it to church," her father said.

"Yes, Dad," Lanie said with a sigh. "Just because my marriage didn't work out doesn't mean I'm not still committed to Jesus. I plan to be here every week for as long as I'm in town."

"That's wonderful, Dear," her mother said. "Perhaps you could come over soon for dinner. We haven't seen you in nearly a week."

Lanie swallowed a sigh. She had enjoyed not being around her father every day, but she knew, living in town, her parents would want to see her more often. "I'll try to get out this week, Mother."

"Good, have a wonderful week, sweetheart."

Elaine drew Lanie in for a hug before turning away to greet a friend.

"Hurry, before anyone else stops us," Lanie whispered. The girls sped up their footsteps as they trotted out to the car.

"I guess I'm glad my folks don't live in town," Layla said, a teasing gleam in her eye.

"Yes, you should be very glad. On the other hand, it is nice having family around."

The two women piled into the car for the short trip to The Diner.

CHAPTER 8

"*D*o you want me to come with you?" Greg asked as he leaned against the doorframe and watched Azarius pack an overnight bag.

"Not this time," Azarius said, rolling a shirt and stuffing it in the duffel bag. It was a tactic he had perfected from his many deployments while in the Army. "I don't know if she'll even want to see me. I'd rather my humiliation happen in private if it's going to happen."

"She's not going to turn you away," Greg said. "I'm telling you, I think she really cares for you."

"We'll find out soon enough. At least Star Lake isn't too far away, so worst case I'll be out some gas and maybe a night's stay somewhere." Azarius ducked into the bathroom and grabbed his razor and deodorant.

"You have to stop thinking like that," Greg said when he came back into view. "Think positive for once in your life."

Azarius sighed. He knew Greg was right. His negativity was part of what had driven Lanie away in the first place, but he'd learned long ago it was effective in protecting his heart. Unfortunately, it also kept him from getting close to anyone, and now he'd finally met a woman he wanted to get close to. He pulled the string, closing the bag, and threw it over his shoulder.

"Okay, hold down the fort and wish me luck."

Greg stepped out of the way, so he could pass by. "You don't need luck if you just tell her the truth."

Azarius set his jaw and nodded. The truth. Hopefully, he would be able to do, but he'd been deflecting so long he wasn't sure he knew how to tell the truth any longer. He flicked his hand in a wave and headed down the stairs, grabbing his keys from the entry way table as he stepped out of the front door and pulled it shut behind him.

He opened the door to his lime green Mustang, tossing the duffel bag on the passenger seat before settling down in the black leather driver's seat. The leather molded to his body, providing a modicum of comfort to his anxiety-ridden heart.

Two hours later, he slowed the car as he entered the small town of Star Lake. The green sign had boasted less than five thousand residents, and the existence of a solitary street light enforced that idea. As he passed through the small downtown area, he realized he had no idea how to find Lanie, but surely in a place this small, he could just ask in one of the businesses and find her.

When the store fronts faded into residential houses, he turned the car around and headed back for the main corner. A diner on the corner looked well lit, so he chose that and pulled into a spot in front.

Though lighted, the diner was mostly empty. A stubbled man in a ball cap and a flannel shirt stood behind the counter, a younger man in a checkered shirt sat at the counter, and a large woman with big hair and red lips filled a table.

All eyes turned to him as he stepped through the door. Not

unfriendly, the eyes were still wary, and the silence pressed down on him.

"Ahem, hello, I'm from out of town, but I'm hoping you can help me. I'm looking for Lanie Hall."

There was a moment of silence as the three looked from one to the other. The woman spoke first. "I assume you mean Lanie Perkins who came back to town a few weeks ago."

Perkins? The name confused him until he remembered that must be her maiden name. She had been Lanie Hall for most of the time he had known her, and if she had changed it back after the divorce, she hadn't told him.

"Yes, I am sure that's who I mean. Can you tell me where I can find her?"

"Well, I don't know if we should be sharing that information," the flannel-clad man said, crossing his arms and leaning back against the counter.

"Oh, I don't see the harm, Max," the woman said. "He said he was her friend." The way the woman emphasized the word friend made Azarius slightly uncomfortable, but if she led him to Lanie, that was all that mattered. "Lanie is working down at Perkins Ice Cream Parlor. Across the street."

Azarius nodded; he remembered the sign from his first time through town. "Thank you." He turned to leave, but the woman's voice stopped him.

"Shouldn't you at least tell us your name?"

"It's Azarius, Azarius Jacobson." He tapped his forehead in a mock salute before turning and exiting the diner. The ice cream parlor was a stone's throw from the diner, so Azarius didn't bother driving.

As he approached the ice cream parlor, his heart sped up in his chest. He had no idea how she would receive his showing up in her hometown unannounced.

The bell jingled overhead as he pushed open the door. Lanie

stood on the opposite end of the room near the cash register. Her face was focused downward as she spoke.

"Welcome to Mr. Perkins, what can I...?" Her voice trailed off as she looked up and saw him for the first time. "Azarius? What are you doing here?"

"Hi, Lanie. I needed to tell you some things."

He had hoped to see a smile or some sort of joy at seeing him again, but her face remained stoic. "Tell me? You rarely gave me a straight answer about anything, and then you didn't even try to stop me from leaving."

"I didn't know I was supposed to try to stop you from leaving. I thought giving you your space was what you wanted."

Her face softened slightly. "Fine. What's so important that you had to drive two hours to see me?"

Azarius sighed. "You aren't going to make this easy for me, are you?"

"No, I'm not," she said, leaning against the back wall as if trying to put as much space between them as possible. "I thought we were friends if not more after the last night, but I still don't even know when your birthday is."

He forced himself not to roll his eyes. Azarius should have just told her his birthday, but ignoring it was easier than telling most people why he didn't like birthdays. "I told you my birthday isn't a big deal. I didn't want you to make a big production of it because I'm terrible at reciprocating."

"I never said I had anything big planned. I just wanted you to share a part of your life with me. It's like you keep me at arms' reach most of the time. I wanted you to want me, but I always had to be the one calling or the one coming over. It's like you couldn't be bothered to contact me first."

Azarius thought back over the last few months and realized she was right. Other than the first few times they hung out, it had always been her asking to come over. Perhaps it had been his emotional wall to protect himself or perhaps he had just been being lazy, but he knew if he was going to have a chance with her, he needed to change that right now.

"You're right," he said, crossing the remaining distance until he was on the other side of the counter. "I can't apologize enough to you, but when you left, it made me realize how much I cared for you. I don't know if you can, but I'd like to give it another shot. I miss you, Lanie."

"I miss you too," she said, and the words lightened his heart, "but I don't know if it would be a good idea. I mean I live here now, at least for the time being, and I assume you'll still be in Dallas."

"I will, but we could spend weekends together until we figure it out. We could take turns driving, or to prove to you how serious I am, I'll drive every weekend."

"We can't let what happened, happen again," she said with a slight hesitation as if testing the waters.

"I'm okay with that," he said, leaning forward on the counter. "While that night was great, and I do look forward to a repeat performance someday, what I realized was that I felt complete just having you around, even if all we were doing was watching television, and I was miserable without you."

Lanie's hazel eyes bored into his soul. He resisted the urge to look away, to turn tail and run. He wanted her to see how serious he was even if her penetrating gaze made him squirm. "Will you let me in?" she asked.

And there it was. The one question he had hoped she wouldn't ask because he didn't know if he could. "I'll try. There's stuff in my past that has made me the way I am, but I really want to try, Lanie."

"I want to believe you, Azarius, I do, but I don't know. I don't know if my heart can take any more of this roller coaster of being up when I'm with you and down in the dumps when you don't call for days."

A tightening like a squeeze from a vice surrounded his heart. What if she said no? What was he going to do?

"I need some time," she continued. "Can you give me a week and let me think about it?"

It wasn't what he hoped to hear. He had hoped she would jump into his arms where he could smell the sweet scent of her shampoo, but he couldn't blame her for being protective of her heart. After all, it was why he was so guarded. "I'll give you as long as you need," he said.

Even though Lanie nodded, the gesture was like a dagger in his heart. "Well, I guess I'll be heading back then. Is it okay if I text you?" It was a cheap substitute to having her there, but it would be better than nothing.

For the first time since he had walked in, a smile touched her lips and almost reached her eyes. "Sure, I'd like that. I find myself checking my phone in hopes of a message from you."

"Me too," he said. Azarius wanted to walk around the counter and kiss her, hug her, or touch her in some way, but he felt he was already on shifty ground, so instead he sucked in his disappointment, flashed her a smile, and walked out of the small ice cream shop.

~

*L*anie sagged against the counter as Azarius walked out the door. His showing up had been a complete surprise and a part of her had wanted to race around the counter into his arms, feel his lips on hers and his arms around her. She wanted to inhale the manly scent she couldn't seem to erase from her mind, but then she'd remembered him avoiding her questions. She'd remembered all the nights she'd checked her phone every five minutes hoping to hear from him only to be disappointed and had stopped herself.

To his credit, he had apologized, and his face had seemed earnest. Lanie had never considered him a player, but she wanted to be sure he meant it. She wasn't certain her heart could take much more of the roller coaster experience it had been on lately.

"Lord," she whispered softly, "please give me a sign. I'm so confused, and I could really use your help."

Less than an hour later, the overhead bell jingled, and Paula's large frame filled the doorway. Her eyes swept the empty room before she stepped inside and let the door close behind her.

"Where's your friend, dear? I thought he'd still be here."

"What friend?" Lanie asked, feigning ignorance. The last thing she needed was Paula in her business. If Paula knew, then the whole town would know shortly, including her father, and she couldn't imagine him approving of Azarius. Her father wasn't overtly racist, but he'd always discouraged her from dating black men stating that children of mixed marriages didn't fully belong in either the white world or the black world, a statement Lanie had never understood or agreed with. Plus, black or white, he wouldn't understand her jumping into a relationship so soon after her divorce from Denny.

"Why, your nice African American friend, Azarius. He stopped into The Diner looking for you. I told him where to find you. He seemed a man on a mission."

"Oh, yes, he did," Lanie said. "He was returning something he had borrowed. Thank you for telling him where to find me." She hated lying, but Paula couldn't know the truth, at least not yet.

The lie wasn't convincing enough though. Paula pursed her lips as her left eyebrow inched up her forehead, but she let the topic drop. "Well, I'm happy to have helped. I hope you have a wonderful evening, Lanie."

"You too, Paula," Lanie called. When the door closed behind the large woman, Lanie sighed with relief. Her secret was safe for a little longer.

～

*T*he next few days flew by for Lanie. She spent the mornings either unpacking or visiting with Layla at the inn. After a quick lunch, she would work her shift at the store and then head home or to her parent's house for dinner. She'd kept herself so busy that she hadn't had much time to think about Azarius's visit or maybe she was just avoiding thinking about it. Though Azarius sent her a text each night, he had never hounded her for an answer, which was good as Lanie still didn't have one.

As she tugged on her jeans for the day, she was forced to suck her stomach in more than usual. "Diet," she said aloud, checking her reflection in the mirror. "It's time to start that diet. And get some concealer," she added, noticing a few red splotches on her face.

Lanie leaned in for a closer look. She'd rarely had skin blemishes, even as a kid. While her weight had never been something to brag about, Lanie had always taken pride in her smooth skin, but today not only did she have a few red splotches, but a pimple had also erupted on her face.

"I better cut back on the greasy food, too," she said, though she couldn't remember the last greasy meal she'd had.

With a shake of her head, she turned off the bathroom light and headed out the door.

Layla was in the kitchen when Lanie arrived at the inn, a large plate of scrambled eggs in front of her.

"Ugh, what did you put in that?" Lanie asked, covering her nose. "That stinks."

"The same thing I always do," Layla said, shoveling a forkful in her mouth. "Since when does it bother you?" she asked after swallowing her bite.

Lanie's stomach tilted and churned. "I don't know. Since today I guess. The smell is making me nauseated."

Layla's eyes narrowed and scanned Lanie's face. "You feel nauseated?"

"That's what I said."

"Anything else unusual?"

Wrinkles appeared on Lanie's face as she scrunched it in confusion. "Unusual? What do you mean? My pants are a little tight, and I have these crazy red spots on my face, but..." Lanie paused as the implication hit her.

"No," she said, sinking into the seat and shaking her head. "No, no, no. It couldn't be."

"Would you get back together with him if you are?" Layla asked.

"What?" Lanie asked. The fog in her mind clouded Layla's words.

"Denny. Would you get back together with him if you're pregnant?"

Lanie rubbed a hand across her face. "It wouldn't be Denny's. We separated months ago, and it was longer than that since we were intimate."

Layla's eyes widened. "Then whose baby would it be?"

A notch in the table garnered Lanie's attention, and she dropped her eyes as she chose her words. "My friend Azarius's- you know the one I told you about."

"Wait, the one who didn't want the same relationship you did?" Layla asked between bites.

"Yeah, that's the one."

"I thought you didn't want a relationship with him because of that."

"I didn't. I was actually planning to call it off the last night I went over, but my divorce papers came in that day, and even though I was expecting them, the news sort of hit me emotionally. I went to see Azarius, and we ended up sleeping together."

A low whistle escaped Layla's lips. "Is that why he came to town?"

A shrug of her shoulders showed Lanie's nonchalance. "He said he wanted to try again, that he realized how much he cared for me after I left."

"That's good though, right?"

"It would be if he weren't so secretive. I like him, but I don't know if I can trust him. He won't even tell me his birthday. Plus, my father would have a conniption fit."

"He won't tell you his birthday?" Layla asked. "Why not?"

Lanie shook her head. It was a question she still didn't have the answer to.

"Well, you can't worry about your father. He comes from a different generation, but I'm sure he would come around. What are you going to do though?"

Tears pricked the back of Lanie's eyes. "I guess I'm going to take a test to see for sure, and then... I don't know."

Layla reached across the table and squeezed Lanie's arm. "It will be okay."

~

Fear parched Lanie's throat as she entered the general store. Though she knew she needed to do this, it didn't make the process any easier.

"Welcome to Star Lake General, can I help you find anything?"

The voice belonged to a teenage girl with horn-rimmed glasses and a blonde ponytail. Lanie envied her carefree expression. Probably the most stressful thing in her life was finals and if the boy behind her in math class liked her. Lanie missed those days, but she didn't need the pity of a teenager.

"No, thank you, I'm good." Lanie grabbed a basket from the stack and headed to the far right of the small store. She might as well grab the few other things she needed.

A few bagged salads and some vegetables found their way into her basket, along with a tube of toothpaste. Then Lanie found herself staring at the pregnancy tests. Even in this small store, there were five different options. She grabbed one that claimed it held two tests and gave accurate early results. A few final items finished her trip, and she made her way to the front to pay.

The same perky blonde stepped to the register and began scanning her items. Though she said nothing as the pregnancy test glided over the scanner, Lanie felt the girl's eyes glance at her left hand. Pregnancy outside of marriage was prevalent in the current year, but Star Lake moved to its own time, and it was an anomaly here.

Lanie kept her eyes downcast as she paid the checker and scurried out of the door, the bag clasped to her chest like a life jacket in a storm.

Though tucked away in the bag, the small box grabbed her attention every few minutes on the drive home, and once she stepped inside her house, it was the first item she removed. She placed it on the bar and stared at it a moment. The simple white box held her future, and the thought of that sent Lanie's heart racing.

It took every ounce of strength for her to put away the other groceries before sneaking off to the bathroom with the accusatory white box. Once inside, Lanie locked the door, not knowing why as she lived alone but feeling it necessary.

The instructions were pretty straight forward. Either pee on the stick or catch some in a cup and put the stick in the cup. Not having brought a cup with her, Lanie chose option one, hoping it would be accurate.

Afterwards, she wiped off the stick and placed it on a few pieces of toilet paper. Then she washed her hands and sat back down on the toilet seat to wait the three minutes the test needed.

Conflicting emotions washed over her as she waited. On one hand, she found herself hoping it would be negative. She could put the night out of her mind and start fresh. Another part of her, smaller but not non-existent, wanted it to be positive. The desire to have a baby had been creeping in on her, and maybe if a child was involved, Azarius would be less secretive and settle down. But then there was her father, who would not only be upset she was pregnant out of wedlock but would have an issue with Azarius's skin color.

A peek at her watch revealed only a minute had passed, but Lanie couldn't take the suspense any longer. She sat up a little straighter and let her eyes wander over to the stick.

CHAPTER 9

*A*zarius lay on his bed nursing his wounded ego. When Lanie had asked for a week to think about their relationship, he had agreed because he didn't believe she would need that long. He knew she was interested in him, and he had believed his apology would smooth over any reservations she still held, but it was now Friday, and he still hadn't heard her decision. Though he sent her a text each night to let her know he was thinking about her, he had been careful not to ask the one question that was constantly on his mind.

The doorbell rang, but Azarius made no move to get it. Not only was Greg downstairs, but Azarius didn't care who was at the door. He wasn't expecting anyone, nor did he care to see anybody, but as the voices carried upstairs, his mood changed.

"I'm not sure that's a good idea," Greg said.

"It's important, Greg, and I won't take no for an answer," Lanie replied.

Azarius sat up and regarded his appearance. Baggy sweats covered his legs, and his oversized t-shirt sported a small stain in the middle of his chest, but there was little time to change. He whipped off the t-shirt and grabbed a clean one from his drawer, pulling it over his head as the sound of footsteps on the stairs reached his ears.

A knock sounded at the door, and he opened it, glad his hair was short and therefore always decent, though when he went out, he spent more time on it. Lanie stood on the other side with a tight smile on her face.

"Hi, Azarius," she sighed. "Do you have a minute?"

Curiosity piqued, he gestured her inside, closing the door after her. "It's good to see you," he said as she sat on the edge of his bed. His small room held no other place to sit, only a dresser and a stand for the television.

"Thanks," she said, biting her lip. Her shoulders rose and fell in a sigh. "I don't know how to say this, so I'm just going to come out with it." She reached into her pocket and pulled something out, holding it out to him.

As soon as he recognized the white stick, his heart dropped. No wonder confusion clouded her face. He took the piece of plastic and stared at the display. Two blue lines filled the two windows. Pregnant! Had it been anyone else, he would have asked if it were his. After all, he and Lanie had never had the "let's be exclusive" discussion, but Lanie was different, and he knew she had been with no one else.

"It was one time," he said as he sank down on the bed next to her.

"It only takes once, Azarius," she said with an eye roll.

"I know. I just didn't expect it is all. What do you want to do?"

"Do?" Frustration dripped from her words. "There's no option here, Azarius. I don't believe in abortion, so I guess I'm having a baby."

"Then I guess I'm having one too," he said, though the words scared him to death. Azarius wanted children; he loved his nieces and nephews and believed he would make a good father, but he hadn't expected to be one so soon. Living with Greg had been enough of an adjustment. Could he live with a woman again?

"Azarius, you don't have to do that," Lanie said. "I didn't tell you expecting you to be heavily involved, but I thought you should know."

As she had yet to look at him, Azarius grabbed Lanie's face and turned it to face his. "I promise to be there for you. I take my responsibilities seriously."

"But you hate having a roommate. What if you hate living with me? I'm not the neatest person," she stammered. "I throw my clothes on the floor and don't get me started on dishes."

His hands moved to her shoulders. "I know I said I liked living alone, but Greg has kind of grown on me, and you'll be the same. We can make it work, Lanie. I came to Star Lake, remember?"

"I know, but that was before this. You haven't met my father. Not only will he not be pleased about the baby, but," - she paused and dropped her eyes - "he's kind of racist."

Azarius squeezed her shoulders. He had lived through racism before. "Look, he's from a different generation. You aren't racist and that's all that matters. I'm not having a baby with your father."

A small laugh escaped Lanie's tight lips, but it didn't reach her eyes. Azarius hated that their union, which he remembered fondly, was now causing her pain.

"How are we going to make this work?" she said. Liquid pools resided in her eyes, creating a glossy look.

"One day at a time," he said and pulled her into his arms. The sweet smell of her hair eased his nerves, and he ran his hand in a caressing gesture up and down her arm.

"Thank you, Azarius," she said, looking up at him. "I don't think I could have done this if you had said you didn't want the baby."

"I told you that night I don't run from commitments and I would be there for you no matter what."

Her hand found his cheek, and as her glistening, hazel eyes stared into his, he leaned down and placed his lips upon hers. It had only been a few weeks, but he had missed the feeling of her soft lips, and as unplanned as it was, he was glad the baby had brought her back to him.

~

*H*ours later when Lanie had left, Azarius ventured downstairs. Greg was parked on the couch in his usual position in front of the television. He glanced up as Azarius entered the living room.

With a deft movement, Greg lowered the volume and sat up straighter. "So, what happened?"

Azarius sat on the opposite end of the couch. "It was heavy. She's pregnant."

Greg let out a low whistle. "What are you going to do?"

With a shrug and a sigh, Azarius answered, "I'm going to be a father. I gotta tell you though I am excited and scared to death at the same time."

"I think that's natural," Greg said. "You going to move there or is she coming back here?" His eyes widened, and he leaned forward. "Am I going to need to find a new place to live?"

"Not yet. For now, she is deciding to stay in Star Lake, and I have to stay here for work. It's not a perfect situation, but we'll trade weekends."

"Well, I know it's not the way you planned it, but at least it means she's giving you another chance."

Azarius nodded, thanking God for that. Though he wasn't as religious as Lanie, he did believe in God, but he wondered if that difference would cause problems for them later on. Now that she was gone, the doubt crept in, and he began to wonder about a lot of things. Could he really do this? What if he were an awful father?

He hadn't had one growing up for most of his formative years. It had just been his mother and him for his first ten years until his mother died and he was adopted. His adopted father had been okay while he was around, but Azarius had no idea what kind of father he would be. For the first time in a long time, he found himself praying.

CHAPTER 10

*L*anie bit the inside of her cheek as she paced the floor. Azarius was supposed to be driving in to meet her parents for the first time, and they were planning to tell them about the baby, although Lanie thought going in for a root canal sounded more appealing.

She checked her watch for the hundredth time and sighed. Her heartburn had been on overdrive this morning, and she had barely slept. Conversations of how this might go played over and over in her head, but none felt right.

The crunch of tires on gravel grabbed her attention, and she smiled as Azarius's turbo Mustang pulled into her drive. Then she snorted as she thought of strapping a car seat in his tiny backseat. Would Azarius give up his mustang? And what if he drove like a crazy man with the baby in the backseat?

Lanie shook her head, forcing the questions from her mind. They had months to plan all that out. Today she needed to focus on her parents and what she was going to say to them. A baby had not been her plan, but she had been delighted that Azarius was willing to help raise the baby, and she enjoyed the feel of his arms again.

His muscular frame stepped out of the car. The air had warmed again, and the bright colors of spring stood out against his dark skin. She opened the door before he reached it and raced into his arms. The masculine, woodsy smell of him washed over her, calming some of her overworked nerves.

"It's good to see you too," he said with a chuckle.

"I'm sorry. I didn't sleep well thinking about talking to my father, but having you here makes it a little better."

His large hand smoothed her hair. "No matter what happens with your father today, it will be okay. I'm not going anywhere."

Though his words sounded perfect, Lanie still had doubts. She wanted to believe he'd be there forever, but there was still so much she didn't know about his past, and he hadn't opened up about everything.

After a brief tour of her small house, they set out for her parents' place. Though a few miles away, they decided to walk so Lanie could show him the main part of town.

"How long has your family run the ice cream parlor?" he asked when they passed it.

"As long as I can remember," she laughed. "My father's grandfather started it and my father has always wanted me to take it over. I don't know that it's in my blood though."

The door to The Diner opened as they approached, and Lanie sighed. Paula was hurrying their direction with a large smile on her face and an eagerness for gossip.

"Lanie, I see your friend has returned. Did he forget something again?" Her eyes dropped to their clasped hands. "Or is there more to the story?"

"Paula, this is my," Lanie paused. What did she call him? Her boyfriend? Her friend? They still hadn't finalized that discussion.

"Boyfriend," Azarius said, reaching out his right hand to shake Paula's. "I believe we've partially met, though I don't remember catching your name."

"I'm Paula Monroe. Delighted to officially meet you, Azarius. Will we be seeing more of you then?"

"I'm sure you will," he said. "Now if you'll pardon us, we have an appointment we must keep."

Paula's head snapped back in slight surprise, but as Azarius's tone had been nothing but respectful, she could say nothing. "Of course. Well, till next time then."

"You handled her so well," Lanie said, surprise threading her voice.

Azarius chuckled. "I met a lot of people like her in the Army. I learned very quickly how to be polite but distant."

"You'll have to teach me that skill," Lanie said with a smile.

"I'll be happy to teach you that and a lot more." Azarius squeezed her hand and returned the smile.

Her parents' house loomed in front of them before she was ready. As her heartbeat accelerated, sweat broke out on her palms and Azarius looked down at her.

"Sorry," she smiled up at him. "I just have a bad feeling this isn't going to go well."

Lanie led the way up the stairs and squared her shoulders before ringing the bell.

The door opened to reveal a smiling Elaine, but her smile faltered when she noticed Azarius. "I see you've brought a friend. Hello, I'm Elaine." She stuck out her hand and Azarius shook it in return.

"Nice to meet you ma'am. I'm Azarius."

"Hi Mom, Is Dad here too?"

Elaine's eyebrows rose on her head, but she nodded and stepped back, opening the door wider. "Yes, he is. Come on inside."

Lanie flashed a tight smile at Azarius before stepping into the entrance. The feeling of doom descended on her shoulders as they entered the family room where her father sat.

"Bob," her mother said, grabbing his attention. "Lanie's here with a friend."

Her father looked up and turned off the television.

"Hi, Dad," Lanie said. "Can we have a few minutes of your time?"

Her mother and father exchanged concerned glances, but Elaine pointed to the couch. Lanie took a deep breath and sat on the edge. Azarius followed suit and sat next to her. He folded his hands into his lap as if unsure where else to put them.

Lanie cleared her throat. "Dad, this is my boyfriend, Azarius." She glanced to him, and he nodded, encouraging her to continue.

"Boyfriend?" Bob said, leaning forward in his chair. Lanie did not miss the disapproval in his voice. "That's a bit quick, don't you think?"

Lanie forced herself to take another deep breath before continuing. "We began hanging out several months ago when Denny and I separated, Dad, but we just started dating."

Bob's eyes narrowed as his arms crossed. "What does hanging out involve these days?"

"Not what you think, Dad." Lanie shook her head, trying to prepare herself for the worst. She dropped her eyes to her lap, unable to meet her father's eyes as she revealed the next part. "But we did have one night where we let things go too far."

Nothing but stony silence from her parents. Azarius squeezed her hand in silent encouragement. Lanie shot him a grateful smile and then looked back at her parents.

"Mom, Dad, I'm pregnant."

Silence fell like a blanket of snow. Elaine's eyes were wide saucers; her hand covered her mouth. Bob's eyes were daggers of ice, and the set of his jaw created a stony exterior. After a long moment, his eyes switched to Azarius.

"What are your plans regarding this baby?"

Azarius shifted in his seat. "I plan to be there, Sir. I don't run from commitments. I already told Lanie that I want to be in the baby's life."

"In the baby's life?" Bob roared, leaning forward. "What does that mean? You'll do weekend visits? Send the child a card on holidays? Or do you plan to step up, be a man, and marry my daughter?"

"Marry?" The word came out strangled and slightly squeaky from Azarius's mouth, not a surprise to Lanie. If the man didn't like having a roommate, why would he want a wife? "We haven't really discussed that, Sir."

"Well, then it's probably high time you did," Bob said.

"Dad, we're adults. You can't force us to marry," Lanie said, trying to control the anger building up inside her.

"No, I can't force you to marry, but I can strongly recommend it. Children need both of their parents in their life, and occasional visits will not be enough. It's important for children to have a strong man in their life."

"It's also important they have two loving parents in their life, even if they don't live together. We told you as a courtesy, not so you could lay demands on us. Azarius and I will figure it out." Lanie bolted up from the couch and turned back to Azarius, her hand outstretched. "Let's go, Azarius."

His deep brown eyes regarded her before glancing to her parents and then back. He stood, though his posture displayed his continued uncertainty.

"Lanie," Elaine began.

"No, Mom," Lanie said, cutting her off. "I hope you guys will be a part of the baby's life, but you will have to be accepting of whatever we decide to do. I know two parents are important for a child, but not if they fight all the time or hate each other. I'm not saying that will happen, but if you force us into a marriage we aren't ready for, then it might."

"If you aren't ready for marriage, you shouldn't have been sleeping together," Bob said in a soft voice.

Lanie knew he was right, but her indignation wanted the last word. "We made a mistake Dad. I know you can't understand that living in the perfection you do, but we did, and we are trying to make it right the best way we know how." Lanie grabbed Azarius's hand and pulled him out of the room and out of the house. She didn't stop until the outside breeze smacked her in the face.

"Lanie, stop," Azarius said, halting his feet and forcing her to stop as well.

She turned to him, blinking back the tears that threatened to spill over her lids.

"Maybe your dad is right," he continued. "I grew up without a father, and it affected me. It probably is part of the reason I like living alone, but I don't want my baby... our baby to grow up like that, so... maybe we should think about getting married."

A sad combination of a snort and a laugh tumbled out of Lanie's mouth. "That's a heck of a proposal, Azarius. Just like I always dreamed."

His brows furrowed together and he dropped her hand to place both arms around her. "I know it's not, Lanie, and one day I'll make it up to you. I messed up, but I don't want to keep messing up."

Lanie blinked as she tried to process his words. "What are you saying, Azarius?"

"I'm saying let's get married. Let's elope and show your father we're serious."

"Elope?" Confusion clouded Lanie's mind, and she struggled to clear a path. "But what about our friends? Our family?"

"We can have another ceremony later and invite everyone. Let me at least look into it. Lanie, we're having a baby together. I want you as my wife."

Lanie wanted to say yes, but the pervading feeling that he was suggesting marriage solely because of the baby wouldn't leave her. She already had one failed marriage; she didn't want another. The memory of the night Denny moved out popped into her brain. She had spent hours online researching divorce, shocked by what she had found. The statistics on first marriages lasting was only about fifty percent and that number dropped to thirty three percent for second marriages. Lanie had no idea how long second marriages that occurred only because of an impending child lasted, but she feared the statistic was not a good one.

"Tell me your birthday," she said, throwing it out as a challenge. If he avoided the question like he had every other time, she would have her answer. They would never be able to make a marriage last, but if he….

"October 15th," he said without hesitation. His eyes fixed on hers, and she found her resolve melting in their chocolaty depths.

"Let me think about it, Azarius. I know you mean well, but there is still so much I don't know about you, that we don't know about each other. What if we get married and hate each other? That wouldn't be any better for the baby."

His eyes remained locked on hers, searching her soul. "Okay, take however long you need, but know that I don't run away from obligations, and whatever it takes, I will make it work."

Oh, how good his words sounded, and he had given up his birthday, but was it the start of something new or simply because he'd been backed against a wall? She needed time to think, to process, to be sure - if such a thing existed.

Knowing he needed some sort of response, she nodded and hugged him, savoring the security of his arms if only for a moment, before heading back towards her house.

∾

*L*anie wandered aimlessly around her house that night. Azarius had stayed another few hours, and they'd cuddled on the couch and watched a movie, but Lanie's mind had been elsewhere.

Even now, in the stillness of her house, she couldn't get her mind to stop. Scenario after scenario played through her mind. Maybe a marriage could work. He could move here, or she could move back to Dallas with him, but did she want to move back? Though returning to Star Lake had never been in her plans, there was something about the small-town atmosphere she liked, and she'd enjoyed reconnecting with Layla.

Her eyes fell on her Bible. In the commotion of the last few days, she hadn't been reading on a daily basis. She picked up the black leather-bound book and held it to her chest. "Lord, I know we didn't do things right. I understand now why you wanted intimacy to belong in a marriage and not outside of it, but we want to do better. We want what's best for this child. Please show me what I should do."

Lanie let the silence cover her, and she listened for that still small voice. The one she could only hear when she was focused and willing to listen.

CHAPTER 11

"*H*ow did meeting the parents go?" Greg asked as Azarius returned that evening.

He fell into the oversized grey chair and collected his thoughts before answering. "I haven't met a lot of parents in my time, but that was definitely the worst experience. Her father hates me; I have no idea if he will even accept this baby. Her mother seemed nice, but we didn't chat for long. Oh yeah, and I asked Lanie to elope."

"What?" The TV picture faded to black, and Greg turned his full attention to Azarius. "You did what?"

Azarius ran his hands over his face. "It just slipped out. Her father was asking if I was going to marry her, and the very word felt like a noose you know? But then Lanie stormed out of the house. I could tell she was upset, and I thought maybe we should get married, and the words just slipped out."

"What did Lanie say?"

With a sigh, Azarius leaned back and shook his head. "She

didn't jump on the idea. She told me it was an awful proposal, and it was. I keep messing everything up."

"Yeah, I can't say that was a great proposal, and my sister said women live for that day, but she ought to give you points for trying."

"I don't know. Maybe I'm not cut out to be married. Maybe Krista was a warning and this botched proposal is another sign."

]"Don't say that, man. I know what happened with Krista was hard, but Lanie isn't Krista. And you want to be a father. You tell me that every time you come back from your sister's house. You're ready, even if you don't think you are."

Azarius sat forward and dropped his hands. "You're right. I do want to be a father, and I'm excited about this baby. I'll just have to figure out a way to make everything else work."

After dinner that evening, Azarius lay in his bed staring up at the black netting. His life felt out of control, and he wondered if this was why Lanie prayed. Did she find comfort in speaking to God?

Though he felt foolish, he opened his mouth and let the words fall out. "God, I don't know if you know who I am or even if you listen to people who haven't been following you, but I've messed up, and I'm hoping you can help me right things. I didn't have a father growing up, but I want to be one to this child. Help me to know what to do for the baby and for Lanie."

He waited, wanting some audible voice to reassure him, but nothing came. With a sigh, he rolled over on his bed and closed his eyes. Maybe something would come to him in the middle of the night.

No epiphany awaited him in the morning when he awoke, but a message from Lanie blinked on his phone.

-I thought about your offer. Let's do it. I'll be there later today.-

Azarius shook his head, wondering what had changed her mind.

Deciding he didn't care, he showered and dressed before heading downstairs.

Sunday was his favorite day, not because he went to church - he honestly couldn't remember the last time he had been - but because it was a day he could rest and not have to worry about work. He liked his job, but the late hours sometimes took a toll on him, and Sundays he claimed entirely for himself. He didn't even go to the gym on Sundays.

The downstairs was still dark and quiet as he made his way down the narrow steps. Greg usually slept in until mid-morning, so Azarius often had the mornings to himself. Not much of a coffee drinker, he headed straight for the griddle. Pancakes had always been what his mother had made when she had time in the mornings, and he had an affinity for them, but the weekends were the only days he had time to make them.

As he pulled out the large ceramic mixing bowl with a pouring spout, he remembered the last time his mother had made pancakes for him. At only ten, he'd had no idea how sick she was, and she had hidden most of her symptoms well. She'd made the pancakes extra special that day with chocolate chips for his birthday, and they had laughed and told jokes as they ate.

The next morning, he had awoken to a silent house and gone in search of his mother. It wasn't like her to let him sleep past school time. He had found her still and silent in her bed, and thinking her asleep, he had tried in vain to wake her. When she wouldn't rouse, he had climbed in bed next to her and cried until his tears ran dry.

The next-door neighbor found him like that a few hours later and gently led him out of the room and to her house. Years later he discovered she had been checking on his mother every day at eleven am for months. She knew to come over when the phone wasn't answered that day, though he had no memory of it even ringing.

It was only then he understood the cancer his mother had been battling. Not having the money to afford expensive treatments and with a less than stellar chance of living even with the treatments, she had opted to just take medicine to cope with the pain and spend her final days at home with him.

After that, he had been placed into foster care for a time until he met Mary. Mary was a spirited white woman recently married and ready to take on the world. Her marriage hadn't lasted, but the adoption had and though it had been strange growing up in a white world at first, Azarius had come to appreciate it. Now he had an insight into both cultures that helped him view the world in a different light. Perhaps if more people had his insight, there would be less racial hatred. And Mary was still his best friend and confidant. He told her everything. In fact, he needed to call her this morning and tell her about Lanie.

She already knew a little about Lanie as he had mentioned her the last time they spoke, but that was before the fateful night and definitely before the news of the baby.

He turned his attention to the mixing of the pancake batter, determined to call his mother after breakfast.

The smell of the pancakes woke Greg from his slumber, and he padded down the stairs rubbing sleep from his eyes. Lean and lanky, his baggy sweatpants barely hung on his hips and his loose shirt engulfed his frame. Short spikes of blond hair stuck up all over his head.

"You cooking?" he asked as he stumbled over to the coffee maker and grabbed the pot.

"Yep, you want some?" Azarius flipped the pancakes with a deft motion, keeping the circular shape.

"Of course, but not until I get some coffee. I still don't understand how you function without it." Greg filled the pot with water and poured it into the coffee maker and then shuffled to the cupboard for the coffee grounds. A few minutes later the sound of coffee dripping into the glass pot joined the sizzling sound of the pancakes.

Azarius turned the stove off, loaded the pancakes up on a plate, and brought it to the small table. He had to shove some papers to the far back as the table seemed to be the catchall place for all the bills and random papers throughout the week.

As he returned to the kitchen for plates, butter, and syrup, Greg sat at the table with a steaming mug.

"So, Lanie's coming over later," Azarius said as he placed a plate in front of Greg. "She agreed to elope, so I'm assuming she'll stay tonight so we can go tomorrow."

"That's good, right?" Greg asked as he stabbed a pancake and dropped it on the plate. "Where are you going to go? The court house?"

"I don't know. That seems so plain, and I already ruined the proposal for her. I'd like to do something nicer." He speared his own pancake and scooped out a pat of butter.

"You know, I heard someone at work talking about this bed-and-breakfast that does elopements. They have different packages you can choose from. You want me to find out more about it?"

Azarius nodded as he finished chewing. "Yeah, that would be great. It would be good to do something special for her."

They finished the rest of breakfast in silence, and then while Greg retired to his second home, the living room couch, Azarius cleaned the table and put the dishes in the sink for later. Then he headed back upstairs to call his mother.

The phone rang only twice before his mother's voice came through. "Azarius! How are you, son?"

"I'm good, Mother," he said as he paced his small room, "but I have some news."

"Oh, yeah? About work?"

Azarius shook his head before remembering his mother couldn't see him. "No, work is fine." He adjusted the row of sunglasses on his dresser. "I um got a girl pregnant."

"Oh, Azarius," she sighed. "Do you love her at least?"

"I think I do, Mother. She completes me though I didn't realize it until she left."

"Wait? She left?"

"She did." He sat on the edge of the bed. "Lanie's pretty religious, and I think she regretted our night together."

"So where does that leave you two?"

"When she told me about the baby, I told her I wanted to be a part of his or her life." Azarius grabbed the pillow with her lingering scent and held it in his lap. "I met her parents. They weren't exactly pleased."

"Well, it isn't the way I would have wanted it to happen for you either, but sometimes life doesn't turn out the way we hoped. I assume though you will be involved."

"Of course. I asked her to elope."

His mother whistled on the other end. "That's a big step. Are you sure? What about the religious difference? Don't you think that will cause problems?"

"Actually, Mom, I think there might be something to her relationship with God. I've found myself praying the last few days, and while I haven't heard an audible answer, I feel different."

"Well, if it makes you happy, I'll support you. So, tell me about this girl who managed to snag your heart."

Azarius smiled as he began discussing Lanie's finer points. "She was in radio when I met her, though she recently got out of that for the time being, but she has the most beautiful voice and smile. Whenever I'm feeling down, all she has to do is smile at me and everything just seems better."

"She sounds lovely, and I can't wait to meet her. And Azarius… I applaud you taking responsibility for your actions. Your mama would have been proud."

Tears pricked his eyes at the mention of his mama, who would never get to meet Lanie. However, maybe she was up in heaven looking down on him. While Azarius wasn't sure of her religious status, he did remember going to church with her on occasion and she had been the one who told him about God in the first place, so perhaps she had been a believer.

"Thanks Mom. I'm sure you'll get to meet her and your grandchild soon."

Azarius smiled as he ended the call. His mother might not be typical, but he loved the fact that she always supported him, and somehow, he knew that when they met, Lanie and his mother would get along well.

～

*L*anie's stomach knotted as she pulled up to Azarius's apartment. Was she really going to go through with this? Even though she knew Texas had a seventy-two-hour waiting list - she'd researched it extensively the last few days - she was here to get the ball rolling as both parties had to be present to sign for the marriage certificate.

She had never expected to be eloping, but she'd had the big wedding once already and it hadn't turned out as planned. Maybe eloping wouldn't be bad, and at least it would keep the stares she feared from coming. Even though it was a quick marriage, at least she would be married when she started to show. Lanie just hoped her parents would forgive her one day.

Grabbing her overnight bag from the passenger seat, she exited the car, took a deep breath, and locked the door. She hadn't planned on staying with Azarius again until after they were married, but they would need to hit the courthouse early tomorrow for her to get back to work in time, and money was still tight.

The chime of the doorbell echoed and fell silent. Then footsteps sounded, and the door opened. Greg smiled at her from the other side.

"Hey, Lanie, long time no see."

Lanie returned the smile. Though they had only had the one heart to heart session, they had spoken by text a few other times and Lanie considered Greg a friend. "I know. I'm sorry." She shrugged. "Things got complicated."

"Well, at least you know he's serious now."

"Yeah, I guess. He upstairs?"

Greg nodded and motioned up the stairs. Lanie leaned in for a quick hug before tackling the ten short steps to the second floor.

Azarius's door was closed, but that wasn't unusual. He didn't like people in his room most days, but he had given her the green light to enter whenever.

The room was barely lit as she entered. Only the glow from the television that seem to constantly play eighties videos lit the room. Azarius looked up from the far side of the bed where he was packing a bag.

"Hi, you ready?"

Lanie blinked in confusion. "Ready? Ready for what?"

A slow smile spread across Azarius's handsome features. "It's a surprise. Did you bring a dress?"

"No, I didn't figure I'd need one to go to city hall. You do know we can't get married for another three days..."

"Oh, but we can." He closed the bag and came around the bed to grab her hands, lacing his fingers through hers. "Greg found a bed-and-breakfast in Oklahoma that performs ceremonies with no wait."

"What?" Though he was speaking English, Lanie couldn't comprehend the words.

"We can get married tonight. We'll even stop at a dress shop on the way, and I'll buy you a dress. It will be my gift to you."

"Tonight?"

"Yes, tonight. Say you will, Lanie. It's only a four-hour drive."

Lanie opened her mouth to answer, but words failed her. She had accepted the idea of being married again next weekend, but tonight? Azarius's chocolate brown eyes pulled her in, and she nodded. "Okay, let's do it."

A large smile broke out on his face, and he grabbed her face and pulled her in for a quick kiss. "Great. Do you have your divorce papers?"

"Yes, they're in my bag," Lanie said, patting the overnight bag.

"Good, mine too."

Lanie blinked at him. "Wait, you were married before?"

Azarius nodded. "It was finalized a year ago, but we had been separated years before that."

Another seed of doubt sprouted in Lanie's mind. What else was she going to find out about him? "How did I never know you were married?"

"Because I never told you. I don't talk about it much."

"But, don't you think that was important? How long were you married?"

"Five years, but we only lived together for three. Krista is partly why I'm so guarded about relationships." Azarius sat on the bed and patted the spot beside him. "Sit. I'll tell you about her. I can see you are curious and I don't want to start our marriage with this hanging over our heads. I promised to try to be more open, so I might as well start with this."

Lanie dropped her bag on the floor and sat down next to Azarius. He shifted slightly to face her and grabbed her hands.

"I don't know if I ever told you, but I liked you from the moment I saw you. I wanted to ask you out at the radio station, but before I got the nerve, you announced your engagement to Denny. It's stupid, but I kept hoping you would break it off, but when you got married, I had to leave."

"You left because of me?" Lanie had never known he had feelings for her back then, though he had said a few statements that had made her think he had.

Azarius nodded. "I was blindsided by your engagement, and I

wanted you to be happy, but I couldn't stick around to watch it. It hurt too much, you know?"

Lanie pursed her lips together and nodded for him to continue. This was the most he had ever shared about his past.

"I took a remote tour after that. Remember when I told you I re-enlisted?"

She nodded.

"Well, on that tour I met Krista. She was a nurse, and I met her after spraining my ankle one day. We married over there, but Krista's deployment ended before mine. When I got back, things had changed, but I couldn't figure out why. At first, I thought it was that our interests weren't similar enough. It turned out the Army was about all we had in common, but a year later, I found out she was having an affair."

"Oh, Azarius, I'm so sorry," Lanie said.

Azarius shrugged his broad shoulders. "We tried counseling, and for a while I thought it was better, but then she took another deployment, and a fellow soldier sent me pictures of her and a new man over there. I filed for divorce after that, but she fought it for a time for whatever reason. She finally agreed a year ago. So there you go. That's the condensed version of why I'm guarded."

Lanie smiled and squeezed his hands. For the first time, she felt confidence in their relationship. "I'm so glad you told me, though I wish you had told me sooner."

He nodded as a playful smile tugged the right side of his mouth up. "I know. I'm going to work on not hiding so much, but I'll need your help. Think you're up for the task?"

"Well, I guess I have to be," Lanie laughed. "Since we plan on getting married."

"Speaking of which," he said, "we should be going before the place closes. You ready?"

"Ready as I'll ever be," she smiled.

Azarius stood first, helping her up and then grabbed his bag from the bed. Lanie rescued hers from the floor and the two made their way down the stairs.

"Heading out?" Greg asked from the couch.

"Yep, thank you for the info, man."

Azarius extended his hand, but Greg stood and pulled him into a hug. Then he turned to Lanie. "I guess the next time I see you, you'll be Lanie Jacobson," he said, pulling her into a hug as well.

"Lanie Jacobson," Azarius chuckled. "Sounds like an author's name."

Lanie rolled the name around in her head and decided she liked the sound of it. "Wish us luck," she smiled.

"You don't need it," Greg said. "You two were made for each other."

Azarius wrapped his arm around Lanie and pulled her close. "I agree."

~

Five hours later, Azarius pulled into the driveway of a large two story yellow house with white shutters. 'Forever Yours Bed and Breakfast' was scrolled across a sign that hung over the door and though there weren't many trees, the front of the house was landscaped beautifully.

Lanie sucked in a breath and turned to Azarius. "This is much nicer than a courthouse."

"I'm glad you like it. Shall we see what they offer?"

Lanie nodded and unbuckled her seatbelt. In the backseat, an elegant cream dress lay across Azarius's garment bag. She grabbed the dress and her overnight bag as he pulled out his suit and duffel bag. With fingers laced together, they walked up the cement walkway to the front door.

Before the chime inside had finished sounding, the white door swung open. An elderly woman with grey streaks in her dark hair stood on the other side. Her friendly smile soothed the last few raw nerves Lanie had.

"Welcome to Forever Yours," she said, clasping her hands in front of her. "I'm Stella White. Are you here to get married?"

"What gave it away?" Azarius asked.

The woman laughed a deep, hearty laugh and winked at Lanie. "You've got yourself a keeper here. I can tell. Well, come on inside and decide which package you'd like."

Stella stepped back and opened the door wide enough for Azarius and Lanie to step through. The white wall paper with gold striping grabbed Lanie's attention as they followed the woman to an ornate desk.

"Here we are. We offer five different packages, though if you want to get married tonight, you'll have to choose one of the pre-made cakes we have. Do you have guests?" Stella asked, looking past them as if she expected a crowd to enter at any moment.

"No, it's just us," Azarius said. "We plan to have a party back where we live later."

"Oh, well in that case, you probably only need to look at package one and two. The main difference is that package two includes a night stay in our honeymoon suite."

Azarius glanced Lanie's direction, and she felt the heat flood her face. "It would be a late drive back," she said.

"We'll take package two then," Azarius said to Stella.

"Wonderful."

As Azarius took care of the bill, Lanie wandered around the room. It was decorated with Victorian touches from the wallpaper to the settees. Along one wall rows and rows of frames hung in even spaces. Lanie leaned in closer and realized they were pictures of couples who had been married here. Underneath each one was the date they were married, but Lanie wondered how many were still together.

"If you'll come with me, I'll show you where you can change," Stella said, breaking into Lanie's thoughts.

Lanie nodded and followed the woman down a hall carpeted in a soft rose color to a white door with 'Bride' stenciled across the top in black. Across the hall was a similar door marked 'Groom.' With a final smile at Azarius, Lanie opened the door to her room and shut it behind her.

The room contained another settee, a full-length mirror, a small vanity and stool, and a clothes rack. Lanie hung the dress and tossed her bag on the settee, then rifled through it for her makeup bag and brush.

As she brushed her hair out in front of the mirror, the nerves started again. In less than an hour, she would be Lanie Jacobson and the thought both thrilled and terrified her.

CHAPTER 12

*A*zarius hung the garment bag on the rack in his room and unzipped it. Though it wasn't a full suit, he had a dark suit coat and pants he had acquired years ago for a wedding or something. He didn't own a white button down shirt, but the pale blue one he had brought would suffice.

He peeled off his current shirt and flexed in the mirror. His arms were looking buff, but he'd need to do some more work on his chest to look his best for Lanie, though she hadn't complained last time.

Azarius grabbed the blue shirt off the hangar and poked his arms through. Thankfully, the buttons didn't stretch, though he wasn't sure he could have buttoned the one around his neck if he'd had to, but as he didn't have a tie that wasn't a problem, so he flipped the collar to make it lay just right.

The pants and the coat added the final touches, and he smiled at his reflection in the mirror. He hadn't been sure he would ever remarry, but he was looking forward to this union with Lanie and the prospect of being a father, even if it wasn't the way he planned it.

Azarius ran his hands down his sleeves one more time for good measure and then grabbed his divorce papers from his bag, tucking them in his suit coat pocket. Then he opened the door to the hall and peeked out. The door across the way was still closed, but Stella stood down the hall talking to an older man with a balding hairline.

"Oh, Azarius," Stella said as he approached, "I'd like you to meet John. He's our Justice of the Peace who will be performing the ceremony."

"Nice to meet you, Azarius," John said, sticking out his hand. He had a kind face underneath his bushy eyebrows which seemed out of place with his lack of hair. "Shall we get the paperwork started and Stella can wait for Lanie?"

Azarius nodded and followed John down the hallway to a small office. John crossed behind the desk and picked up a white sheet lying on top.

"Okay, so you need to sign here. Lanie will sign underneath and Stella will sign as your witness. Have either of you been married before?"

"Yes, both of us." Azarius reached into his inside pocket and pulled out the divorce decree.

"Great. I just need to make a copy of this for when I file," John said, grabbing it and turning to a small printer. "Hopefully, you have better luck with this one."

As the printer whirred to life and spat out a copy of his papers, Azarius signed his name to the line.

"Wonderful. If you'll come with me, I'll take you to the chapel room where we perform the ceremony and we can wait for Stella and Lanie."

Azarius followed John out of the office and down the hallway. He glanced back at the rooms, but Lanie's door was still closed. Was she backing out?

John took a right and Azarius followed him to a hallway enclosed by glass. It led to another large building he hadn't noticed from the front.

As John pushed open the door, the smell of flowers hit his nose. The room was set up similar to how he imagined a small church would look. Rows of white chairs lined both sides of a red carpeted aisle. A raised platform sat at the far back of the room surrounded by beautiful flowers in whites, pinks, and reds.

"Okay, here's where we'll stand," John said, stepping up on the platform. "Lanie will enter through that door, obviously, and when she gets here, we'll start the ceremony."

Azarius nodded and rolled his shoulders back. He wasn't nervous exactly, but he was ready to get the ceremony part over with. As the time crept on, he found himself rocking back and forth on his heels.

"I'm sure they're almost ready," John said with a kind smile.

Before Azarius could reply, the sound of music filled the room. The far door opened and Lanie stepped into view. She was a vision in her satin cream dress. The neckline dipped low and showed off her bare shoulders. Her auburn hair was piled loosely on her head with only a few tendrils hanging down. He was glad now that she hadn't modeled the dress for him in the store. He hadn't understood her adamant refusal then, but he did now. It would have ruined this moment.

She glided up the aisle, her dress skimming the floor. A bouquet of white roses clutched in her hands. A tentative smile adorned her face as she reached the podium and stepped up. When she turned to face him, Azarius realized they hadn't bought any rings. In a panic, he turned to John with wide eyes. John, seeming to understand his predicament, just smiled and held up a hand.

"Azarius and Lanie, you have come here today to declare your love for one another and pledge to spend your lives together. I haven't known either of you long, but I can see the love you have for each other, and I believe your union will be blessed and happy. Azarius, do you take Lanie to be your lawfully wedded wife, to have and to hold for as long as you both shall live?"

"I do," Azarius answered.

"Lanie, do you take Azarius as your husband to have and to hold as long as you both shall live?"

"I do," Lanie said, her eyes focused on Azarius.

John motioned Stella to join them on the podium. As she stepped up, Azarius realized she held a cushion with two thin gold bands on it. Of course, the package he had paid for had included rings. They were not what he wanted to symbolize their love forever, but they would work for now.

"Azarius, please take a ring and Lanie's hand and then repeat after me," John instructed.

Azarius grabbed the smaller gold band and Lanie's left hand.

"With this ring, I thee wed," John said and Azarius repeated the words, sliding the ring on Lanie's finger.

Lanie went next, sliding the ring on his finger as she repeated the words.

"By the power vested in me by the great state of Oklahoma, I now pronounce you husband and wife. You may kiss the bride."

Elated, Azarius leaned forward and placed his lips on Lanie's. They had kissed before, but it felt different this time with her as his wife, and from the look in her eyes as they pulled back, he knew she felt it too.

Stella tucked the pillow under her arm to clap. "Wonderful, so beautiful. Rosie has your cake ready, and I'd love to get a picture of the two of you for the wall."

Lacing his fingers through Lanie's, Azarius led the way down the aisle and back to the main building. Stella led them to a grand fireplace in the living room and they smiled for the camera before following her to the kitchen.

A small but pretty cake sat prominently displayed in the center of the large table.

"You want it here?" Stella asked. "Or I could send it up to your room with some dinner."

"Let's do that," Lanie said.

Azarius smiled and nodded his agreement. He was glad they were married, but hanging out with people he didn't know had never been his strong suit.

Stella led them back to their changing rooms where they grabbed their bags and then followed her up the stairs. She stopped in front of a white door at the end of the hall. "Here you go," she said, handing them a key on a large plastic frame. "I'll give you some time to get situated before I send up dinner and the cake."

"Thank you," Lanie said.

Stella smiled and nodded, then waved goodbye and headed back down the stairs.

"Well, shall we?" Azarius asked as he reached for the doorknob.

Lanie bit her lip and nodded. Azarius couldn't tell if she was excited, nervous, or both. The same emotions battled inside him as he opened the door.

A king-sized bed with a red comforter sat squarely in the middle of the room. White pillows floated at the top like clouds. On one pillow was a red rose and on another was a plate of chocolate covered strawberries. Azarius's stomach rumbled, and he realized he hadn't eaten in hours. Those strawberries would be at the top of his list.

Lanie stepped forward, but Azarius grabbed her arm before her foot could land in the room. She turned wide eyes on him as he smiled and scooped her into his arms.

"We might as well do this part right," he said and carried her over the threshold.

Lanie laughed as he set her down and then she reached behind her and closed the door.

Azarius picked up their bags, bringing them further into the room. A small couch sat under the window to the right and a table was on the left of the bed. Directly across from the bed was a wardrobe which probably housed a television along with some drawers.

Beyond the table was an open door, and Azarius stepped inside and flicked the light on. A large heart-shaped tub took up most of the real estate in the room, but there was also a toilet, a small sink, and a single person shower encased in glass.

Flicking off the light, he turned back around to face Lanie.

"Well, wife," he said, walking to her and putting his arms around her. "What would you like to do first?"

Her hands wound up around his neck and pulled him closer. "I think we should try out the strawberries and the bed," she said in a husky voice.

"A woman after my own heart," he said, dropping his lips to hers and backing her up until she fell onto the bed.

CHAPTER 13

*L*anie awoke in Azarius's arms and almost jumped out of bed before remembering they had gotten married the night before. With a small sigh, she rolled closer to him, enjoying the feel of his chest under her hand and his arm laying loosely around her.

One eye popped open, and he turned to her. "Hello wife, how did you sleep?"

"Surprisingly well," she said, running her hand over the faded tattoo on his chest. She had never noticed it before but the tattoo was of a pair of hands in a praying position. Perhaps Azarius was more religious than she originally thought.

"Surprisingly, huh?" A playful smile tugged at his lips as he pulled her closer and planted a kiss on her forehead. "That was the best sleep I've had in ages, but I'm not surprised. I knew you comforted and completed me."

Lanie smiled and snuggled down deeper against Azarius. "I suppose we should get up soon. I need to get back before my shift starts."

"Mmm, I don't want to get up yet. I won't get to make it down until Friday, and I'm not ready to let go of you yet."

"I don't want to get up yet either, but I'd also rather not anger my father any further."

That got Azarius moving. His eyes snapped open, and he pulled his arm away from Lanie, who immediately missed the warmth and security. "Come on," he said as he rolled over and planted his feet on the floor. "No way am I making your father hate me any more than he already does."

"He doesn't hate you," Lanie said as she stood beside him. "He dislikes the situation. You just happen to be a part of it, but maybe once he finds out we're married, the situation will resolve."

"Let's hope so, but until then, I'm not taking any chances."

～

Four hours later, she was kissing him goodbye and climbing back in her car to return to Star Lake. It felt odd leaving this time. As much as she and Denny hadn't been a connected couple, they hadn't spent many nights in different places after they got married, and she felt as if she shouldn't be leaving Azarius. Perhaps she should move back to Dallas - she did have a job waiting for her, but she had just rented her house, and if she moved in with Azarius, there was still Greg to consider. She liked him as a person, but having him as a roommate while married didn't seem right.

Maybe one day Azarius would move to Star Lake, but she knew his job was important to him and the commute would be awful from her small town. Well, they'd figure it out. For now, weekends would have to work.

She pulled into her driveway later than she'd hoped. She had only thirty minutes to change and get to the store. With a quick flick of her wrist, she turned off the car and darted inside. There was no time for a full shower, but she peeled off her clothes and ran a wet rag across her face and under her arms.

Her reflection caught her attention in the mirror and she focused on her belly. It was pudgier than she remembered though not large. Lanie placed her hands on her tummy, but there was no movement. She wondered when she would begin to feel the fluttering sensations and then she remembered she hadn't set an appointment with the OB yet. Hopefully the store would be quiet enough she could sneak a call in to schedule it.

After pulling on a new pair of jeans and a clean shirt, Lanie raced back out of the house and to the ice cream shop. She unlocked the door with just minutes to spare.

Her first task was to take all the chairs down and give the tables another quick wipe. Then she needed to check the dishes and remove any from the dishwasher that had been washed before.

Lanie was in the middle of this process when the bell jingled and Bert walked in. "Hi, Bert, what can I do for you?"

Bert fumbled with his brown bow tie as he shuffled into the room. He wore a matching brown and cream checkered shirt and brown pants. "Hello, Lanie, I was wondering if you had a date to the Summer Fling next week."

"Aren't you seeing Amelia?" Lanie asked.

"Well, she said she needed a break, so I thought I'd see what else might be out there."

Lanie bit her lip to keep from smiling. It wasn't a romantic proposal even if she had been looking, so she was thrilled to have a real excuse to say no. "Oh, Bert, I appreciate the offer, but I'll have a date to the dance." At least she hoped she would. She had forgotten to ask Azarius, but as it was on a weekend, she assumed he would be there.

Bert's face crumpled in and Lanie felt bad for him. She didn't

384 | LORANA HOOPES

know Amelia well, but she hoped the girl would come around. The two seemed perfect for each other.

"I'm sorry Bert. Can I get you an ice cream? On the house?"

That appeared to lighten his load a little as he shuffled toward the bar and took a seat. "I'll have the triple chocolate brownie with caramel, fudge, and whip cream. Oh and don't forget the cherry."

Ah, their most expensive dessert on the menu. That made sense as to why it perked him up slightly. Lanie smiled and shook her head as she turned to scoop the dessert.

"Here you go, Bert," she said a few minutes later as she set the dessert in front of him.

"Thank you." He reached for the bowl, but before he picked up the spoon, his eyebrows crammed together and he tilted his face up to hers. "Lanie, is that a wedding ring on your hand?"

"What?" Lanie glanced down at her left hand and froze as she realized she hadn't taken off the simple gold band from the night before. She thought about fibbing as quick remarriages were frowned upon nearly as much as unwed mothers in Star Lake, but she didn't want to start her marriage out with a lie. And people would know soon enough when she started to show. "It is, Bert. It's the reason I can't go with you to the dance. I married my friend Azarius last night."

Bert said nothing, but Lanie could see the wheels turning in his mind.

"That was quite fast," he finally managed and Lanie sighed. This would be a statement she had better get used to as she was bound to hear it more often in the future.

"Yes, I suppose it was, but sometimes you just know, right?"

He dipped his spoon in the dessert and brought it to his mouth. "Yes, I suppose you do," he mumbled through his bite.

Lanie sighed softly. Bert had been easy to convince, but she knew there would be other people who would not be placated so easily.

When Bert finished his ice cream, he pushed the bowl back across the counter to her and left, leaving the parlor empty and Lanie able to call the nearest OB for an appointment. The nearest OB was almost an hour outside of town and was booked for the next two weeks, but Lanie didn't think that would be a problem. Nothing happened early in pregnancies, right?

As she hung up the phone, the bell above the door jingled and Paula made her entrance, her dark hair flying behind her.

"Lanie Perkins," she said, splaying her hands on the counter, "Bert just told me you got married yesterday. To whom did you marry and why were we not invited?"

Lanie sighed. She had hoped Bert would keep the information to himself or at the very least that he wouldn't run into Paula for a while, but secrets didn't remain secret very long in a small town. "I did, Paula. It was rather a spur-of-the-moment decision, but we will have a party soon and invite everyone."

"Do your parents know?" Paula asked, leaning back and cocking one hip to the side.

"Not yet, but I assume they will soon."

Paula's mouth dropped open at the implication of the snarky comment, and Lanie quickly hurried to amend the situation. The last thing she needed was Paula angry with her.

"Look, Paula, I'll tell my folks, but I'm thirty years old. I'm allowed to marry who I want when I want and I don't need anyone's permission."

That seemed to soothe Paula's fragile ego for the moment as her face softened and she leaned forward. "Was it at least that handsome friend of yours or did you pick up a random stranger on the street?"

Lanie let the dig go and smiled back at Paula. "It was my handsome friend whom I've actually known for years though we just recently began hanging out again after my separation. You can rest assured I didn't marry a stranger." As the words left her mouth,

Lanie wondered how true they were. He had opened up about his ex-wife, but there was still so much in Azarius' past she didn't know, and she wondered how long it would take to peel away all the layers and finally feel like she knew him, the real him.

"Well, that is nice," Paula said, but her face told a different story. Lanie knew Paula would keep digging until she knew the real reason for the marriage.

After Paula, Lanie enjoyed a steady stream of customers. Some knew of her hasty marriage and asked questions, but others either didn't care or didn't know. Still, by the end of the evening, Lanie was exhausted.

A minute before closing time, the bell jingled again. Lanie nearly threw her hands up in frustration but smiled when she saw it was Layla. She gestured her inside and then locked the door behind her.

"I'm so glad it's just you. It's been busy tonight," Lanie said, sinking down into a chair and dropping her head onto her hands.

"For you or for Paula?" Layla joked as she pulled out the chair across from Lanie. Lanie groaned and rolled her eyes.

"You could have told me at least," Layla said. "I thought we were friends."

Lanie's head shot up. "Oh, Layla, I'm so sorry. I meant to tell you first, but I got in late today, and then Bert saw my ring and it just spiraled out of control from there."

"It's okay, I'm just teasing you. I guess that means the test was positive then?"

Lanie slapped her forehead. The stress of telling her parents and deciding what to do had weighed so heavily on her mind that she had forgotten to tell Layla. "Yes, but no one knows that part yet except for you and my parents. Azarius asked me to elope the night we told them. I wasn't going to at first, but then I thought about how people would react when I started to show, and I took him up on his offer."

Layla nodded, her dark hair rustling against her shoulders. "What about the secrecy thing? You guys work that out?"

Lanie's lips twisted together as she broke away from Layla's gaze. "Some, he told me about his ex-wife, but I didn't ask for more and he didn't volunteer any more. I'm hopeful now that we're married, he'll share his life with me."

A small sigh escaped Layla's lips. "I hope so for your sake, Lanie, but what are you going to do if he doesn't?"

Lanie shook her head. She had no idea.

CHAPTER 14

*A*zarius walked into his apartment with an extra bounce in his step. Some happy tune he couldn't place whistled from his lips.

"How did it go?" Greg asked from the couch.

"It was amazing. Lanie looked like an angel in her dress. I forgot rings, but they had simple bands for us," he said, looking down at the band on his left hand. Though small, the gold band stood out against his dark skin. "I'll have to get better ones soon as she deserves something with diamonds."

"Yes, she does. I'm glad you finally came around. Did you two have your heart to heart?"

Azarius shifted his weight and turned his face as he dropped his bag in the oversized chair. "Uh, not exactly. I told her about Krista but not my mama yet, but I will."

"You need to man. She deserves the truth, and she isn't going to run."

Azarius plopped down next to his bag. "I guess I know that, but I still worry, you know?"

"You don't have to worry about her. Lanie is all in when it comes to you as long as you stay all in."

As long as he stayed all in. That did seem to be his issue, didn't it? But this time would be different. He promised himself this time he was all in.

His day proved to be busy, but Lanie was never far from his mind. He waited as patiently as he could until nine pm when he knew she would be done at the diner before dialing her number. It rang two times before her angelic voice filled the earpiece.

"Hello?"

"Hello, wife, how was your day?" Azarius lay back against his black pillow and folded one arm behind his head.

There was a slight pause before she answered. "It was eventful. I forgot to take my ring off before I went to work and now half the town knows I got married."

"Well, that's okay, right? We knew they would find out eventually."

"Yeah, I guess I just wasn't expecting it to be so quickly." Another quick pause and her voice came again, lighter this time. "How was your day?"

A smile crawled across his lips. "It was great. I got to wake up with the most beautiful woman I know and call her my wife. The only thing that would have made it better was if I got to come home to her too."

"We'll have to figure that out soon. Oh hey, I scheduled the first appointment with the OB if you want to come. It's for the end of June. Also this weekend there's a Summer Fling. I know you say you don't dance in public, but would you be interested in going?"

Azarius's heart leapt. He wasn't much of a dancer, but the chance to see Lanie again and hold her in his arms was too good to pass up. "Of course I'm interested. You tell me when, and I'll be there. I'll stay the weekend if that works for you."

"I'd love that. I miss you already," she said.

"I miss you too." The feeling didn't go away as he hung up the phone. Instead, it intensified, growing and churning in his stomach. He couldn't remember ever feeling this way about a woman before, not even Krista.

~

*W*hen Friday finally rolled around, Azarius could barely wait for work to end so he could see Lanie again. Even though they had spoken every day of the week, it wasn't the same and he really wanted to hold her in his arms again. He missed the smell of her hair and the feel of her soft skin against his.

The house was dark as he pulled in, and he briefly wondered where Greg was, though it was possible he was sitting in the dark. He often did that when he had headaches, and he suffered from migraines often.

Azarius threw the Mustang in park and turned off the ignition. His plan was to be back on the road in half an hour, so he needed to pack a bag as quickly as possible. He should have done it last night, but work had run late, and he'd fallen into bed bone tired.

Not bothering to flick on the lights, he bounded up the stairs and clicked his bedroom light on. His bag still sat near the bed from the road trip to Oklahoma.

One at a time, he pulled open the drawers and grabbed the needed items. A few shirts, pants, socks, and underwear. Then he moseyed into the bathroom to grab his lotions, toothbrush, and shower items. He added those to the bag and grabbed a jacket for good measure. Mid-June in Texas normally meant warmer weather, but sometimes a cold front would sneak in, and he didn't want to be left unprepared.

As he opened the front door and stepped outside, he realized he still hadn't seen or heard Greg. Maybe he had gone to visit his folks. They did live close in town, so he could walk there if needed.

With a shrug of his shoulders, Azarius locked the door behind him and jogged back to the car. He had made great time and should see Lanie before she turned in for the night. The thought sent an extra tingle of joy through him and a smile across his lips. He turned the radio up and nodded his head to the beat as he pulled out of the driveway and back on the main road.

Two hours later, he was parking in front of Lanie's house. Her porch light gleamed, a welcoming beacon in the dark night. Reaching over, Azarius grabbed his bag and climbed out of the car, locking it behind him. The front door opened before he had a chance to knock and Lanie rushed into his arms.

The bag fell from his hand as he wound his arms around her and planted his lips on hers. Heat swirled through them, dispelling any chill in the surrounding air. When they broke apart, he smiled down at her. "I guess you did miss me."

"More than you know," she said. With her fingers firmly locked with his, she pulled him into the house, pausing only long enough for him to rescue his bag.

～

*S*unlight streaming in through the windows woke Azarius the next morning. A glance to his left revealed Lanie's auburn hair splayed across his arm. He tightened his grip on her shoulder, relishing the feel of her against him. The realization that he had almost lost her made him squeeze her a little tighter, and she opened her eyes.

"Hey you," she said, her voice still heavy with sleep.

"Hey, sorry, I was enjoying the scent of your hair, go back to sleep."

She tilted her head to smile up at him. "What is it with you and my hair?"

"I don't know," he said, pushing her head back against his chest, "but yours has always smelled fantastic."

A giggle escaped her lips, and she batted his chest playfully. "I love you, funny man."

The words permeated his heart and a feeling of joy coursed through his body.

"We should probably get up," Lanie said as her finger lazily traced a pattern on his chest. "My parents probably know, but we should stop in and tell them before the dance in case they don't."

That sounded like torture to Azarius, but he would do anything for Lanie, and so after another kiss on her forehead, he released her from his grip. She leaned up and planted her lips directly on his, nibbling slightly on his bottom lip and sending a tingling sensation through him.

"You better stop that if you want to get up," he said.

She winked at him, but pulled back, and he immediately missed the warmth. Sighing, he rolled over and out of the bed.

As Lanie padded to the shower, he wandered into the kitchen to make some tea. He filled the tea kettle and set it boiling on the stove while he opened cupboards in search of some tea bags. Lanie loved green tea almost as much as her coffee, so she was sure to have a few bags around somewhere. His search yielded a stash in the pantry, and he pulled out the box.

Lanie entered the kitchen as the tea kettle began whistling. "Shower's free," she said, planting a kiss on his cheek.

"I'll jump in as soon as I finish my tea," he said, returning her kiss and filling a mug.

She filled a mug as well and sat down at the small table across from him. As he sipped the warm tea and took in her porcelain skin from across the way, he knew he could no longer be content with only seeing her on weekends. He'd have to make the decision to either move here with her or convince her to move back with him, but it could wait until after the dance tonight. Maybe by then he'd have an idea of what to do.

A few hours later, they pulled up in front of Lanie's parents' house. Though they were married now, Azarius's mouth still dried up at the prospect of seeing her father again.

"Come on, it can't be any worse than last time," Lanie said, sensing his discomfort.

"Yeah, I know," he said with a shrug. "I just wish we could win them over."

"We will one day," she said and turned off the engine.

The walk up to the door felt like the green mile to Azarius. Lanie squeezed his hand as she rang the doorbell. Again her mother was the one to answer it.

"Lanie, Azarius, come on in," her mother said with a smile, but Azarius noted it didn't quite reach her eyes.

"Hi mom, sorry we didn't call first, and you've probably already heard the news, but Azarius and I wanted to make sure you heard it from us before you were accosted at the dance."

"I'm not sure to what news you are referring," her mother said. "But you should share with your father too."

They followed the older woman into the living room. Lanie's father looked up as they entered. "Well, hello again. To what do we owe this pleasure?"

Lanie opened her mouth to speak, but Azarius stepped forward and spoke first. "We wanted to say again how sorry we are that we didn't do things right the first time, but I took your words to heart. The Army taught me to follow through with commitments and so Lanie and I eloped last weekend. We hope you'll be able to give us your blessing now as we want to move forward."

Her mother clasped her hand to her mouth and collapsed into a chair. "Oh, Lanie, you eloped?"

"It was my idea, ma'am. I wanted Lanie to be married before she started showing and people began asking questions."

"But we plan to have a big party to announce it mom," Lanie said, stepping in.

There was a moment of silence as her parents looked back and forth at each other. Then her father rose from his chair and approached. "Army, huh? What's your rank, son?"

"I'm a sergeant, and I'm still in the reserves sir."

Bob's eyes narrowed even more. "Well, I certainly can appreciate your service. I too served my country. One more question. What is your stance on God?"

"Dad," Lanie said with a shake of her head.

Azarius took a deep breath. "To be honest sir, until I met Lanie, I believed there was a God, but I didn't have a relationship with him. However, after hearing your daughter talk about him and seeing her faith, I started looking and praying." He smiled as Lanie turned to him with wide eyes. "I hadn't told you yet, but I did. I started praying, and with your help, I'd like to deepen that relationship. I know I may not know exactly how to be a strong leader yet, but I'd like to try."

Lanie's father narrowed his eyes as if he were trying to decide if Azarius were telling the truth. Lanie's bottom lip was curled in under her top teeth as she looked from her father to Azarius and back again.

"I don't approve of the way this started, but I do see that you are trying to make a difference," her father said. He extended his hand. "Welcome to the family."

Relief flooded Azarius as he shook the outstretched hand. Maybe they could be a real family after all.

CHAPTER 15

*L*anie couldn't believe how well the interaction with her parents had gone. "Were you serious about what you said about praying?" she asked Azarius as she backed out of her parents' drive.

"I was and I am," he said with a smile that showed off his white teeth. "Are you pleased?"

"Pleased and surprised," she said as she pulled into a space in front of The Diner. "I honestly thought that might be the one thing we'd fight over in the future."

"Well, now we have nothing to fight over," he said, flashing a wink at her.

"Good, now come and meet my friends. I want to show you off." She parked the car and opened the door, but as she stepped out a pain shot through her abdomen and she doubled over.

Azarius rushed to her side, concern etched on his face. "Are you alright?"

She took a deep breath, hoping to ease the pain. "Yeah, I think I'm just hungry." The pain receded, and she stood, flashing him what she hoped was a confident smile, but he didn't look convinced. "Come on, it's nothing."

Lanie led the way into The Diner, waving to the people she knew as she made her way over to the back booth Layla was holding down. She slid in across from Layla and patted the seat next to her for Azarius to sit.

"Layla, I want you to officially meet my husband, Azarius. Azarius, this is my friend Layla."

"It's nice to meet the man who's made my friend smile again," Layla said as she shook Azarius's hand.

He nodded, forcing a smile on his face, but Lanie could still see the concern residing in his eyes.

Max appeared a few minutes later, clad in his usual flannel. "Back for food this time, huh?" he asked Azarius as he plopped three menus on the table top.

"Max, behave," Layla said, raising her eyebrow at him. "This is Azarius, Lanie's husband."

Something akin to a snort came out of Max's mouth as he leaned back and folded his arms across his chest. "Husband, huh? Well, congrats I guess."

"Thanks, Max," Lanie said. "Maybe our nuptial will spur you into action, huh?" She cringed again as Layla kicked her shin under the table, but it was worth it. If her friend wasn't going to push him, someone ought to.

Max opened his mouth to speak, but thought better of it and turned back to the kitchen without a word.

"Is that guy the owner?" Azarius asked in a hushed voice.

Layla belted out a laugh, throwing back her head and letting her dark hair swish back and forth. "Yeah, he's the owner. He's a little gritty on the outside, but he's really a sweetheart underneath all that gruff."

"Max is Layla's boyfriend," Lanie explained.

"Oh, I see." Azarius unfolded the menu and glanced over the

contents.

"Yeah, he is an acquired taste," Layla said with a smile.

Lanie grinned back before another shock of pain shot through her. She tried to keep her face passive as she reached over and pushed on her abdomen. It was odd to have cramps if she were pregnant, wasn't it? As the pain receded again, she pushed the thought from her mind and decided to enjoy lunch with her friends. After this it would be time to get ready for the Summer Fling Dance and she had the perfect dress. She couldn't wait to show Azarius.

~

Two hours later, Lanie was curled up on the couch watching cartoons with Azarius. She wasn't much for cartoons herself, but if it meant laying in his arms, she didn't care what they watched. As she looked up at him though, an old doubt resurfaced and tumbled from her mouth before she could stop it.

"Azarius, why didn't you tell me your birthday the first time I asked?"

"Huh?"

He kept his face turned to the television, but she had felt him stiffen slightly and she knew he had heard her. Well, two could play this game. She maneuvered to a sitting position, so she was blocking his vision.

"You heard me. Why didn't you tell me when your birthday was?"

He sighed and shifted his glance to her eyes. "I told you, I don't want anyone to make a big deal of my birthday because I don't reciprocate well. I'll probably forget yours at least once in this marriage."

"I know, but that doesn't seem like the real reason or at least not the whole reason. I just want the truth."

"That is the truth, Lanie," he said.

She knew there was more and the fact he wouldn't tell her miffed her. "Fine, I thought you were going to open up to me, share your life, but I guess not." She stood and walked to the bedroom, her feet stomping on the floor harder than she intended.

"Lanie." She heard his voice behind her, but she shut the door and locked it, blocking out his noise. As she did, another wave of pain coursed through her abdomen and she fell against the bed, clutching her stomach. She might be angry at him for concealing the whole truth, but wasn't she doing the same thing?

The pain had gotten worse, but she hadn't told him about it and she didn't even know why. Shouldn't she be sharing everything with him now that he was her husband? Yet, she couldn't stop from telling herself that she'd take care of it Monday after he left, that surely it wasn't anything to worry about. She fell asleep with that thought in her head, curled up with her hands over her stomach.

Incessant knocking at her door woke Lanie sometime later. She opened her eyes, concentrating on her stomach, but the pain was gone. At least for now. Rolling off the bed, she trundled to the door and opened it.

"I don't want to fight, Lanie, I'm sorry," Azarius said. "I'll tell you whatever you want to know."

Lanie shook her head as she stepped into his arms. "No, I should be the one apologizing. I know you'll tell me when you're ready." *Just like I'll tell you about the pain when I'm ready.*

His arms wound around her, and Lanie sighed against his muscular chest. "It's almost time for the dance. You still want to go?" She tilted her head up to look at him.

He leaned down to place a kiss on her nose. "I'll go wherever you want to go. I know I'm not the best at expressing my feelings, but I promise to work on it."

"It means everything, right?" she said with a smile, remembering the song he had once sent her via text.

His arms tightened around her. "That's right. It means everything."

An hour later, Lanie and Azarius walked arm and arm into the large red barn. Pink, white, and blue balloons hung from the ceiling amid streamers of the same color. A few tables filled the right side, each covered in a different table cloth cover. Amid those, a small table with a speaker system blared songs for those on the dance floor. At the very back, a long table was laden with a myriad of cookies and bowls of fruit punch.

"Never see anything like this back in Dallas, huh?" Lanie said, squeezing Azarius's arm.

"There might be a reason for that," Azarius said with a smile.

Lanie punched his arm and led him to the dance floor.

"Lanie, I don't dance in public," Azarius said, planting his feet.

"You do today. Come on, it's a slow song. You just put your arms around me and sway. Please." She put on her best puppy dog face and batted her eyes at him.

He rolled his eyes and shook his head, but followed her to the floor. "Fine, but don't say I didn't warn you."

As his arms wound around her, Lanie breathed in his manly scent, put her head on his shoulder, and sighed. The grey shirt he was wearing tonight hugged his chest and his arms, accentuating his well-toned muscles. She couldn't imagine any place she'd rather be.

"See, this isn't too ha....." Lanie never finished her sentence as the worst pain yet shot through her stomach. Her hand clutched at Azarius's arm as she crumpled downward.

"Lanie? What's wrong?"

Lanie shook her head, the pain too strong to talk over. With a strength she didn't know he had, Azarius scooped her up in his arms and headed for the door.

"What's going on?" Layla's concerned voice reached Lanie's ears as the cooler air hit her skin.

"I don't know," Azarius said. "She just collapsed, holding her stomach. She's grabbed it a few times today. Where's the closest doctor?"

"Closed for now, but there's an ER clinic on the far side of town. Come on, I'll drive."

"Where are we going?" Max's voice had joined the conversation.

"The ER, come on."

Moments later the car door opened and Lanie felt Azarius sliding her into the backseat. Then he climbed in beside her. The feel of his hands smoothing her hair warmed her heart. She remembered a time a few months back when she had done the same for him.

He hadn't wanted her to come over, insisting he didn't feel well, but Lanie had promised to work and let him rest. When she got there, he had curled up on the couch with his head on her lap and she had stroked it until he felt better. It had been a loving gesture then, but she had never expected the gesture to be returned.

The car roared to life, and Lanie could tell by the erratic driving that Layla was behind the wheel. A few minutes later, Lanie rolled forward as Layla slammed on the brake and threw the car into park.

Azarius helped her out of the car before picking her up again and striding into the ER.

"Can I help you?" a woman's voice said.

"My wife is having stomach pains, and she's pregnant."

"She's what?" Max's voice broke through the haze of pain.

"Sssh! Not now."

Layla's voice hushing Max was the last thing Lanie heard before the darkness took her over.

CHAPTER 16

When Lanie opened her eyes, the first thing she noticed was the cold, numb sensation inside her veins. The awful searing pain was gone, but the emptiness in its place was even worse. It reminded her of that old Robert Frost poem "Fire and Ice." She had always thought the fire would be the worse, but she would gladly trade the ice she felt now for the earlier fire. She splayed her hands across her abdomen, but there was nothing.

It's just too early, that's all. I didn't feel anything yesterday either.

But the truth nibbled at her brain. The pain earlier hadn't been natural. Even though this was her first pregnancy, she knew that. Of course she knew that, but God wouldn't take her baby, would he?

Not when she had come back to the fold. What was that old story? The one about the shepherd who rejoices when the lost sheep returns or the prodigal son. That's what she was - the prodigal daughter. And Azarius had started praying. Surely that gave them some points, some cushion from the grief of life. He might never have started praying had there been no baby.

"Lord, I know we didn't do it right in the beginning, but if you'll save this baby, I promise we'll do it right from now on. We'll be there every Sunday. We'll attend Bible studies. I'll join the choir. We'll do whatever you want us to do if you'll save the baby."

Lanie waited for some warmth, some sign of healing, but the cold emptiness remained. Maybe God was no longer listening. Maybe he had turned his back on her because of her divorce and her sexual slipup.

"Ah, you're awake."

Lanie turned to the door. An elderly nurse with a kind face and blue scrubs smiled at her.

"How are you feeling?"

"Cold," Lanie replied.

"Oh, well, let me get you a blanket."

Lanie nodded, though she knew no blanket would warm up the cold she felt.

The nurse exited the room and returned a moment later with a folded blanket in her arms. "Here you go, fresh out of the warmer. That should help."

She spread the blanket over Lanie's body, but it made no difference. The bitter cold still ate at her insides.

"You have people waiting to see you, but I'll send the doctor in first, okay?"

"Is it gone?" Though Lanie was certain she had lost the pregnancy, she needed to hear the words.

The woman's face held her smile, but her eyes dropped a little. "I'll send in the doctor to talk to you shortly."

She exited the room, leaving Lanie in silence. She hadn't said yes, Lanie reasoned. Maybe the baby wasn't gone; maybe there were just complications. She could handle complications, but the loss? If the baby was gone, would Azarius be gone too? As much as she wanted to believe he had married her for her, a shred of doubt that the marriage had occurred only because of the baby remained.

The door opened, and a young man in a white coat entered. He didn't look much older than Lanie, except for his receding hairline. "Hello, Lanie, I'm Dr. Fredrickson, how are you feeling?"

A darkness like nothing she'd felt before descended on Lanie, and her eyes narrowed. "Why does everyone keep asking me that? How do you think I'm feeling?"

The doctor appeared not to register her anger as his voice did not change in emotion or inflection. "I'm sure you are feeling a lot of things. Probably guilt and anger at the loss of your pregnancy."

Lanie squeezed her eyes shut and shook her head. *No, it wasn't true.* If she didn't listen to him, it wouldn't be true.

"And those feelings are completely normal," he continued. "But Lanie, it's important that you also know this wasn't your fault. It was an ectopic pregnancy. It never had a chance, and the pain you felt today was your body rejecting it. The good news is that it didn't rupture, and there appears to be no damage to your fallopian tubes so you'll be able to get pregnant again. In fact, a lot of women get pregnant within months of a miscarriage like this."

Lanie continued to shake her head. Waves of denial and anger fought within her.

"I'll give you some time, but your family would like to see you."

Family. The word elicited a single tear from her right eye. She had no family. Her chance at a family had died with the fire and only the ice remained, and the ice was so much worse.

～

*A*zarius paced the floor of the hospital, worry lines etched in his face. He needed word on Lanie's condition. In his brain, he knew it wasn't cancer, but he couldn't help fearing he'd lose Lanie just like he'd lost his mother. He didn't think he would survive if something happened to her.

A young doctor approached the waiting area. "Azarius Jacobson?" he asked after glancing at his clipboard.

"That's me," Azarius said and Lanie's two friends joined him.

"Well, physically your wife is going to be fine. She's resting now. Emotionally though, well, you need to speak with her. Lanie's not herself right now, and she might not be for a while. She's going to need time and a lot of patience."

"Can I see her?"

"Yes, but I suggest one at a time, and remember patience." He motioned for Azarius to follow him down the sterile hallway.

This, this was the green mile. Azarius had thought the walk to her parents' house had been bad, but the fear and sadness he felt now were so much worse.

Azarius knocked gently on the door before pushing it open. Lanie lay still and stiff under the white sheet. She glanced his way as he entered and then returned her focus to the television up on the wall which was playing some game show. He wondered what she was thinking behind her expressionless face.

"Hey Lanie. How are you?" he asked when he reached her bedside.

"I lost our baby, Azarius, how do you think I'm feeling?"

"We... we lost the baby?" He couldn't keep the shock from his voice. The baby was gone. The baby that had brought them together. Did that mean they would fall apart now? Or were they strong enough to survive this? Fear they weren't flooded his veins.

"Not we, Azarius. Me. I lost the baby. It was ectopic."

Azarius blinked at the flat tone of her voice. He had never heard her normally bright cheery voice so empty.

"It wasn't your fault, Lanie," he said reaching for her hand. Though she didn't pull it away, she made no move to return the gesture and her hand remained limp like wilted lettuce in his hand.

"It it was an ectopic pregnancy, there was nothing you could have done."

"It's our punishment, don't you see? We're being punished for intimacy outside of marriage."

Azarius sighed and sat down on the edge of the bed. "Lanie, I know I'm new to this religion thing, but I don't think God works that way. Ectopic pregnancies happen all the time. Did the doctor say anything else?"

"He said there was no damage, that we'd be able to try again."

"Well, that's a good thing. I'd say we're lucky then."

"Lucky?" she snorted. "We eloped to save ourselves from the embarrassment of having a child out of wedlock, and now there is no child."

Azarius shook his head. His words were coming out all wrong. "Lanie, I don't care about all of that," he began.

"You don't care about our baby?" Lanie's voice dripped with venom as she turned fiery eyes on him. "That's all we had holding us together."

"That's not true."

"It is true, and you know it!" Her voice rose in volume until the last two words were almost shouted. "You know what? Just get out."

"Lanie…"

"Out!" she screamed. "You can go back to your secrecy and riddles and the other women you probably have on the side."

Azarius sucked in his breath. She's not herself, he had to remind himself. "I'll go for now, Lanie, but I'm not leaving forever."

She said nothing, just returned her gaze to the television.

Unsure what else to do, Azarius sighed and exited the room.

Layla stood as he entered the waiting room. "How did it go?"

Azarius shook his head. Tears stung the back of his throat, but he would not cry in front of this woman he barely knew.

"It's okay," she said, touching his arm. "She's hurting right now, but it will get better."

Azarius nodded and covered her hand with his own to show he understood. Then he walked down the hall. He needed to be alone.

He rounded the corner and leaned against the wall, but before he could let the emotions out, his phone rang. The area code was Dallas, but he didn't recognize the number. Swallowing the knot of emotion in his throat, he punched the button.

"Hello?"

"Is this Azarius Jacobson?"

The unfamiliar professional voice dispelled the last of his emotion, and he stood straighter. "Yes, this is Azarius."

"Mr. Jacobson, we have you listed as an emergency contact for Greg Weaver."

Azarius's heart tightened. "Yes, is everything okay?" This couldn't be happening. First Lanie and now Greg.

"He was in an accident last night."

"I'm on my way," Azarius said, not waiting for more details from the woman. He looked around and spying a nurse at a nearby desk, he headed her direction.

"Hi, do you have some paper, so I can leave a note?"

The woman held up a finger and only then did he see the phone attached to her ear. Nodding, he stepped away from the desk to give her some privacy to finish the call.

"I'm sorry, what did you need?" she asked a moment later.

"Some paper to leave a note."

She looked down at the desk which was cluttered with papers and shifted through them until she found a blank one. She handed it to him with a pen and then turned to her computer.

Azarius scribbled a quick message to Lanie about Greg's accident and folded the paper. "Can you make sure the patient in room 108 gets this?"

The nurse nodded, but as she took the paper, Azarius wondered if his folded slip wouldn't get lost in the clutter of the desk. With a sigh, he headed for the exit, dialing a cab on his way. Lanie needed him, but she didn't want him around right now, and he needed to make sure Greg was okay. Maybe the drive would clear his head and he would find some way to convince Lanie he wasn't going anywhere.

CHAPTER 17

*A*zarius entered Greg's room in the Dallas hospital both anxious to make sure Greg was okay and take him to task for his poor timing.

Greg's right leg was suspended in the air, encased in a cast and a bandage was wrapped around his head as well.

"Dude, what happened?" All thoughts of giving Greg a hard time flew from his mind at the image of his friend broken and battered.

Greg's lips pulled into a lopsided smile. "It's worse than it looks, really. Az, I met a girl."

"Where? In the hospital?" Azarius wondered if the head trauma was affecting Greg's memory.

"No, last night. I met her after work. I called an Uber for a ride home, and she was the driver. She's beautiful, Az. Long dark hair and emerald eyes."

"That's great, Greg, but what about the accident?"

"Oh, yeah, we got in a heated discussion about the best

LOVE CONQUERS ALL | 409
LOVE CONQUERS ALL | 409

television show, and she missed a stop sign. Neither of us saw the other truck."

"I hope she has insurance," Azarius said.

"I'm sure she does, but it's not like that, man. She's been here every moment since the accident."

Azarius glanced around the room to make sure he hadn't missed the beautiful mystery woman. "Greg? How much head trauma did you sustain? There's no one here."

"She went to get some food. She'll be right back."

As if his words held summoning power, a woman entered the doorway. "Oh, sorry, I didn't know you had guests. I can come back later."

"No, Jada, this is my bro, Azarius, the one I told you about."

Jada's eyes lit up, and a smile stretched across her face. She hurried into the room, dropping the food on the table before coming to Azarius's side. Before he knew what was happening, she had grabbed his hand and was pumping it up and down.

"I'm so happy to meet you. Greg has told me such good things, and I know you must be worried about me, but I'm normally a very good driver, and I do have insurance so Greg will be taken care of." The words spilled out one after the other from her mouth and all Azarius could do was stare. He had never heard anyone speak so quickly.

"I wish we had met under different circumstances, but Greg said you were visiting your wife." Her hand flew to her mouth. "Oh, I'm so sorry we cut your visit short. Yours was the only name I had before we got in the accident. I guess his license still shows his sister's place, and they tried to call her, but she wasn't answering, so then they asked me if he had any other family as he had a brain bleed and they thought they might have to do surgery. He had called you his brother; I didn't realize you aren't brothers by blood, but I told them to look you up. I didn't mean to ruin your weekend though."

The irony of this woman, who appeared to have only one speed when she spoke, liking Greg, who rarely spoke full sentences, hit Azarius and he laughed. A full bellied, throaty laugh that pushed away his sadness and fears for a moment.

Jada's eyes grew wide, and she glanced to Greg, who appeared just as surprised as she was.

"I'm sorry," Azarius said, composing himself. "It's just that you two are like polar opposites, which probably means you're perfect for each other. It's nice to meet you, Jada, and you're right - I do wish we had met under better circumstance, but if Greg likes you, then I like you." He turned to Greg. "And what about you? What is the damage here?"

"Broken leg, concussion, mild brain bleed, and bruised ribs," Greg said. "I'll live."

"You will, but you'll need someone to take care of you and I can't stay. Lanie had an ectopic pregnancy and lost it."

Jada sucked in her breath. "Oh no."

"Oh man, I'm sorry," Greg said. "Is she doing okay?"

"Not really," Azarius said with a shake of his head. "She's angry and hurt. I need to show her I'm not going anywhere."

"How are you going to do that?" Greg asked.

"By doing something I should have done a long time ago. I'm going to tell her the truth. And I'm going to commit. I'm going all in, but it means I won't be in the apartment to take care of you."

"I can do it," Jada said. "I don't believe in living together, but I can check up on him, and I'll pay for someone to be there with him when I can't."

Azarius turned to her. "How can you afford that on an Uber driver pay?"

"It pays more than you think," she laughed, "but it wouldn't be paid with my Uber pay." She bit her lip as if unsure if she wanted to disclose the thought on her mind, then drew her shoulders back and looked him in the eye. "I'm an heiress. My father owns Vizio

Technology. I don't drive because I have to; I drive because I want to. It keeps me grounded, and I like meeting all the different types of people."

Now Azarius knew they were a match made in Heaven. For all of Greg's positives, handling money was not one of them. Azarius looked to Greg.

"It will be fine, man. I know it seems fast, but when you know, you know, right?"

Azarius nodded. He felt the same way about Lanie. It might have taken them a decade to get together, but he'd known she was special the first time he saw her. "Okay, well, can I get you anything from the house? I'm going to start getting things in order and then take care of some business tomorrow."

The shop he needed to visit would be closed tonight, but hopefully they'd be open tomorrow. He didn't want to be away from Lanie for long, especially in her present state. She might think she didn't want or need him, but he was determined to show her differently.

"Yeah, I could use a few things," Greg said, "but just drop them by tomorrow. I can't use any of them tonight anyway."

Azarius took notes on his phone of the items Greg would need for the next few days and then headed to the apartment.

As he stepped inside, he realized it might be one of his last times in the place. He wouldn't miss the apartment per se- it was nothing fancy - but it did hold memories of his time with Lanie, and while he knew he would be making more memories, a sentimental piece tugged at his heart.

He gathered up Greg's items and then packed a bag of his own. He would probably have to hire someone to pack up the rest of the items, but that could wait. Three months still remained on the lease.

After those tasks were finished, Azarius climbed into bed. Only the faintest whiff of Lanie's shampoo remained on his pillow, and he missed her warmth.

"Lord," he said quietly, "please be with Lanie now. Comfort her and heal her pain. Work on her heart and help me to know exactly what to say to show her how serious I am."

~

"He's not here?" Lanie asked as Layla helped her pack up the next morning. There wasn't much, but Layla had run to her house the previous night and grabbed toiletries and comfortable clothing. She had then stayed until visiting hours ended when Lanie had been left alone with her thoughts.

Torturous, sad, and lonely thoughts. Yet, somewhere in the midst of those thoughts, an arm of comfort had surrounded her, easing the guilt and numbing the pain. Just as He stated in the Bible, God had been there at her lowest, offering her comfort if only she would accept it

It wasn't an immediate erasing of pain, and Lanie knew there would still be rough days ahead, but she had woken this morning with a desire to apologize to Azarius. He certainly hadn't earned the lashing she delivered the night before.

Layla bit her bottom lip and shook her head. "No, I'm sorry, honey. I haven't seen him since last night. He seemed pretty shaken up though."

Lanie's lips pursed together forming a tight seal. Of course he was. She had told him to leave and practically kicked him out of the room and out of her life. "Well, that's a problem for another day, I guess," Lanie said. She had no more energy to give today.

Layla placed her arm on Lanie's shoulders. "I don't think he's gone for good. One thing I can tell for sure is when a man loves a woman, and he loves you."

"Right," Lanie nodded, "that's why it took a decade for you to realize Max loved you."

Layla feigned shock before throwing her head back and laughing. "Well, maybe I can't see it when it's aimed at me, but I can tell with anyone else." Her laughter rang throughout the room - a ray of hope in the midst of the darkness, and Lanie tucked that ray of hope away to remember later when the sadness knocked again.

"All ready?" An elder orderly with closely cropped grey hair pushed a black wheelchair into the room.

"Is that really necessary?" Lanie asked with a roll of her eyes. "I can walk."

A single shake of his head confirmed her fears. "Sorry, hospital policy. Everyone gets a ride out. Think of it as curbside service."

He flashed a wink and a smile, earning a small one in return. With a sigh, Lanie walked to the chair and sat down.

"Now that wasn't so hard, see?" He patted her shoulder with a tan, weathered hand that had probably comforted many patients before her. Then he turned the chair around and pushed it out the door.

It felt good to leave the sterile walls, but hard. This building held the last memory of her child, but also the realization she'd never know if she had lost a son or a daughter.

Before the black cloud could cloak her again, Lanie pushed the thought away and squared her shoulders. It would do no good to dwell in the past. She needed to focus on the future, whatever it might hold.

~

*L*anie stood in front of her bathroom mirror Monday wondering if she really could go into work. Her father had offered to give her a few days, but she'd insisted the business of routine would help her feel better. Now she wasn't so sure.

Dark circles still clung to her eyes, and a sadness she wasn't used to seeing had taken residence on her face. Part of it was losing the baby, but another part was not hearing from Azarius. She knew she had been hard on him, but she had hoped he would fight for their marriage, that he would be there to take her home or at least call to check up on her, but none of that had happened.

His arms could have at least eased some of the pain on her heart. After all, it was his baby too. She looked back to the warm comfort of her bed which beckoned to her with soft sheets and the promise of cloaking darkness. She could crawl in bed, pull the covers over her head, and let the darkness steal the rest of the day. Her father would understand.

The chime of the doorbell halted her decision. She wasn't expecting anyone, but it was probably her mother checking up on her. Not bothering to even brush her hair, Lanie shuffled to the front door and pulled it open.

Still raw with emotion, tears streamed down her face before words could form at the vision in front of her. Azarius stood with his arms by his side and a bag at his feet, an angel in the midst of the wilderness.

"I thought you were gone," Lanie sobbed. Her knees gave out, but before she could hit the floor, he stepped over the threshold and wound his arms around her.

"For better or for worse, remember?" he whispered in her ear and Lanie melted into his strong chest, letting his arms bear most of her weight. The tears poured out, a continuing landslide of tears down her cheeks and still he held her. He held her until her shoulders stopped shaking and her breath slowed. Only then did he lift her face to look in her eyes.

"Where did you go?" she asked. "Why weren't you there when I was released?"

Azarius kissed her nose. "Let me bring my bag in and I'll tell you everything."

Reluctantly, Lanie stepped from his embrace and let him grab his bag and shut the door. Azarius patted his pocket and grabbed Lanie's hand, leading her to the couch.

"I left you a note, but I'm guessing from your reaction you never got it."

Lanie shook her head.

Azarius nodded; he should have known as much. "After you told me go," he began, "I got a call from a Dallas hospital. Greg had been in an accident and they couldn't reach his sister."

"Oh no, is he okay?" Lanie asked, squeezing Azarius's hand tighter.

"He will be," Azarius said. "He'll have some healing to do, but he met a new friend who I think will take good care of him. Lanie, I know you wanted me to leave, but I hope it was only the anger talking."

Lanie nodded; she still couldn't believe how she had lashed out at him. "It was mostly that, but," her eyes dropped to her lap.

"But what?" His finger tilted her chin up again. "You can tell me anything."

"I was... I am afraid that now that there's no baby, you won't want to be married any longer. There's still so much you haven't told me, and I..." her words trailed off.

Azarius sighed. "Lanie, I know the baby is what brought us together, but it wasn't the reason I married you. That night, that fateful bad decision night, I knew I was falling for you. It broke my heart when I saw your note the next morning, and when you first left for Star Lake, I was a mess. I had no idea how much I cared about you until you were gone."

He shook his head and smiled. "You can ask Greg - well, when he gets out of the hospital. I moped around all day and spent most of the time in my room in the dark. It was Greg who convinced me to drive out to see you that first time, and I didn't even know about the baby then, but I knew I wanted to be with you. But you didn't seem ready, and I thought I'd lost you again. Then you showed up on my doorstep with the news of your pregnancy, and I was terrified and elated at the same time. I knew this was our chance, but I tried to play it safe, to keep my secrets and live in both sides, and I've realized I can't do that."

Lanie bit the inside of her lip. She wanted to ask him to spill it, just get to the meat, but she forced herself to listen. He was finally opening up to her the way she had wanted from the first day, and she wasn't going to mess that up.

Azarius took a deep breath and blew it out. His eyes dropped to their hands, and he laced their fingers together before meeting her eyes again. "I told you once that I lost my mother when I was very young. It was actually the morning after my tenth birthday. She was sick with cancer, but I didn't know that. She had hidden it from me because we were poor and she couldn't afford the expensive treatments."

Pieces began to click into place. Of course he would have a negative association with his birthday, who wouldn't?

"I woke up that morning to a quiet house which was unusual. Even on her worst days, my mama would be up and fixing breakfast when I woke up, but that morning it was quiet. I knew something was wrong, and I went to her room. She lay in bed, looking peaceful, and I thought she was just asleep but after shaking her and hollering for her to wake up, I knew something was wrong, but I had no one to call, so I climbed up in bed with her and lay there until the neighbor showed up."

Lanie sucked in her breath and tears welled up in her eyes. "I'm so sorry, Azarius. Is that why you avoid your birthday?"

"I don't avoid it," he said.

"Yes, you do," she countered.

"Okay, I guess I do. Those memories are hard to deal with every year, so I found if I treated it like any other day, it got easier. Anyway, the neighbor came and took me to her house for the afternoon, but then CPS came. I had no idea who my father was, and most of my mother's family were either dead or too poor to take me in, so I landed in foster care. Some places were better than others, but on the whole it wasn't an experience I would want to repeat. It taught me to hold information close and keep people at a distance.

"Then I landed at Mary's house - my mother. She had just married, but found out she couldn't have kids and so she decided to foster in hopes of adopting. I was thirteen and a handful, but she kept me anyway, even after the divorce of her first husband. My mom and I became close friends, and little by little she got me to open up."

"I don't understand then," Lanie said, interrupting him. "If your mom got you to open up, why are you still so distant?"

"I wasn't finished," Azarius said with a smile. "I didn't have many close relationships, but it's because I was looking for someone like my mother. When I met you, I thought I had finally found someone I could open up to. Before I could tell you though, you were engaged and then married, and my world was thrown upside down again."

"Azarius, I never knew," Lanie interrupted. Would it have made a difference, she wondered?

"I know you didn't, and that was my fault. I should have told you in the beginning, but I was too scared to. Krista was the first person I opened up to, and you know what happened with her. Needless to say, my trust in people diminished about then. The only person I've told since is Greg, and that's only because I met him right after Krista left me and he helped me through some hard times. I'm sorry I didn't tell you earlier, but I need you to know that I love you and when you collapsed, I was reminded of my mother again. All I could think was that I needed you to be okay because I couldn't... I can't imagine my life without you."

Tears began to stream out of the corner of Lanie's eyes.

"Hey, hey, why are you crying? I thought me being open was what you wanted."

"It is," she sniffled. "Now I can really see a future with you, but the baby..."

He wiped a tear from her cheek. "I know. I'm sad about the baby too, but we have plenty of time to start a family. In fact, we have the rest of our lives to do that, if you'll let me stick around." He reached into his pocket and pulled out a small black box. "I'm glad we got married when we did, but I always regretted not having a better ring for you."

Lanie gasped as he opened the lid. A beautiful sparkly diamond sat nestled in between intertwining rings of silver and gold. "Oh, Azarius," she said with a sigh. "It's perfect. It means everything."

He smiled as he slipped her old band off and slid the new ring on her finger. "You mean everything."

With no words left to say, Lanie circled her arms around his neck and met his lips.

EPILOGUE

"Ugh, nothing fits," Lanie said, throwing yet another skirt on the bed. Though barely out of her first trimester, her belly had ballooned in size the last week and none of her clothes fit.

"Go naked then," Azarius said, wrapping his arms around her and nuzzling her neck.

"I can't do that," she said, turning to kiss him. "Your mother will be there, remember?"

"Oh, right. Well, then how about that maxi dress you wore a few weeks ago? It was stretchy, right? It's supposed to warmer today, and we'll be inside anyway."

"That is a great idea. I knew I married you for a reason." She flashed him a smile and then bounced into the closet to grab the dress.

"I thought it was my mysterious allure," he called from behind her.

Lanie popped her head out of the closet. "No, that I always hated, remember?"

Azarius laughed. "My rugged good looks?"

Lanie tugged the dress over her head. It sat a little off kilter with her baby bump, but it looked okay. "Yes, those I love," she said walking back to him and tilting her face up to kiss him again. "Now, we better go or we're going to be late."

The barn was already packed when they arrived. A huge banner that read "Congratulations Azarius and Lanie" hung across the front door. Layla had insisted on throwing them both a "belated wedding" party and a "congratulations on the new baby" party." Lanie had convinced her to throw them both at the same time. Because Layla had asked, nearly the whole town had shown up.

Of course, it probably helped that the town had officially adopted Lanie and Azarius into the fold. Even the few staunch grinches had changed their tune when Azarius began helping the local businesses with a marketing plan that had drawn more tourists this past summer than ever before.

She and Azarius had even officially taken over Perkins from her father and increased revenue so much that they'd hired a few local teens to take the afternoon shift, leaving Lanie time to write and Azarius time to run the advertising.

"Hey bro, long time no see," Greg, no longer on crutches, but still limping slightly embraced Azarius as soon as they opened the door. With him was a stunning, petite woman with dark hair and the greenest eyes Lanie had ever seen.

"Lanie, you look amazing," Greg said, embracing her next. "I want you to meet Jada, and while I don't want to steal your thunder, I did want to share we just got engaged last night."

"Oh that's wonderful," Lanie said as Azarius issued congratulations as well. Greg looked happier than she could remember seeing him, and as she shook Jada's hand, she had a feeling their relationship would be a good one.

Before they could take another step farther into the barn, a stout woman with long blond hair gathered Azarius into a hug. Mary, this had to be Mary. Though they'd spoken on the phone, Lanie had yet to meet her mother-in-law as Mary didn't travel very often.

"It's good to see you too, Mother," Azarius said. "I would like you to meet Lanie."

Mary turned warm brown eyes on her, and Lanie could see why Azarius confided in his mother. She had a presence like warm cookies on Christmas Day that just made you want to spill everything.

"It's so nice to meet you," Lanie said, holding out her hand, but Mary pulled her in for a hug.

"It's nice to meet the woman who's finally completed my son. I knew when he first talked about you that you were special, but seeing you - I can see that you two were made for each other."

Lanie smiled at Azarius and squeezed his hand.

Her parents came next, and Lanie was surprised to see a smile on her father's face as he approached.

"I have to say I had my doubts, but you have proven to be a good man, Azarius," her father said, shaking Azarius's hand.

"Thank you, sir. That means a lot coming from you."

"And we know it's early," her mother said, "but we brought you a baby gift to say congratulations. I know you don't know the gender of the baby yet, but I know babies love loveys, so..." She pulled a bright yellow ducky out of the bag she was holding.

"Oh, it looks just like my old lovey," Lanie sighed. "Thank you, Mother."

"You are welcome, Dear. We're so proud of you both."

Her parents moved along, and more guests approached to issue well wishes - Bert and Amelia (who were evidently back together after their break), Barnard, Paula, Presley and Brandon, and people whose names Lanie wasn't even sure she knew. Layla and Max brought up the rear.

"Thank you for this party, Layla," Azarius said. "You went above and beyond."

"Well, I was happy to do it, though I'm not sure why we had to do it on this specific day." Layla said pointedly at Lanie.

Lanie smiled and shook her head. That was a secret only for her and Azarius.

"Why did you pick my birthday for this party?" Azarius whispered when they were out of ear shot of everyone else.

"I thought you needed a happy memory for once around it," Lanie said. "I didn't tell anyone else, so we don't have to make a big deal about it."

Azarius pulled her in for an unexpected hug. "You are amazing, Lanie. Did you know that?"

Lanie laughed as she squeezed him back. "Okay, I'm amazing. Can we go sit now? My feet are killing me?"

"Almost," he said.

Music flooded the barn, and he led her to the center of the dance floor.

"I thought you didn't dance in public," she said with a smile as she locked her arms around his neck.

"There are a lot of things I do now that I didn't do before," he said, turning her in a slow circle. "Like sharing a house."

Lanie smiled. "Good thing you got over that one because it won't be much longer before it's even fuller. Oh, I finished the book by the way."

He tilted his head. "What book?"

"Our story, silly. You told me the day we eloped that Lanie Jacobson sounded like a good author's name, so I decided to try it out. I've been writing in the afternoons while you market, and I think I finally finished it."

"That's amazing, Lanie. What's it called?"

"Love Conquers All," she said.

He nodded slowly. "Love Conquers All," he said. "I like it. It's a good title."

"No," Lanie said with a shake of her head. "It's a great title. It means everything."

Azarius smiled and pulled her closer. "It means everything."

The End!

WOULD YOU LEAVE A REVIEW?

As an author, I highly appreciate the feedback I get from my readers. It helps others make an informed decision before buying my book. If you enjoyed this book, please leave a review at your retailer.

Do you like free books? I'm offering a free sample of my next book Free Sample!

IT'S NOT QUITE THE END!

~

If you like boxed sets, turn the page for a sneak peek at another one!

AUTHOR'S NOTE

If you're anything like me, you read a lot. Okay, I don't read as much as I used to now that I'm writing, but I do pick up a book once a week to read and hone my skills. Plus, I joined a book club to make me read a book a month.

So, I understand that books can get expensive which is why I've boxed up another set just for you. Turn the page for a sneak peek.

And if you've enjoyed reading this author's note so far (and really, how could you not?) I am offering, for today only, a page where you can sign up for my weekly newsletter for the low, low price of absolutely nothing.

Included in this weekly newsletter are many wonderful things like pictures of my adorable children, chances to win awesome prizes, new releases and sales I might be holding, great books from other authors, and anything else that strikes my fancy and that I think you would enjoy.

Even better, I solemnly swear to only send out one newsletter a week (usually on Tuesday unless life gets in the way which with three kids it usually does). I will not spam you, sell your email address to solicitors or anyone else, or any of those other terrible things.

Join me here and receive a free novella as my thank-you gift for choosing to hang out with me. It's fun and entertaining. I promise.

Prayers and blessings,

Lorana

NOT READY TO SAY GOODBYE YET?

While we must leave Star Lake for now, I have more great characters to introduce you to. Check out the Lawkeeper series and meet a whole new cast of characters.

The Lawkeepers Collection begins with Lawfully Matched

She thought she was marrying a rancher...

But he isn't who she expected when he shows up.

He is looking for vengeance...

But he ends up opening his home to a stranger.

When tragedy strikes....

Will Jesse and Kate find love?

Read on for a taste of The Lawkeepers Series....

THE LAWKEEPERS PREVIEW

*B*oston, Massachusetts 1883

*M*ary Katherine Whidby grabbed the local paper and strolled to a corner to read in private. While she hated to leave her beloved Boston, she was quickly approaching the spinster age, and all the surrounding men seemed intimidated by her brains or more likely her strong-willed spirit as her brother Robert liked to remind her.

Mary Katherine, or Kate as her family called her, had always held a grand notion of love, so agreeing to marry a complete stranger caused distaste in her mouth every time she thought about it, but her options had run out when her parents died.

She opened the paper and scanned the offerings:

'Forty-year-old widowed rancher looking for wife who can be a mother to three kids.'

Three kids? Kate shook her head and drew a line through that one. While she wanted kids one day, she did not feel confident stepping into the role immediately.

'Fifty-year-old Pastor seeks wife for companionship and to lead women's socials at local church.'

A pastor's wife wouldn't be too bad, but the age difference was more than Kate could stomach. After all, she was barely twenty-five, which would make this man twice her age, and wasn't the lifespan shorter in the west? Knowing her luck, he would die shortly after she arrived, and she'd be left all alone.

'Thirty-year-old saloon owner seeks wife and possible waitress.'

While this one was closer in age, Kate had no desire, or skills for that matter, to work in a saloon.

The pickings were slim this month it seemed. Just one ad left.

'Thirty-two-year-old farmer in search of brave woman to help on homestead.'

Well, she didn't know much about farming, but no one would say Kate wasn't brave. She had even taken shooting lessons with her brother and father.

Crossing her fingers this man would not be a con man or an abuser, she made her way to the counter.

"Hello Miss Kate, what can I help you with today?" Mr. Gaines, the elderly owner of the newspaper asked. He wore a black vest over his shirt and a pair of old spectacles sat on the bridge of his nose.

Kate cleared her throat, still embarrassed to be doing this. "I wanted to inquire how I might go about answering an ad."

"Hmm, let me see," he said, pushing up his glasses as he read the ad. "Mail-order bride?" He looked up at Kate. "Does that mean we're losing you?"

A heated flush flared across Kate's face. "Well, there isn't much left for me here with mother and father gone."

"Don't you still have a brother?" Mr. Gaines asked kindly.

Kate nodded. "I do, but Robert just married, and he's trying to get his practice up and running. I would just be in the way." She didn't add the fact that his wife Abigail appeared to despise her, and the thought of staying in their house much longer held little appeal.

"Well, if you're sure," he said, though the tone of his voice told her he wasn't convinced. He reached below the cabinet and pulled out a pad of paper and a pencil. "Generally, you write the man back and see if it's a good fit."

"Oh," Kate stammered. She had not realized she would need to reply. "Thank you," she said taking the paper and pencil. "I will return this shortly."

Kate headed back to the corner and sat down at the table, thinking for a moment. She placed the pencil on the paper and scribbled out:

Dear Mr. Easterly,

My name is Kate Whidby. I am a brave twenty-five-year-old woman with dark hair and blue eyes. I am looking for love and adventure in a new area. I saw your ad in my paper, and although I do not know much about farming, I am a quick study and think I could be the woman you are looking for. Please advise if this is acceptable. I would like to travel as soon as possible.

Kate Whidby

She folded the letter and returned to Mr. Gaines. "Do you have an envelope I could use to send this?"

Mr. Gaines supplied one from under the counter and handed it to her. Kate quickly jotted her name and address down and sealed the envelope. She held it out to Mr. Gaines, but he shook his head.

"Take it to the post office. They will send it out and your response will come back through them."

"How long do you think it will take to get a reply?"

"I don't know for sure, but my guess would be about two weeks."

Kate's jaw dropped open. "Two weeks?"

Mr. Gaines nodded and scratched the side of his bald head with the back of the pencil. "Yes ma'am, unless you'd like to telegraph it. That costs considerably more though."

Kate fingered the few coins she had managed to find in her parent's bedroom as she was packing up the last items she'd been able to take. No, she had better be frugal and spend only a little.

"No, two weeks is fine." Perhaps, she could find a temporary job. It would be nice to have some money for the trip.

Kate paid the small fee and left with the letter in hand. After a quick stop in the post office to drop it off, she continued on to the mercantile to pick up a few items.

Once inside the store, she loaded the basket with the necessities —flour, sugar, teas—and then picked up a few pieces of penny candy. Kate felt guilty for imposing on Robert and Abigail by staying with them at their house, especially so early in their marriage, but her parents had rented their house. Kate took care for her parents but had no money to continue the payments after their death, and so she had been forced to give up her home.

"Morning, Miss Kate," Sally, the plump owner of the Mercantile, smiled at her.

Kate had often wondered how Sally had married before she did, but then she would remember the two marriage proposals she had turned down. Funny how she had rebuffed those proposals because she felt she didn't know the men well enough, yet now she was planning to travel across the country and marry a man she'd never met.

"Hello, Sally," she said, laying the items on the counter. "How is business?"

"It is not too bad," Sally said. Then she glanced behind her and leaned forward. "Tell you the truth, it has been a little slow the last few months. John is stressed about it," she whispered.

Kate smiled and leaned in to reply. "Well, I will keep praying it will pick up."

"That is mighty kind of you, Kate. Will I see you at church on Sunday?"

Kate nodded, but the question sent her mind spinning. God was an important part of her life. Would there be proper churches in Texas?

~

*S*age Creek, Texas 1883

*J*esse Jennings removed his hat and wiped the sweat from his brow. Finally, the last fence post was in. With his cattle safe once again, he would now be able to focus on putting the finishing touches on his homestead, so he could marry Pauline.

As he replaced his hat, Sheriff Johnson rode up. Jesse sighed and lifted his gaze to the lawman.

"What can I do for you, Sheriff?" he asked, though he knew the answer to the question. Sheriff Johnson had come around once every few days like clockwork over the past month, trying to enlist Jessie as a deputy sheriff.

Jesse enjoyed the protection the law provided as much as the next person, but he was just a simple rancher, and all he wanted to do was marry his sweetheart and raise cattle.

Unfortunately, time and money had dwindled after some rough winter weather and the previous summer's drought, extending the finishing of the homestead.

"You know why I'm here, Jesse," the older man said as he dismounted his chocolate brown stallion. "There was another robbery last night. This time at Doc Moore's office. No one was hurt, but they took a lot of his supplies. We need more men to help patrol. At least until we catch these varmints." He removed his hat and ran his leathery hand through his salt-and-pepper hair.

"I'm sorry to hear that Sheriff, but as I've told you before, I'm not a lawman, and I need to finish this homestead."

Sheriff Johnson planted his hands on his slim hips and donned his hat again. "Well, I can set with that, but the attacks appear to be becoming more frequent. I just hope you still have a home when all is said and done."

With that, Sheriff Johnson tipped the brim of his black Stetson before re-mounting his horse.

Jesse lifted a hand in a loose wave and watched the sheriff recede from view. Maybe Sheriff Johnson was right. He was young, in shape, and not half bad with a gun.

Once he finished the homestead he'd be able to think about it. Right now, thoughts of Pauline with her long blonde hair consumed his thoughts.

Jesse checked the sun on the horizon. It had sunk low, leaving the sky a brilliant orange and pink color. He had lost track of time and needed to wash up before dinner with his fiancée.

Keep reading for The Lawkeeper boxed set

THE STORY DOESN'T END!

You've met a few people and fallen in love....

I bet you're wondering how you can meet everyone else.

Star Lake Series:

When Love Returns: The first in the Star Lake series. Presley Hays and Brandon Scott were best friends in High School until Morgan entered their town and stole Brandon's heart. Devastated, Presley takes a scholarship to Le Cordon Bleu, but five years later, she is back in Star Lake after a tough breakup. Brandon thought he'd never return to Star Lake after Morgan left him and his daughter Joy, but when his father needs help, he returns home and finds more than he bargained for. Can Presley and Brandon forget past hurts or will their stubborn natures keep them apart forever?

Once Upon a Star: The second book in the Star Lake series. Audrey left Star Lake to pursue acting, but after an unplanned pregnancy her jobs and her money dwindled, leaving her no option except to return home and start over. Blake was the quintessential nerd in high school and was never able to tell Audrey how he felt.

Now that he's gained confidence and some muscle, will he finally be able to reveal his feelings? Once Upon a Star will take you back to Christmas in Star Lake. Revisit your favorite characters and meet a few ones in this sweet Christmas read.

Love Conquers All: Lanie Perkins Hall never imagined being divorced at thirty. Nor did she imagine falling for an old friend, but when she runs into Azarius Jacobson, she can't deny the attraction. As they begin to spend more time together, Lanie struggles with the fact Azarius keeps his past a secret. What is he hiding? And will she ever be able to get him to open up? Azarius Jacobson has loved Lanie Perkins Hall from the moment he saw her, but issues from his past have left him guarded. Now that he has another chance with her, will he find the courage to share his life with her? Or will his emotional walls create a barrier that will leave him alone once more? Find out in this heartfelt, emotional third book (stand alone) in the Star Lake series.

The Heartbeats Series:

Where It All Began: Sandra Baker thought her life was on the right track until she ended up pregnant. Her boyfriend, not wanting the baby, pushes her to have an abortion. After the procedure, Sandra's life falls apart, and she turns to alcohol. Her relationship ends, and she struggles to find meaning in her life. When she meets Henry Dobbs, a strong Christian man, she begins to wonder if God would accept her. Will she tell Henry her darkest secret? And will she ever be able to forgive herself and find healing? Find out in this emotional love story.

The Power of Prayer: Callie Green thought she had her whole life planned out until her fiance left her at the altar. When her carefully laid plans crumble, she begins to make mistakes at work and engage in uncharacteristic activities. After a mistake nearly costs her her job, she cashes in her honeymoon tickets for some time away. There she meets JD, a charming Christian man who, even though she is not a believer, captures her interest. Before their relationship can deepen, Callie's ex-fiance shows back up in her life and she is forced to choose between Daniel and JD. Who will she choose and how will her choice affect the rest of her life? Find out in this touching novel.

When Hearts Collide: Amanda Adams has always been a Christian, but she's a novice at relationships. When she meets Caleb, her emotions get the best of her and she ignores the sign that something is amiss. Will she find out before it's too late? Jared Masterson is still healing from his girlfriend's strange rejection and disappearance when he meets Amanda. She captivates his heart, but can he save her from making the biggest mistake of her life? A must read for mothers and daughters. Though part of the series and the first of the college spin off series, it is a stand alone book and can be read separately.

A Past Forgiven: Jess Peterson has lived a life of abuse and lost her self worth, but when she is paired with a Christian roommate, she begins to wonder if there is a loving father looking down on her. Her decisions lead her one way, but when she ends up pregnant, she must make some major changes. Chad Michelson is healing from his own past and uses meaningless relationships to hide his pain, but when Jess becomes pregnant, he begins to wonder about the meaning of life. Can he step up and be there for Jess and the baby?

Sweet Billionaires Series:

The Billionaire's Secret: Maxwell Banks was the ultimate player until he found himself caring for a daughter he didn't know he had. Can he change to become the role model she needs? Alyssa Miller hasn't had the best luck with past relationships, so why is she falling for the one man who is sure to break her heart? Though nearly complete opposites, feelings develop, but can Max really change his philandering ways? Or will one mistake seal his fate forever?

A Brush with a Billionaire: Brent just wanted to finish his novel in peace, but when his car breaks down in Sweet Grove, he is forced to deal with a female mechanic and try to get along. Sam thought she had given up on city boys, but when Brent shows up in her shop, she finds herself fighting attraction. Will their stubborn natures keep them apart or can a small town festival bring them together?

The Billionaire's Christmas Miracle: Drew Devonshire is captivated by the woman he meets at a masquerade ball, but who is she? Gwen Rodgers is a teacher, but when she pretends to be her friend and meets Drew at a masquerade ball, her world gets thrown upside down.

The Billionaire's Cowboy Groom: Carrie Bliss finally found the man she wants to marry but there's just one little problem. She's technically still married. Cal Roper hasn't seen her in years but his heart still belongs to his wife. When she returns to town requesting a divorce, can he convince her they belong together?

The Cowboy Billionaire: Coming Soon! Hunter Garrison's name is in every paper for a scandal he didn't commit. This time. In an attempt to salvage his reputation, he is tasked with helping a local ranch, but love was not supposed to be part of the deal. Daisy Keller has one focus. Keeping her ranch alive, but when Hunter Garrison shows up on her doorstep, he steals her attention and sparks fly.

The Lawkeeper Series:

Lawfully Matched: Kate Whidby doesn't want to impose on her newly married brother after their parents die, so she accepts a mail order bride offer in the paper. Little does she know the man she intends to marry has a dark past, sending her fleeing into a neighboring town and into Jesse Jenning's life. Jesse never wanted to be in law enforcement, but after a band of robbers kills his fiancee, he dons the badge and swears revenge. Will he find his fiancee's killer? And when Kate flies into his life, will he be able to put his painful past behind him in order to love again?

Lawfully Justified: William Cook turns to bounty hunting after losing his wife. When he suffers a life-threatening injury, he is forced to stay in town with an intriguing woman. Emma Stewart has moved back in with her widowed father, the town doctor, but she still longs for a family of her own, so no one is more surprised than she is when she starts to develop feeling for the bounty hunter, who hides his heart of gold behind a rugged exterior. Can Emma offer William a reason to stay? Can William find a way to heal from his broken past to start a future with Emma? Or will a haunting secret take away all the possibilities of this budding romance?

The Scarlet Wedding: William and Emma are planning their wedding, but an outbreak and a return from his past force them to change their plans. Is a happily ever after still in their future?

Lawfully Redeemed: Dani Higgins is a K9 cop looking to make a name for herself, but she finds herself at the mercy of a stranger after an accident. Calvin Phillips just wanted to help his brother, but somehow he ended up in the middle of a police investigation and caring for the woman trying to bring his brother in.

Lawfully Pursued: SWAT Officer Jesse Calhoun wasn't looking for love, much less with a billionaire's daughter, but Brie is hard to ignore. Brie Carter was just looking for a little fun but when a bet goes wrong, how does she keep from losing the man she's fallen in love with?

The Still Small Voice Series:

The Still Small Voice: Jordan Wright was searching for something after she gave her son up for adoption. What she found was God, and she began receiving visions. But can she trust Him when he asks her to do something big? Kat Jameson had long been a lukewarm Christian, but when her friend dies and she begins seeing lights, she thinks she is going crazy. Then she meets someone with a message for her. Will she be able to give up control and do what is asked of her?

A Spark in the Darkness coming soon! Raven Ryder's past has been anything but pretty, so when the new girl, Kat Jenkins, come into her life spouting about God being the light of the world, Raven can't stand it. But the more she is around Kat, she wonders if maybe she isn't a spark in the darkness of her world. Will she find the courage to take the leap of faith before it's too late.

Blushing Brides Series:

The Cowboy's Reality Bride: Tyler Hall just wanted to find love, but the women he dated wanted more than his small-town life provided. He gets more than he bargained for when he ends up on a reality dating show and falls for a woman who is not a contestant. Laney Swann has been running from her past for years, but it takes meeting a man on a reality dating show to make her see there's no need to run.

The Reality Bride's Baby: Laney wants nothing more than a baby, but when she starts feeling dizzy is it pregnancy or something more serious?

The Producer's Unlikely Bride: Justin Miller had given up on love, but when his image needs help, he finds himself needing the aid of a stranger who just happens to be a romance writer. Ava McDermott is waiting for the perfect love, but after agreeing to a fake relationship with Justin, she finds herself falling for real.

The Soldier's Steadfast Bride: coming soon
The Cop's Fiery Bride: coming soon

Texas Tornado Series:

Love on the Line coming soon
Touchdown on Love coming soon
Run with my Heart coming soon

Stand Alones:

Love Renewed: This books is part of the multi author second chance series. When fate reunites high school sweethearts separated by life's choices, can they find a second chance at love at a snowy lodge amid a little mystery?

Her children's early reader chapter book series:

The Wishing Stone #1: Dangerous Dinosaur

The Wishing Stone #2: Dragon Dilemma

The Wishing Stone #3: Mesmerizing Mermaids

The Wishing Stone #4: Pyramid Puzzle

The Wishing Stone Inspirations 1: Mary's Miracle

authorloranahoopes.com

loranahoopes@gmail.com

To see a list of all her books

authorloranahoopes.com

loranahoopes@gmail.com

ABOUT THE AUTHOR

Lorana Hoopes is an inspirational author originally from Texas but now living in the PNW with her husband and three children. When not writing, she can be seen kickboxing at the gym, singing, or acting on stage. One day, she hopes to retire from teaching and write full time.